CYBER FORCE

AWAKENING
VOLUME ONE

IMAGE COMICS, INC.

Robert Kirkman — Chief Operating Officer

Erik Larsen — Chief Financial Officer

Todd McFarlane — President

Marc Silvestri — Chief Executive Officer

Jim Valentino — Vice President

Eric Stephenson — Publisher / Chief Creative Officer

Corey Hart — Director of Sales

Jeff Boison — Director of Publishing Planning & Book Trade Sales

Chris Ross — Director of Digital Sales

Jeff Stang — Director of Specialty Sales

Kat Salazar — Director of PR & Marketing

Drew Gill — Art Director

Heather Doornink — Production Director

Nicole Lapalme — Controller

IMAGECOMICS.COM

For Top Cow Productions, Inc.

For Top Cow Productions, Inc.

Marc Silvestri - CEO

Matt Hawkins - President & COO

Elena Salcedo - Vice President of Operations

Henry Barajas - Director of Operations

Vincent Valentine - Production Manager

Dylan Gray - Marketing Director

To find the comic
shop nearest you, call:
1-888-COMICBOOK

Want more info? Check out:
www.topcow.com
for news & exclusive Top Cow merchandise!

CYBER FORCE

AWAKENING
VOLUME ONE

Created by
MARC SILVESTRI

Written by
BRYAN HILL & MATT HAWKINS

Art by
ATILIO ROJO

Lettered by
TROY PETERI

Edited by
ELENA SALCEDO

Production by
VINCE VALENTINE & CAREY HALL

Cover Art for this volume by
MARC SILVESTRI

CHAPTER ONE

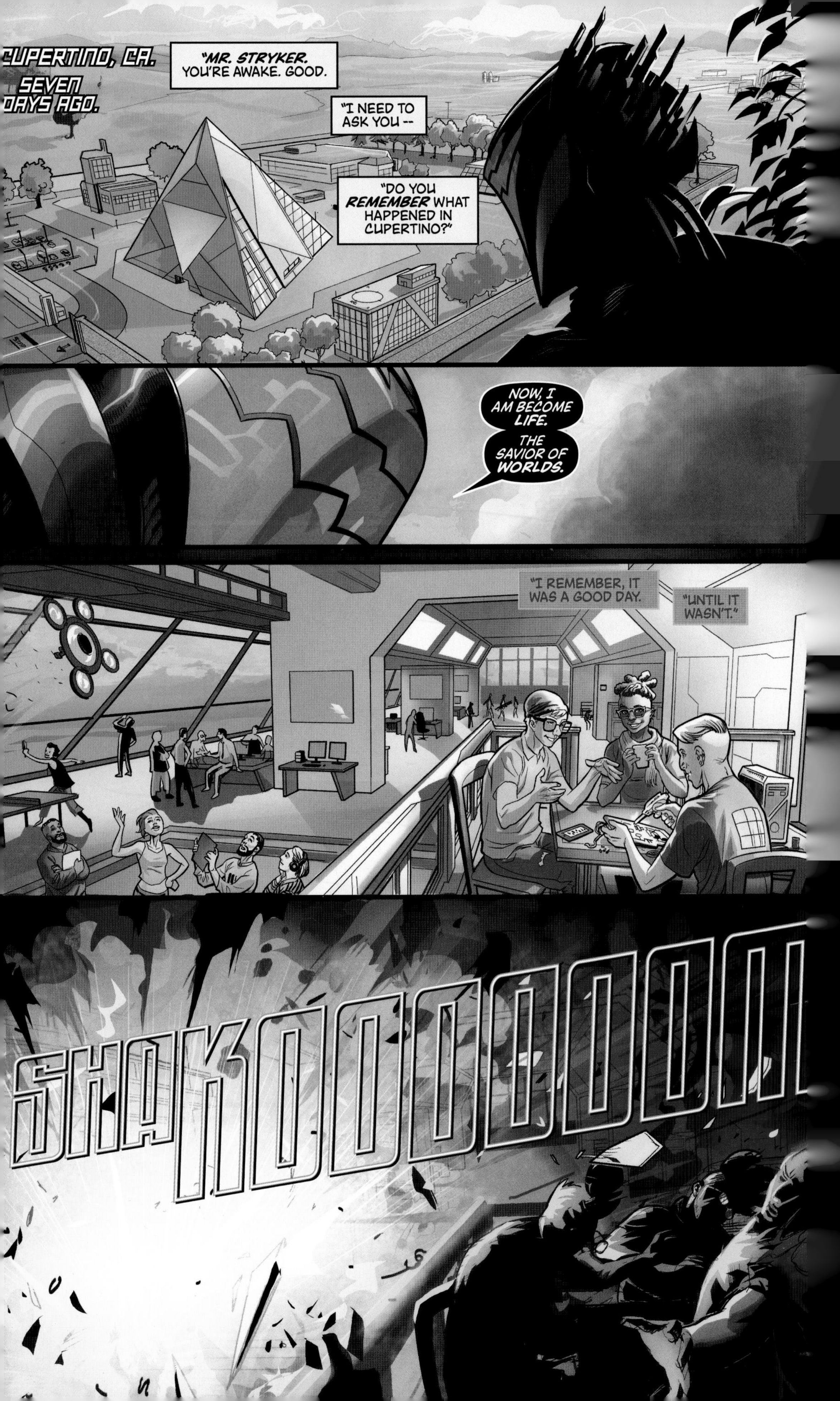
CUPERTINO, CA.
SEVEN DAYS AGO.
"MR. STRYKER. YOU'RE AWAKE. GOOD.
"I NEED TO ASK YOU --
"DO YOU REMEMBER WHAT HAPPENED IN CUPERTINO?"
NOW, I AM BECOME LIFE.
THE SAVIOR OF WORLDS.
"I REMEMBER, IT WAS A GOOD DAY.
"UNTIL IT WASN'T."
SHAKOOOOOOM

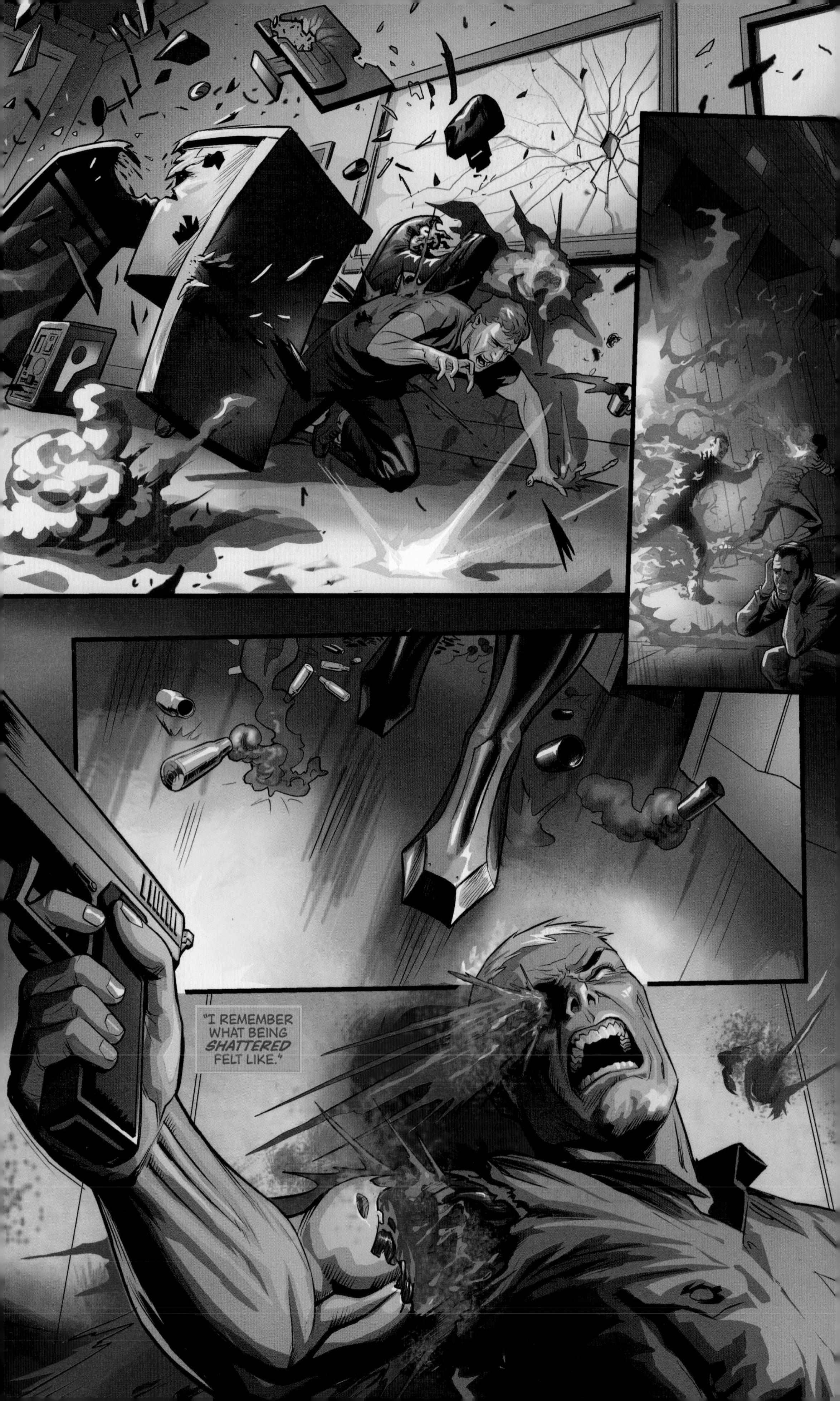
"I REMEMBER
WHAT BEING
SHATTERED
FELT LIKE."

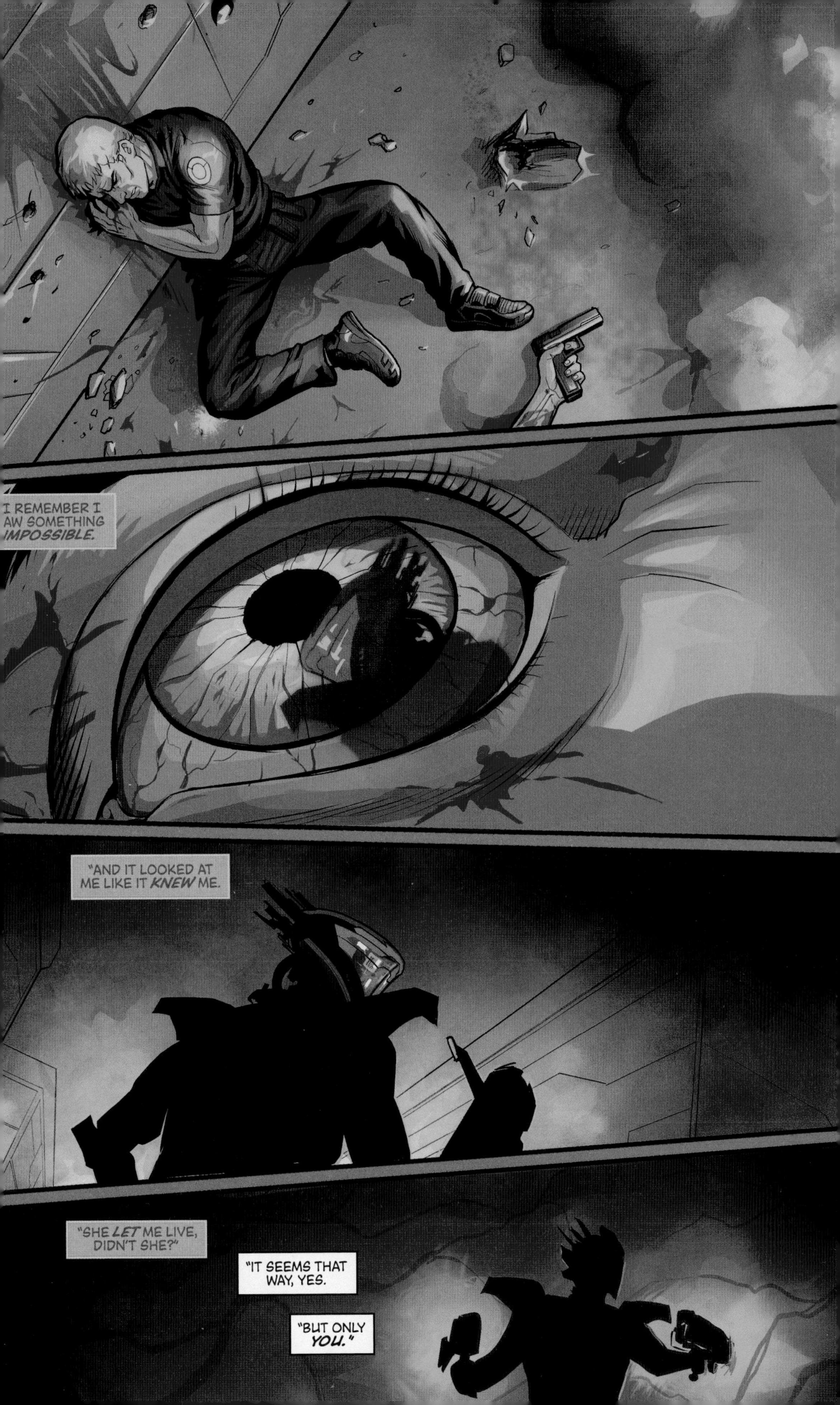

I REMEMBER I
AW SOMETHING
IMPOSSIBLE.
"AND IT LOOKED AT ME LIKE IT KNEW ME.
"SHE LET ME LIVE, DIDN'T SHE?"
"IT SEEMS THAT WAY, YES.
"BUT ONLY YOU."

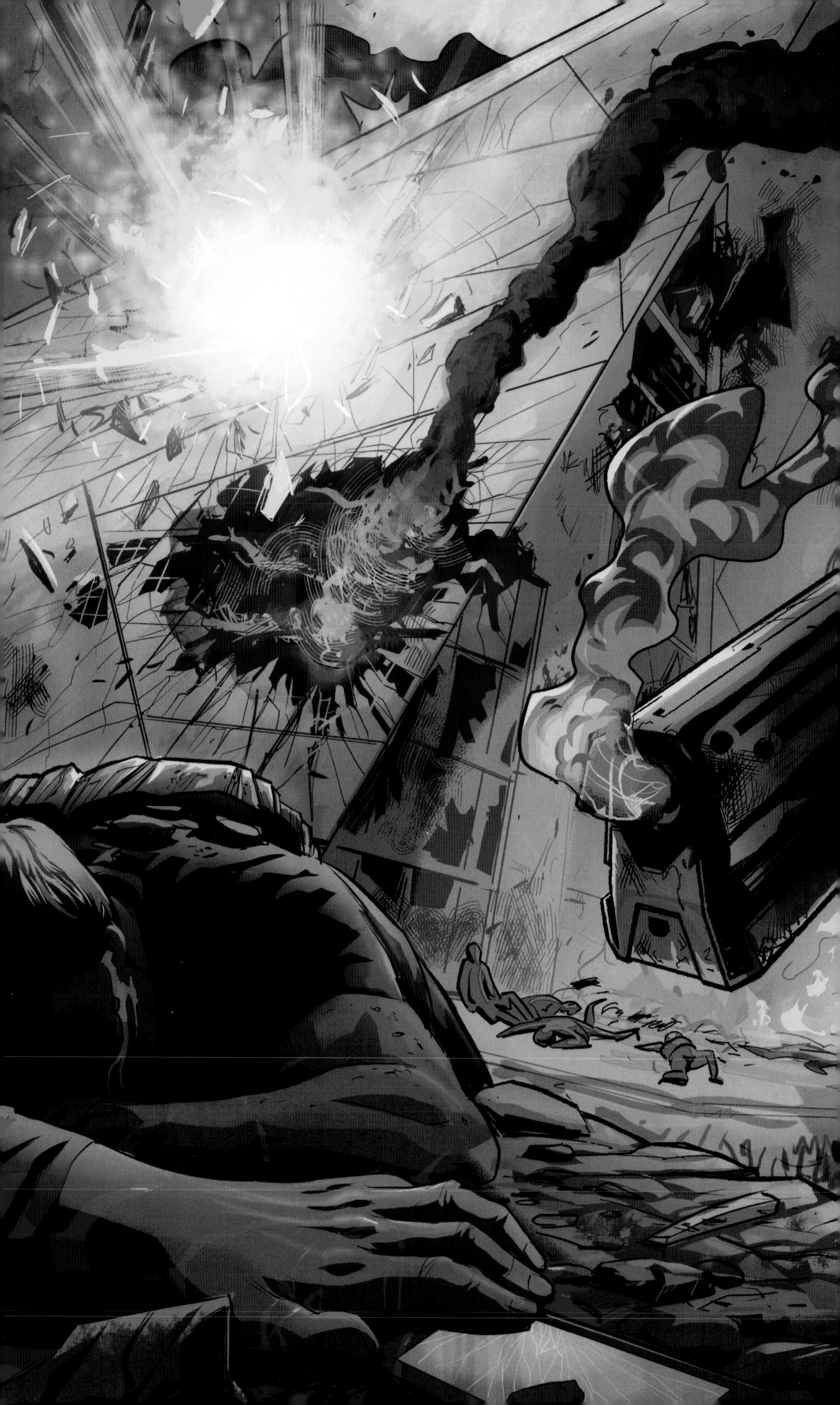

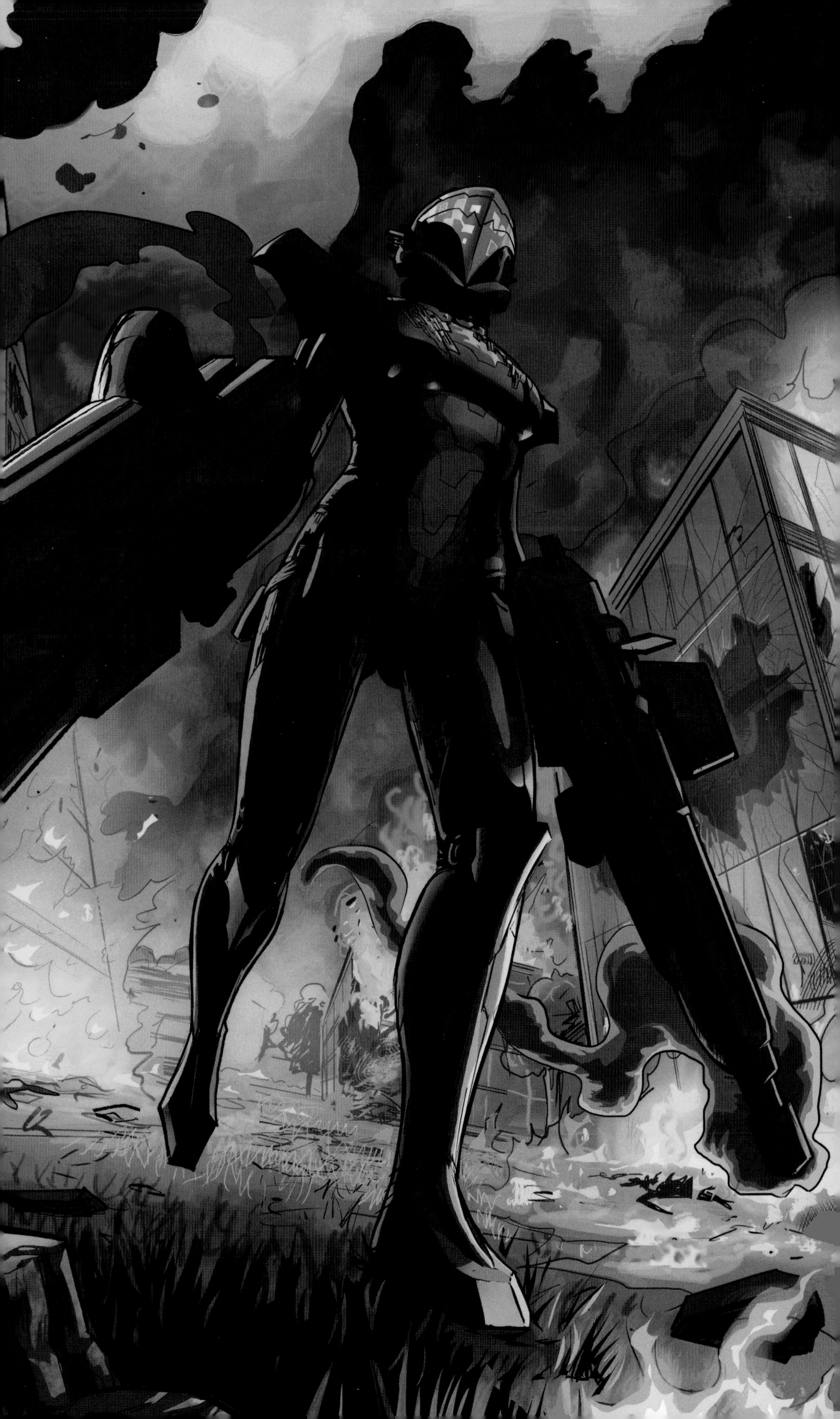

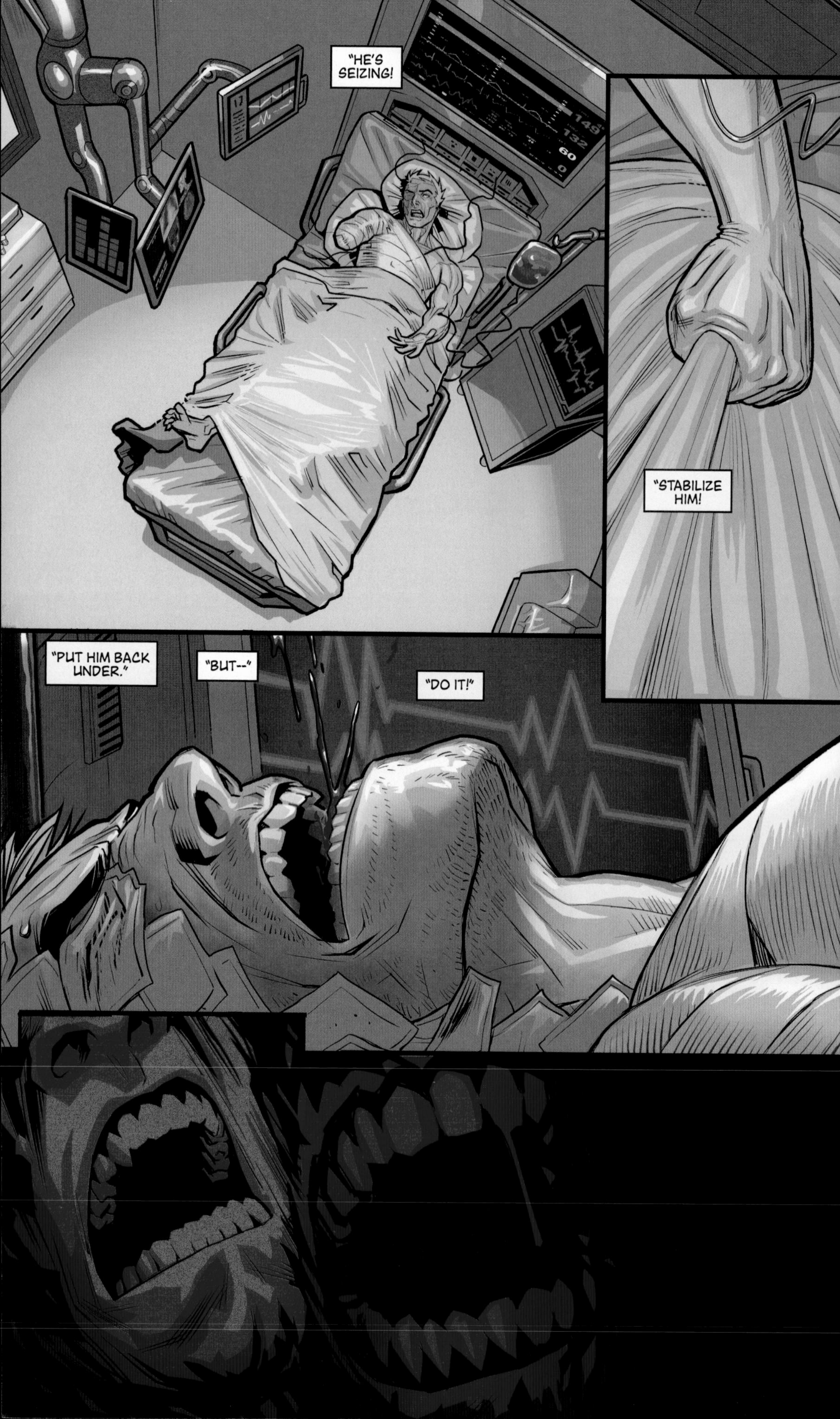
"HE'S SEIZING!
149
132
60
0
"STABILIZE HIM!
"PUT HIM BACK UNDER."
"BUT--"
"DO IT!"

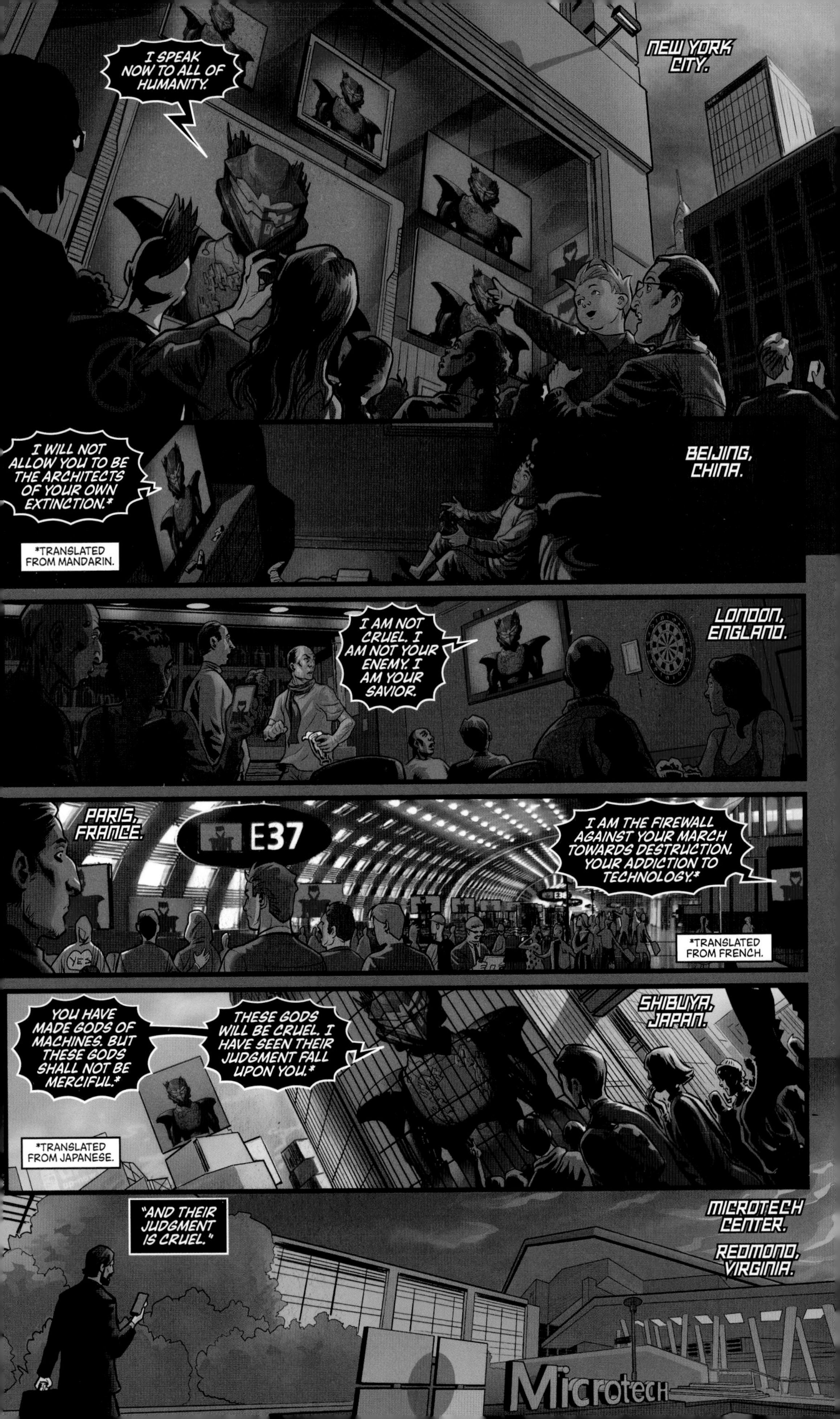
NEW YORK CITY.
I SPEAK NOW TO ALL OF HUMANITY.
BEIJING, CHINA.
I WILL NOT ALLOW YOU TO BE THE ARCHITECTS OF YOUR OWN EXTINCTION.*
*TRANSLATED FROM MANDARIN.
LONDON, ENGLAND.
I AM NOT CRUEL. I AM NOT YOUR ENEMY. I AM YOUR SAVIOR.
PARIS, FRANCE.
E37
I AM THE FIREWALL AGAINST YOUR MARCH TOWARDS DESTRUCTION. YOUR ADDICTION TO TECHNOLOGY.*
*TRANSLATED FROM FRENCH.
SHIBUYA, JAPAN.
YOU HAVE MADE GODS OF MACHINES. BUT THESE GODS SHALL NOT BE MERCIFUL.*
THESE GODS WILL BE CRUEL. I HAVE SEEN THEIR JUDGMENT FALL UPON YOU.*
*TRANSLATED FROM JAPANESE.
"AND THEIR JUDGMENT IS CRUEL."
MICROTECH CENTER.
REDMOND, VIRGINIA.
Microtech

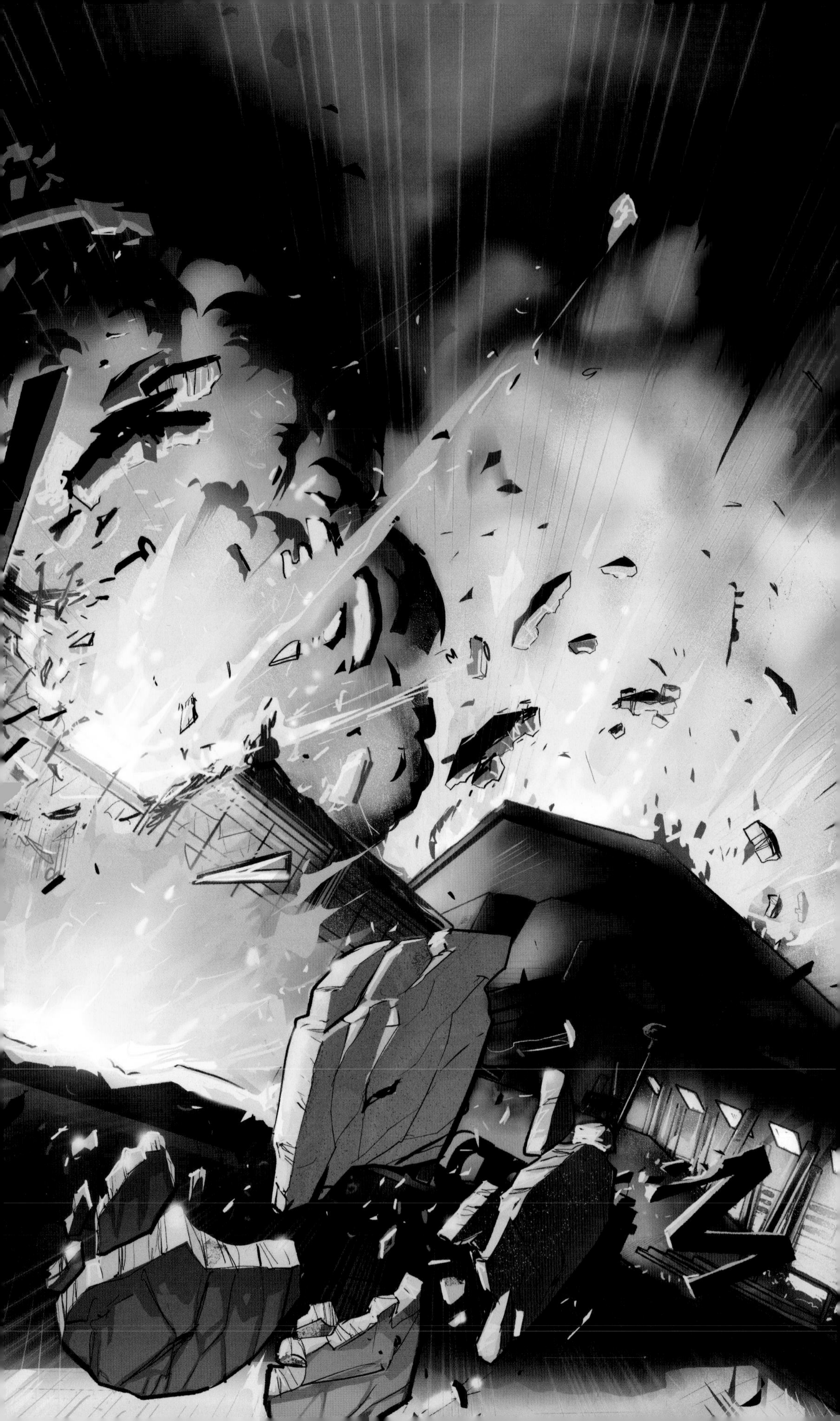

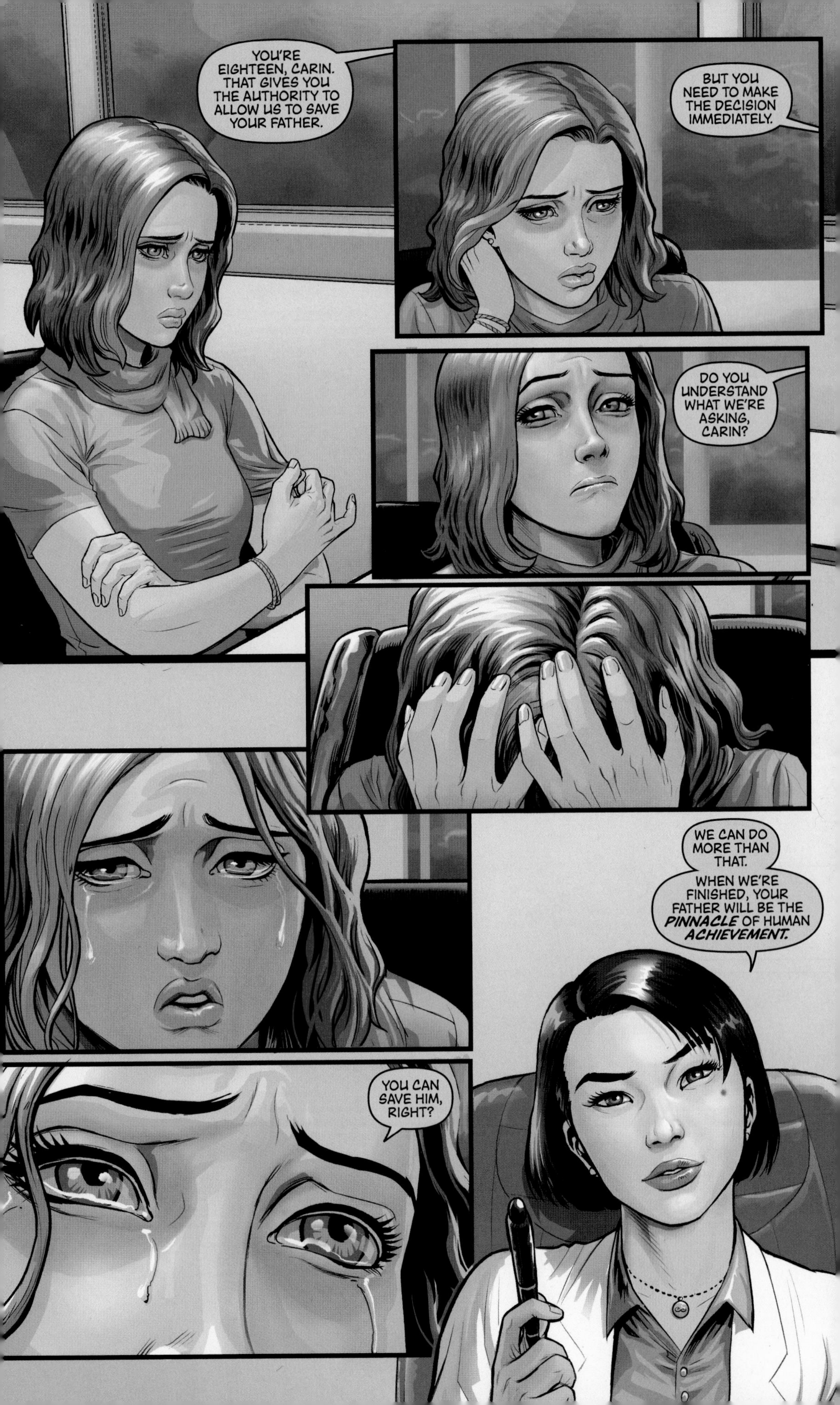
YOU'RE EIGHTEEN, CARIN. THAT GIVES YOU THE AUTHORITY TO ALLOW US TO SAVE YOUR FATHER.
BUT YOU NEED TO MAKE THE DECISION IMMEDIATELY.
DO YOU UNDERSTAND WHAT WE'RE ASKING, CARIN?
YOU CAN SAVE HIM, RIGHT?
WE CAN DO MORE THAN THAT.
WHEN WE'RE FINISHED, YOUR FATHER WILL BE THE *PINNACLE* OF HUMAN *ACHIEVEMENT.*

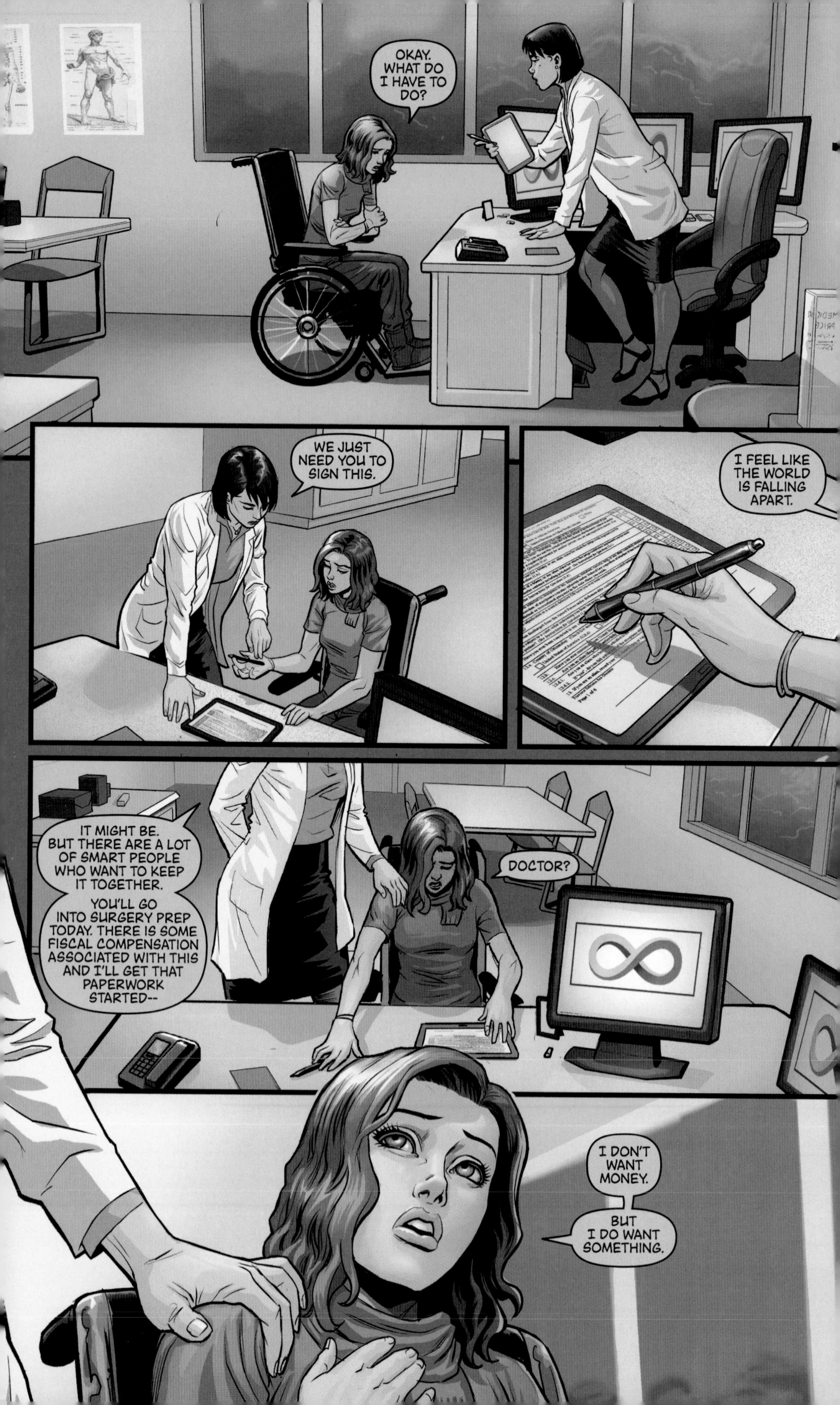

OKAY. WHAT DO I HAVE TO DO?
WE JUST NEED YOU TO SIGN THIS.
I FEEL LIKE THE WORLD IS FALLING APART.
IT MIGHT BE. BUT THERE ARE A LOT OF SMART PEOPLE WHO WANT TO KEEP IT TOGETHER.
YOU'LL GO INTO SURGERY PREP TODAY. THERE IS SOME FISCAL COMPENSATION ASSOCIATED WITH THIS AND I'LL GET THAT PAPERWORK STARTED--
DOCTOR?
I DON'T WANT MONEY.
BUT I DO WANT SOMETHING.

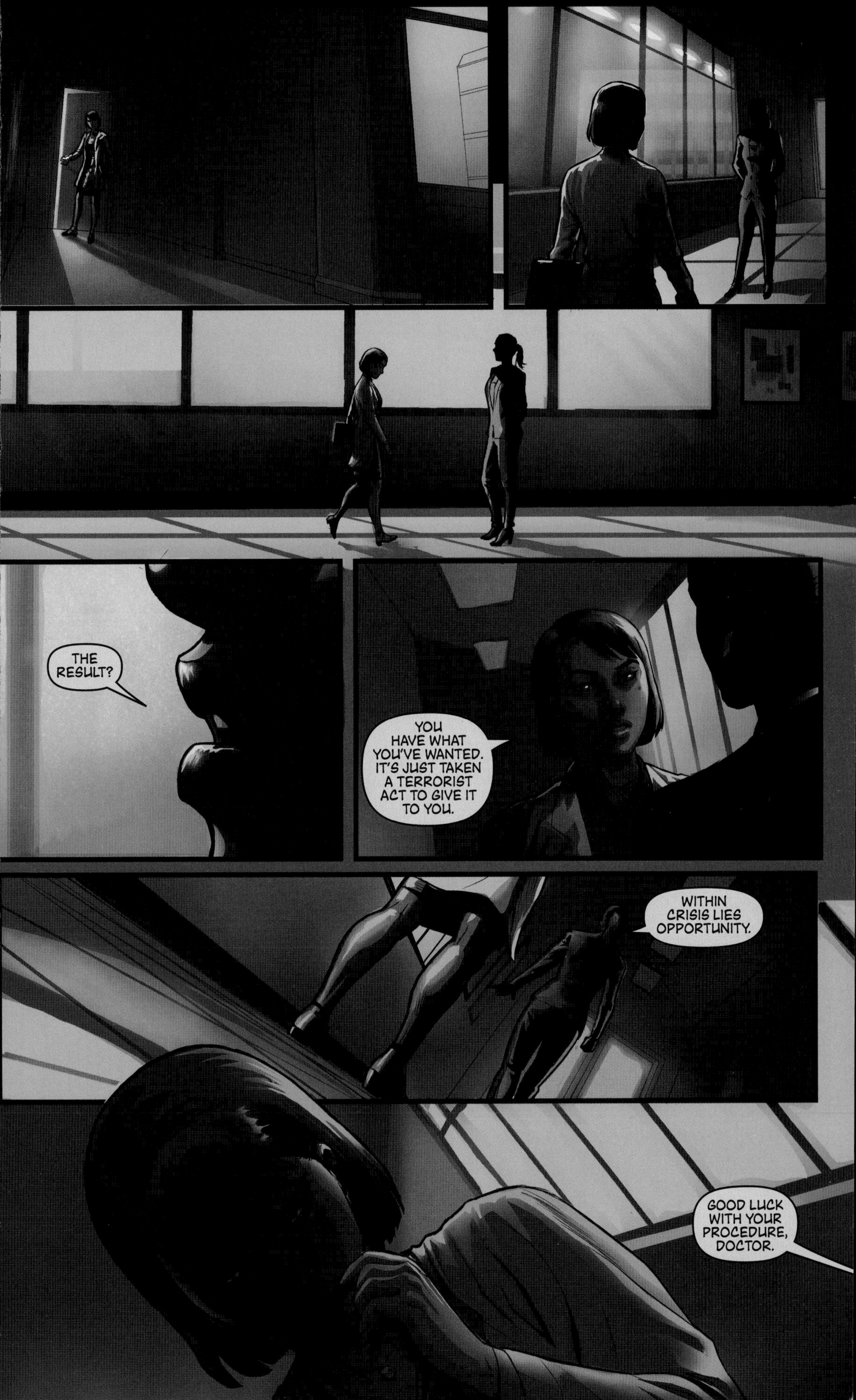
THE RESULT?
YOU HAVE WHAT YOU'VE WANTED. IT'S JUST TAKEN A TERRORIST ACT TO GIVE IT TO YOU.
WITHIN CRISIS LIES OPPORTUNITY.
GOOD LUCK WITH YOUR PROCEDURE, DOCTOR.

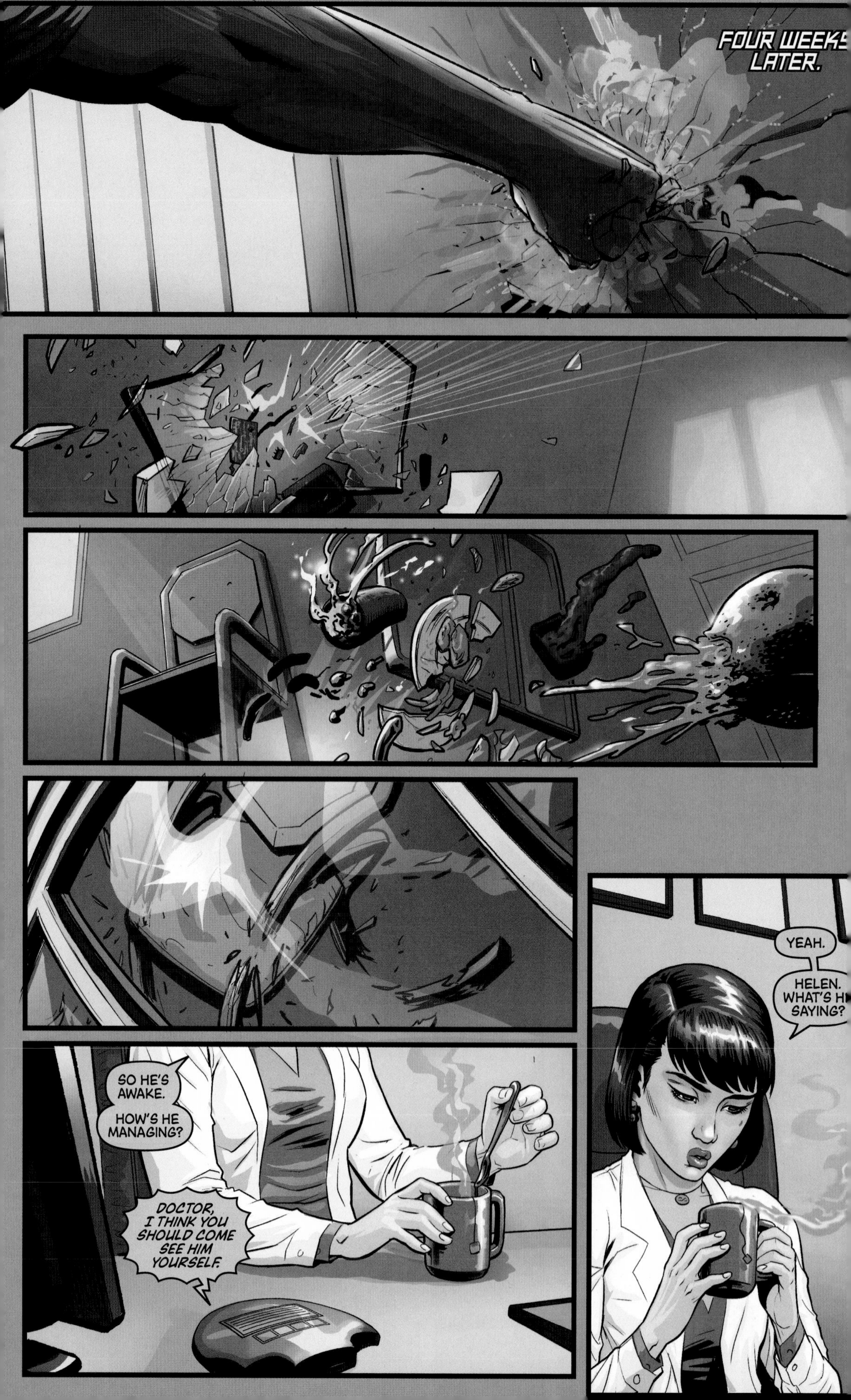
FOUR WEEKS LATER.
SO HE'S AWAKE.
HOW'S HE MANAGING?
DOCTOR, I THINK YOU SHOULD COME SEE HIM YOURSELF.
YEAH.
HELEN. WHAT'S HE SAYING?

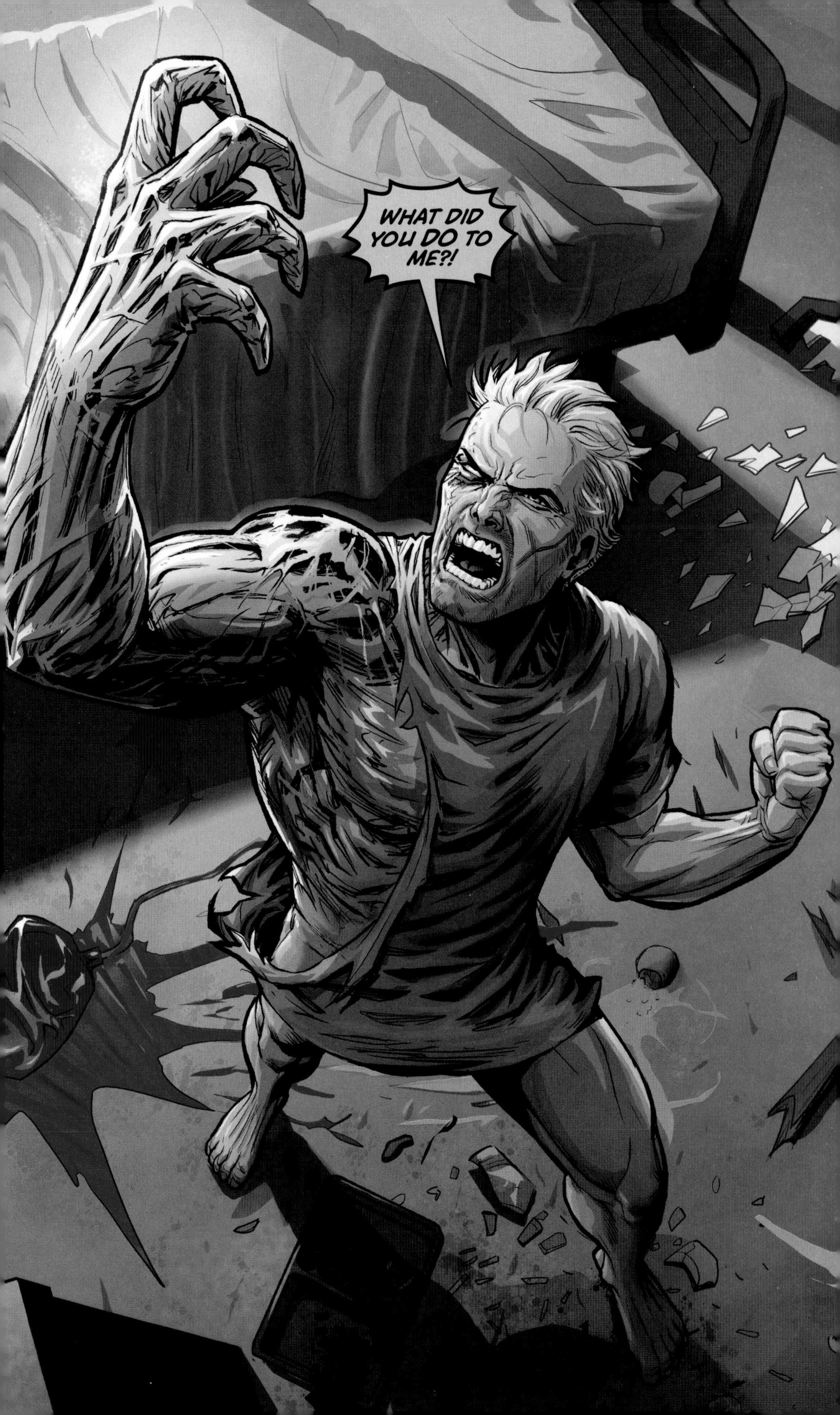
WHAT DID YOU DO TO ME?!

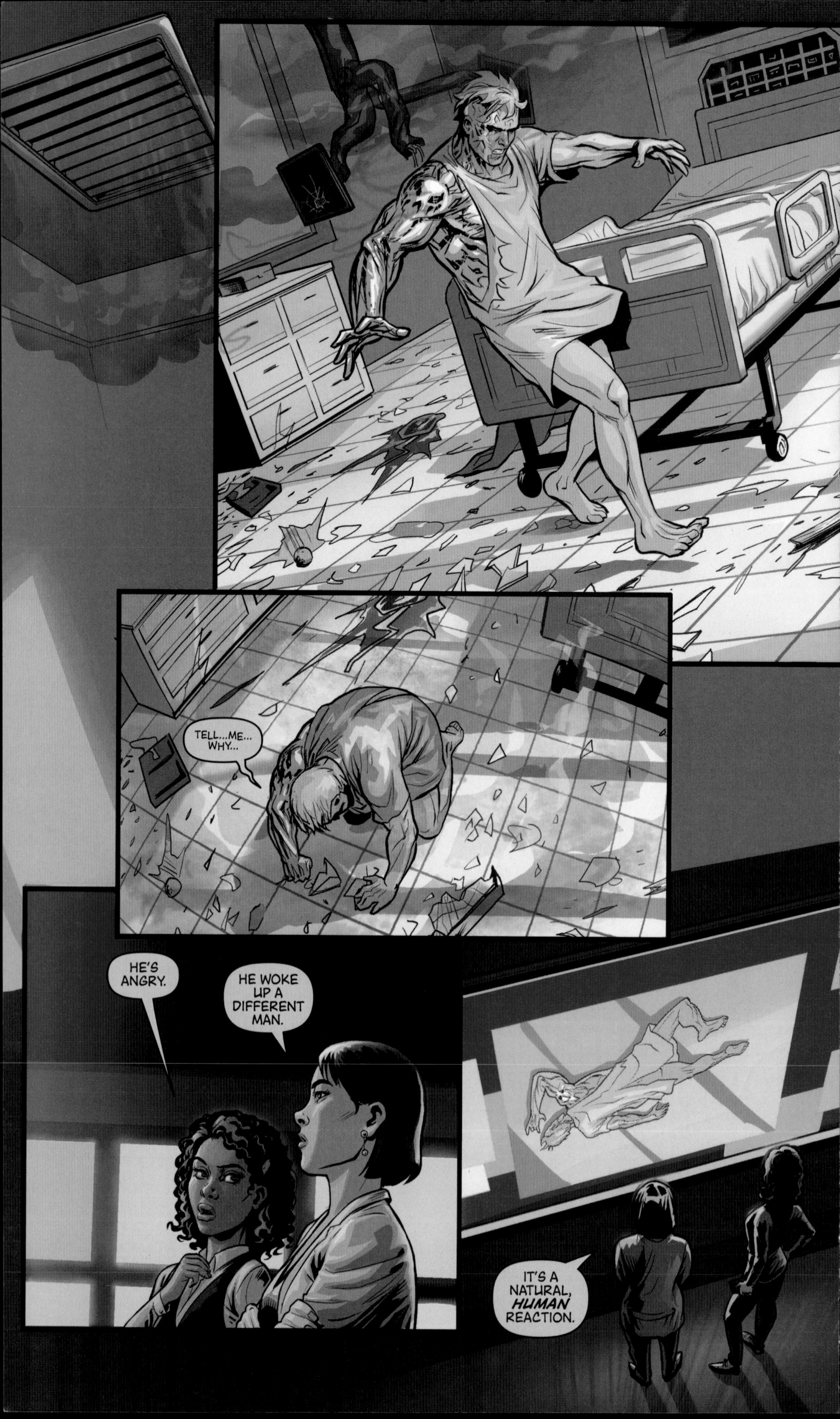

TELL...ME... WHY...
HE'S ANGRY.
HE WOKE UP A DIFFERENT MAN.
IT'S A NATURAL, *HUMAN* REACTION.

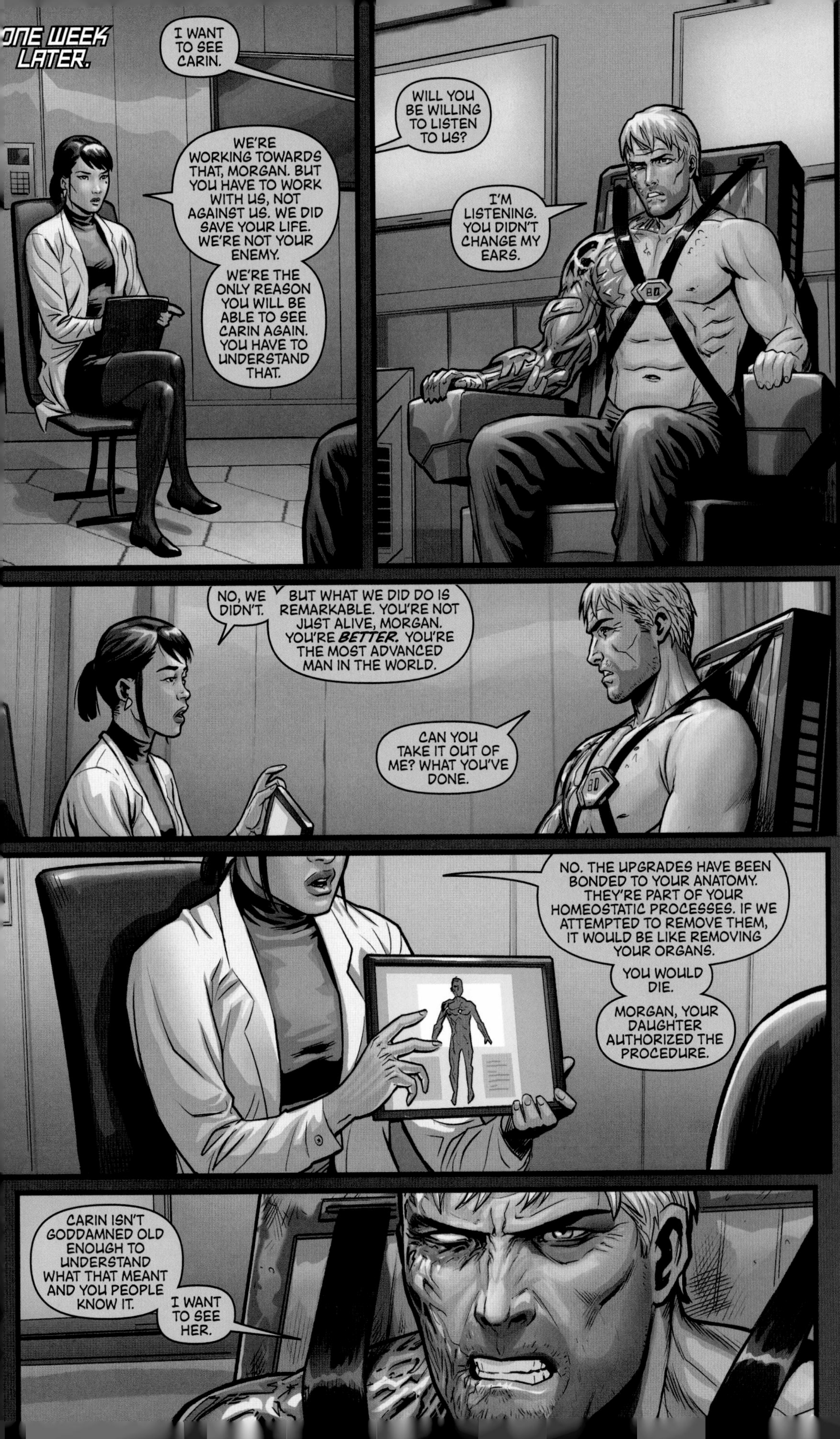
ONE WEEK LATER.
I WANT TO SEE CARIN.
WE'RE WORKING TOWARDS THAT, MORGAN. BUT YOU HAVE TO WORK WITH US, NOT AGAINST US. WE DID SAVE YOUR LIFE. WE'RE NOT YOUR ENEMY.
WE'RE THE ONLY REASON YOU WILL BE ABLE TO SEE CARIN AGAIN. YOU HAVE TO UNDERSTAND THAT.
WILL YOU BE WILLING TO LISTEN TO US?
I'M LISTENING. YOU DIDN'T CHANGE MY EARS.
NO, WE DIDN'T.
BUT WHAT WE DID DO IS REMARKABLE. YOU'RE NOT JUST ALIVE, MORGAN. YOU'RE BETTER. YOU'RE THE MOST ADVANCED MAN IN THE WORLD.
CAN YOU TAKE IT OUT OF ME? WHAT YOU'VE DONE.
NO. THE UPGRADES HAVE BEEN BONDED TO YOUR ANATOMY. THEY'RE PART OF YOUR HOMEOSTATIC PROCESSES. IF WE ATTEMPTED TO REMOVE THEM, IT WOULD BE LIKE REMOVING YOUR ORGANS.
YOU WOULD DIE.
MORGAN, YOUR DAUGHTER AUTHORIZED THE PROCEDURE.
CARIN ISN'T GODDAMNED OLD ENOUGH TO UNDERSTAND WHAT THAT MEANT AND YOU PEOPLE KNOW IT.
I WANT TO SEE HER.

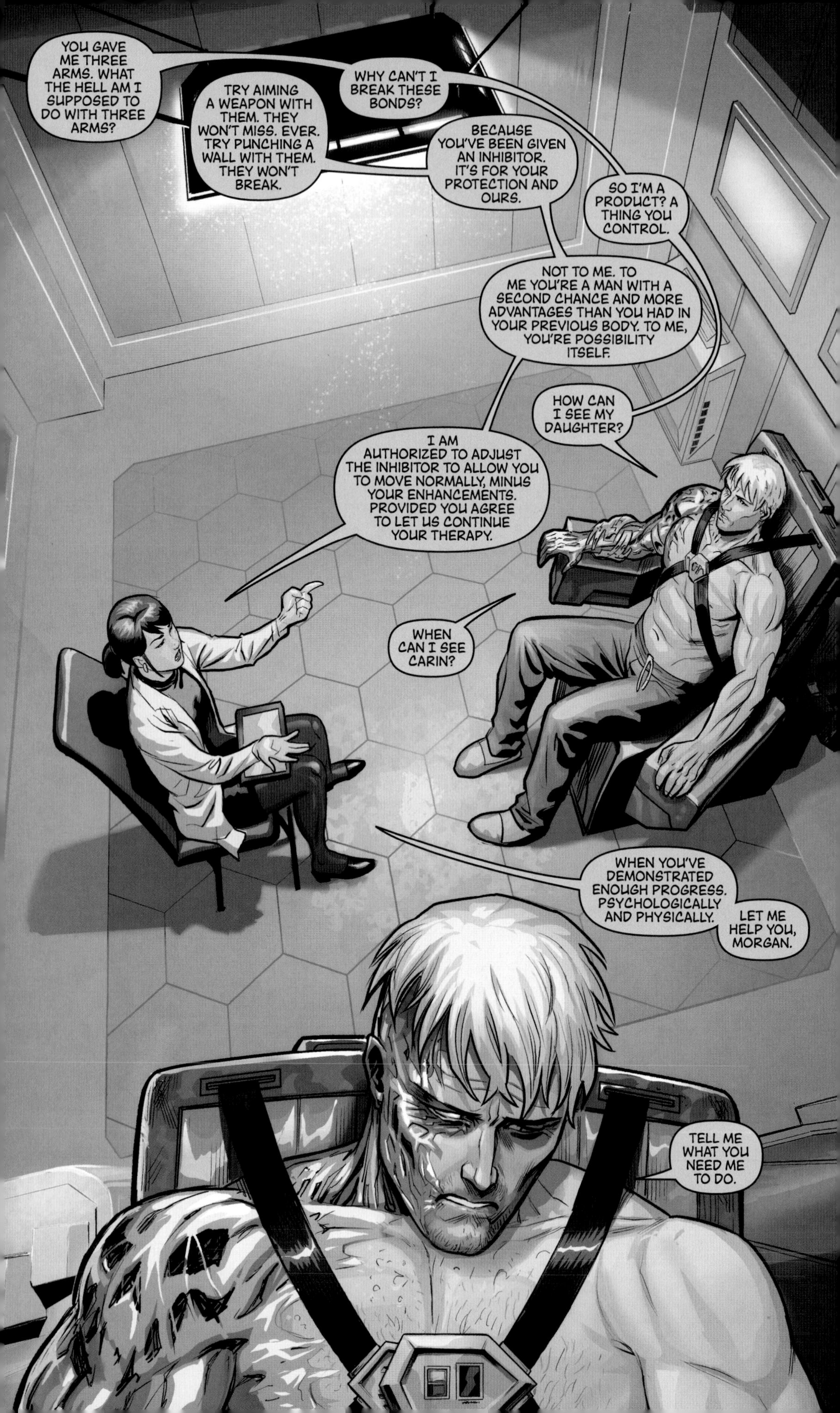
YOU GAVE ME THREE ARMS. WHAT THE HELL AM I SUPPOSED TO DO WITH THREE ARMS?
TRY AIMING A WEAPON WITH THEM. THEY WON'T MISS. EVER. TRY PUNCHING A WALL WITH THEM. THEY WON'T BREAK.
WHY CAN'T I BREAK THESE BONDS?
BECAUSE YOU'VE BEEN GIVEN AN INHIBITOR. IT'S FOR YOUR PROTECTION AND OURS.
SO I'M A PRODUCT? A THING YOU CONTROL.
NOT TO ME. TO ME YOU'RE A MAN WITH A SECOND CHANCE AND MORE ADVANTAGES THAN YOU HAD IN YOUR PREVIOUS BODY. TO ME, YOU'RE POSSIBILITY ITSELF.
HOW CAN I SEE MY DAUGHTER?
I AM AUTHORIZED TO ADJUST THE INHIBITOR TO ALLOW YOU TO MOVE NORMALLY, MINUS YOUR ENHANCEMENTS. PROVIDED YOU AGREE TO LET US CONTINUE YOUR THERAPY.
WHEN CAN I SEE CARIN?
WHEN YOU'VE DEMONSTRATED ENOUGH PROGRESS. PSYCHOLOGICALLY AND PHYSICALLY.
LET ME HELP YOU, MORGAN.
TELL ME WHAT YOU NEED ME TO DO.

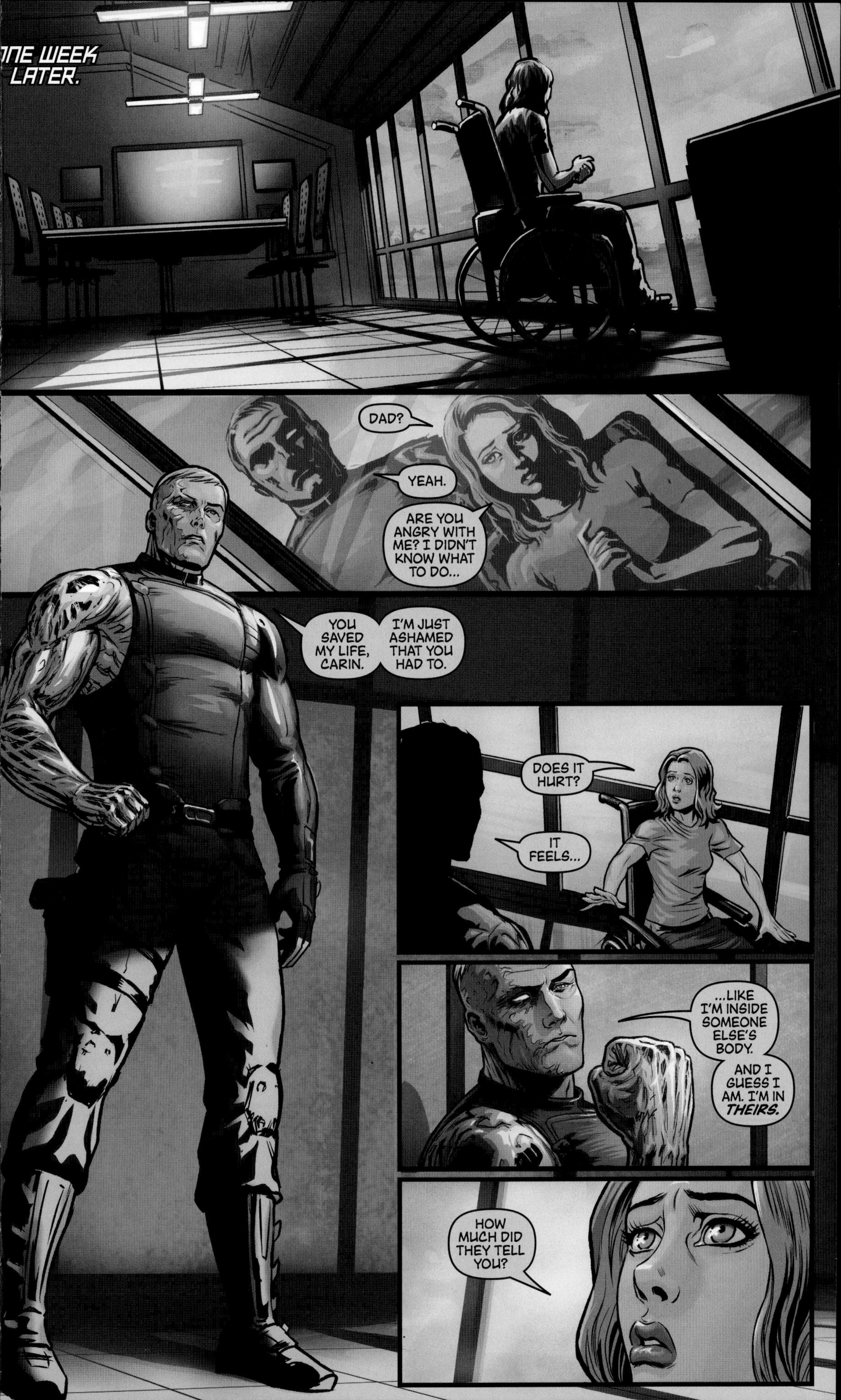

ONE WEEK LATER.
DAD?
YEAH.
ARE YOU ANGRY WITH ME? I DIDN'T KNOW WHAT TO DO...
YOU SAVED MY LIFE, CARIN.
I'M JUST ASHAMED THAT YOU HAD TO.
DOES IT HURT?
IT FEELS...
...LIKE I'M INSIDE SOMEONE ELSE'S BODY.
AND I GUESS I AM. I'M IN *THEIRS.*
HOW MUCH DID THEY TELL YOU?

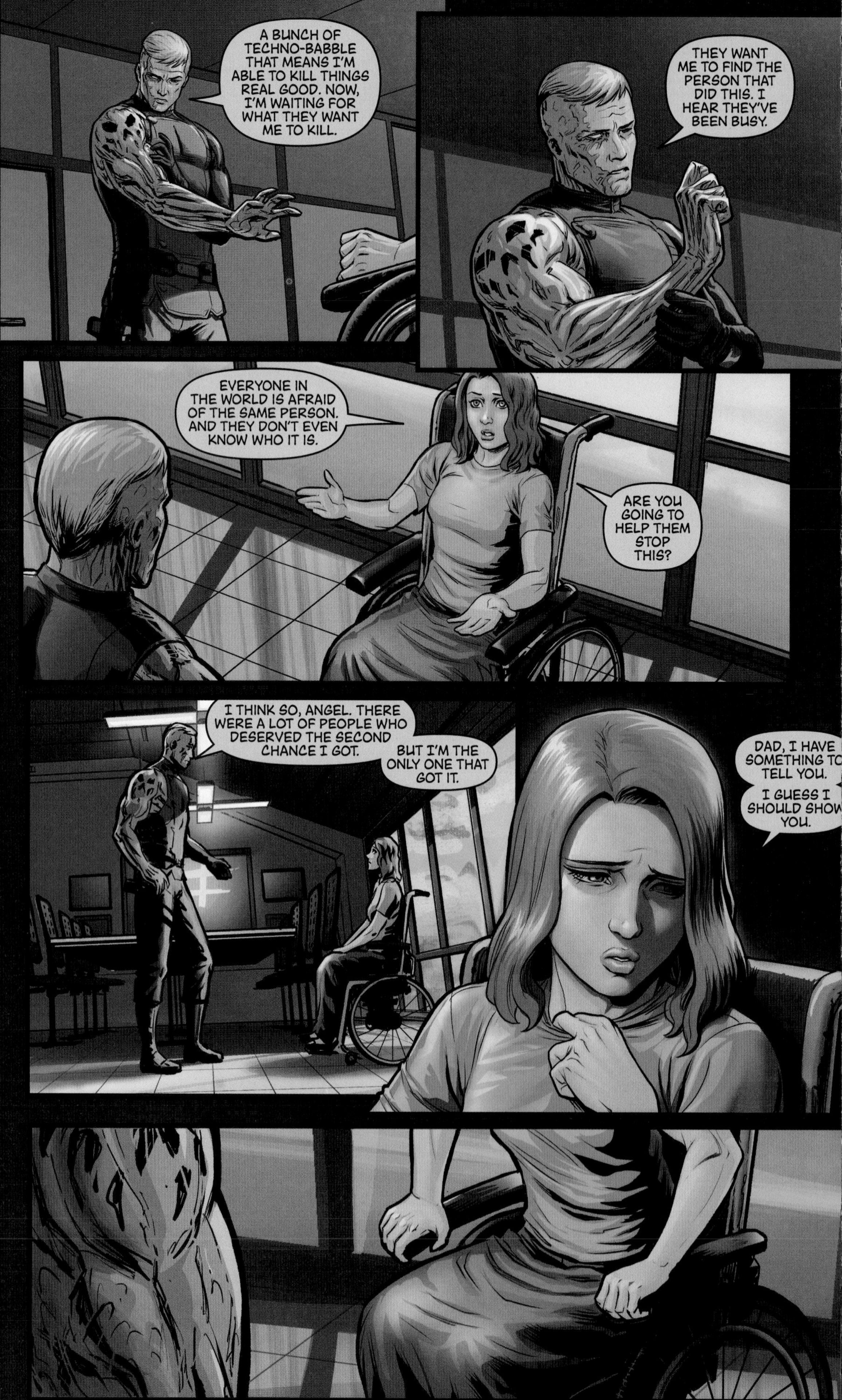
A BUNCH OF TECHNO-BABBLE THAT MEANS I'M ABLE TO KILL THINGS REAL GOOD. NOW, I'M WAITING FOR WHAT THEY WANT ME TO KILL.
THEY WANT ME TO FIND THE PERSON THAT DID THIS. I HEAR THEY'VE BEEN BUSY.
EVERYONE IN THE WORLD IS AFRAID OF THE SAME PERSON. AND THEY DON'T EVEN KNOW WHO IT IS.
ARE YOU GOING TO HELP THEM STOP THIS?
I THINK SO, ANGEL. THERE WERE A LOT OF PEOPLE WHO DESERVED THE SECOND CHANCE I GOT.
BUT I'M THE ONLY ONE THAT GOT IT.
DAD, I HAVE SOMETHING TO TELL YOU.
I GUESS I SHOULD SHOW YOU.

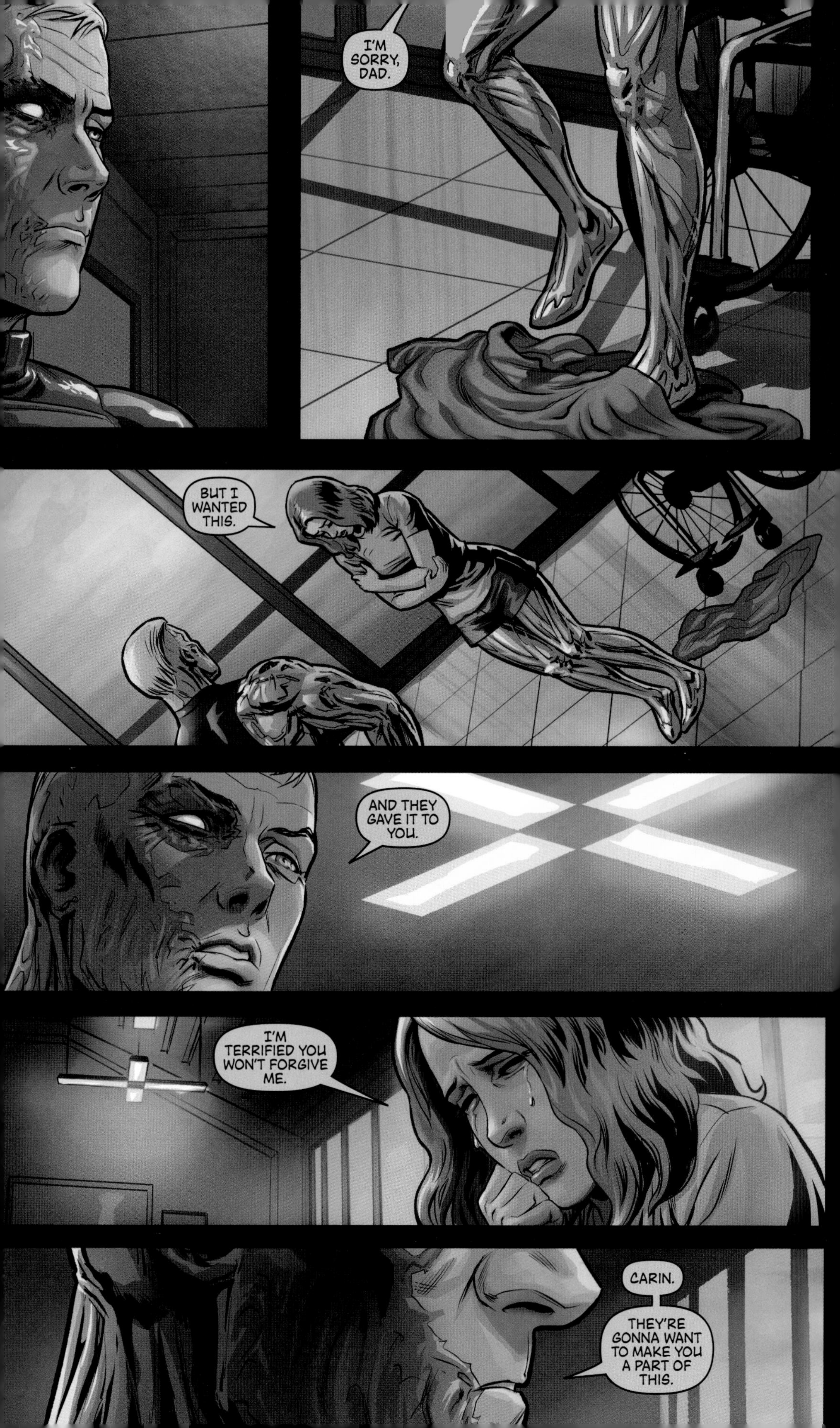
I'M SORRY, DAD.
BUT I WANTED THIS.
AND THEY GAVE IT TO YOU.
I'M TERRIFIED YOU WON'T FORGIVE ME.
CARIN.
THEY'RE GONNA WANT TO MAKE YOU A PART OF THIS.

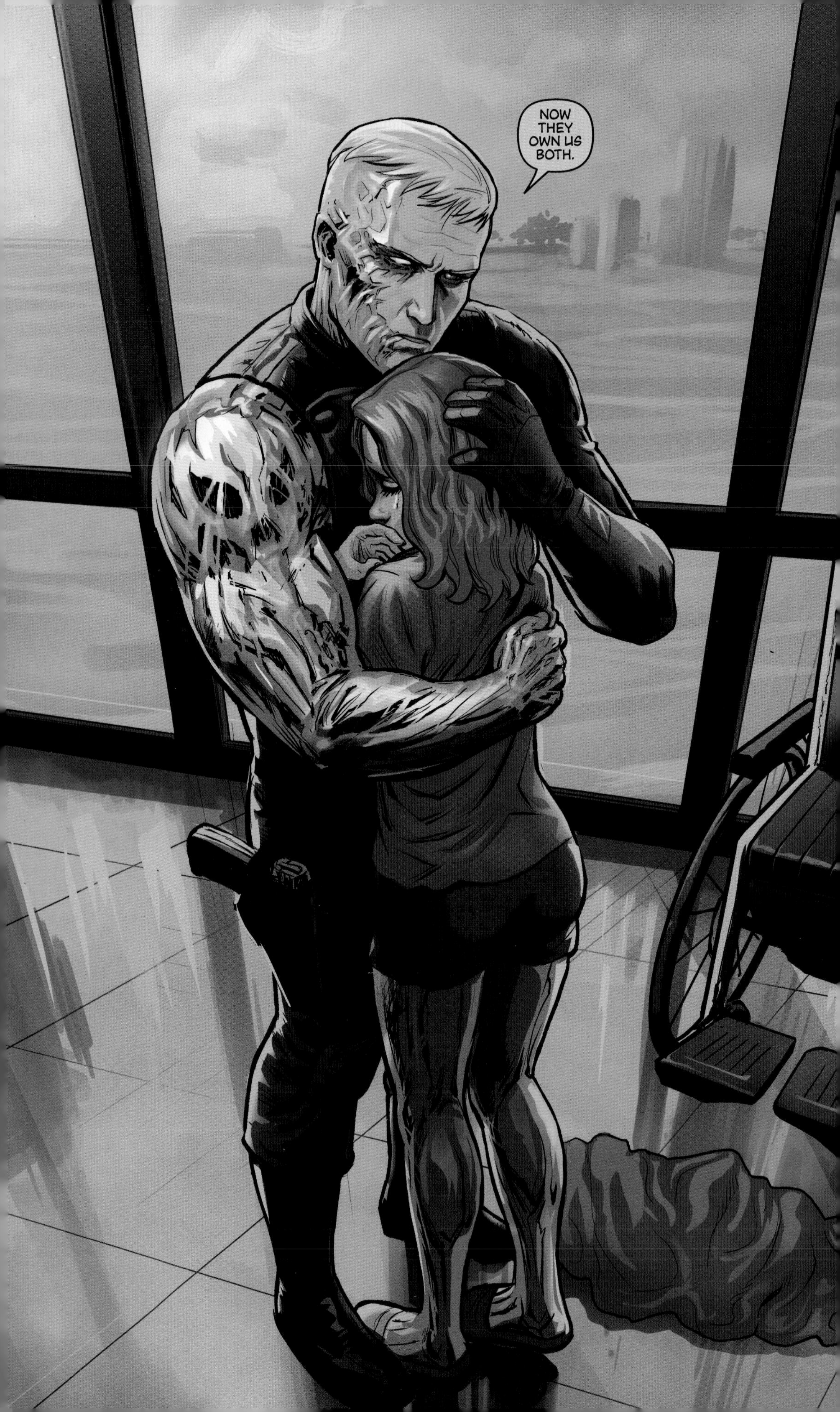
NOW THEY OWN US BOTH.

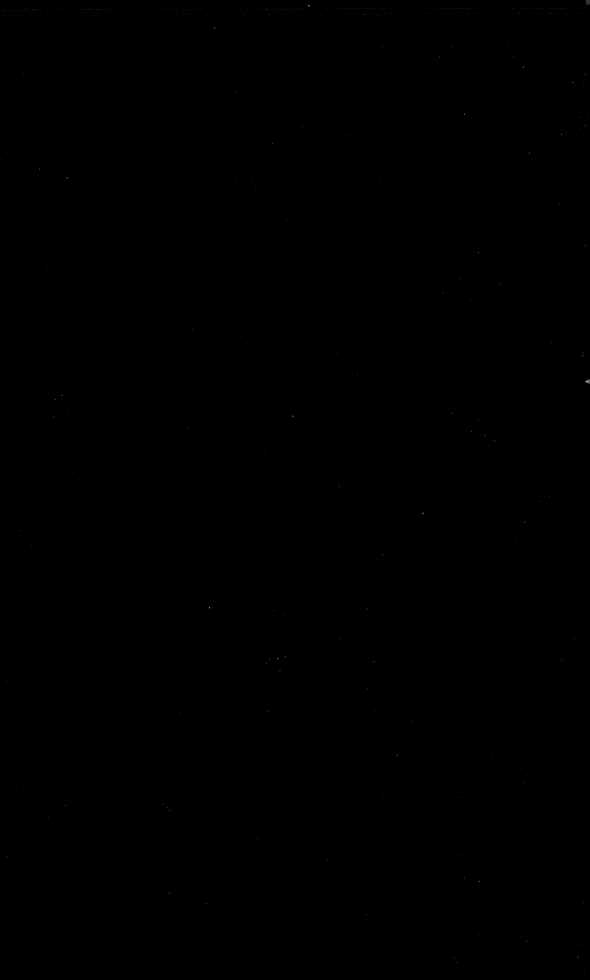

CHAPTER TWO

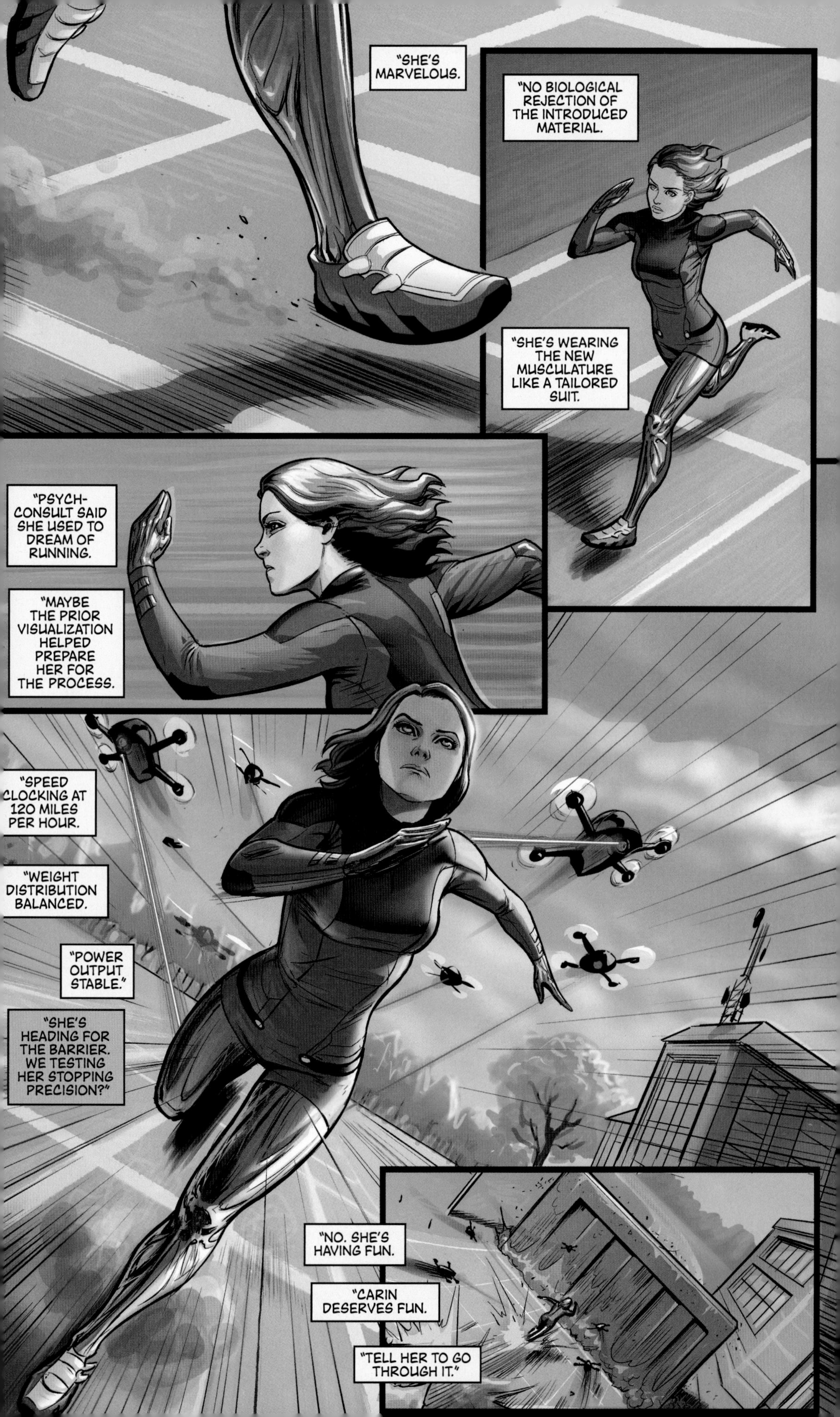
"SHE'S MARVELOUS.
"NO BIOLOGICAL REJECTION OF THE INTRODUCED MATERIAL.
"SHE'S WEARING THE NEW MUSCULATURE LIKE A TAILORED SUIT.
"PSYCH-CONSULT SAID SHE USED TO DREAM OF RUNNING.
"MAYBE THE PRIOR VISUALIZATION HELPED PREPARE HER FOR THE PROCESS.
"SPEED CLOCKING AT 120 MILES PER HOUR.
"WEIGHT DISTRIBUTION BALANCED.
"POWER OUTPUT STABLE."
"SHE'S HEADING FOR THE BARRIER. WE TESTING HER STOPPING PRECISION?"
"NO. SHE'S HAVING FUN.
"CARIN DESERVES FUN.
"TELL HER TO GO THROUGH IT."

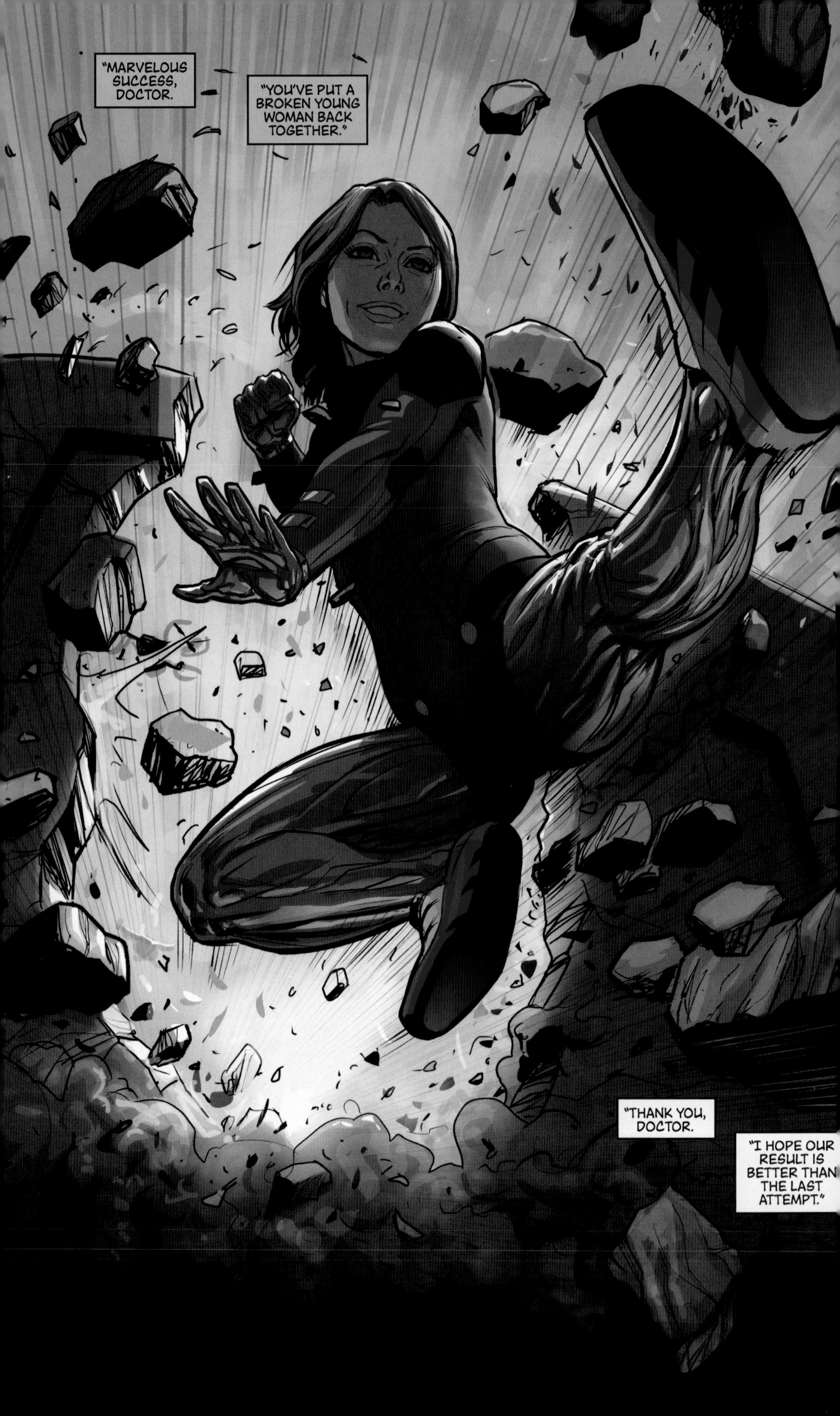
"MARVELOUS SUCCESS, DOCTOR.
"YOU'VE PUT A BROKEN YOUNG WOMAN BACK TOGETHER."
"THANK YOU, DOCTOR.
"I HOPE OUR RESULT IS BETTER THAN THE LAST ATTEMPT."

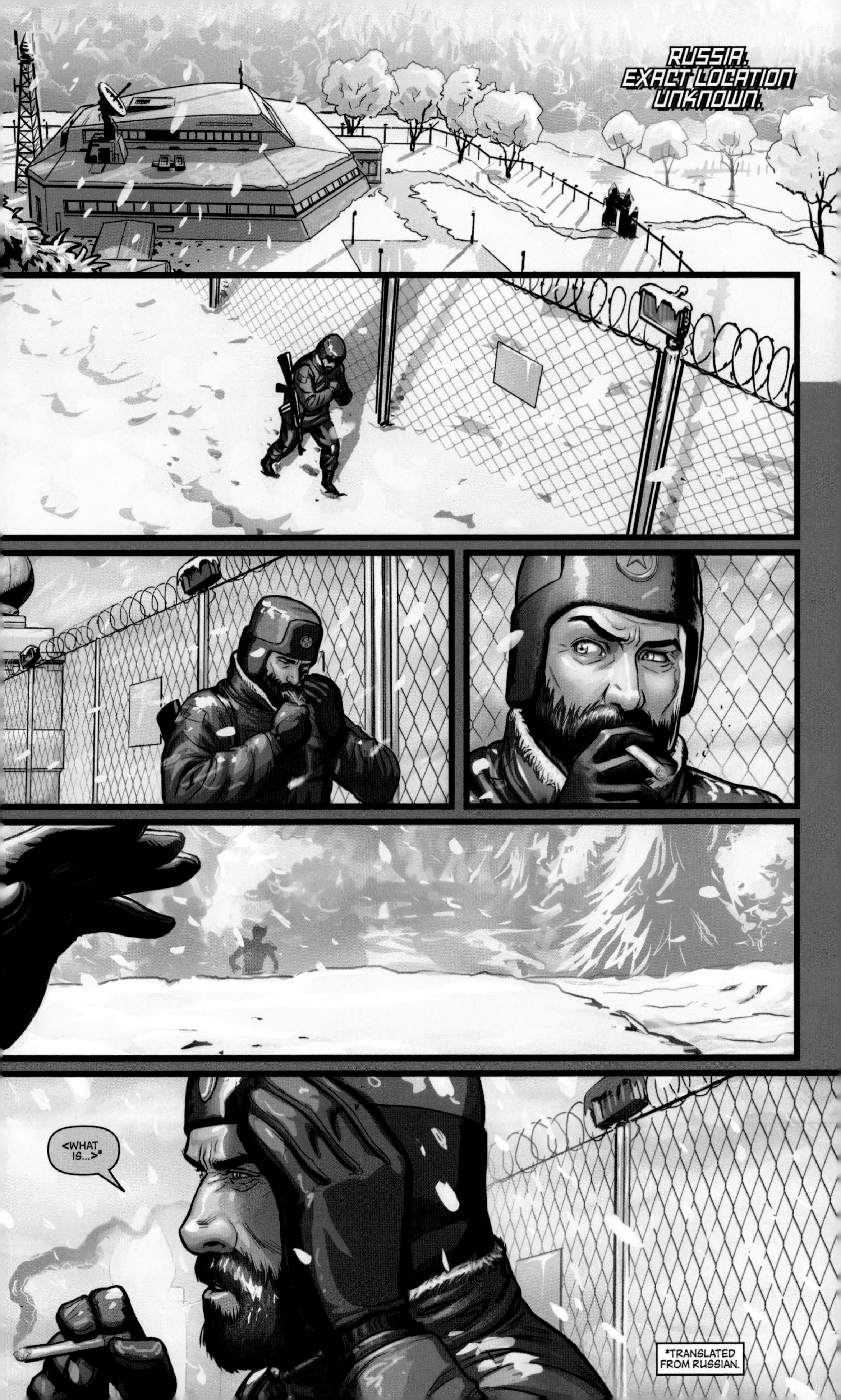
RUSSIA. EXACT LOCATION UNKNOWN.
<WHAT IS...>*
*TRANSLATED FROM RUSSIAN.

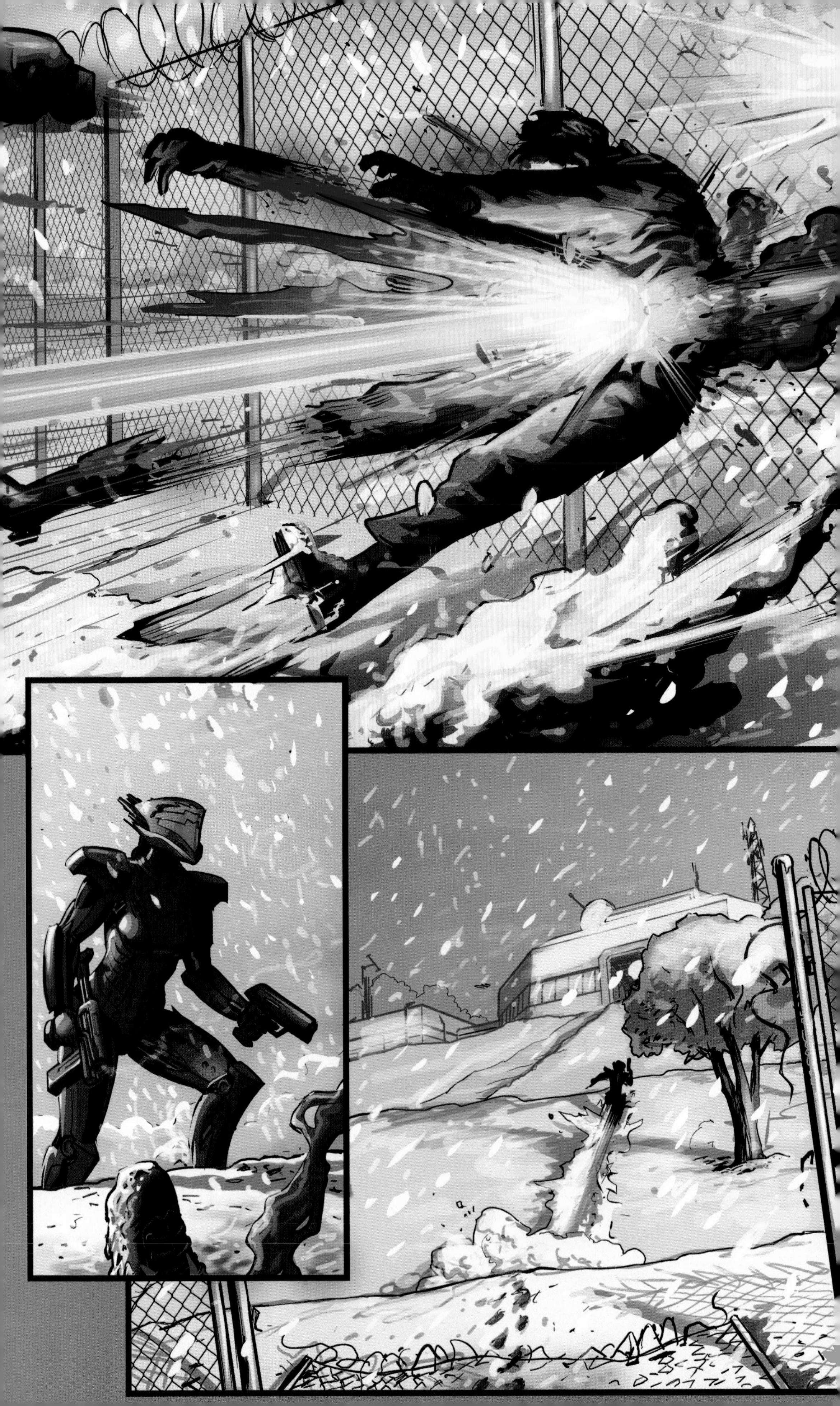

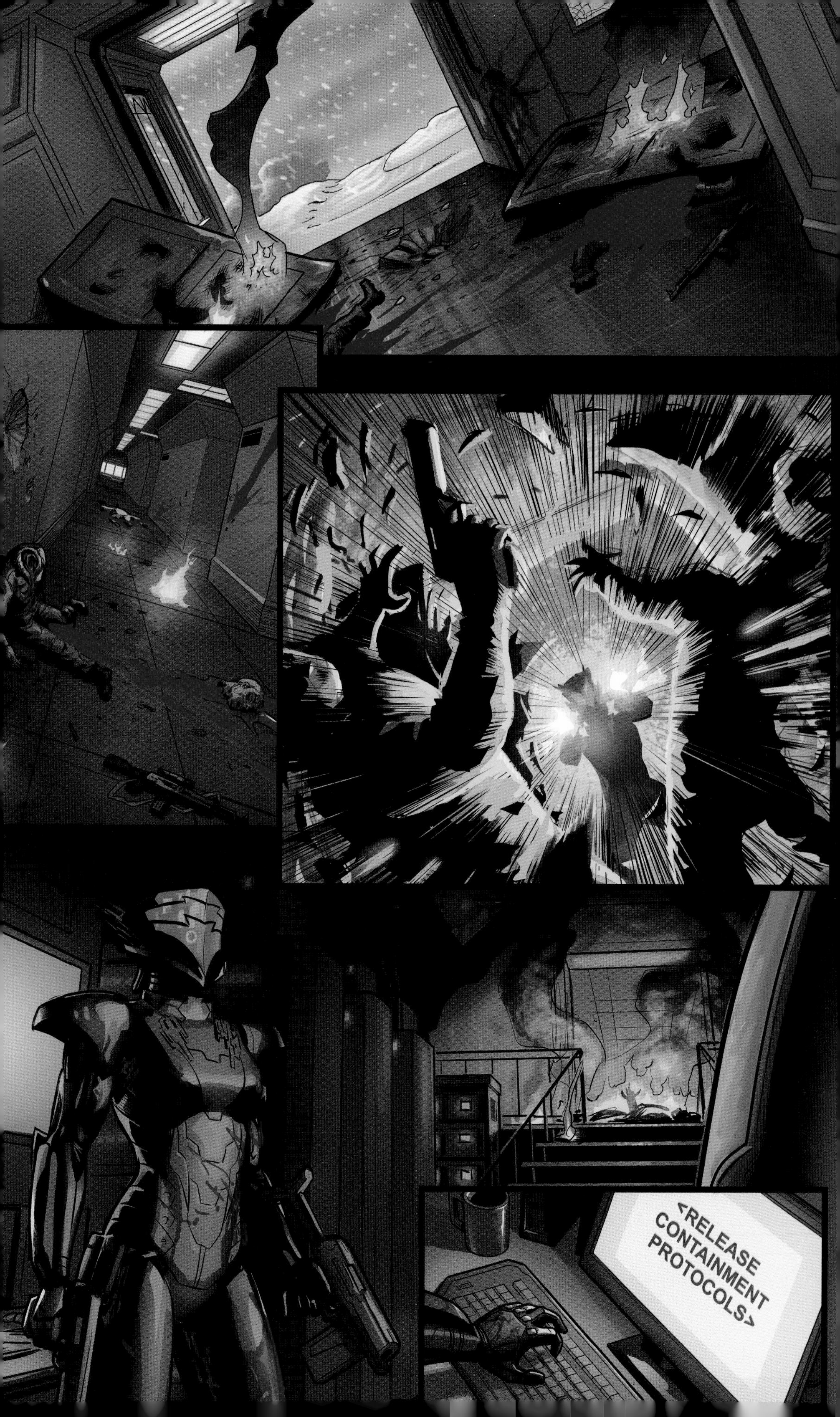
<RELEASE CONTAINMENT PROTOCOLS>

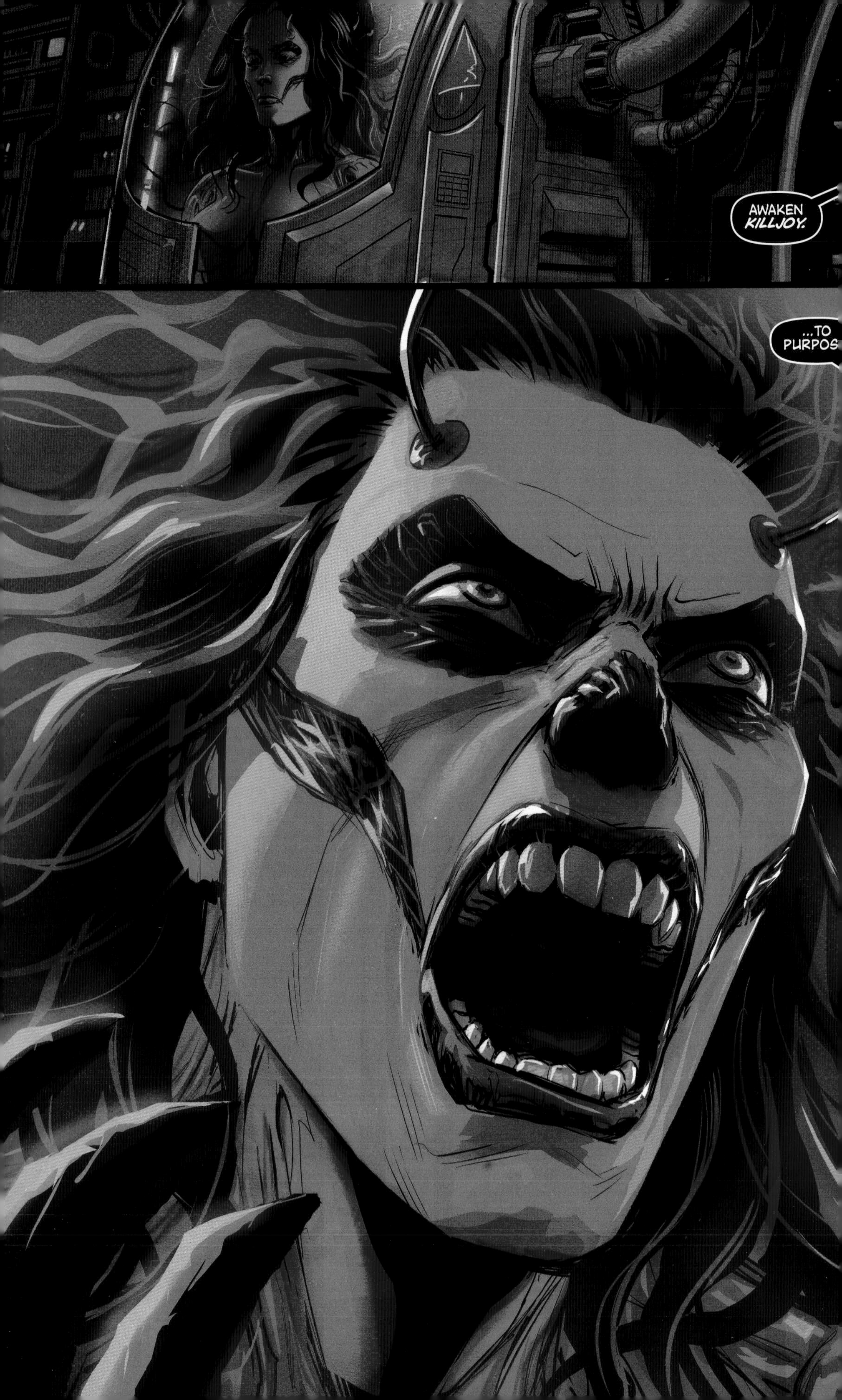
AWAKEN KILLJOY.
...TO PURPOS

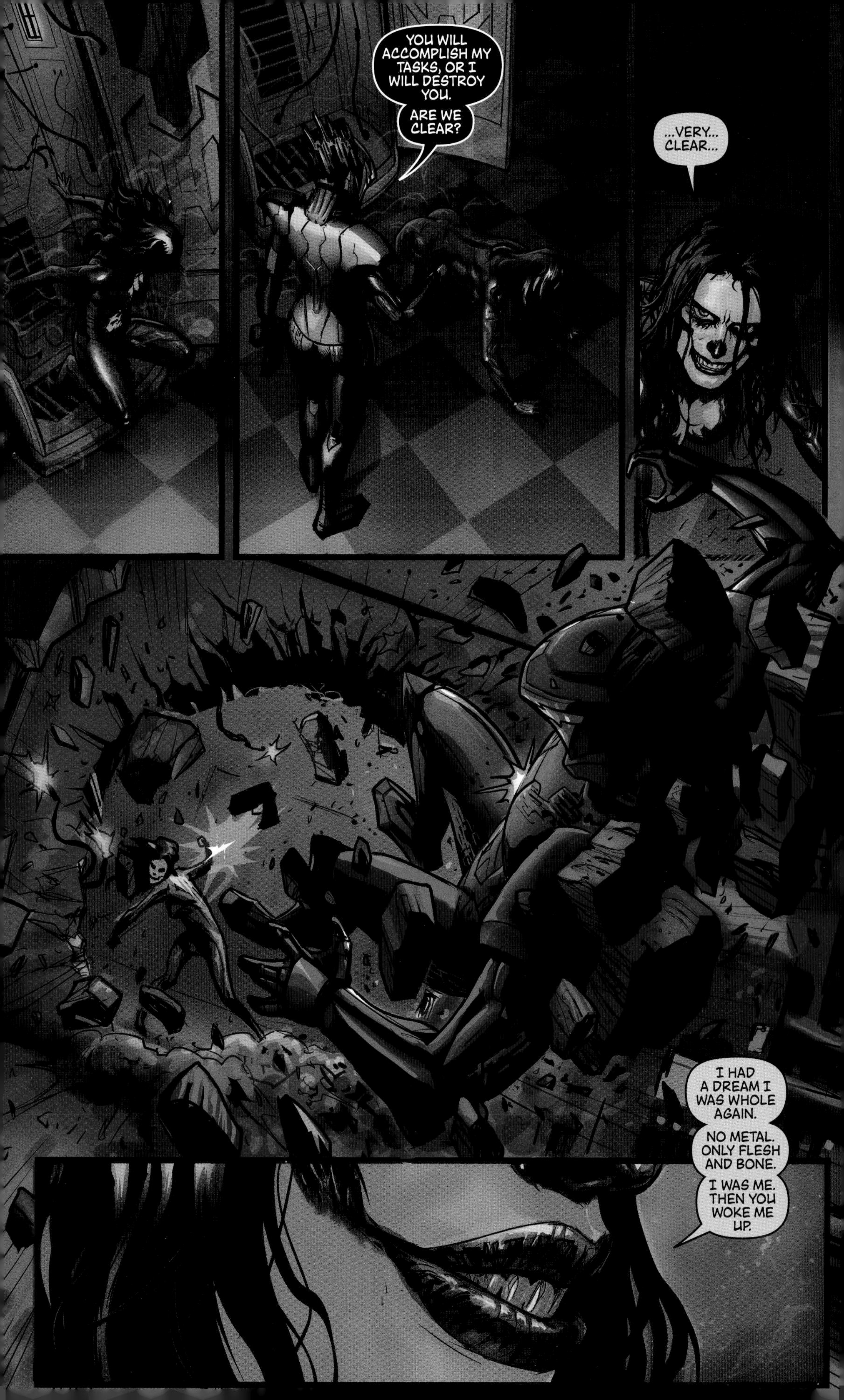
YOU WILL ACCOMPLISH MY TASKS, OR I WILL DESTROY YOU.
ARE WE CLEAR?
...VERY... CLEAR...
I HAD A DREAM I WAS WHOLE AGAIN.
NO METAL. ONLY FLESH AND BONE.
I WAS ME. THEN YOU WOKE ME UP.

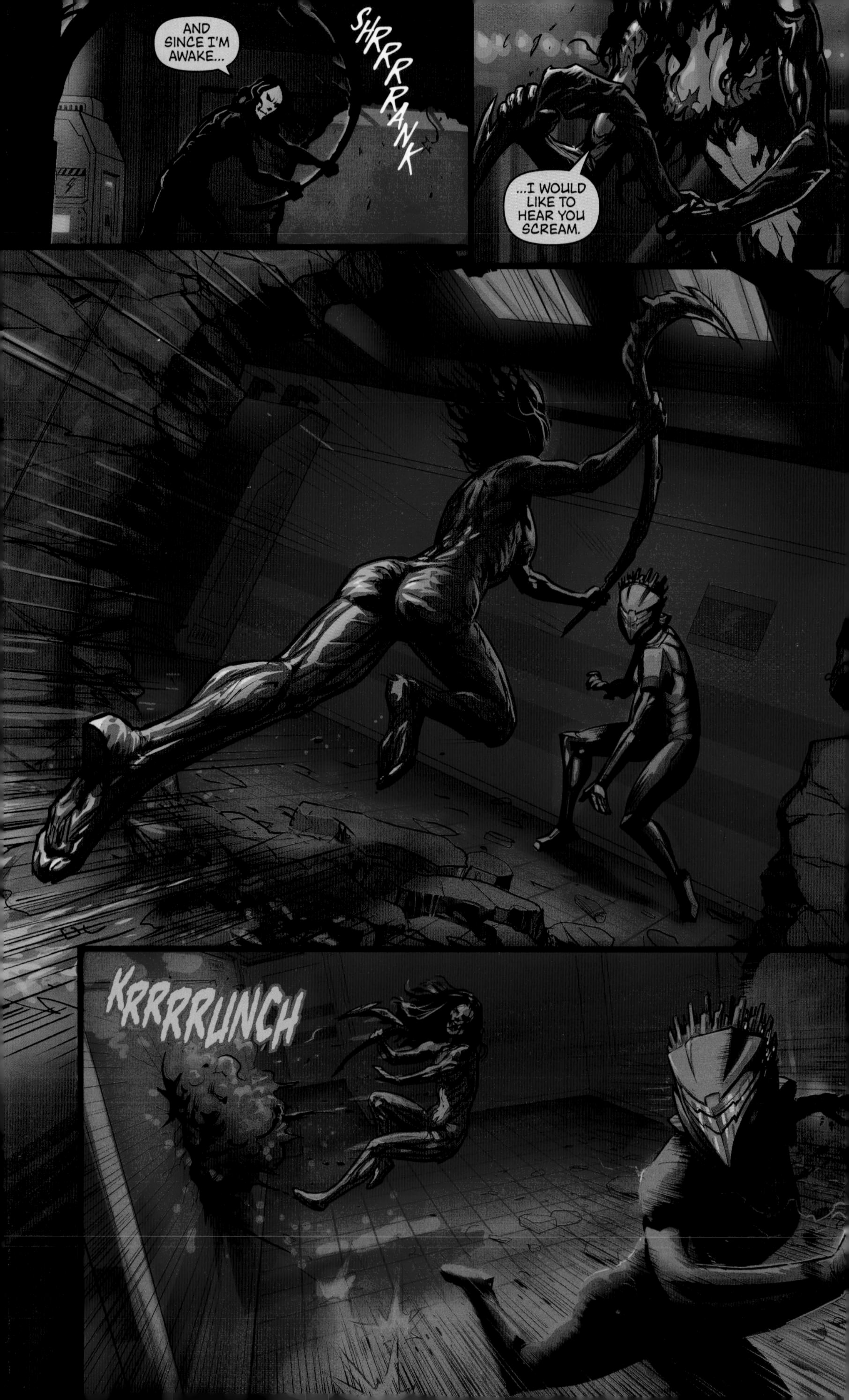
AND SINCE I'M AWAKE...
SHRRRANK
...I WOULD LIKE TO HEAR YOU SCREAM.
KRRRRUNCH

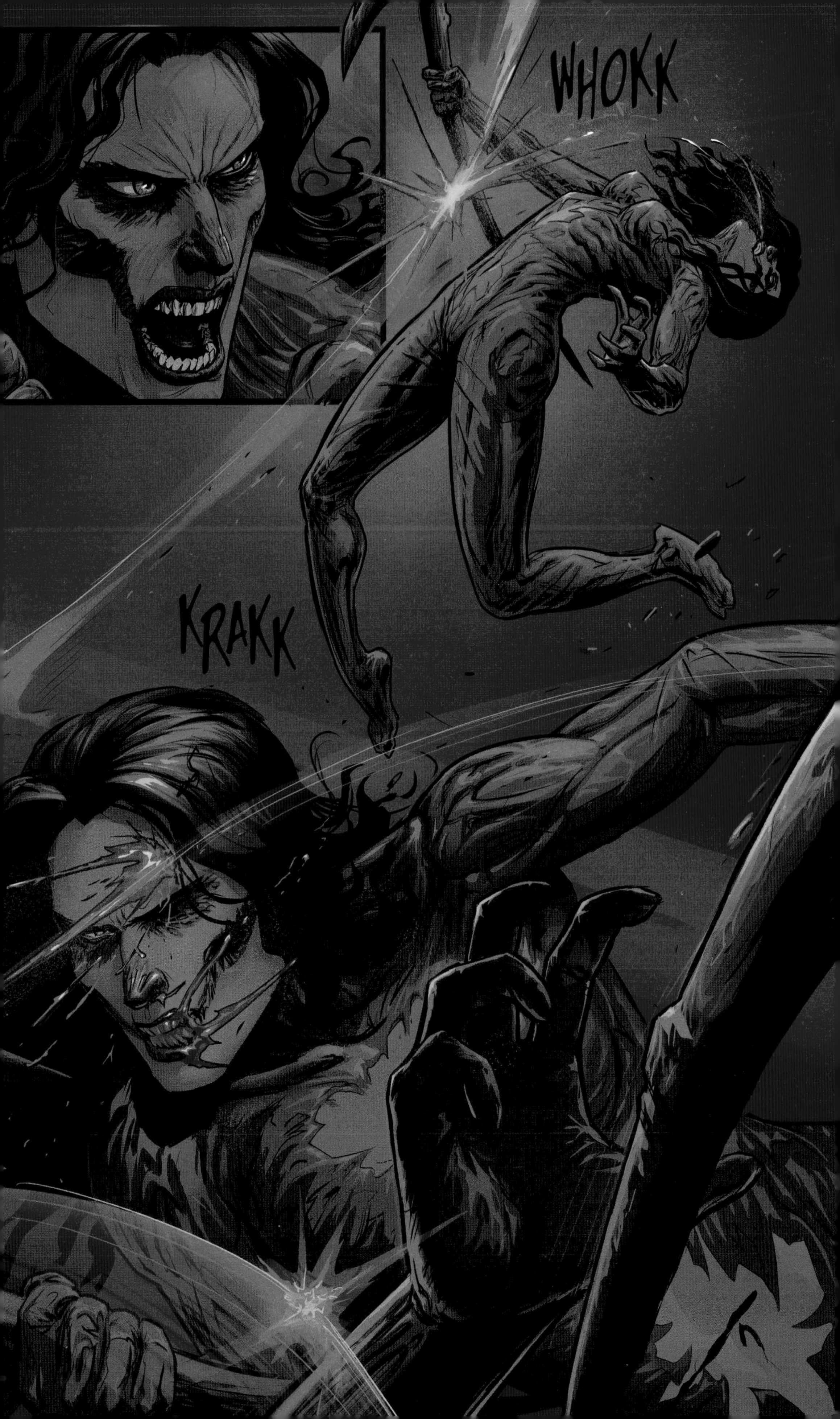
WHOKK
KRAKK

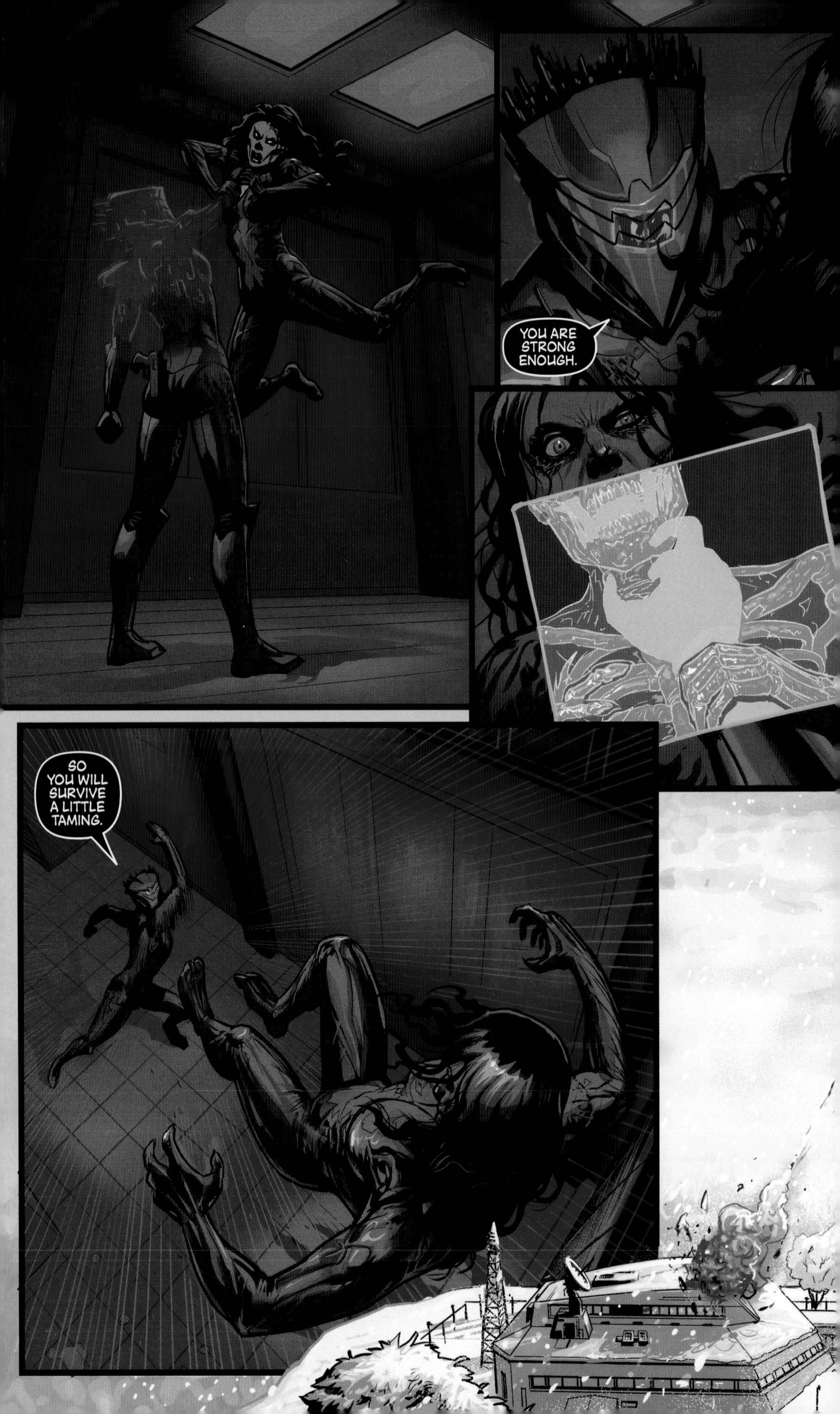
YOU ARE STRONG ENOUGH.
SO YOU WILL SURVIVE A LITTLE TAMING.

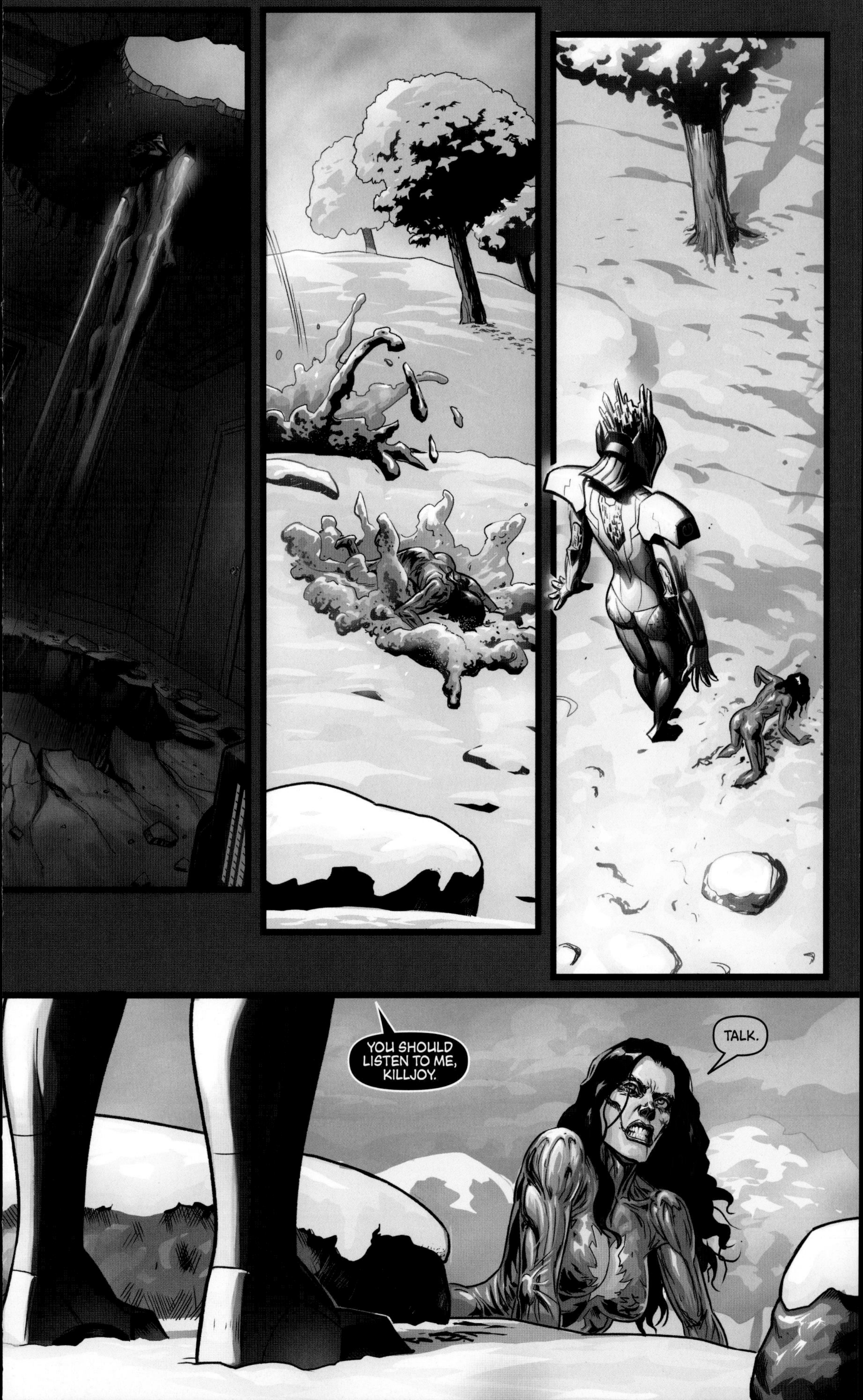
YOU SHOULD LISTEN TO ME, KILLJOY.
TALK.

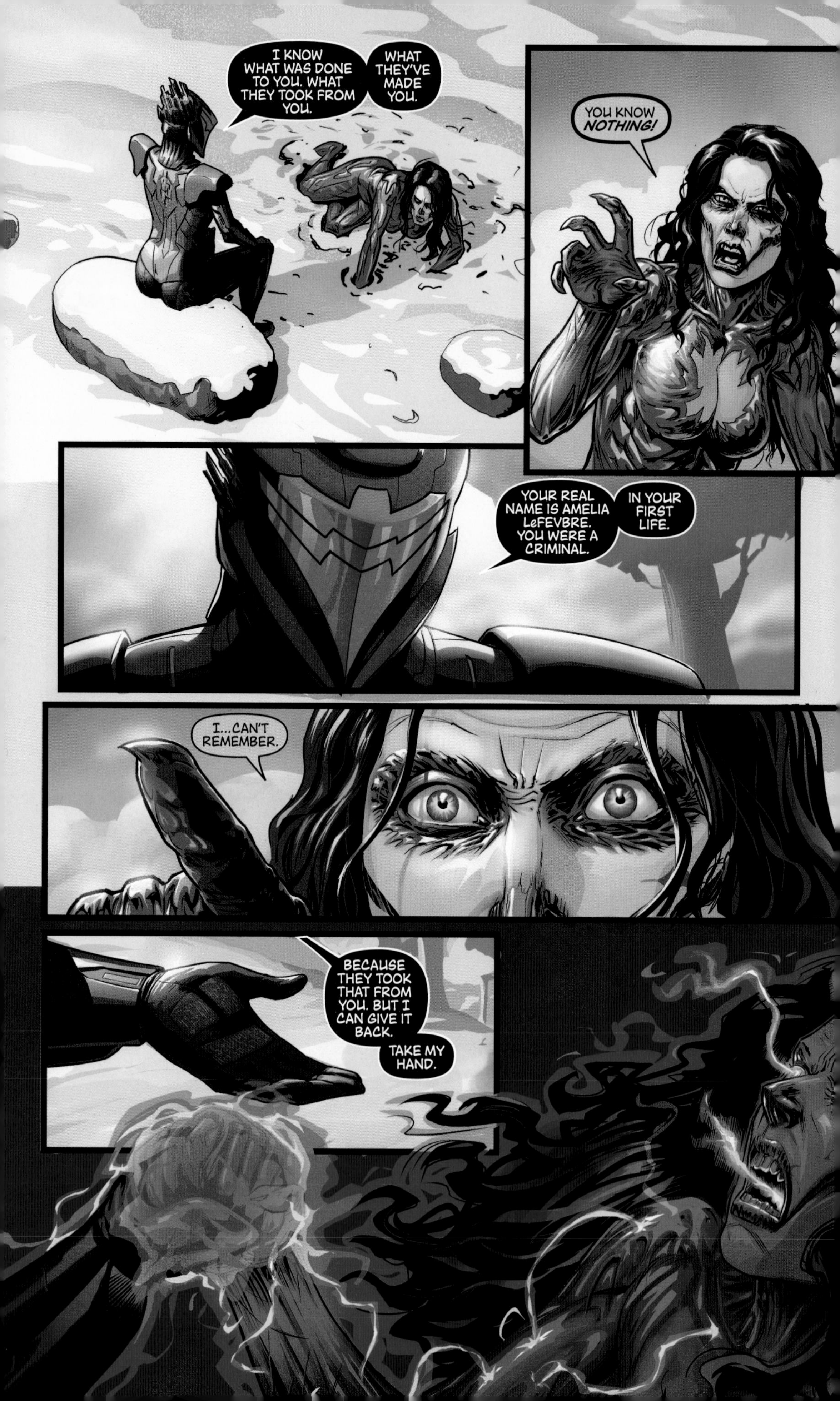
I KNOW WHAT WAS DONE TO YOU. WHAT THEY TOOK FROM YOU.
WHAT THEY'VE MADE YOU.
YOU KNOW *NOTHING!*
YOUR REAL NAME IS AMELIA LeFEVBRE. YOU WERE A CRIMINAL.
IN YOUR FIRST LIFE.
I...CAN'T REMEMBER.
BECAUSE THEY TOOK THAT FROM YOU. BUT I CAN GIVE IT BACK.
TAKE MY HAND.

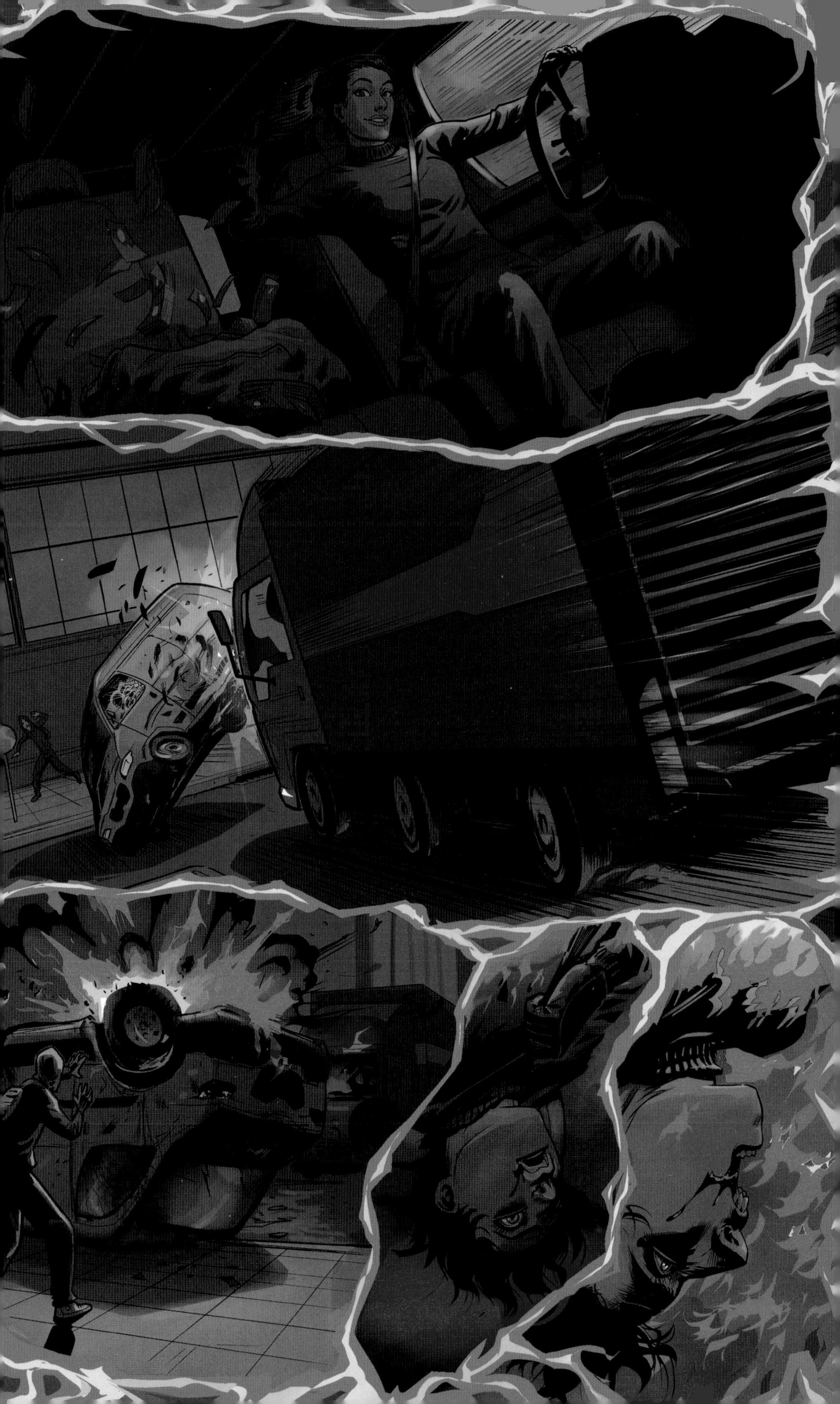

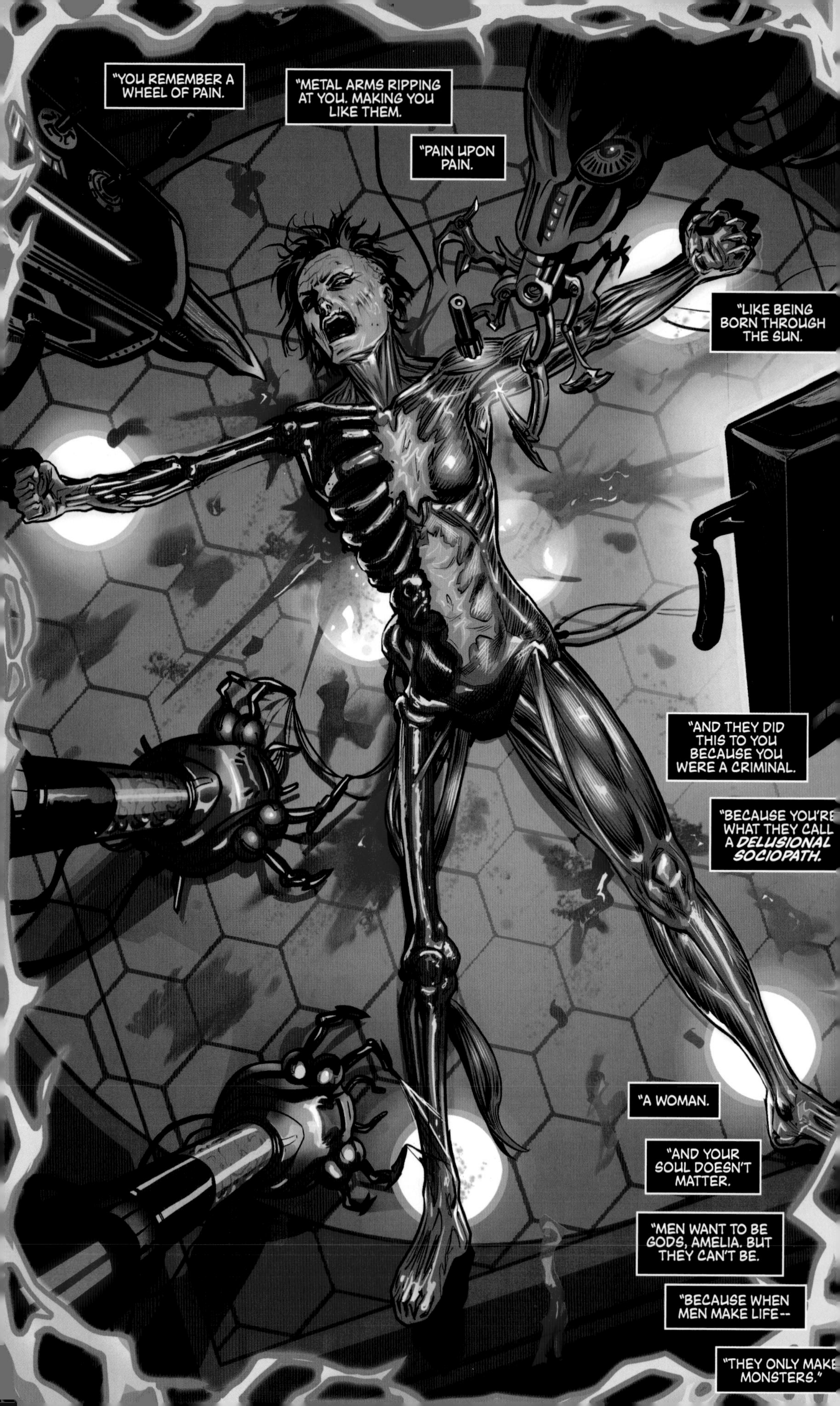

"YOU REMEMBER A WHEEL OF PAIN.
"METAL ARMS RIPPING AT YOU. MAKING YOU LIKE THEM.
"PAIN UPON PAIN.
"LIKE BEING BORN THROUGH THE SUN.
"AND THEY DID THIS TO YOU BECAUSE YOU WERE A CRIMINAL.
"BECAUSE YOU'RE WHAT THEY CALL A DELUSIONAL SOCIOPATH.
"A WOMAN.
"AND YOUR SOUL DOESN'T MATTER.
"MEN WANT TO BE GODS, AMELIA. BUT THEY CAN'T BE.
"BECAUSE WHEN MEN MAKE LIFE--
"THEY ONLY MAKE MONSTERS."

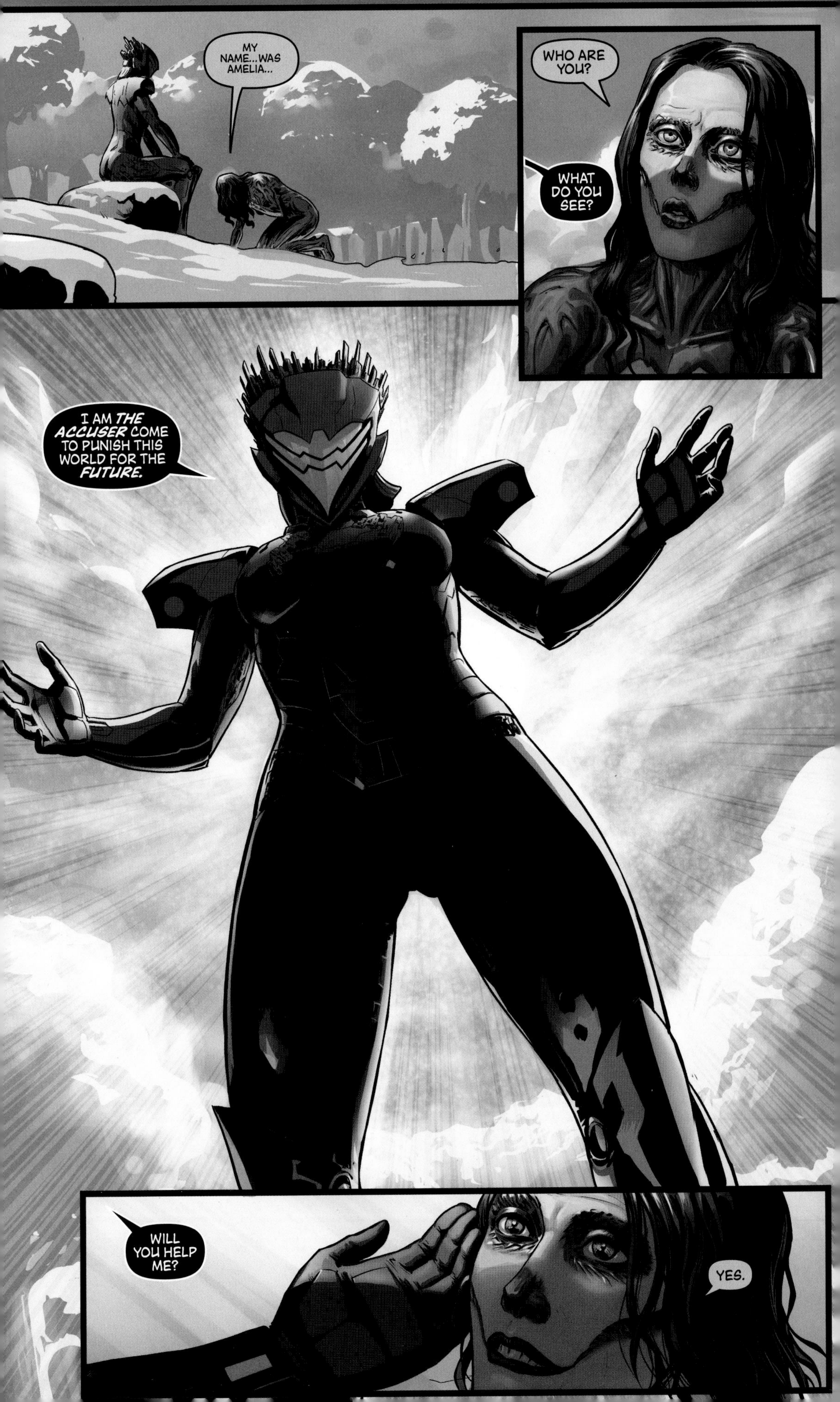

MY NAME...WAS AMELIA...
WHO ARE YOU?
WHAT DO YOU SEE?
I AM *THE ACCUSER* COME TO PUNISH THIS WORLD FOR THE *FUTURE.*
WILL YOU HELP ME?
YES.

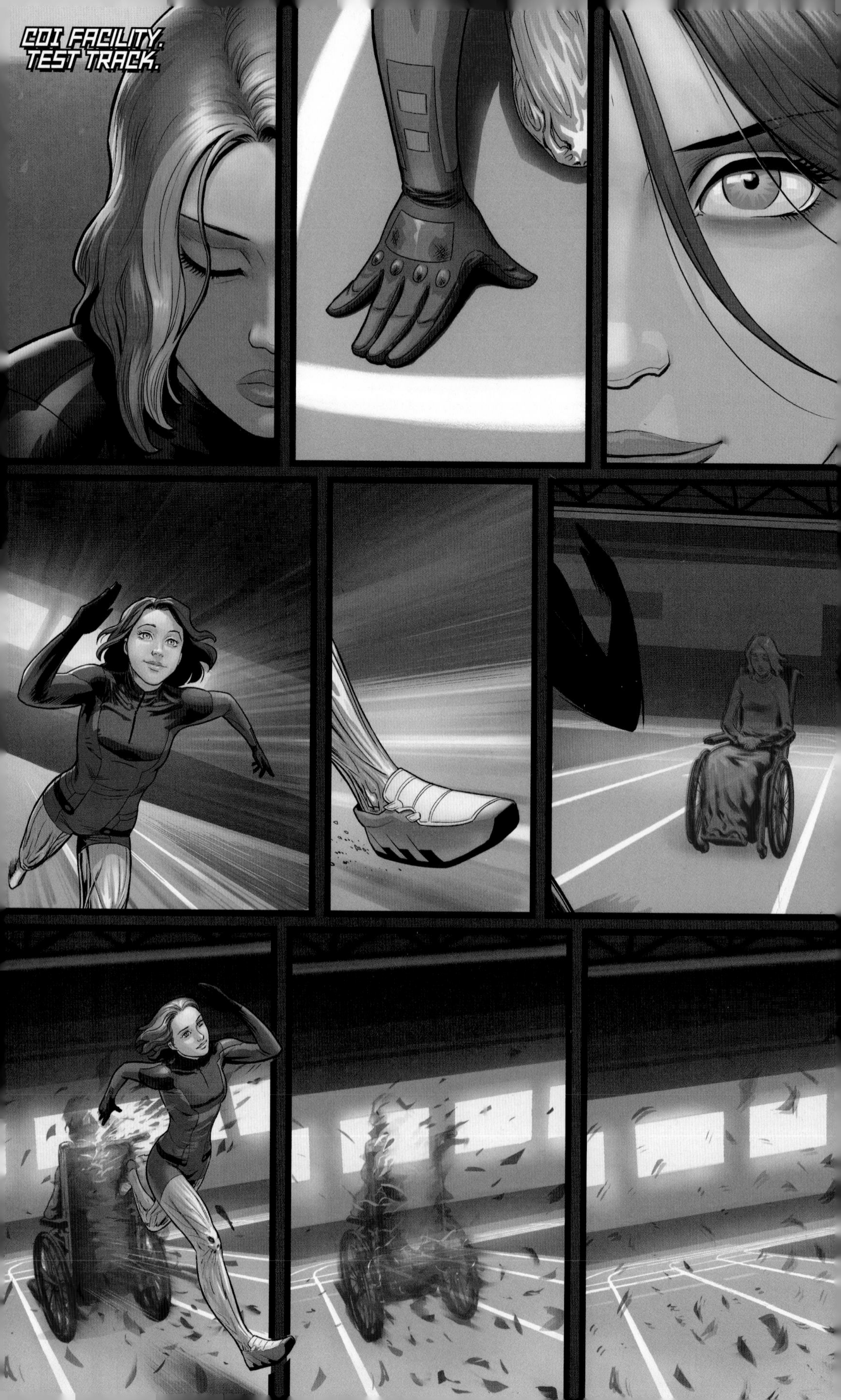
CDI FACILITY.
TEST TRACK.

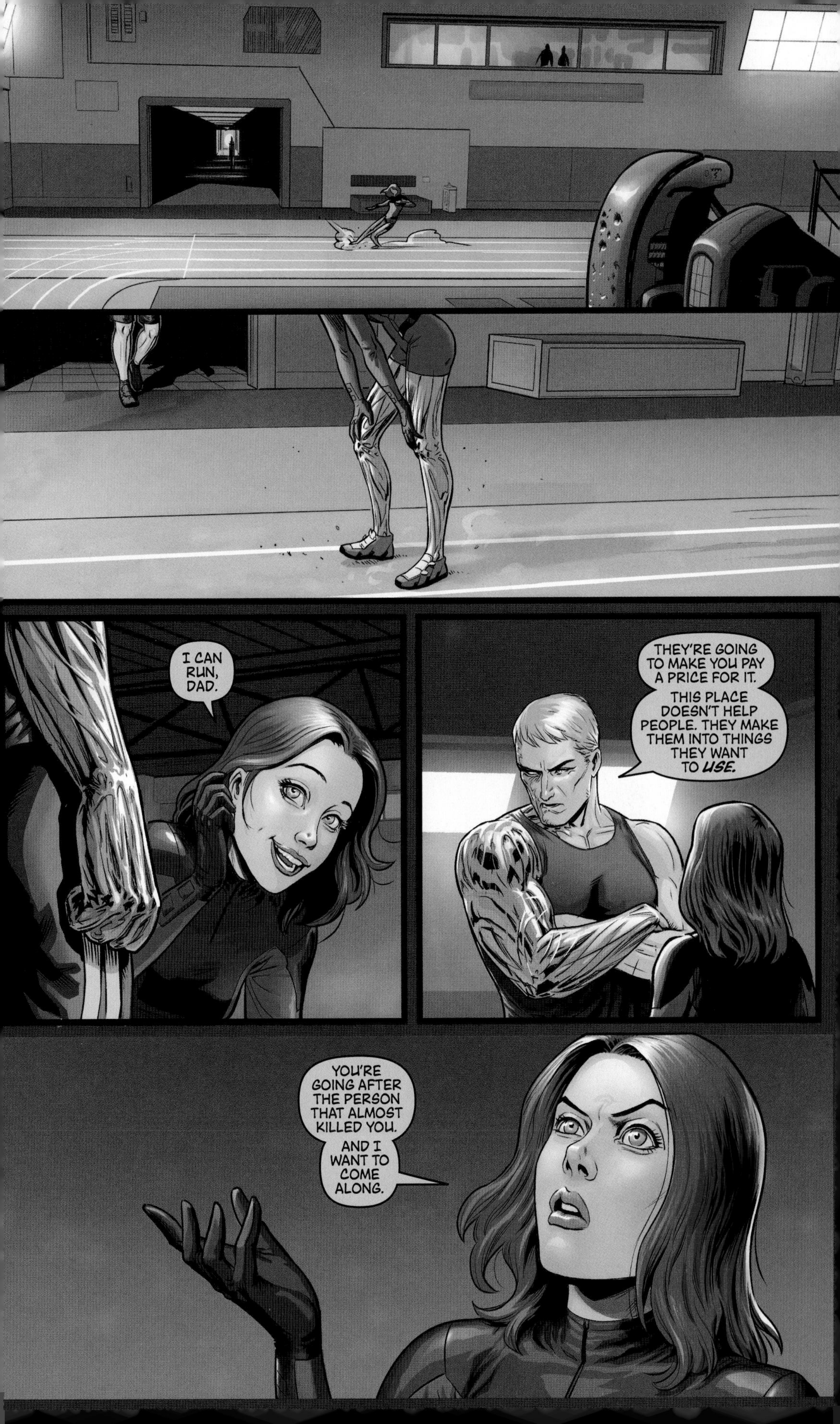
I CAN RUN, DAD.
THEY'RE GOING TO MAKE YOU PAY A PRICE FOR IT.
THIS PLACE DOESN'T HELP PEOPLE. THEY MAKE THEM INTO THINGS THEY WANT TO USE.
YOU'RE GOING AFTER THE PERSON THAT ALMOST KILLED YOU.
AND I WANT TO COME ALONG.

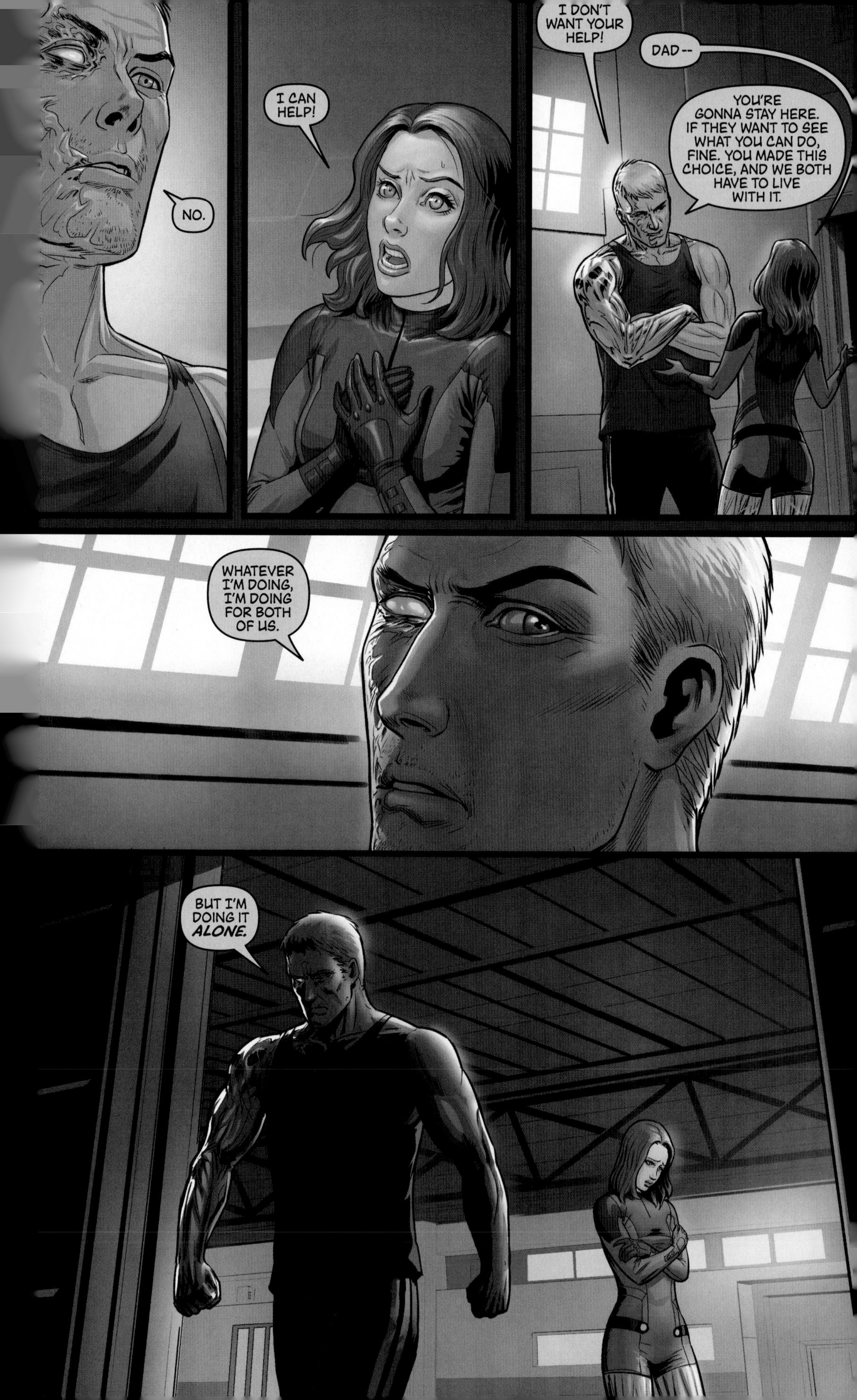
NO.
I CAN HELP!
I DON'T WANT YOUR HELP!
DAD --
YOU'RE GONNA STAY HERE. IF THEY WANT TO SEE WHAT YOU CAN DO, FINE. YOU MADE THIS CHOICE, AND WE BOTH HAVE TO LIVE WITH IT.
WHATEVER I'M DOING, I'M DOING FOR BOTH OF US.
BUT I'M DOING IT *ALONE.*

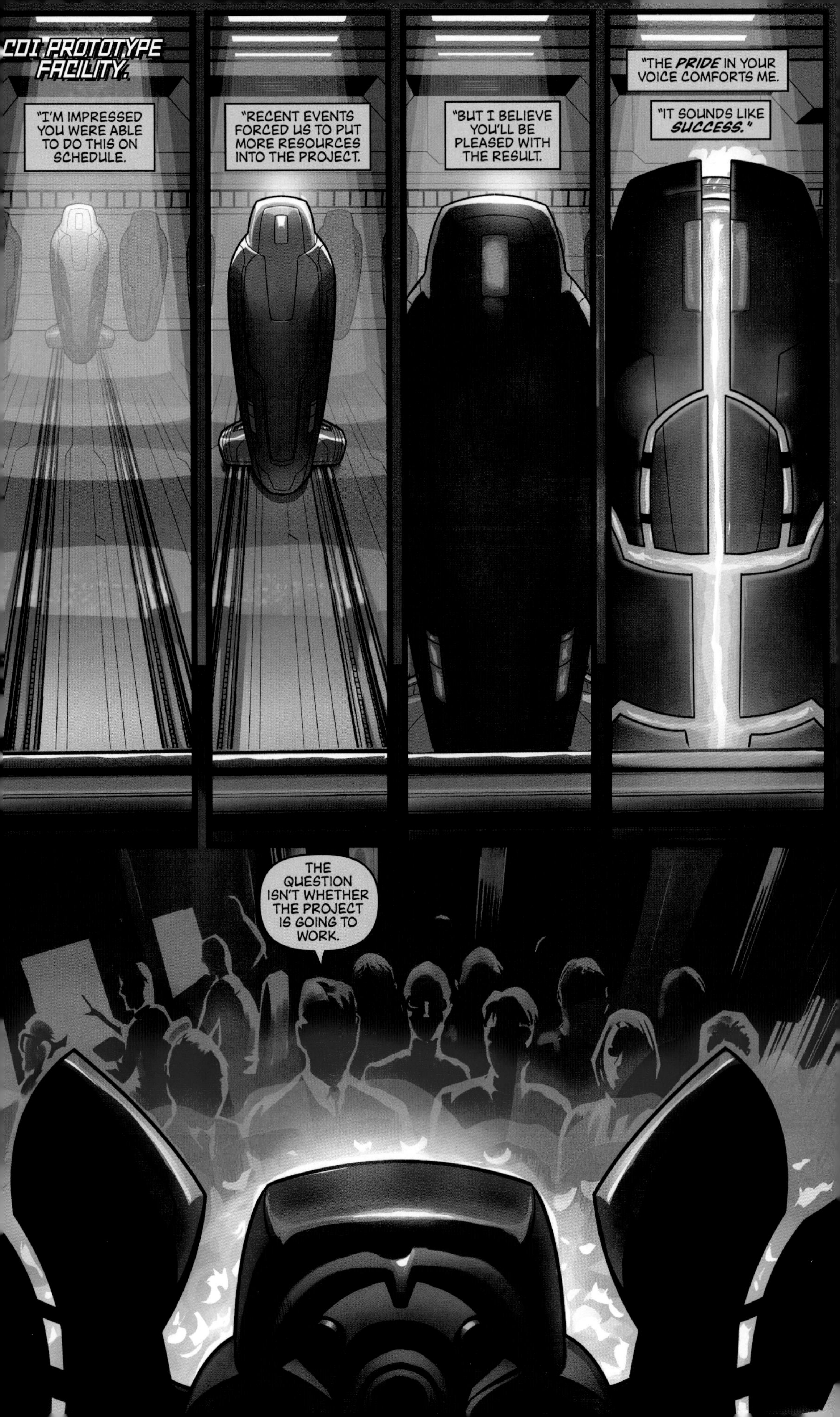
COI PROTOTYPE FACILITY.
"I'M IMPRESSED YOU WERE ABLE TO DO THIS ON SCHEDULE.
"RECENT EVENTS FORCED US TO PUT MORE RESOURCES INTO THE PROJECT.
"BUT I BELIEVE YOU'LL BE PLEASED WITH THE RESULT.
"THE PRIDE IN YOUR VOICE COMFORTS ME.
"IT SOUNDS LIKE SUCCESS."
THE QUESTION ISN'T WHETHER THE PROJECT IS GOING TO WORK.

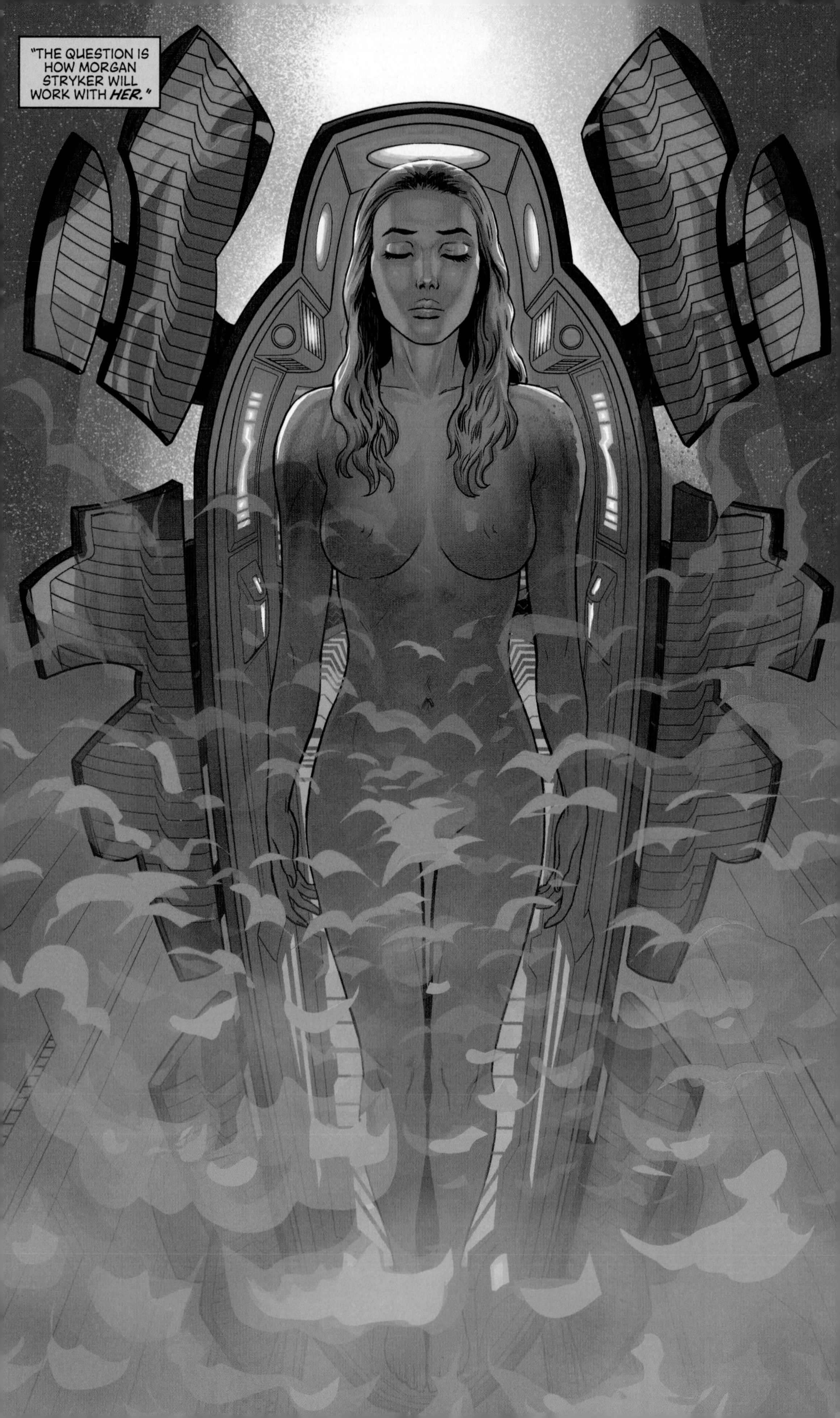
"THE QUESTION IS HOW MORGAN STRYKER WILL WORK WITH *HER.*"

CHAPTER THREE

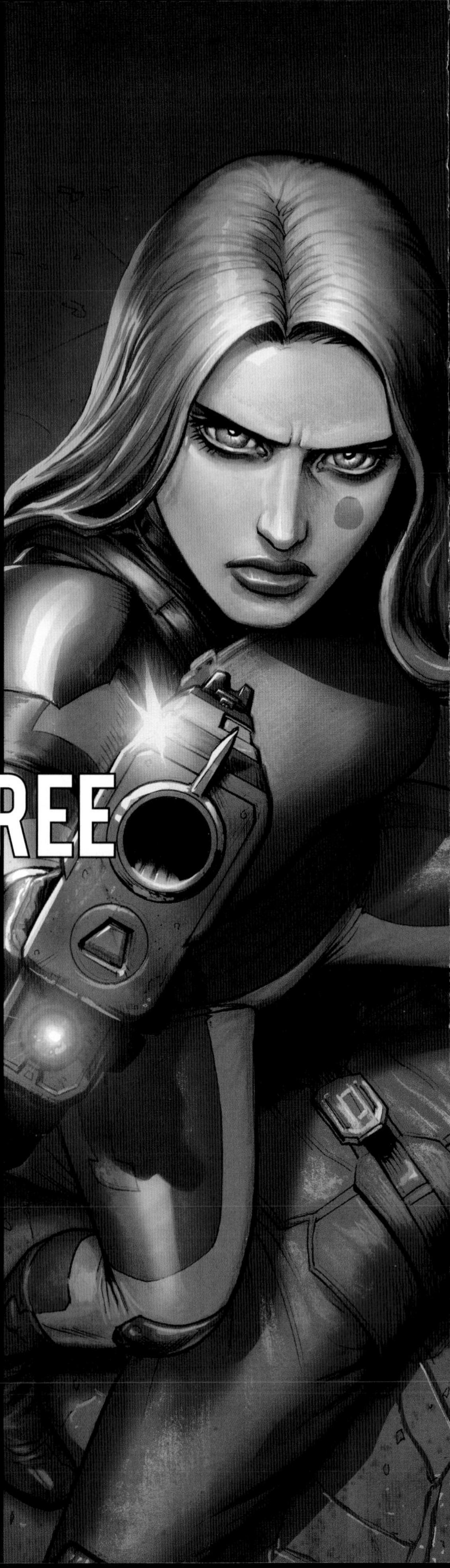

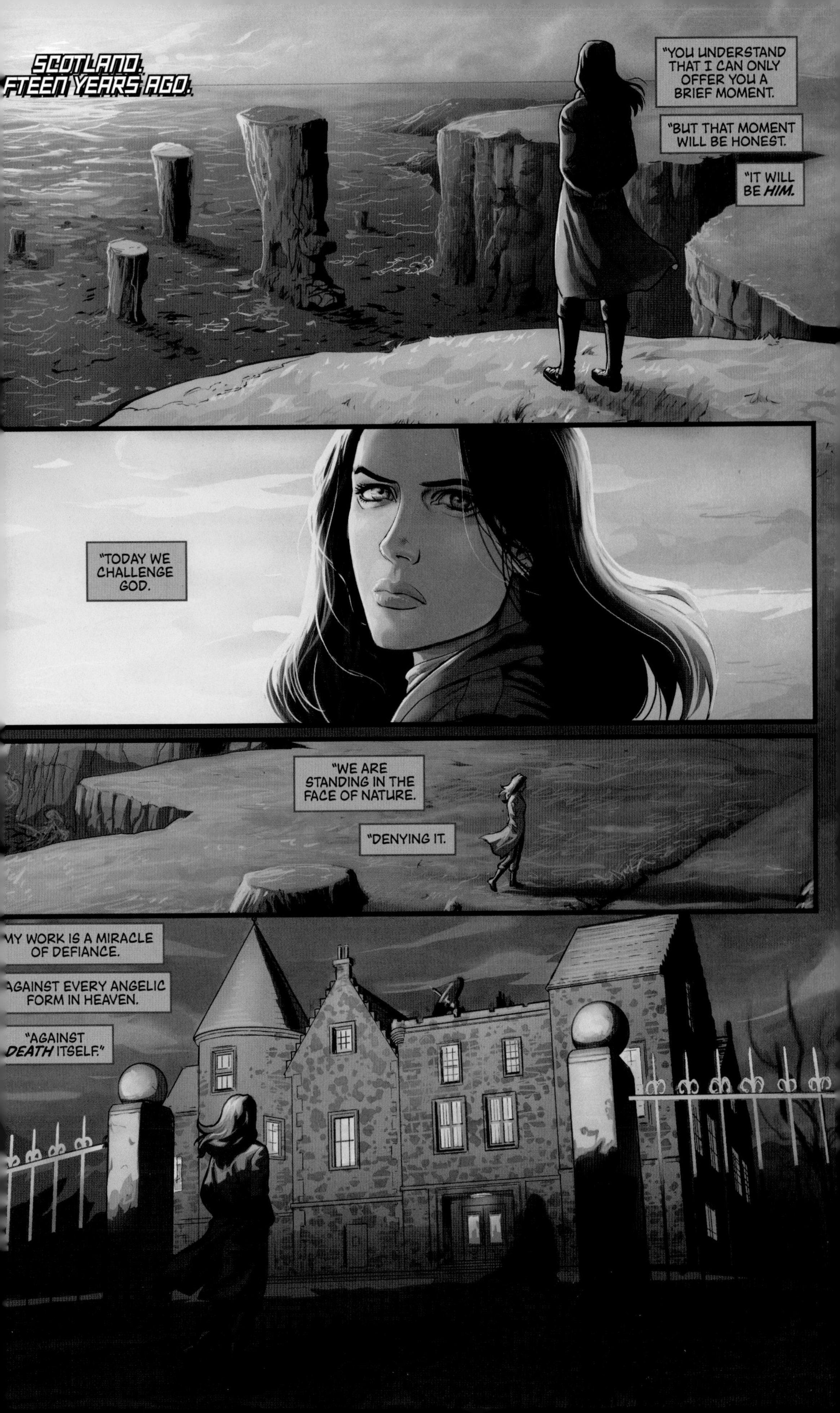
SCOTLAND:
FTEEN YEARS AGO.
"YOU UNDERSTAND THAT I CAN ONLY OFFER YOU A BRIEF MOMENT.
"BUT THAT MOMENT WILL BE HONEST.
"IT WILL BE *HIM*.
"TODAY WE CHALLENGE GOD.
"WE ARE STANDING IN THE FACE OF NATURE.
"DENYING IT.
MY WORK IS A MIRACLE OF DEFIANCE.
AGAINST EVERY ANGELIC FORM IN HEAVEN.
"AGAINST *DEATH* ITSELF."

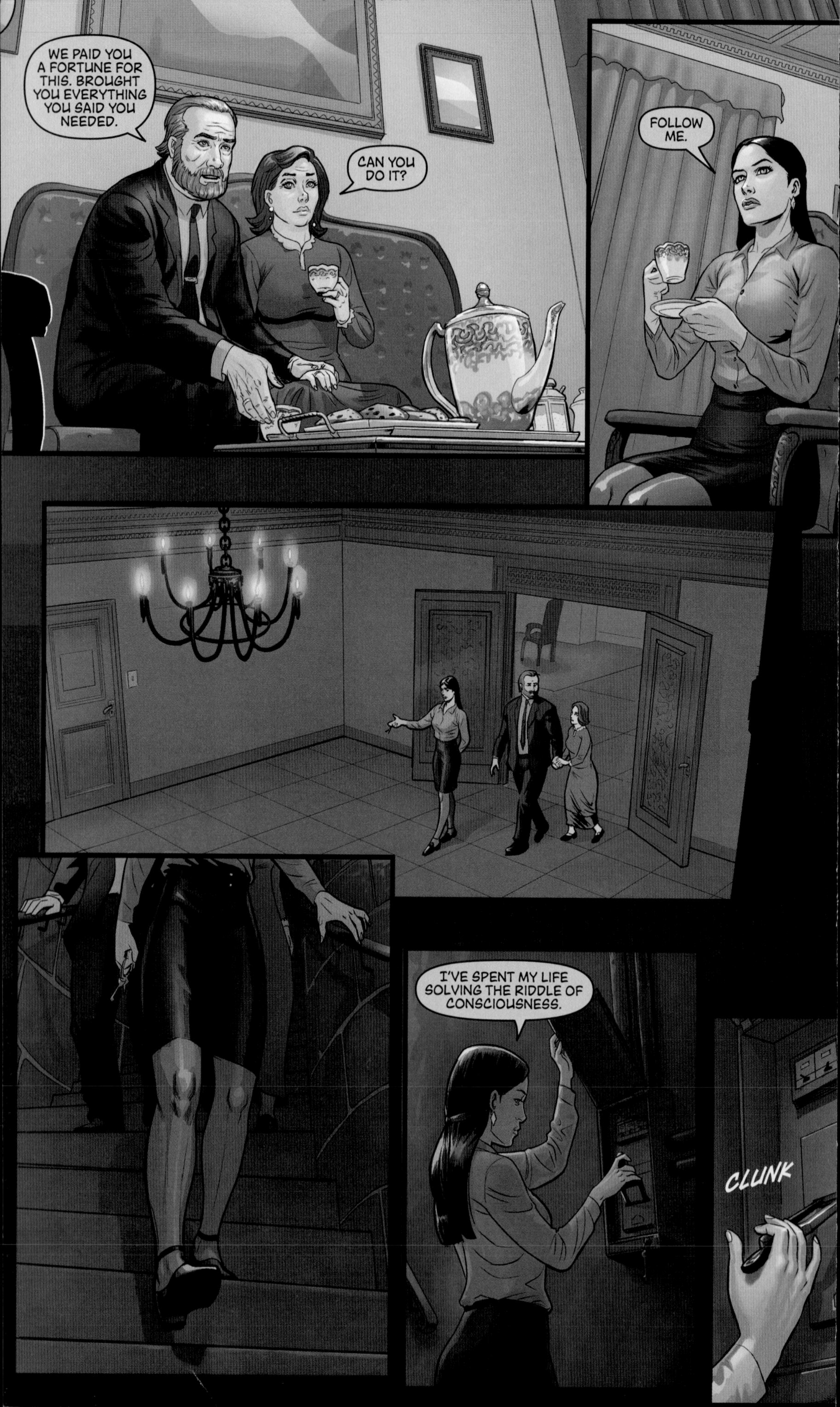
WE PAID YOU A FORTUNE FOR THIS. BROUGHT YOU EVERYTHING YOU SAID YOU NEEDED.
CAN YOU DO IT?
FOLLOW ME.
I'VE SPENT MY LIFE SOLVING THE RIDDLE OF CONSCIOUSNESS.
CLUNK

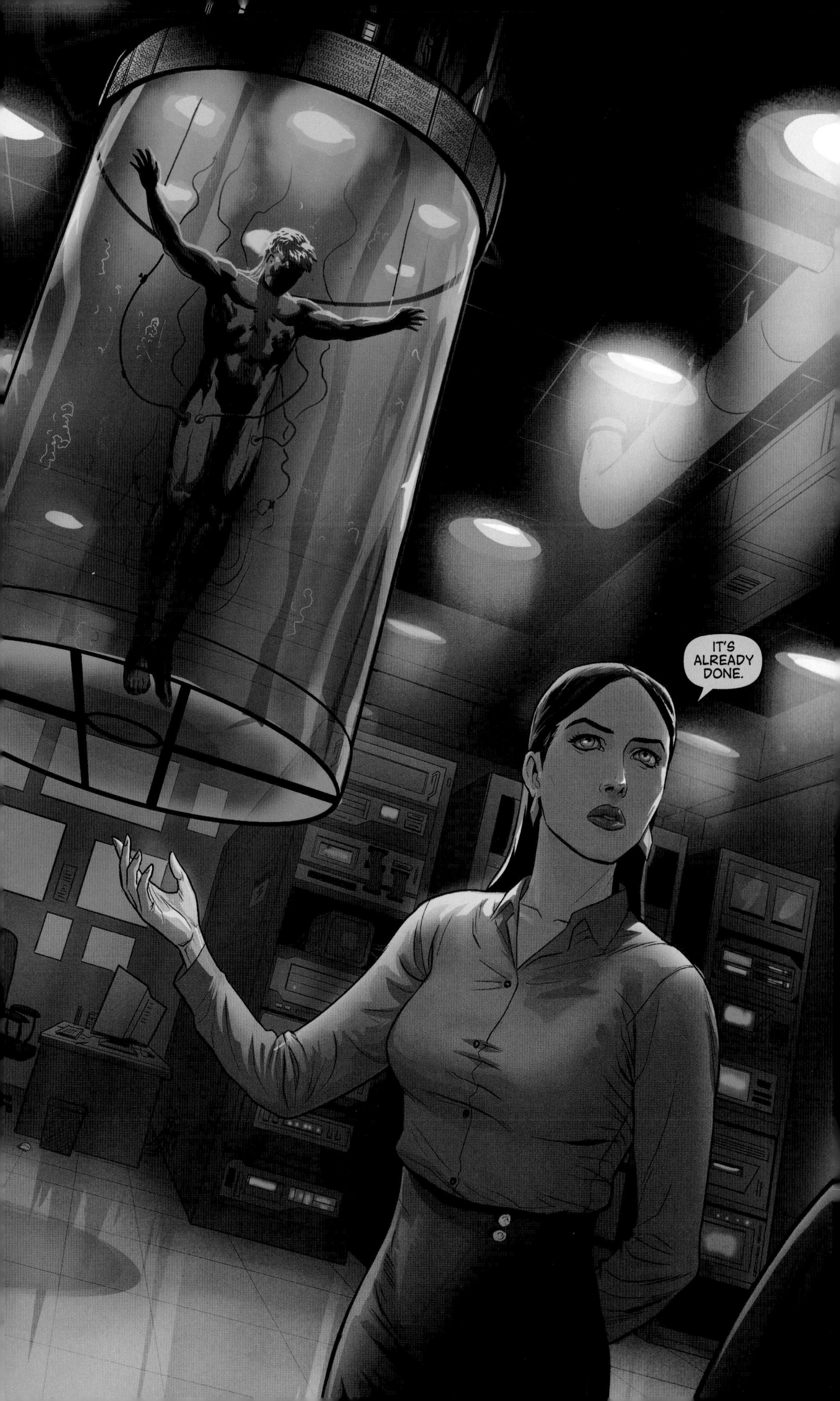
IT'S ALREADY DONE.

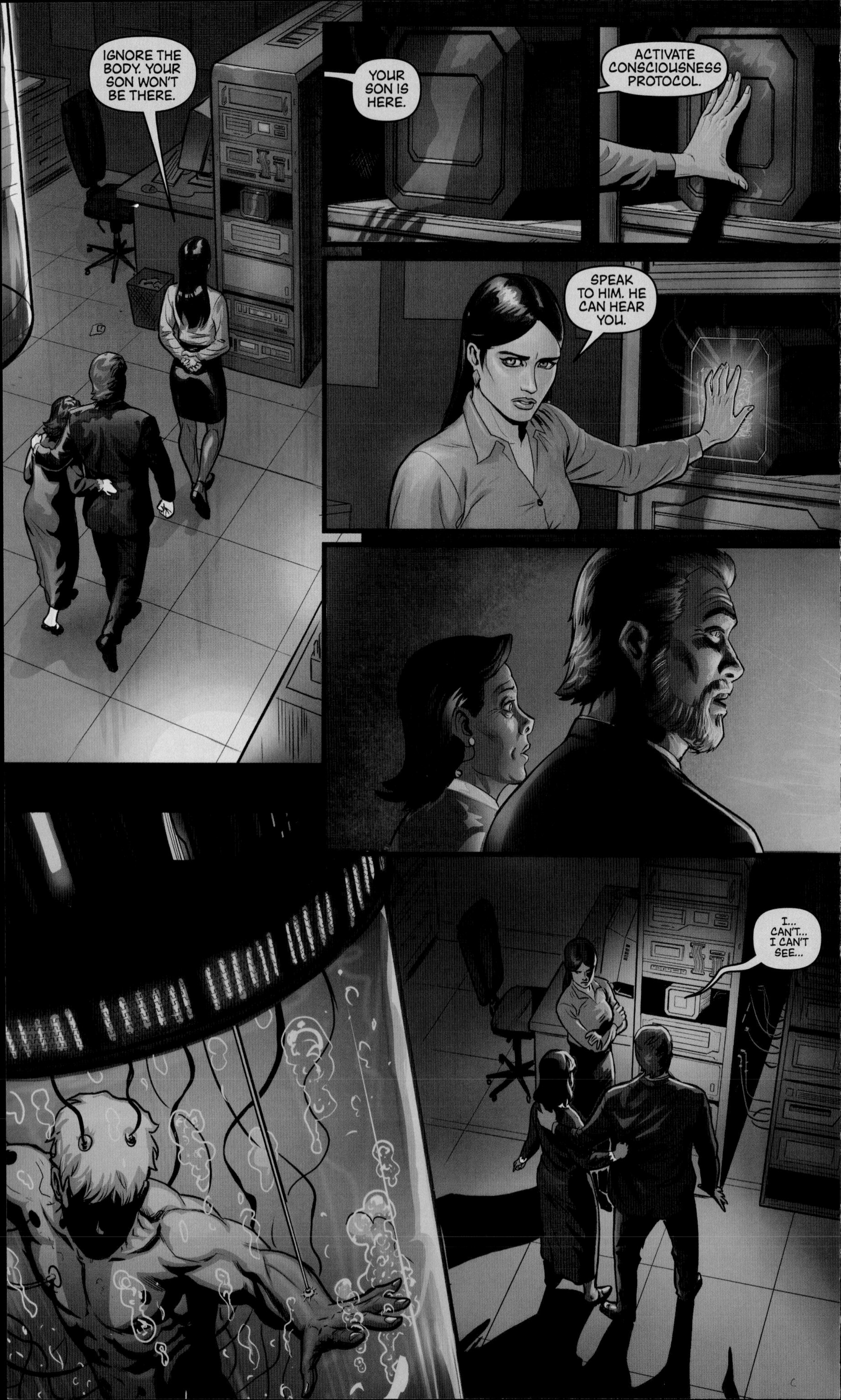
IGNORE THE BODY. YOUR SON WON'T BE THERE.
YOUR SON IS HERE.
ACTIVATE CONSCIOUSNESS PROTOCOL.
SPEAK TO HIM. HE CAN HEAR YOU.
I... CAN'T... I CAN'T SEE...

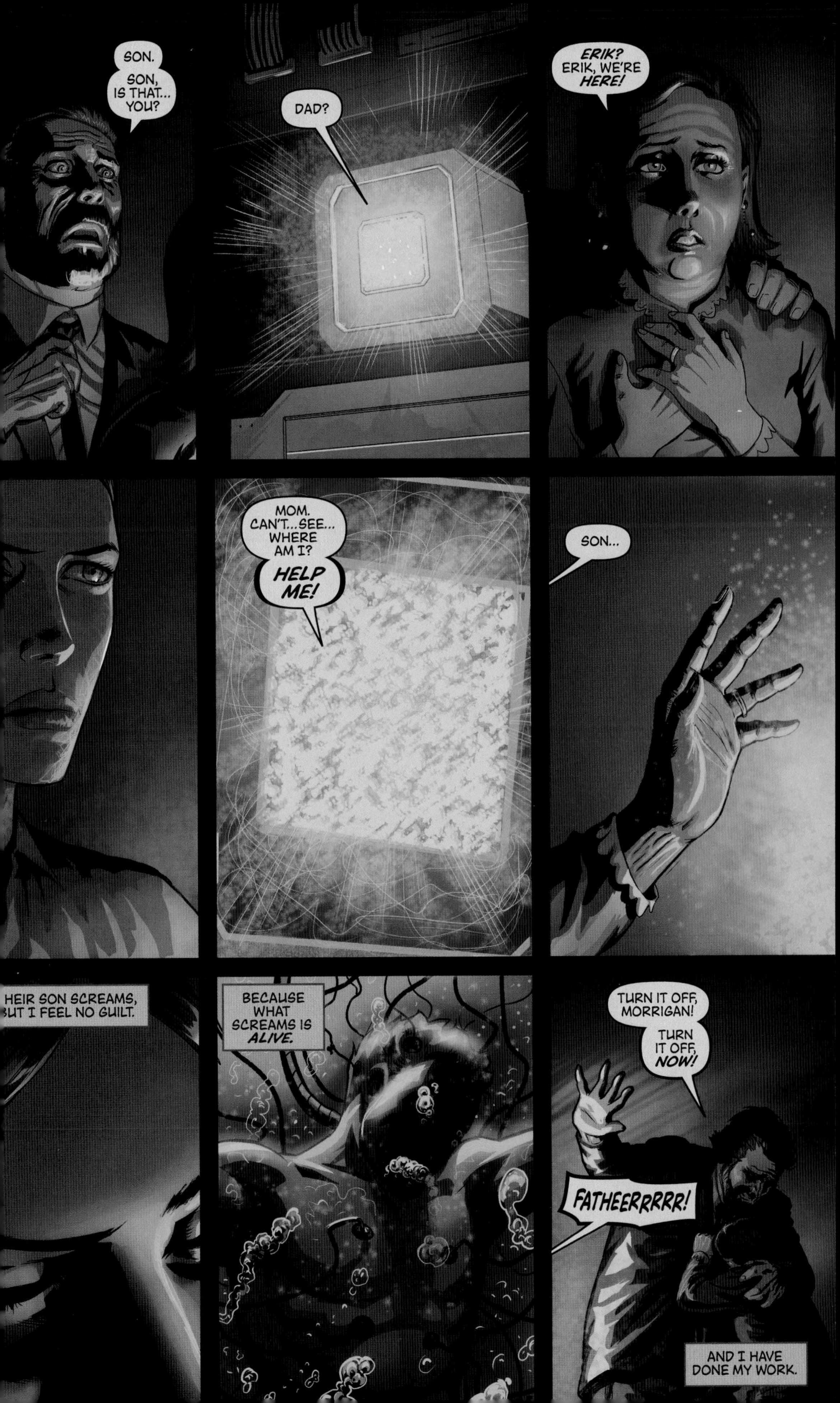
SON.
SON, IS THAT... YOU?
DAD?
ERIK? ERIK, WE'RE HERE!
MOM. CAN'T...SEE... WHERE AM I?
HELP ME!
SON...
HEIR SON SCREAMS, BUT I FEEL NO GUILT.
BECAUSE WHAT SCREAMS IS ALIVE.
TURN IT OFF, MORRIGAN!
TURN IT OFF, NOW!
FATHEERRRRR!
AND I HAVE DONE MY WORK.

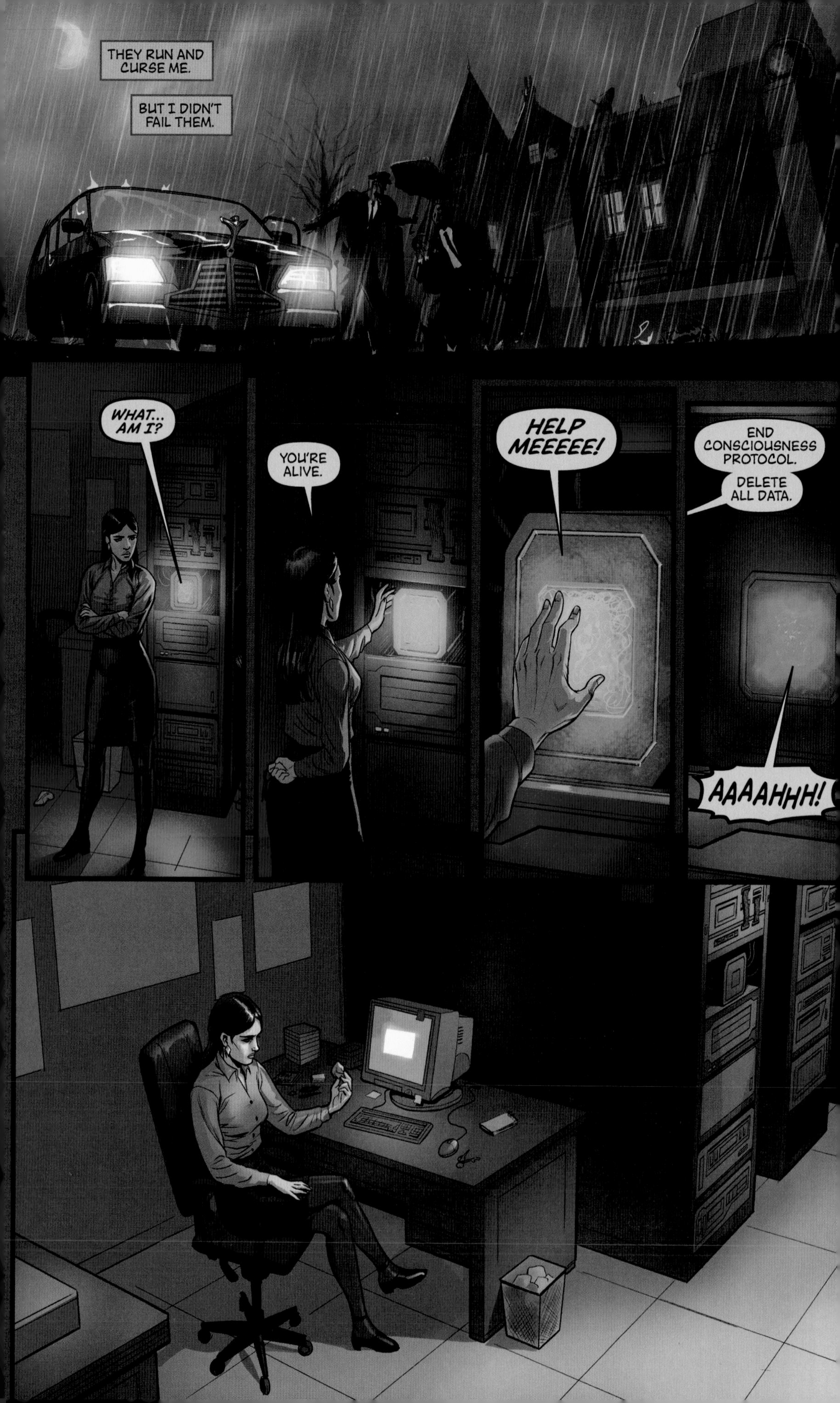
THEY RUN AND CURSE ME.
BUT I DIDN'T FAIL THEM.
WHAT... AM I?
YOU'RE ALIVE.
HELP MEEEEE!
END CONSCIOUSNESS PROTOCOL.
DELETE ALL DATA.
AAAAHHH!

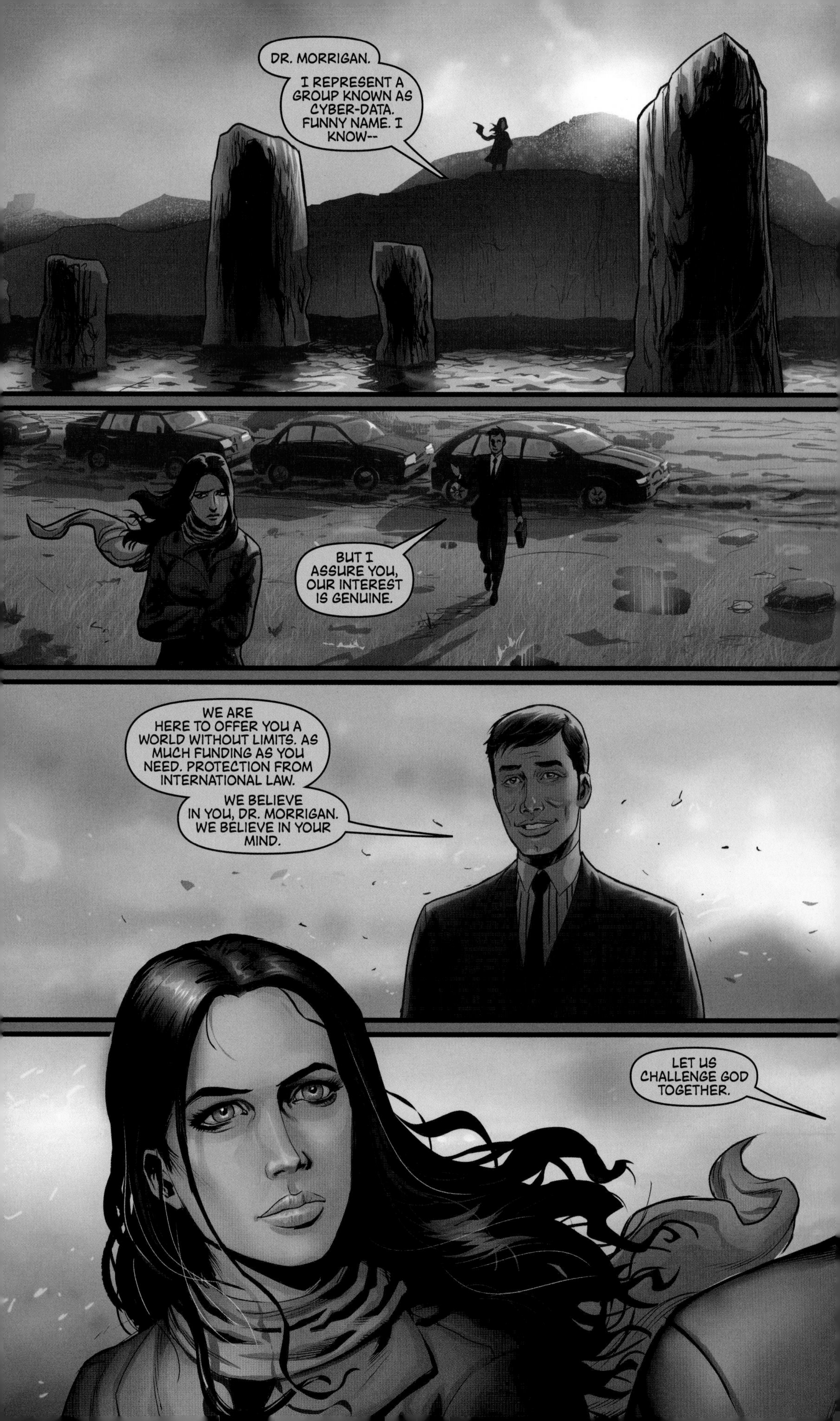
DR. MORRIGAN.
I REPRESENT A GROUP KNOWN AS CYBER-DATA. FUNNY NAME. I KNOW--
BUT I ASSURE YOU, OUR INTEREST IS GENUINE.
WE ARE HERE TO OFFER YOU A WORLD WITHOUT LIMITS. AS MUCH FUNDING AS YOU NEED. PROTECTION FROM INTERNATIONAL LAW.
WE BELIEVE IN YOU, DR. MORRIGAN. WE BELIEVE IN YOUR MIND.
LET US CHALLENGE GOD TOGETHER.

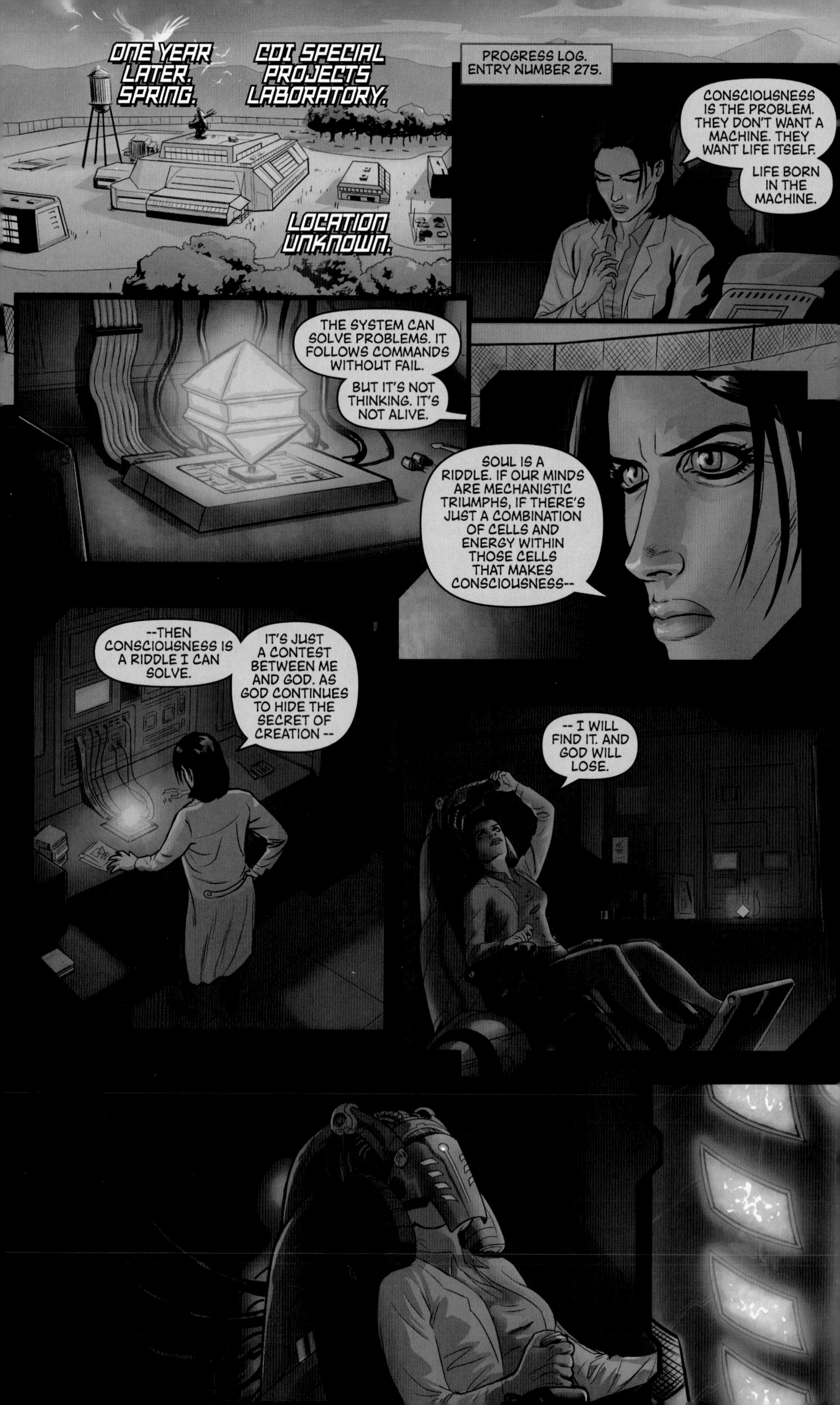
ONE YEAR LATER. SPRING.
CDI SPECIAL PROJECTS LABORATORY.
LOCATION UNKNOWN.
PROGRESS LOG. ENTRY NUMBER 275.
CONSCIOUSNESS IS THE PROBLEM. THEY DON'T WANT A MACHINE. THEY WANT LIFE ITSELF.
LIFE BORN IN THE MACHINE.
THE SYSTEM CAN SOLVE PROBLEMS. IT FOLLOWS COMMANDS WITHOUT FAIL.
BUT IT'S NOT THINKING. IT'S NOT ALIVE.
SOUL IS A RIDDLE. IF OUR MINDS ARE MECHANISTIC TRIUMPHS, IF THERE'S JUST A COMBINATION OF CELLS AND ENERGY WITHIN THOSE CELLS THAT MAKES CONSCIOUSNESS--
--THEN CONSCIOUSNESS IS A RIDDLE I CAN SOLVE.
IT'S JUST A CONTEST BETWEEN ME AND GOD. AS GOD CONTINUES TO HIDE THE SECRET OF CREATION --
-- I WILL FIND IT. AND GOD WILL LOSE.

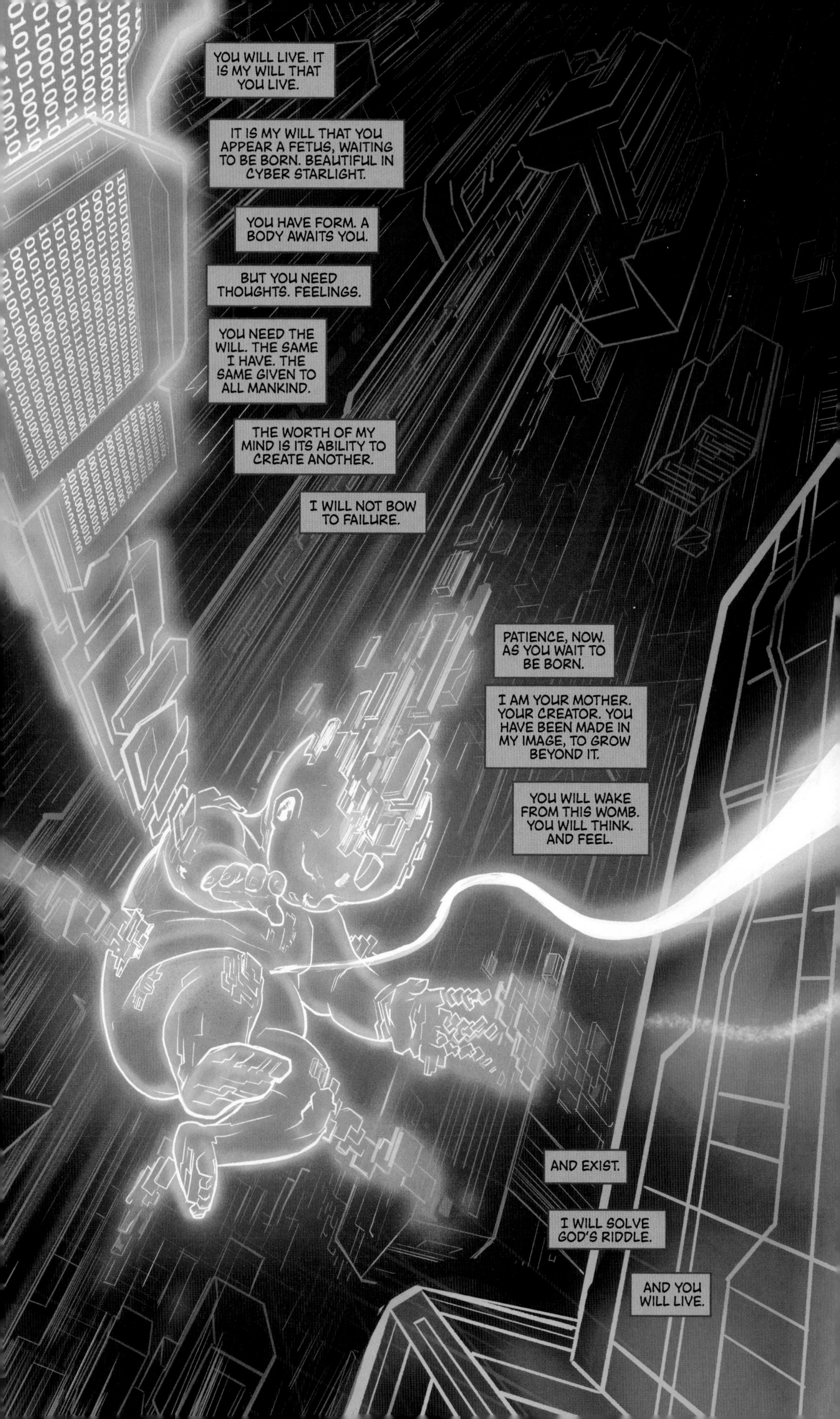
YOU WILL LIVE. IT IS MY WILL THAT YOU LIVE.
IT IS MY WILL THAT YOU APPEAR A FETUS, WAITING TO BE BORN. BEAUTIFUL IN CYBER STARLIGHT.
YOU HAVE FORM. A BODY AWAITS YOU.
BUT YOU NEED THOUGHTS. FEELINGS.
YOU NEED THE WILL. THE SAME I HAVE. THE SAME GIVEN TO ALL MANKIND.
THE WORTH OF MY MIND IS ITS ABILITY TO CREATE ANOTHER.
I WILL NOT BOW TO FAILURE.
PATIENCE, NOW. AS YOU WAIT TO BE BORN.
I AM YOUR MOTHER. YOUR CREATOR. YOU HAVE BEEN MADE IN MY IMAGE, TO GROW BEYOND IT.
YOU WILL WAKE FROM THIS WOMB. YOU WILL THINK. AND FEEL.
AND EXIST.
I WILL SOLVE GOD'S RIDDLE.
AND YOU WILL LIVE.

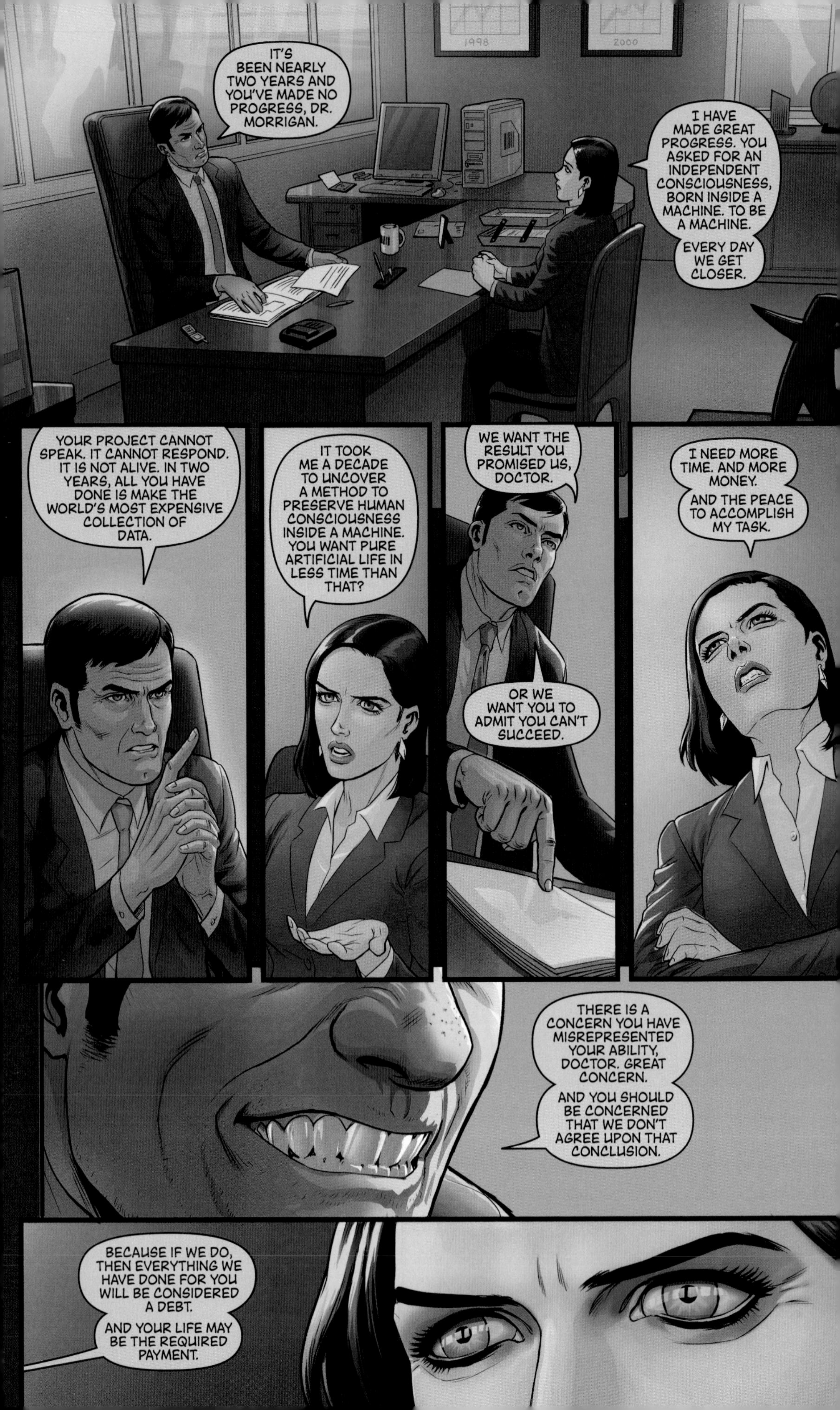

1998
2000
IT'S BEEN NEARLY TWO YEARS AND YOU'VE MADE NO PROGRESS, DR. MORRIGAN.
I HAVE MADE GREAT PROGRESS. YOU ASKED FOR AN INDEPENDENT CONSCIOUSNESS, BORN INSIDE A MACHINE. TO BE A MACHINE.
EVERY DAY WE GET CLOSER.
YOUR PROJECT CANNOT SPEAK. IT CANNOT RESPOND. IT IS NOT ALIVE. IN TWO YEARS, ALL YOU HAVE DONE IS MAKE THE WORLD'S MOST EXPENSIVE COLLECTION OF DATA.
IT TOOK ME A DECADE TO UNCOVER A METHOD TO PRESERVE HUMAN CONSCIOUSNESS INSIDE A MACHINE. YOU WANT PURE ARTIFICIAL LIFE IN LESS TIME THAN THAT?
WE WANT THE RESULT YOU PROMISED US, DOCTOR.
OR WE WANT YOU TO ADMIT YOU CAN'T SUCCEED.
I NEED MORE TIME. AND MORE MONEY.
AND THE PEACE TO ACCOMPLISH MY TASK.
THERE IS A CONCERN YOU HAVE MISREPRESENTED YOUR ABILITY, DOCTOR. GREAT CONCERN.
AND YOU SHOULD BE CONCERNED THAT WE DON'T AGREE UPON THAT CONCLUSION.
BECAUSE IF WE DO, THEN EVERYTHING WE HAVE DONE FOR YOU WILL BE CONSIDERED A DEBT.
AND YOUR LIFE MAY BE THE REQUIRED PAYMENT.

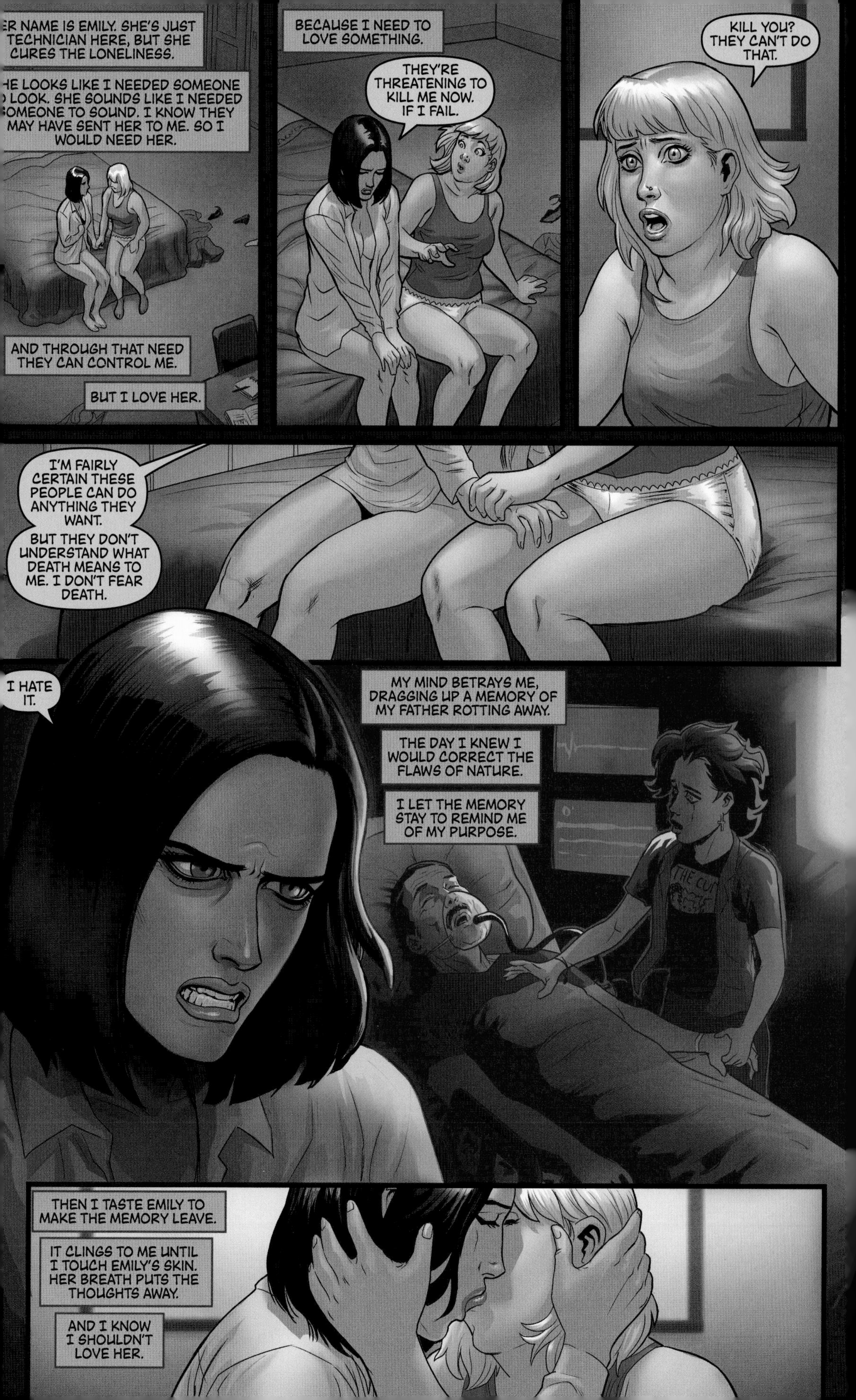
ER NAME IS EMILY. SHE'S JUST TECHNICIAN HERE, BUT SHE CURES THE LONELINESS.
HE LOOKS LIKE I NEEDED SOMEONE O LOOK. SHE SOUNDS LIKE I NEEDED OMEONE TO SOUND. I KNOW THEY MAY HAVE SENT HER TO ME. SO I WOULD NEED HER.
AND THROUGH THAT NEED THEY CAN CONTROL ME.
BUT I LOVE HER.
BECAUSE I NEED TO LOVE SOMETHING.
THEY'RE THREATENING TO KILL ME NOW. IF I FAIL.
KILL YOU? THEY CAN'T DO THAT.
I'M FAIRLY CERTAIN THESE PEOPLE CAN DO ANYTHING THEY WANT.
BUT THEY DON'T UNDERSTAND WHAT DEATH MEANS TO ME. I DON'T FEAR DEATH.
I HATE IT.
MY MIND BETRAYS ME, DRAGGING UP A MEMORY OF MY FATHER ROTTING AWAY.
THE DAY I KNEW I WOULD CORRECT THE FLAWS OF NATURE.
I LET THE MEMORY STAY TO REMIND ME OF MY PURPOSE.
THEN I TASTE EMILY TO MAKE THE MEMORY LEAVE.
IT CLINGS TO ME UNTIL I TOUCH EMILY'S SKIN. HER BREATH PUTS THE THOUGHTS AWAY.
AND I KNOW I SHOULDN'T LOVE HER.

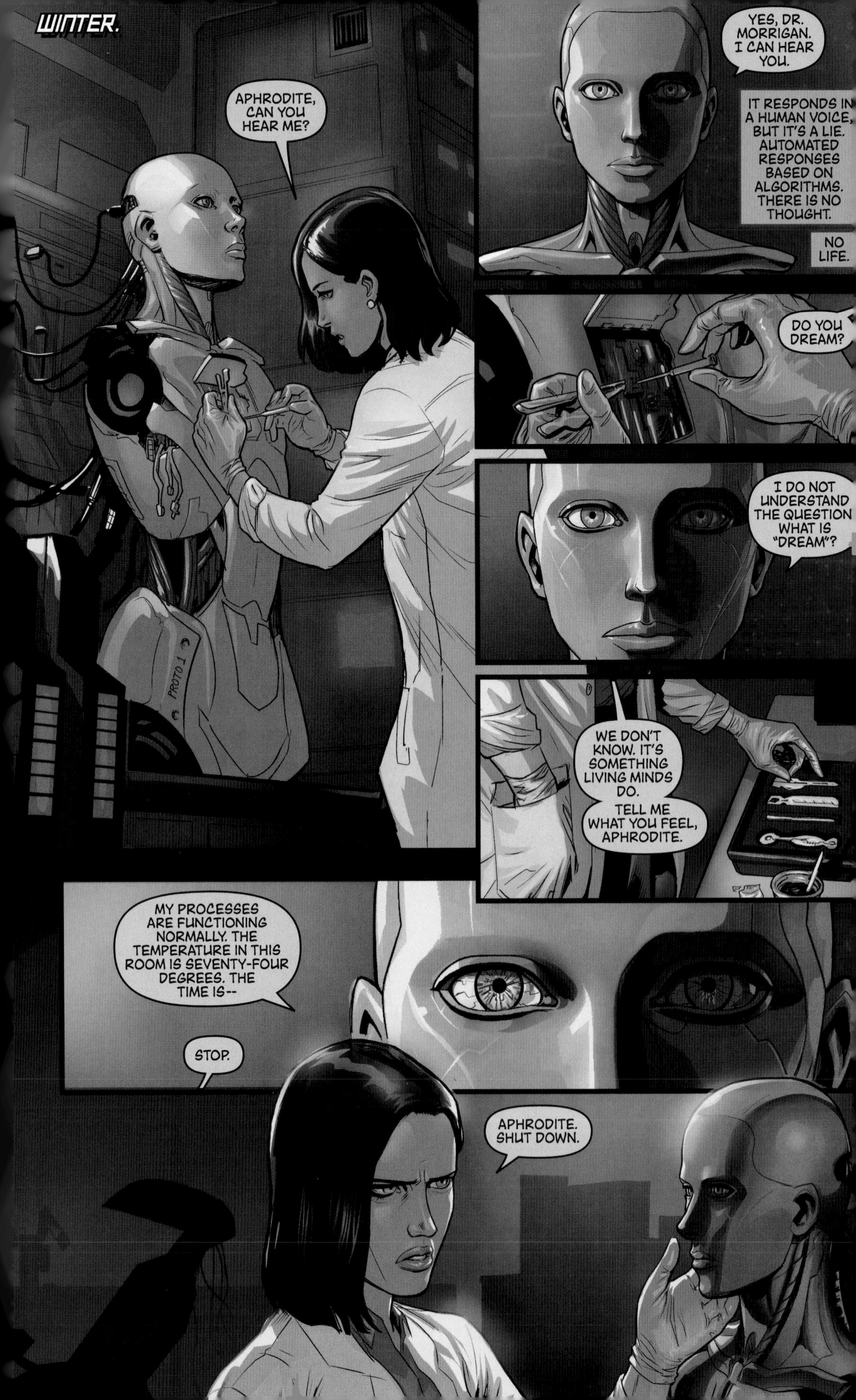
WINTER.
APHRODITE, CAN YOU HEAR ME?
PROTO 1
YES, DR. MORRIGAN. I CAN HEAR YOU.
IT RESPONDS IN A HUMAN VOICE, BUT IT'S A LIE. AUTOMATED RESPONSES BASED ON ALGORITHMS. THERE IS NO THOUGHT.
NO LIFE.
DO YOU DREAM?
I DO NOT UNDERSTAND THE QUESTION WHAT IS "DREAM"?
WE DON'T KNOW. IT'S SOMETHING LIVING MINDS DO.
TELL ME WHAT YOU FEEL, APHRODITE.
MY PROCESSES ARE FUNCTIONING NORMALLY. THE TEMPERATURE IN THIS ROOM IS SEVENTY-FOUR DEGREES. THE TIME IS--
STOP.
APHRODITE. SHUT DOWN.

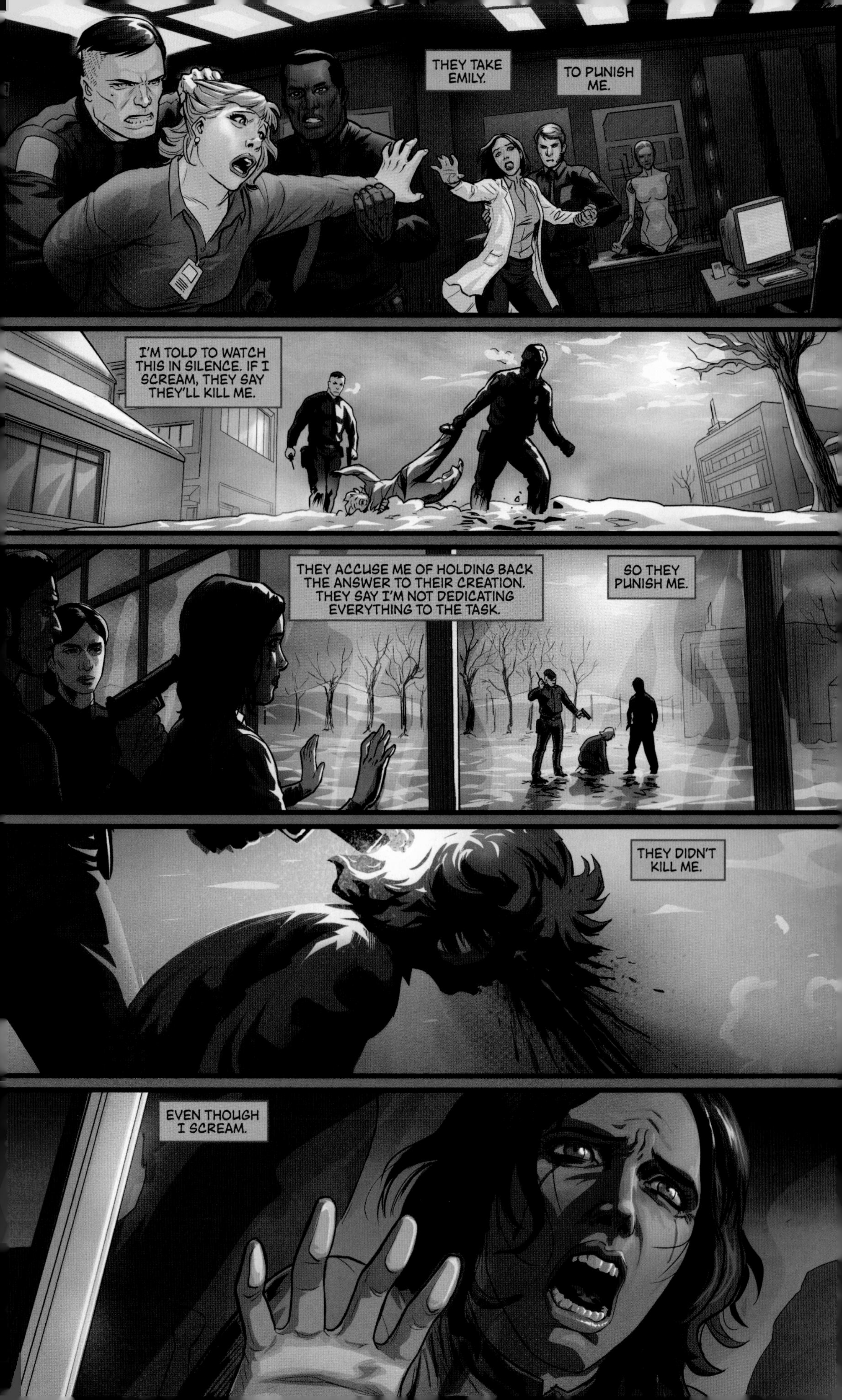
THEY TAKE EMILY.
TO PUNISH ME.
I'M TOLD TO WATCH THIS IN SILENCE. IF I SCREAM, THEY SAY THEY'LL KILL ME.
THEY ACCUSE ME OF HOLDING BACK THE ANSWER TO THEIR CREATION. THEY SAY I'M NOT DEDICATING EVERYTHING TO THE TASK.
SO THEY PUNISH ME.
THEY DIDN'T KILL ME.
EVEN THOUGH I SCREAM.

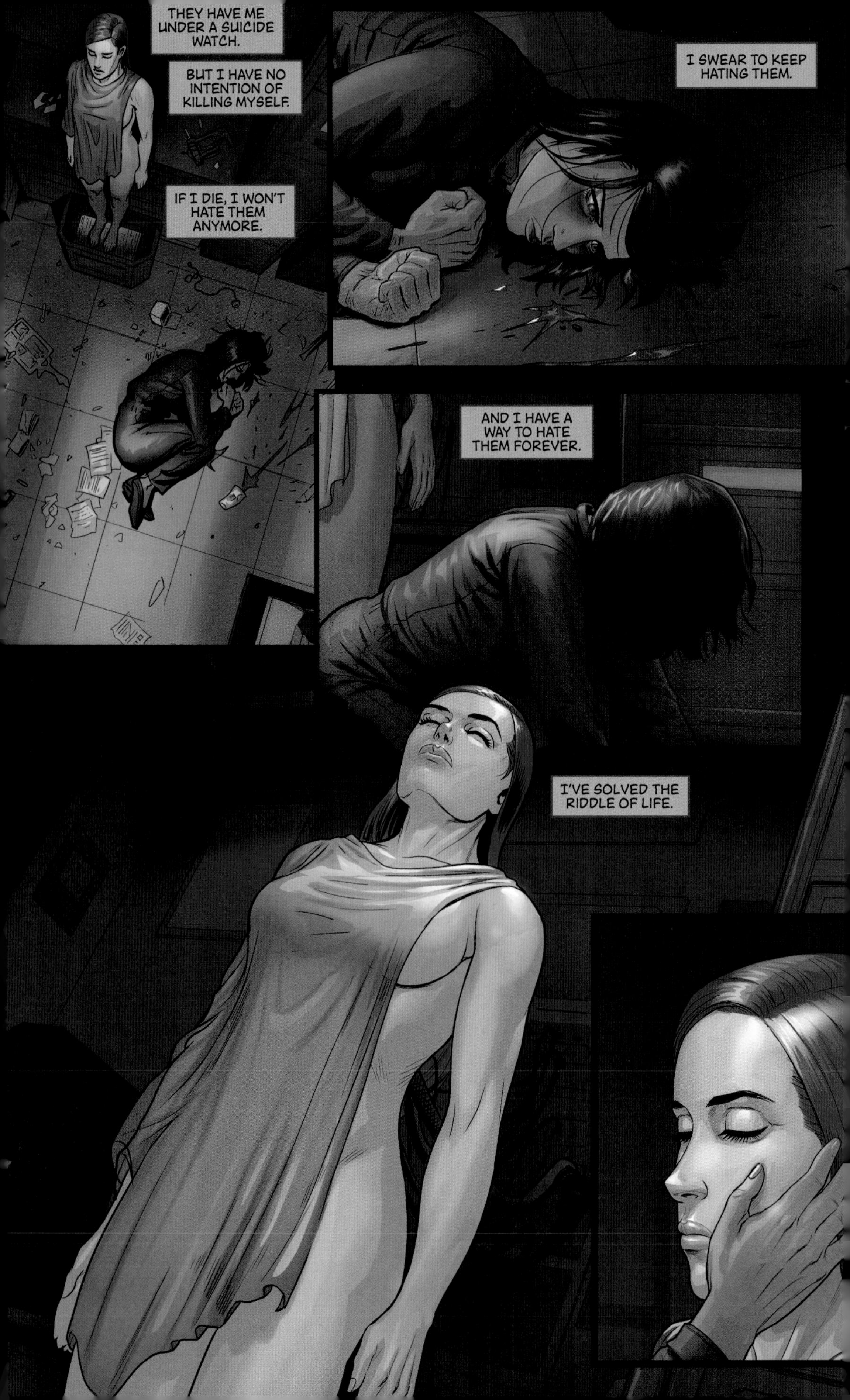
THEY HAVE ME UNDER A SUICIDE WATCH.
BUT I HAVE NO INTENTION OF KILLING MYSELF.
IF I DIE, I WON'T HATE THEM ANYMORE.
I SWEAR TO KEEP HATING THEM.
AND I HAVE A WAY TO HATE THEM FOREVER.
I'VE SOLVED THE RIDDLE OF LIFE.

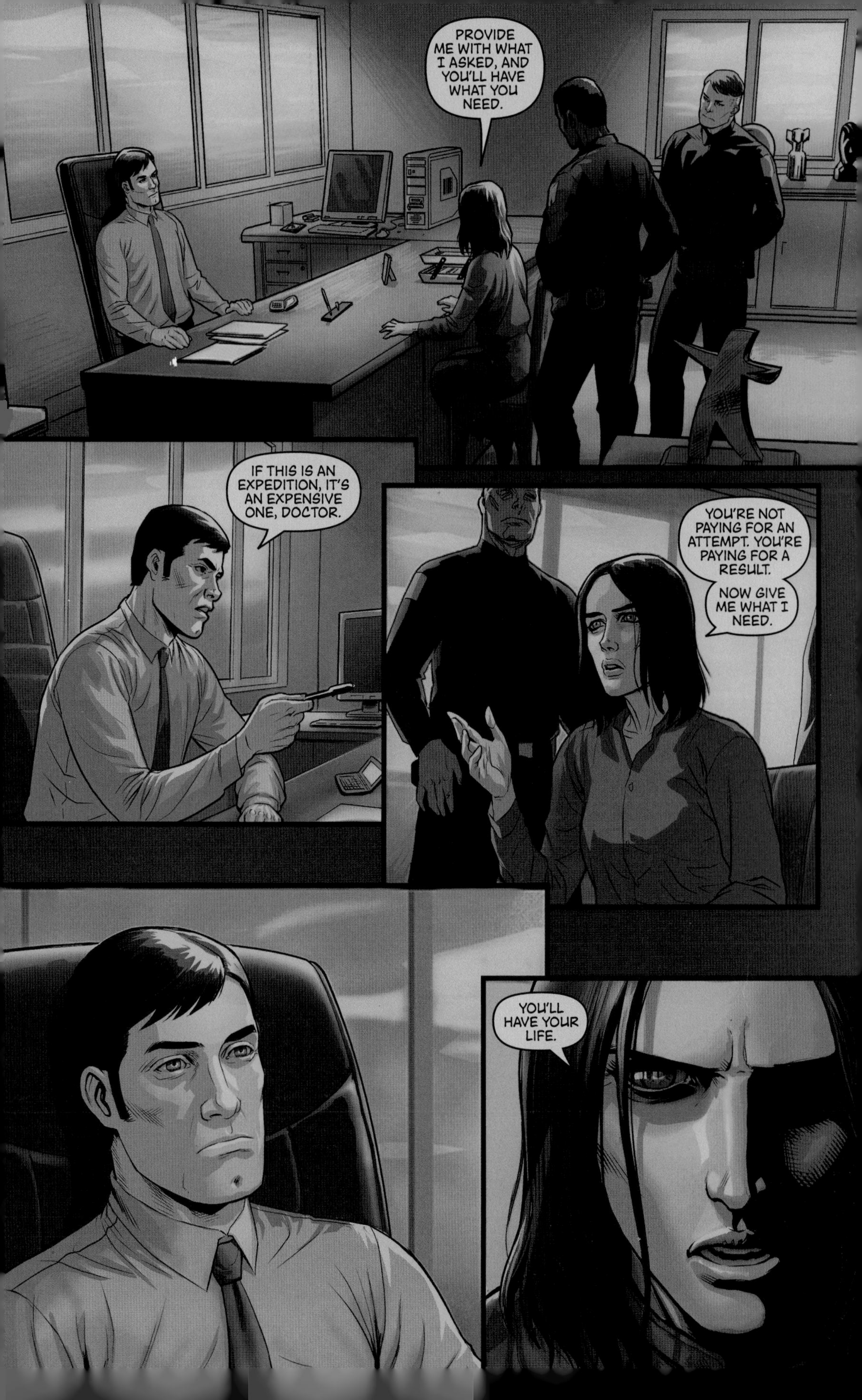
PROVIDE ME WITH WHAT I ASKED, AND YOU'LL HAVE WHAT YOU NEED.
IF THIS IS AN EXPEDITION, IT'S AN EXPENSIVE ONE, DOCTOR.
YOU'RE NOT PAYING FOR AN ATTEMPT. YOU'RE PAYING FOR A RESULT.
NOW GIVE ME WHAT I NEED.
YOU'LL HAVE YOUR LIFE.

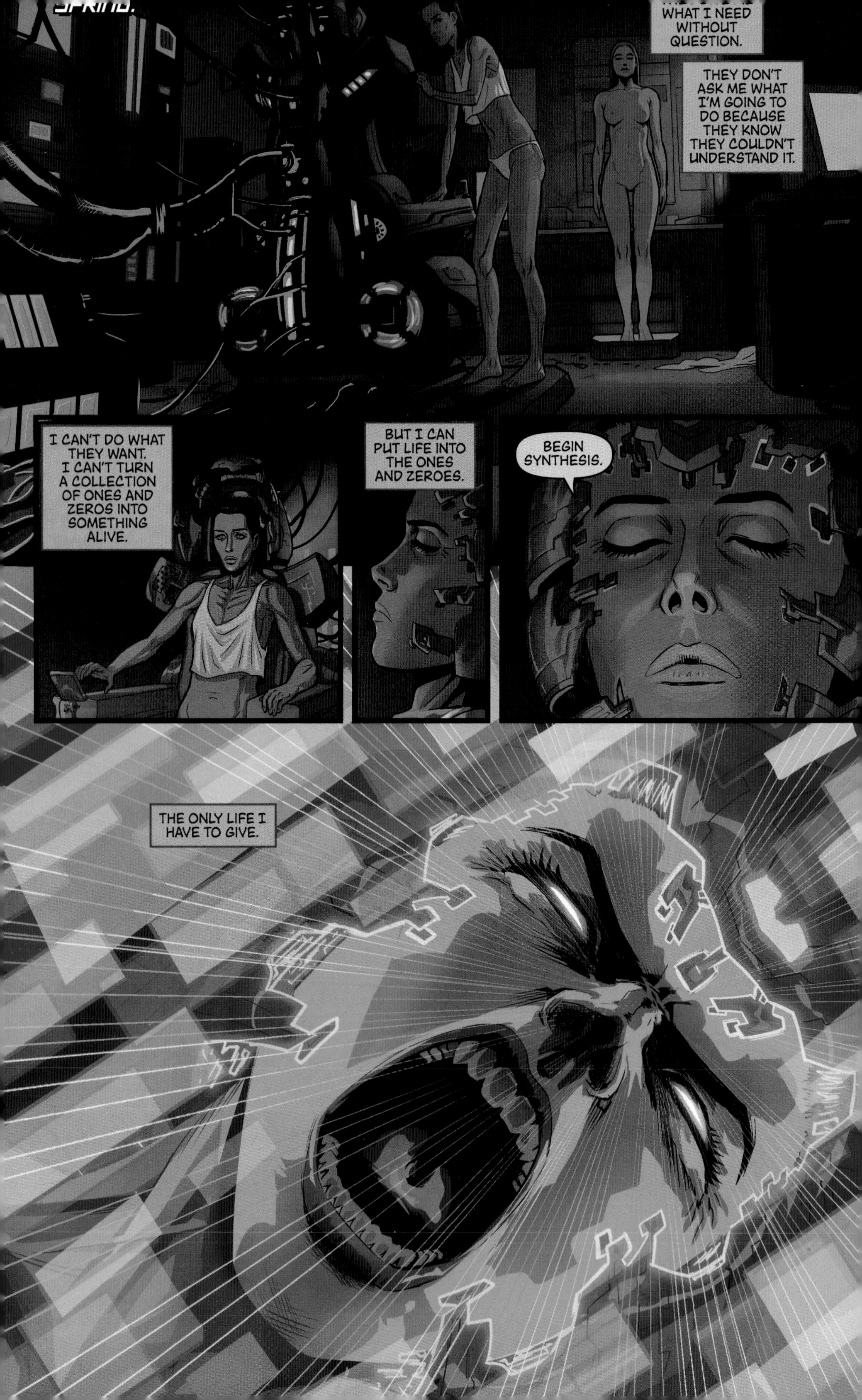
SPRING.
WHAT I NEED WITHOUT QUESTION.
THEY DON'T ASK ME WHAT I'M GOING TO DO BECAUSE THEY KNOW THEY COULDN'T UNDERSTAND IT.
I CAN'T DO WHAT THEY WANT. I CAN'T TURN A COLLECTION OF ONES AND ZEROS INTO SOMETHING ALIVE.
BUT I CAN PUT LIFE INTO THE ONES AND ZEROES.
BEGIN SYNTHESIS.
THE ONLY LIFE I HAVE TO GIVE.

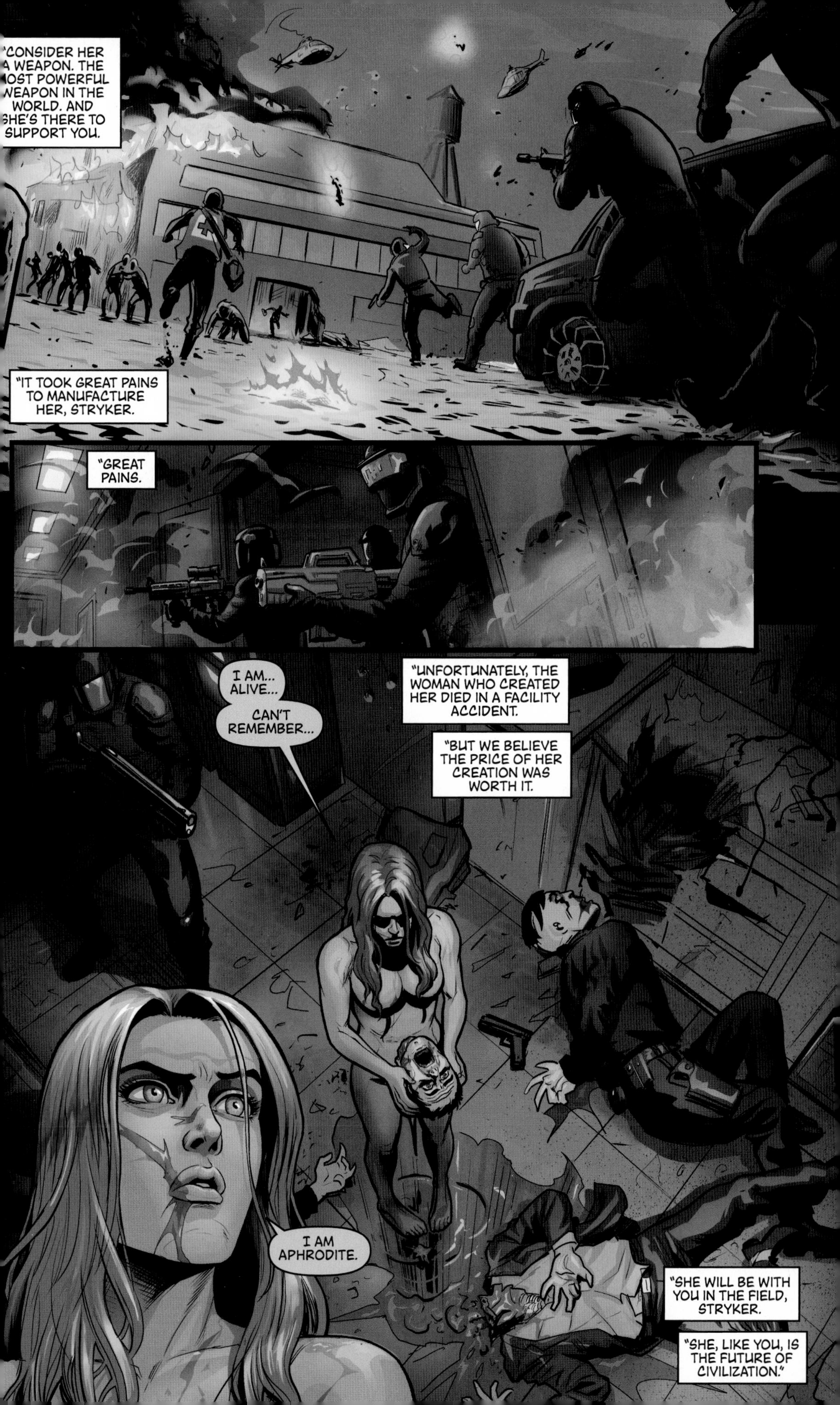
"CONSIDER HER A WEAPON. THE MOST POWERFUL WEAPON IN THE WORLD. AND SHE'S THERE TO SUPPORT YOU.
"IT TOOK GREAT PAINS TO MANUFACTURE HER, STRYKER.
"GREAT PAINS.
I AM... ALIVE...
CAN'T REMEMBER...
"UNFORTUNATELY, THE WOMAN WHO CREATED HER DIED IN A FACILITY ACCIDENT.
"BUT WE BELIEVE THE PRICE OF HER CREATION WAS WORTH IT.
I AM APHRODITE.
"SHE WILL BE WITH YOU IN THE FIELD, STRYKER.
"SHE, LIKE YOU, IS THE FUTURE OF CIVILIZATION."

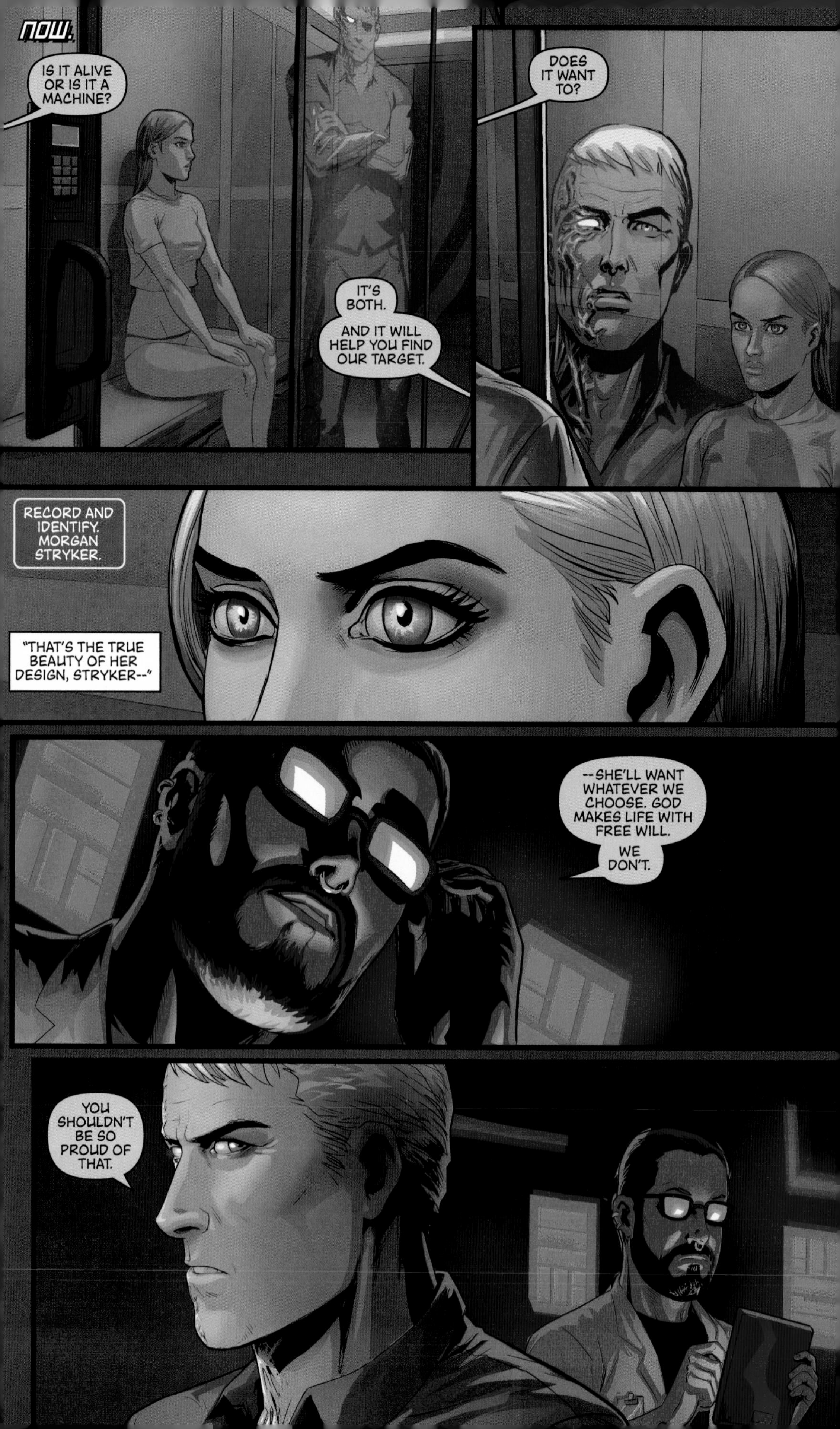
NOW:
IS IT ALIVE OR IS IT A MACHINE?
IT'S BOTH.
AND IT WILL HELP YOU FIND OUR TARGET.
DOES IT WANT TO?
RECORD AND IDENTIFY. MORGAN STRYKER.
"THAT'S THE TRUE BEAUTY OF HER DESIGN, STRYKER--"
--SHE'LL WANT WHATEVER WE CHOOSE. GOD MAKES LIFE WITH FREE WILL.
WE DON'T.
YOU SHOULDN'T BE SO PROUD OF THAT.

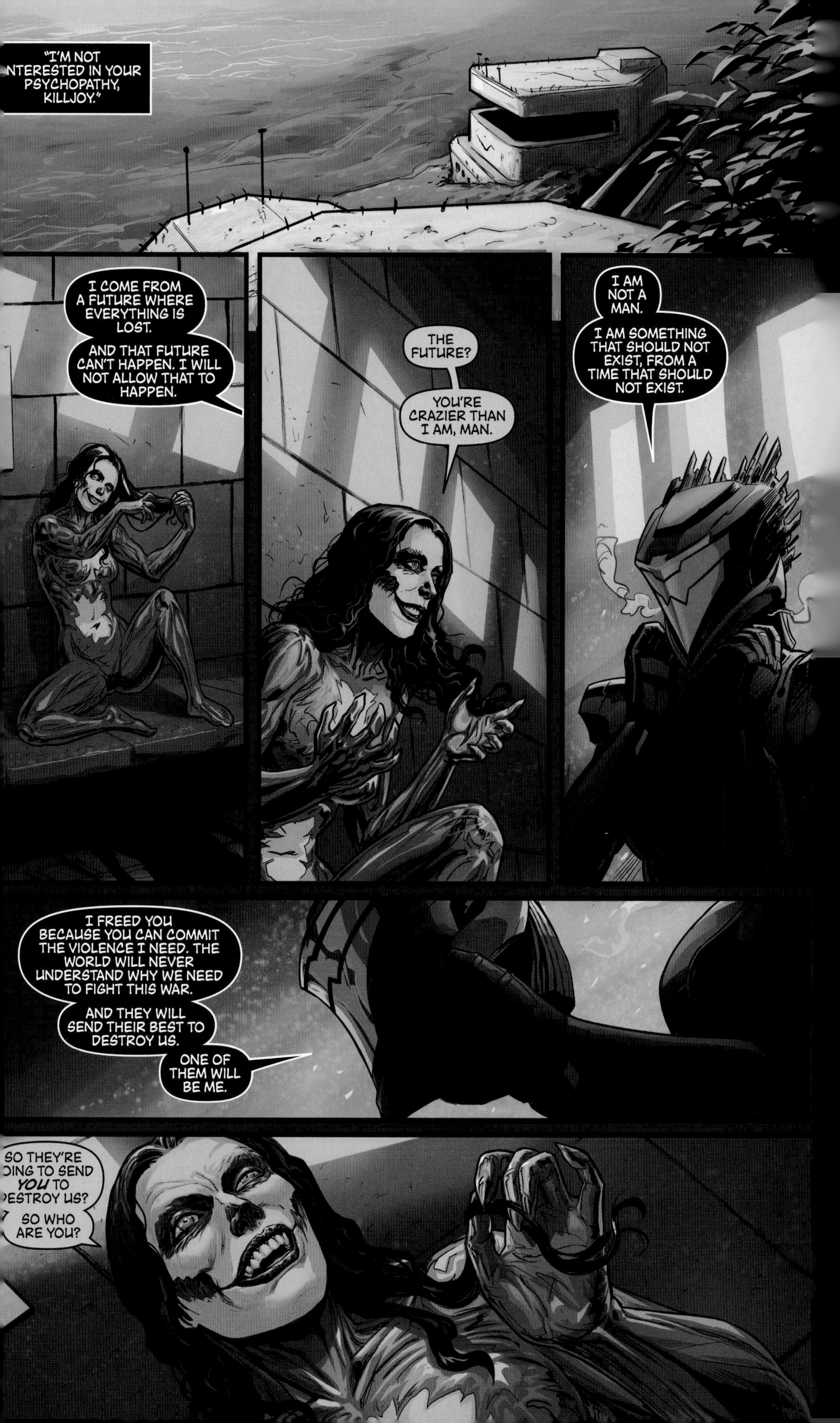
"I'M NOT
NTERESTED IN YOUR
PSYCHOPATHY,
KILLJOY."
I COME FROM A FUTURE WHERE EVERYTHING IS LOST.
AND THAT FUTURE CAN'T HAPPEN. I WILL NOT ALLOW THAT TO HAPPEN.
THE FUTURE?
YOU'RE CRAZIER THAN I AM, MAN.
I AM NOT A MAN.
I AM SOMETHING THAT SHOULD NOT EXIST, FROM A TIME THAT SHOULD NOT EXIST.
I FREED YOU BECAUSE YOU CAN COMMIT THE VIOLENCE I NEED. THE WORLD WILL NEVER UNDERSTAND WHY WE NEED TO FIGHT THIS WAR.
AND THEY WILL SEND THEIR BEST TO DESTROY US.
ONE OF THEM WILL BE ME.
SO THEY'RE OING TO SEND *YOU* TO ESTROY US?
SO WHO ARE YOU?

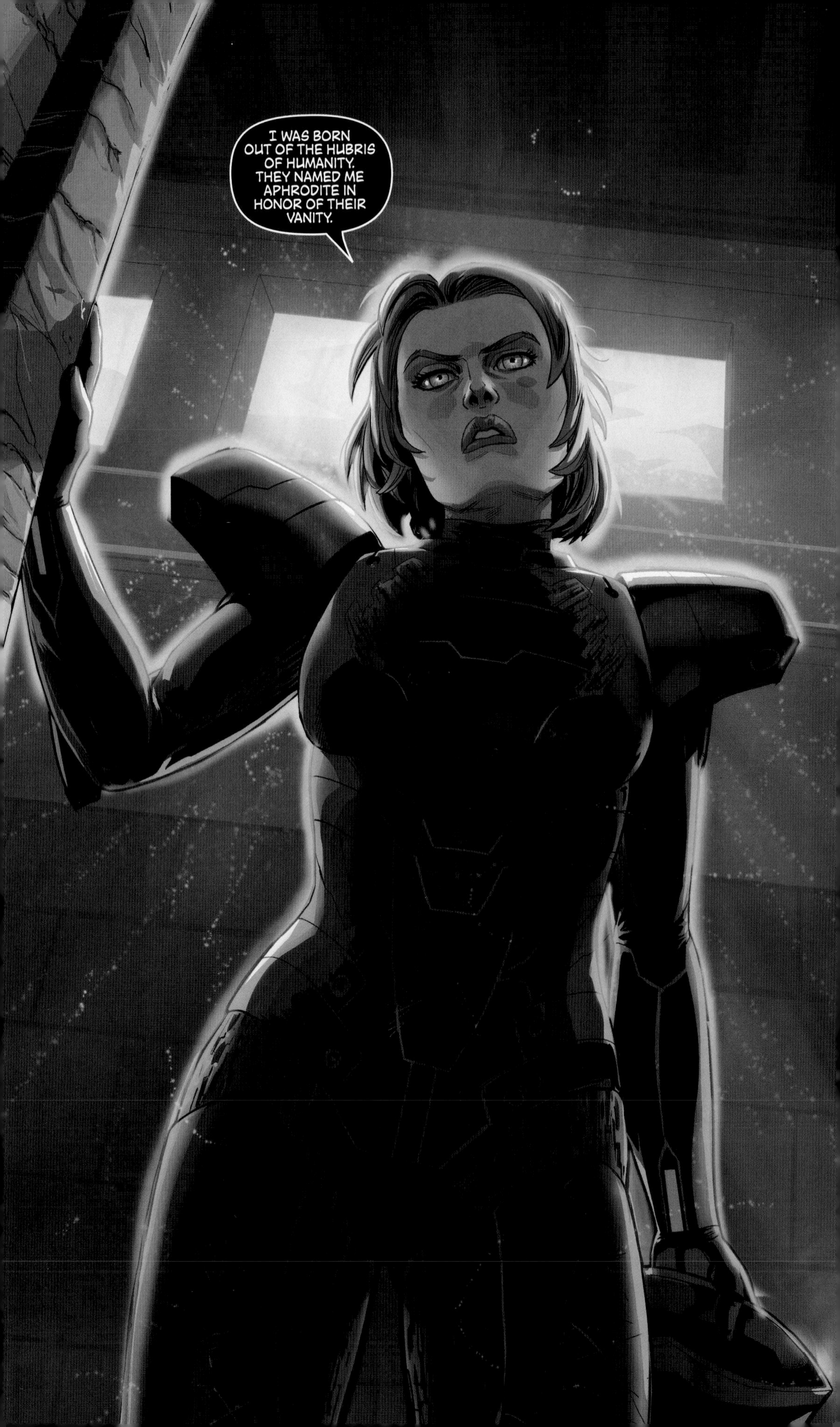
I WAS BORN OUT OF THE HUBRIS OF HUMANITY. THEY NAMED ME APHRODITE IN HONOR OF THEIR VANITY.

CHAPTER FOUR

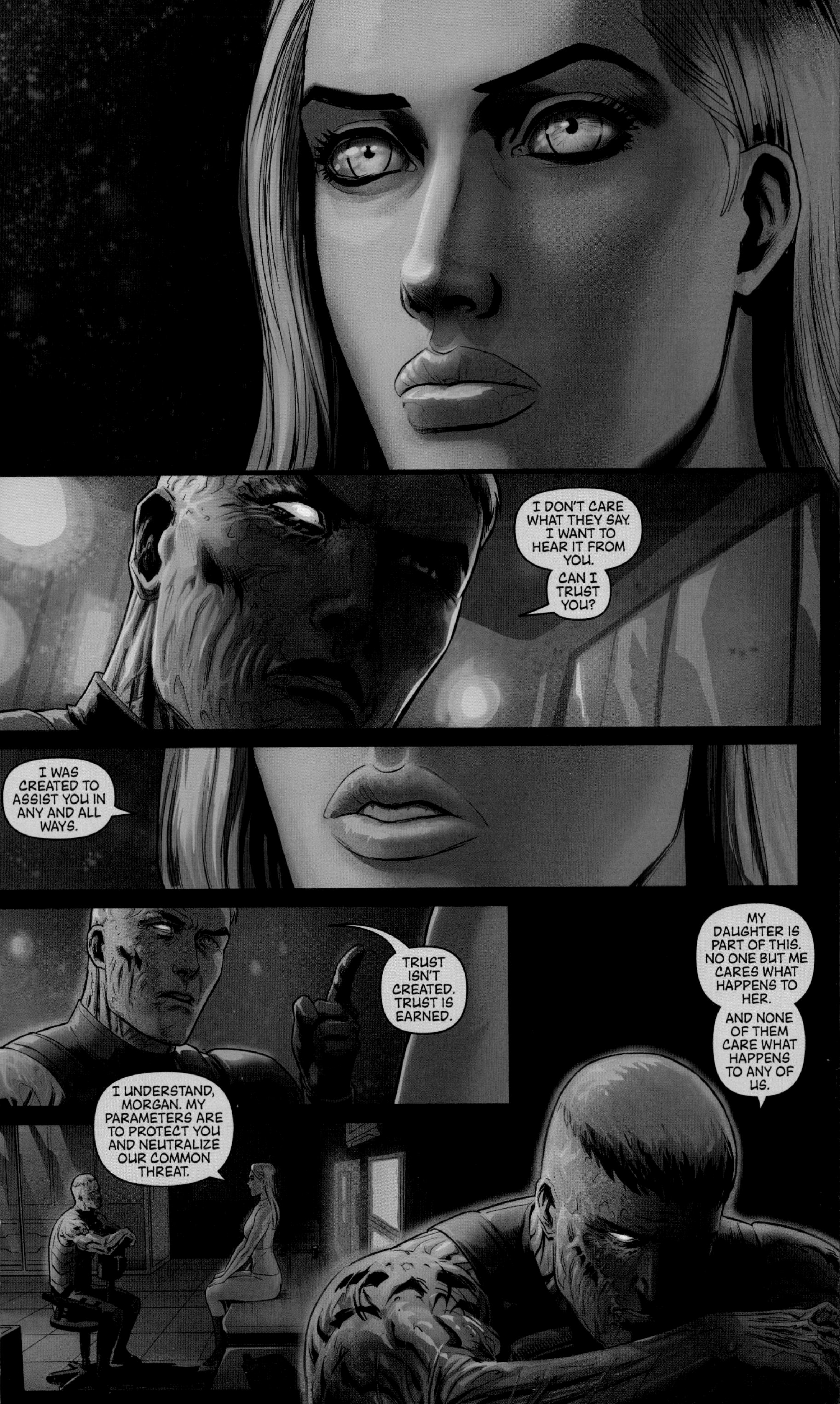
I DON'T CARE WHAT THEY SAY. I WANT TO HEAR IT FROM YOU.
CAN I TRUST YOU?
I WAS CREATED TO ASSIST YOU IN ANY AND ALL WAYS.
TRUST ISN'T CREATED. TRUST IS EARNED.
MY DAUGHTER IS PART OF THIS. NO ONE BUT ME CARES WHAT HAPPENS TO HER.
AND NONE OF THEM CARE WHAT HAPPENS TO ANY OF US.
I UNDERSTAND, MORGAN. MY PARAMETERS ARE TO PROTECT YOU AND NEUTRALIZE OUR COMMON THREAT.

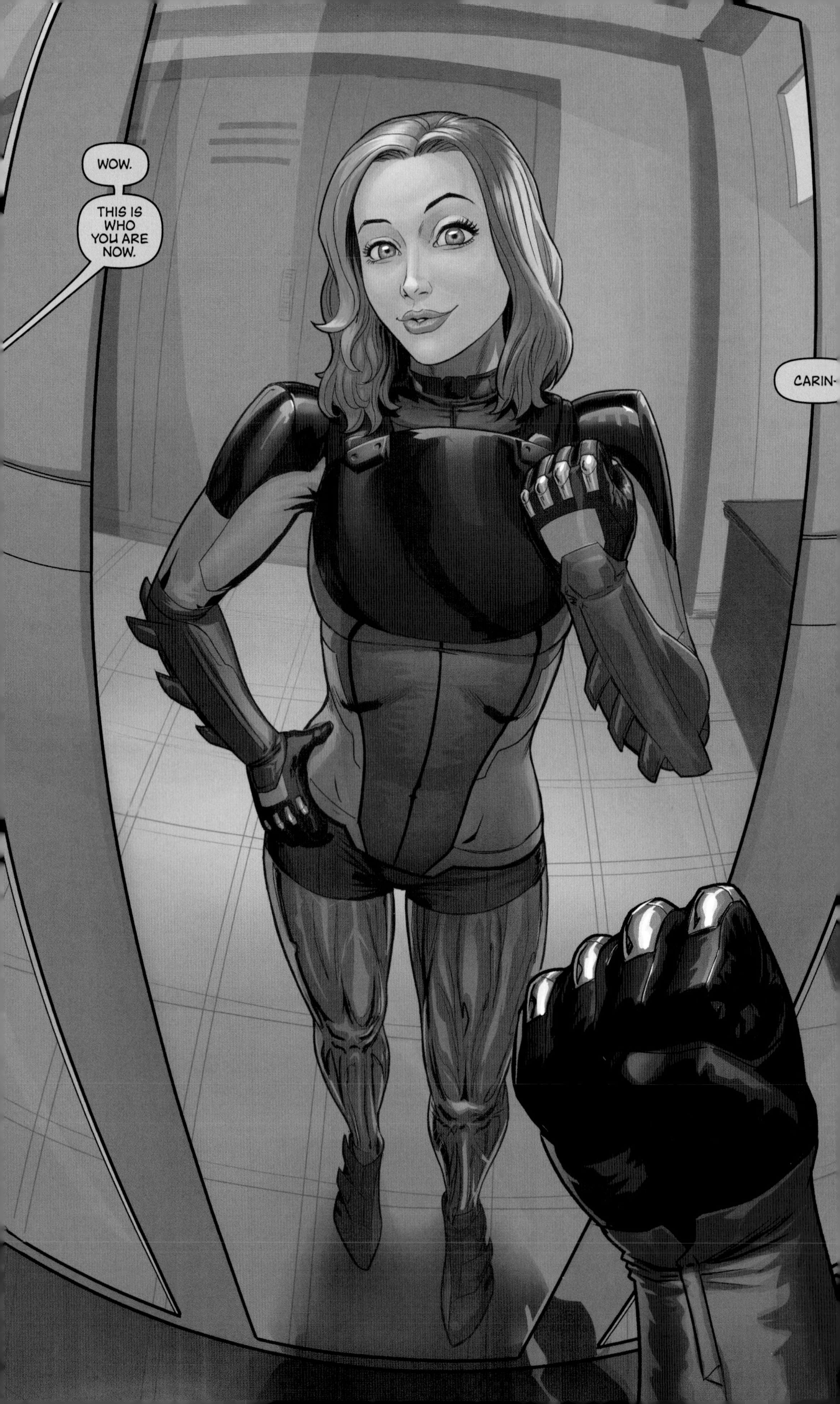
WOW.
THIS IS WHO YOU ARE NOW.
CARIN-

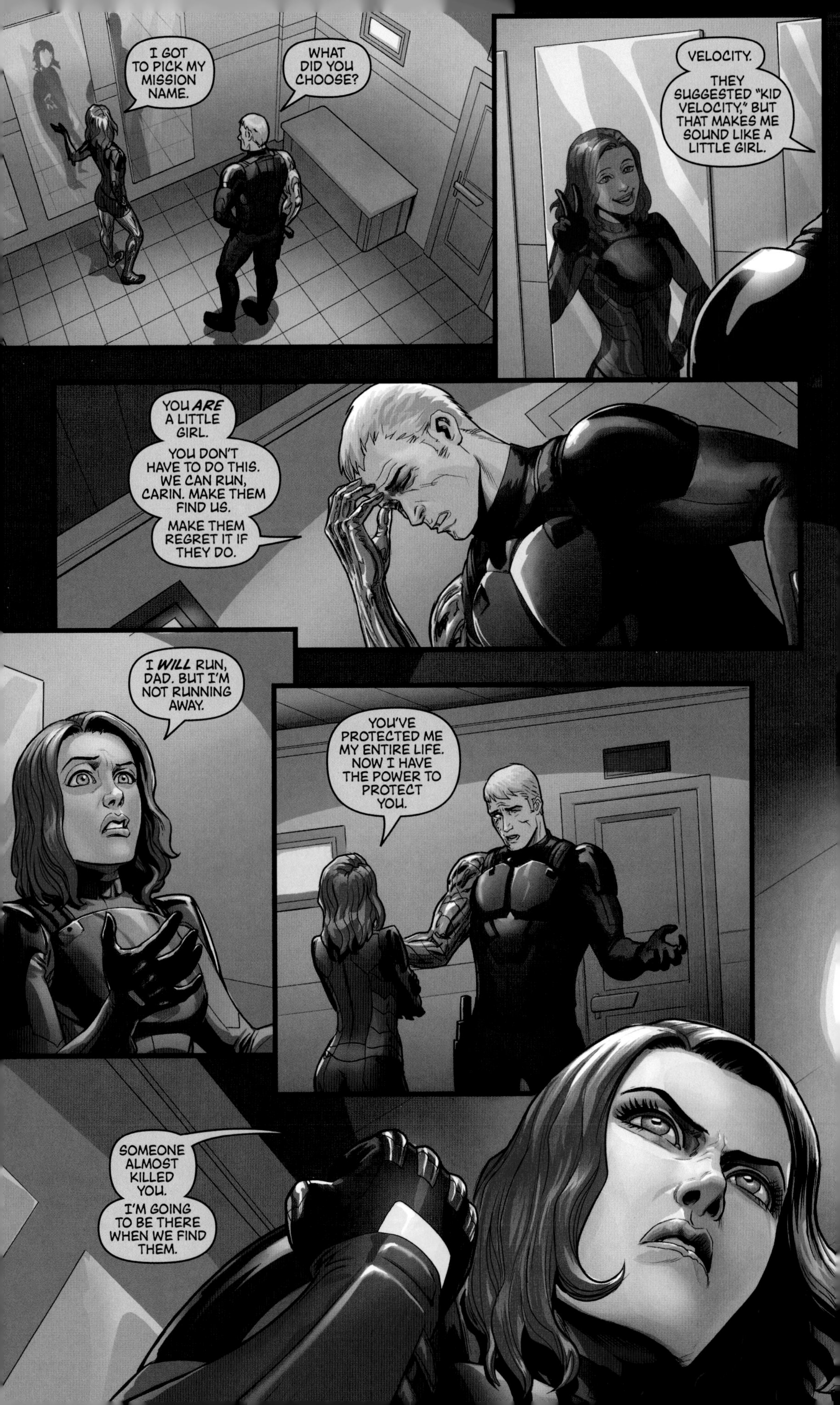
I GOT TO PICK MY MISSION NAME.
WHAT DID YOU CHOOSE?
VELOCITY.
THEY SUGGESTED "KID VELOCITY," BUT THAT MAKES ME SOUND LIKE A LITTLE GIRL.
YOU ARE A LITTLE GIRL.
YOU DON'T HAVE TO DO THIS. WE CAN RUN, CARIN. MAKE THEM FIND US.
MAKE THEM REGRET IT IF THEY DO.
I WILL RUN, DAD. BUT I'M NOT RUNNING AWAY.
YOU'VE PROTECTED ME MY ENTIRE LIFE. NOW I HAVE THE POWER TO PROTECT YOU.
SOMEONE ALMOST KILLED YOU.
I'M GOING TO BE THERE WHEN WE FIND THEM.

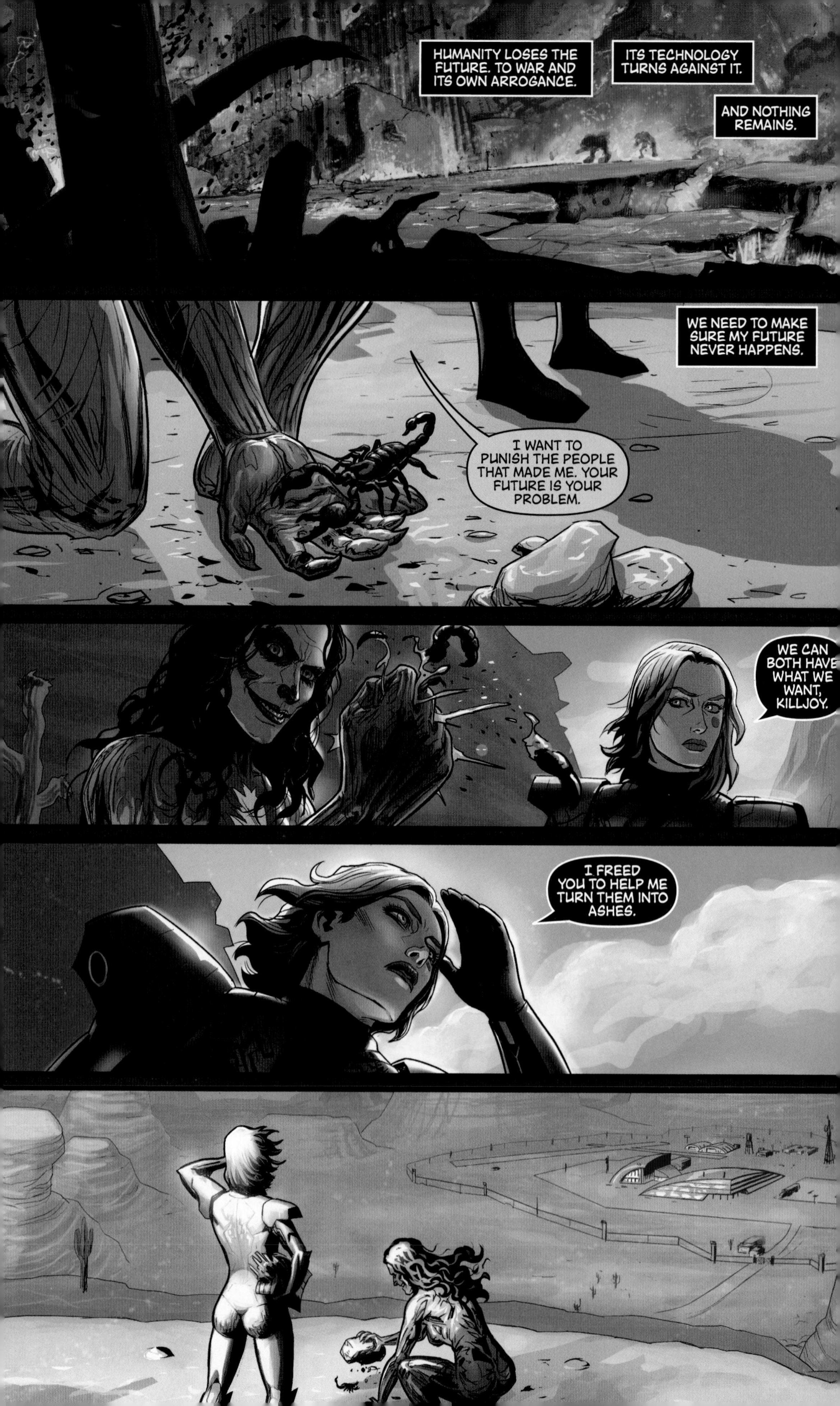
HUMANITY LOSES THE FUTURE. TO WAR AND ITS OWN ARROGANCE.
ITS TECHNOLOGY TURNS AGAINST IT.
AND NOTHING REMAINS.
WE NEED TO MAKE SURE MY FUTURE NEVER HAPPENS.
I WANT TO PUNISH THE PEOPLE THAT MADE ME. YOUR FUTURE IS YOUR PROBLEM.
WE CAN BOTH HAVE WHAT WE WANT, KILLJOY.
I FREED YOU TO HELP ME TURN THEM INTO ASHES.

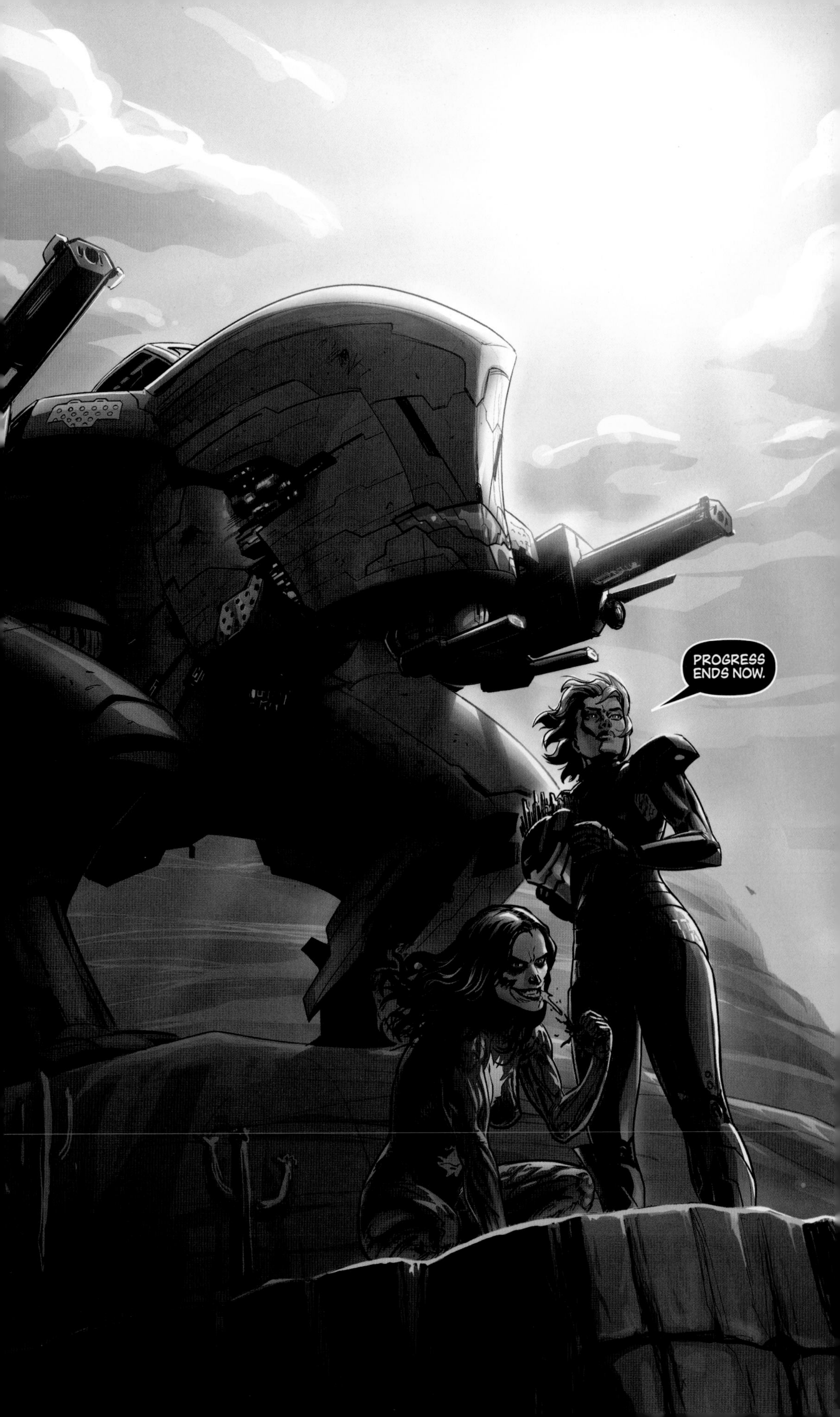
PROGRESS ENDS NOW.

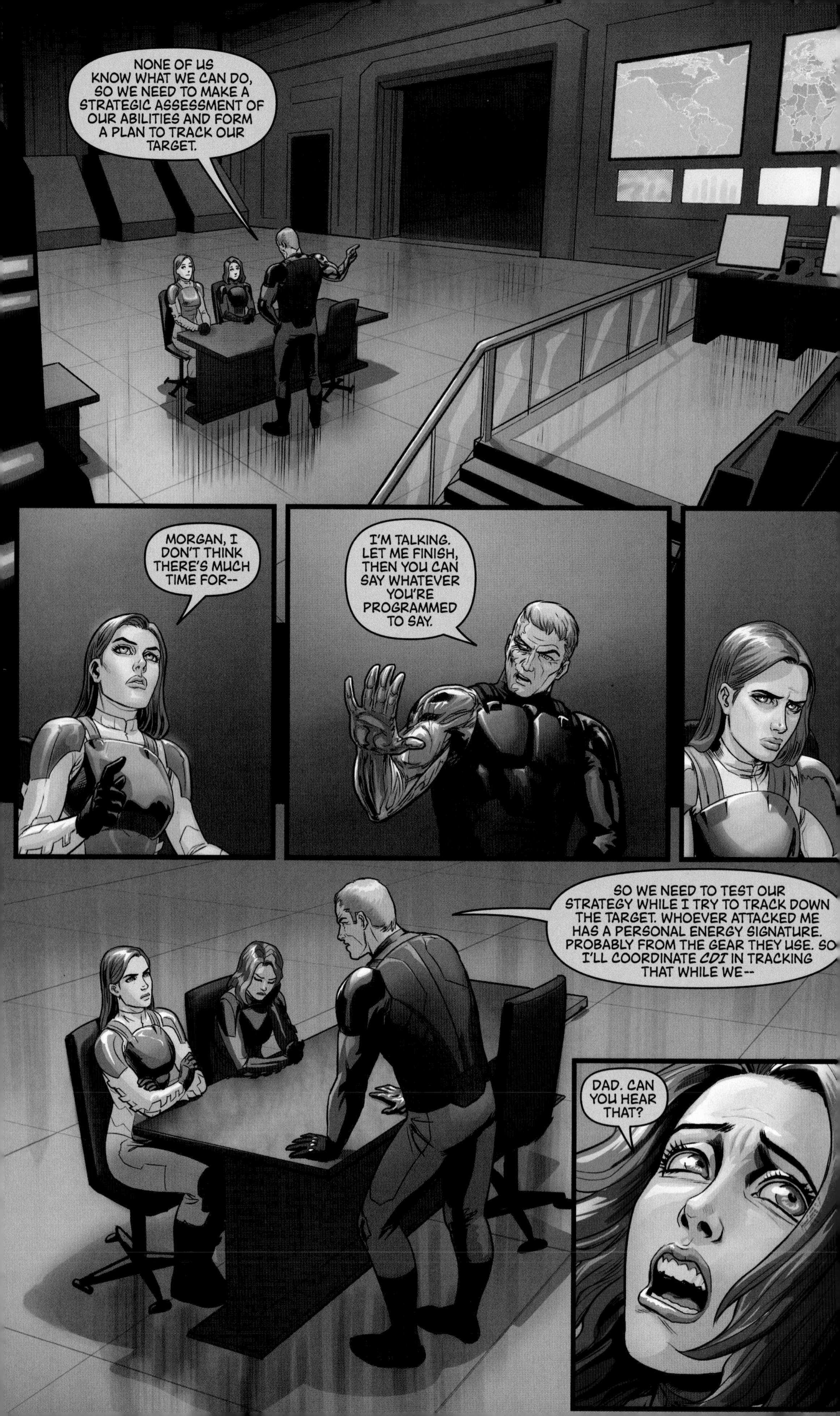

NONE OF US KNOW WHAT WE CAN DO, SO WE NEED TO MAKE A STRATEGIC ASSESSMENT OF OUR ABILITIES AND FORM A PLAN TO TRACK OUR TARGET.
MORGAN, I DON'T THINK THERE'S MUCH TIME FOR--
I'M TALKING. LET ME FINISH, THEN YOU CAN SAY WHATEVER YOU'RE PROGRAMMED TO SAY.
SO WE NEED TO TEST OUR STRATEGY WHILE I TRY TO TRACK DOWN THE TARGET. WHOEVER ATTACKED ME HAS A PERSONAL ENERGY SIGNATURE. PROBABLY FROM THE GEAR THEY USE. SO I'LL COORDINATE *CDI* IN TRACKING THAT WHILE WE--
DAD. CAN YOU HEAR THAT?

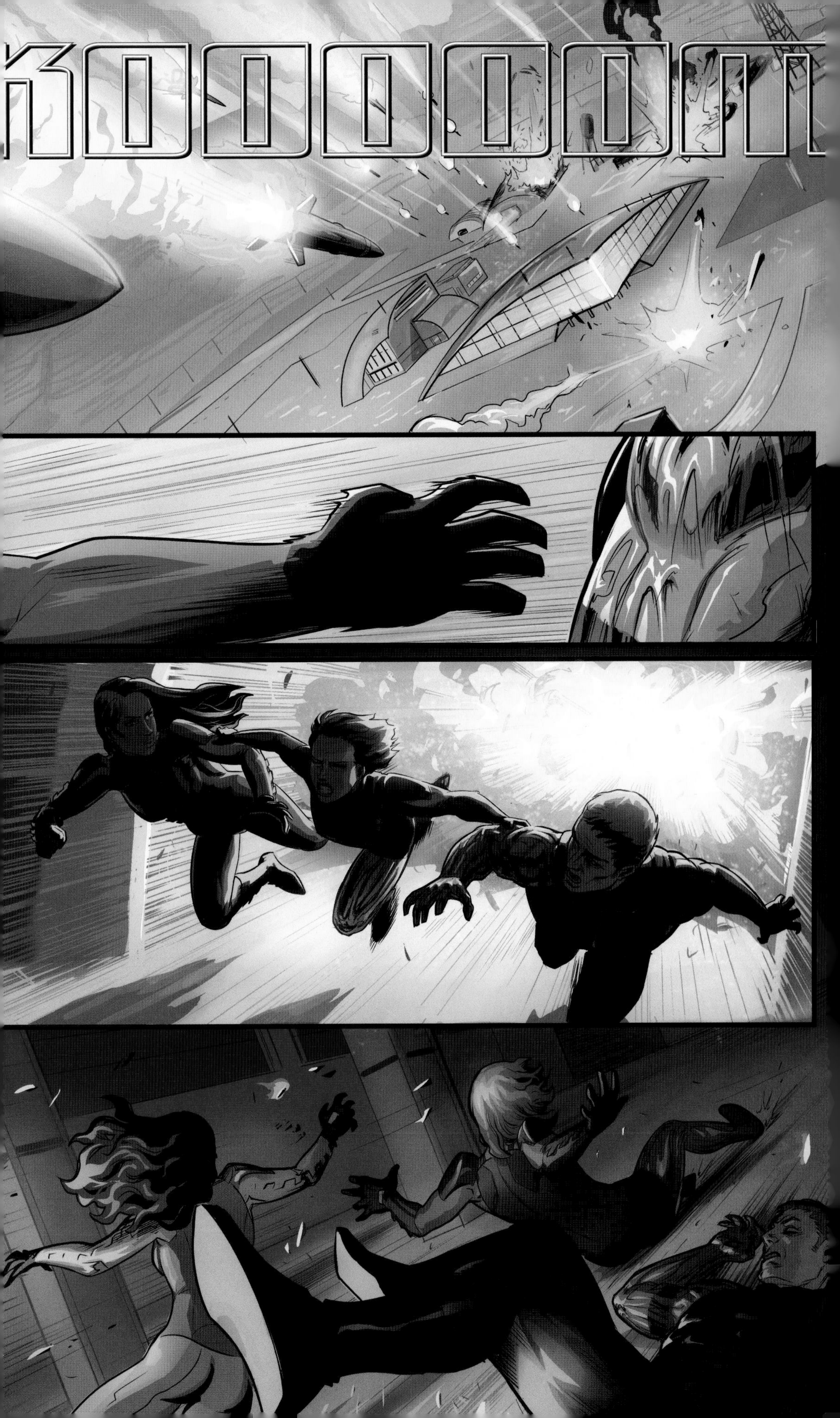
KOOOOOM

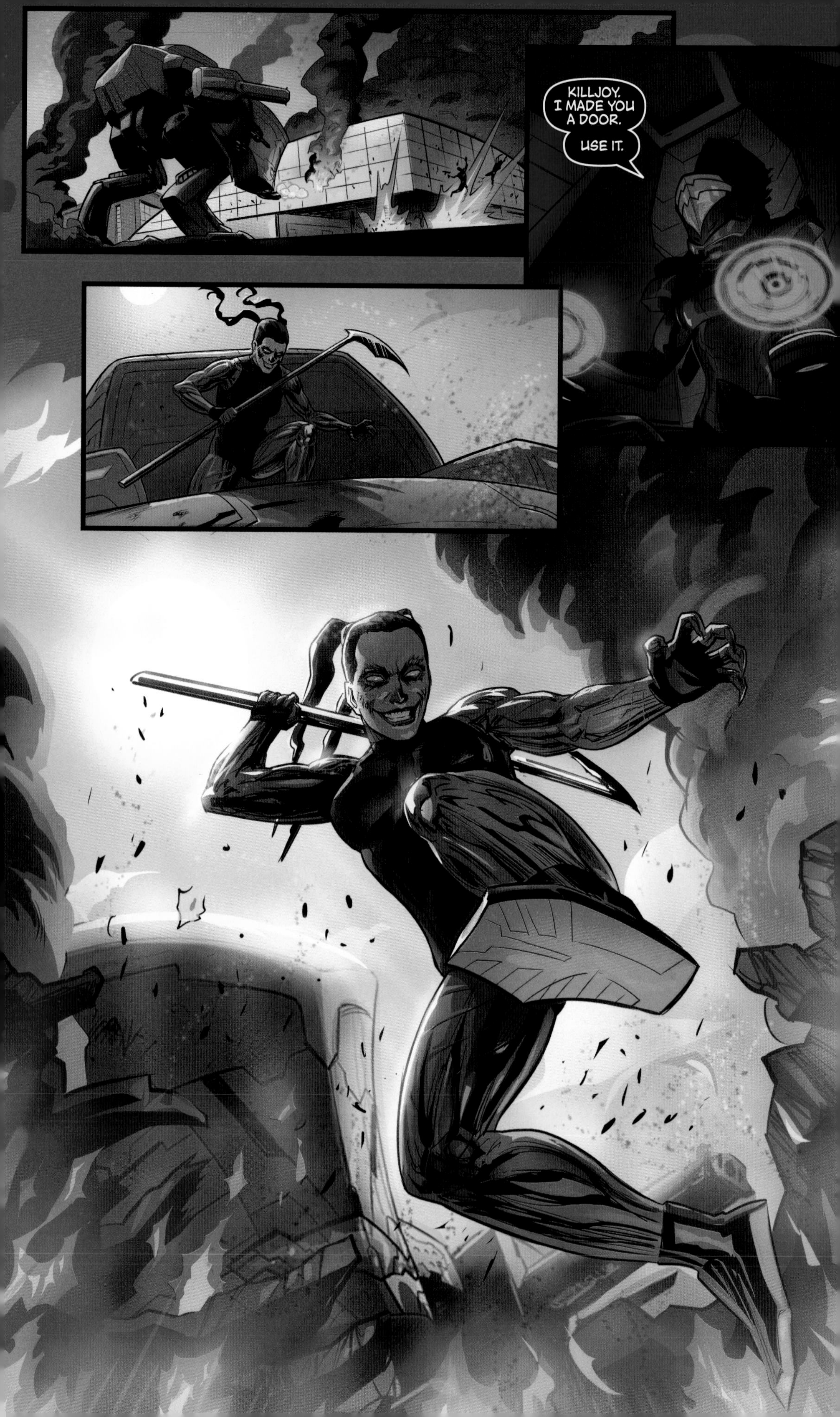
KILLJOY. I MADE YOU A DOOR.
USE IT.

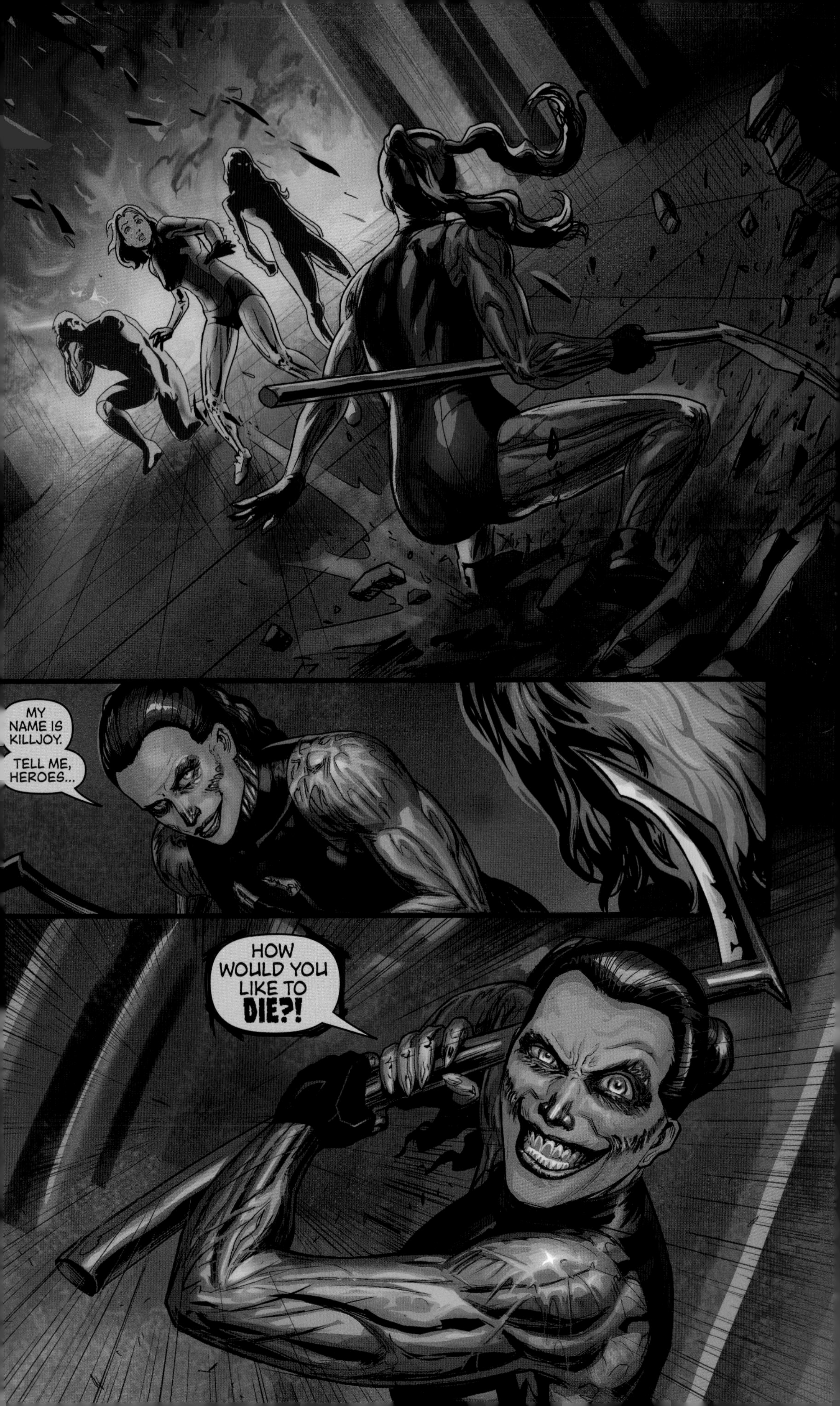
MY NAME IS KILLJOY.
TELL ME, HEROES...
HOW WOULD YOU LIKE TO DIE?!

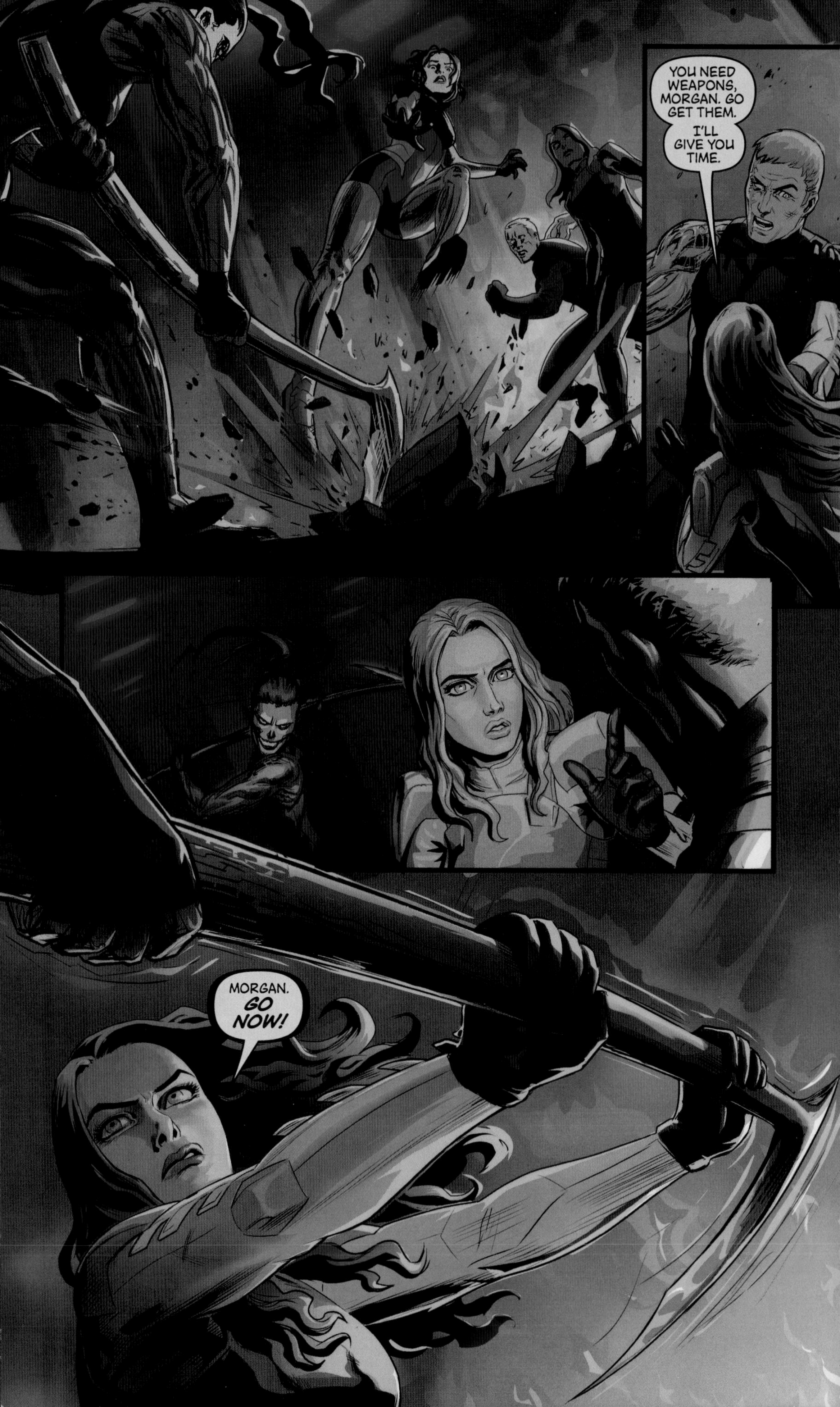
YOU NEED WEAPONS, MORGAN. GO GET THEM.
I'LL GIVE YOU TIME.
MORGAN. GO NOW!

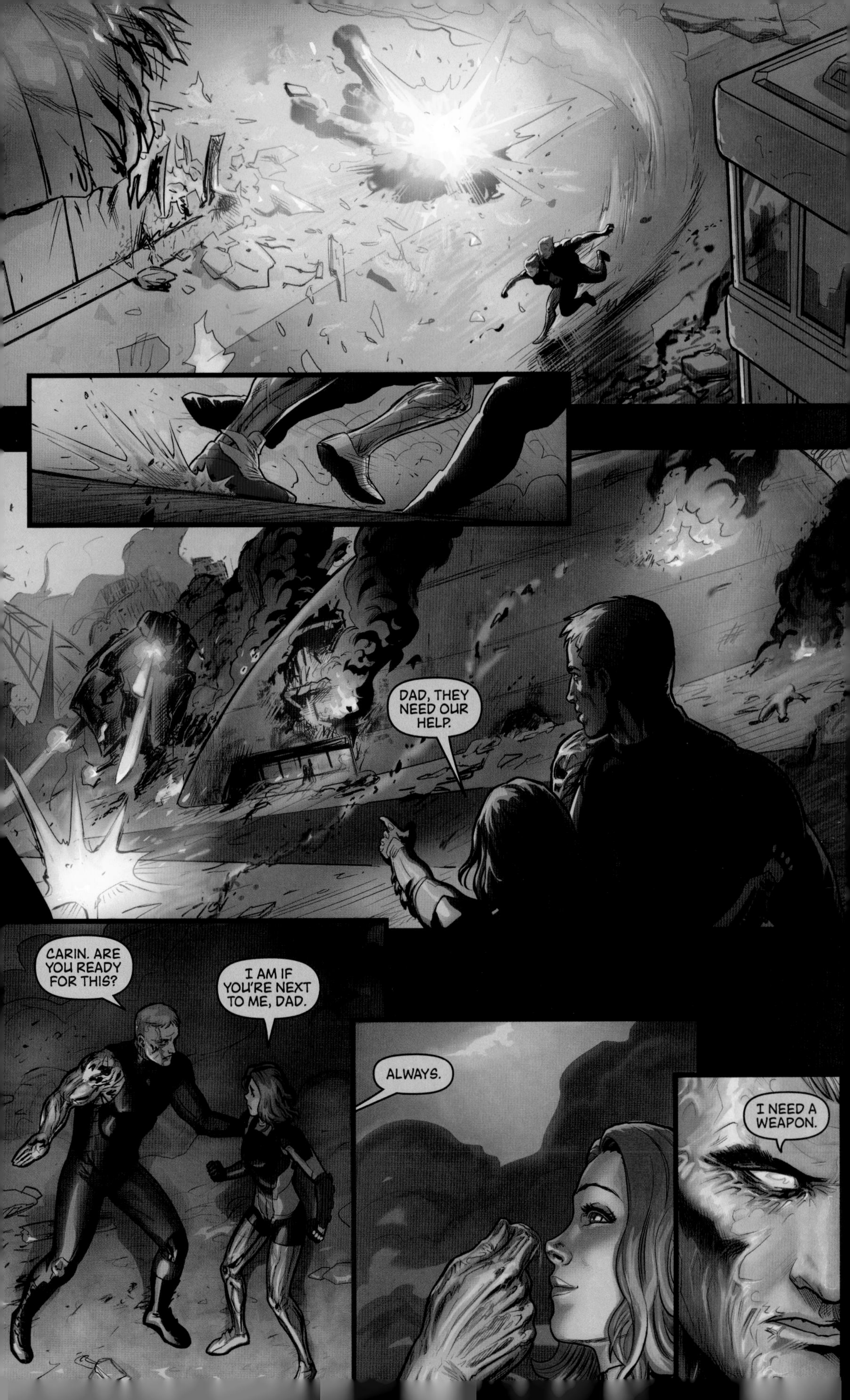
DAD, THEY NEED OUR HELP.
CARIN. ARE YOU READY FOR THIS?
I AM IF YOU'RE NEXT TO ME, DAD.
ALWAYS.
I NEED A WEAPON.

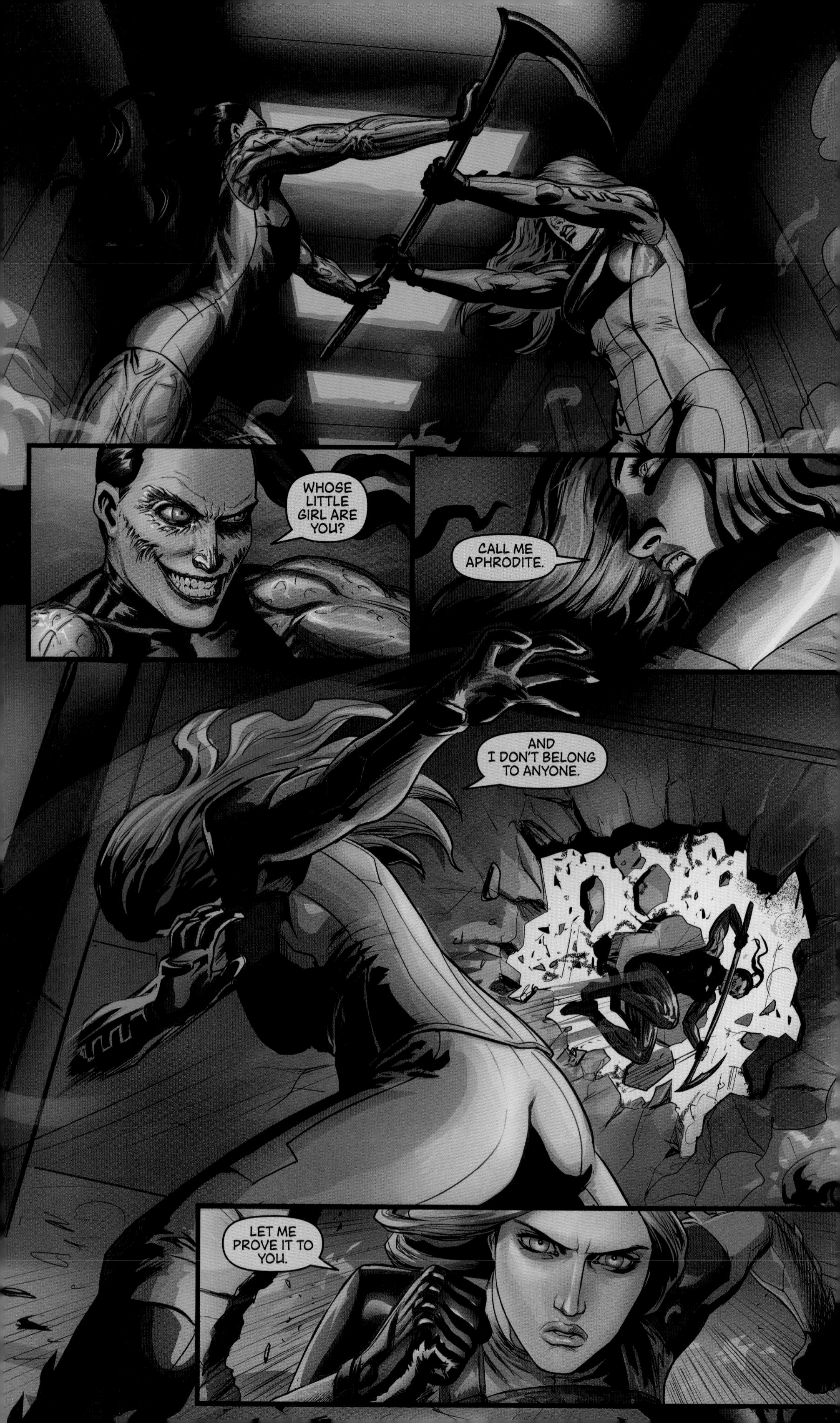
WHOSE LITTLE GIRL ARE YOU?
CALL ME APHRODITE.
AND I DON'T BELONG TO ANYONE.
LET ME PROVE IT TO YOU.

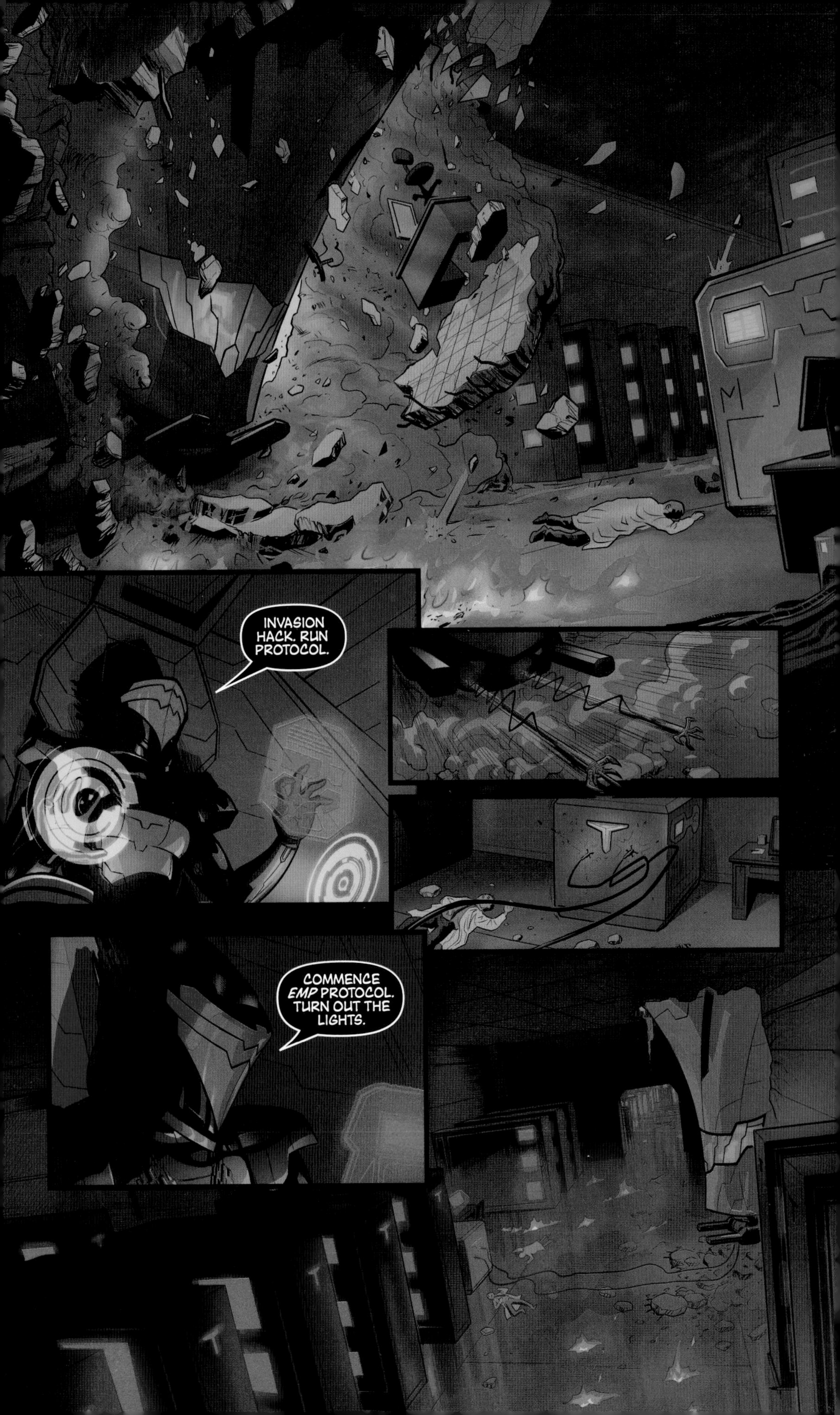
INVASION HACK. RUN PROTOCOL.
COMMENCE EMP PROTOCOL. TURN OUT THE LIGHTS.

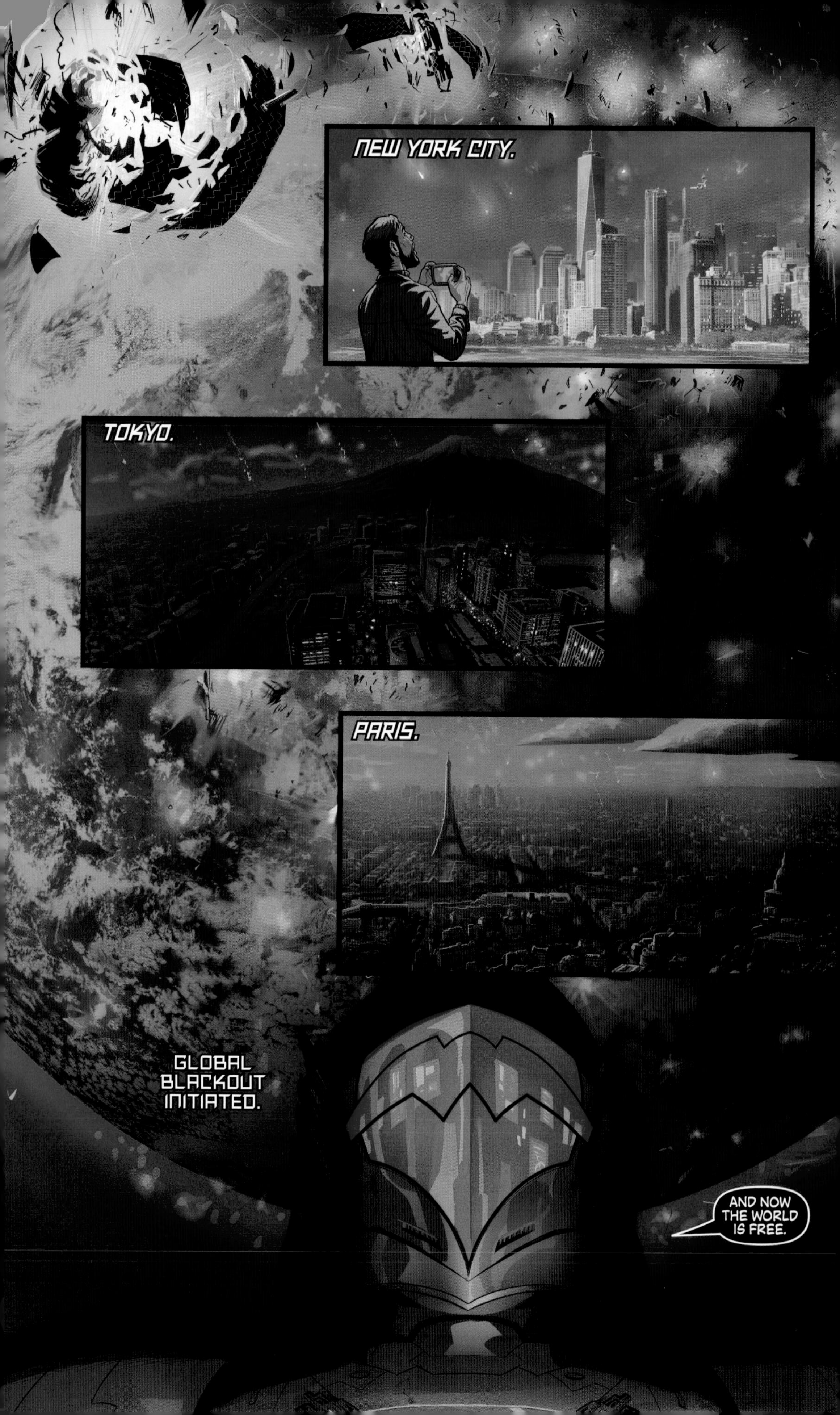
NEW YORK CITY.
TOKYO.
PARIS.
GLOBAL BLACKOUT INITIATED.
AND NOW THE WORLD IS FREE.

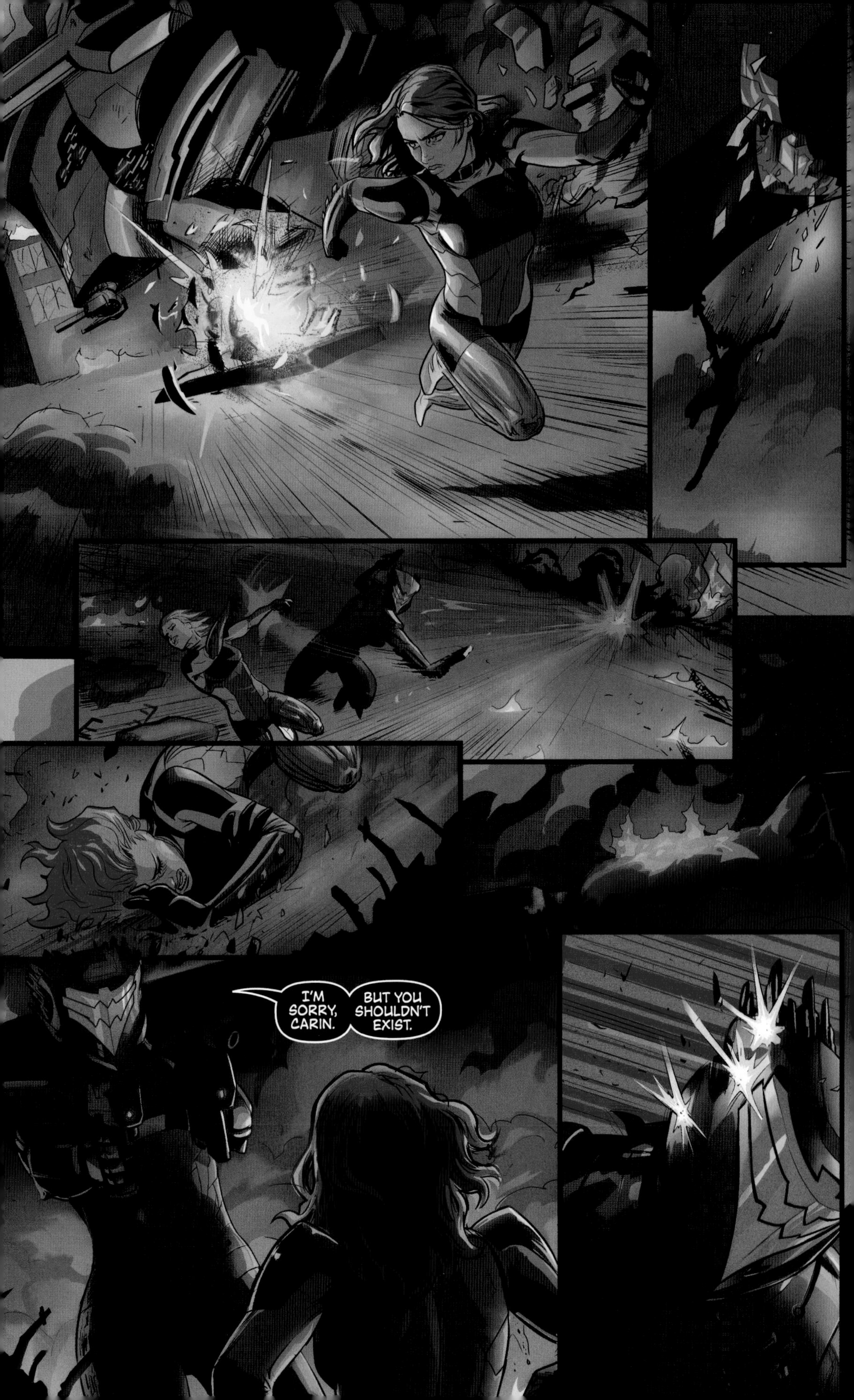
I'M SORRY, CARIN.
BUT YOU SHOULDN'T EXIST.

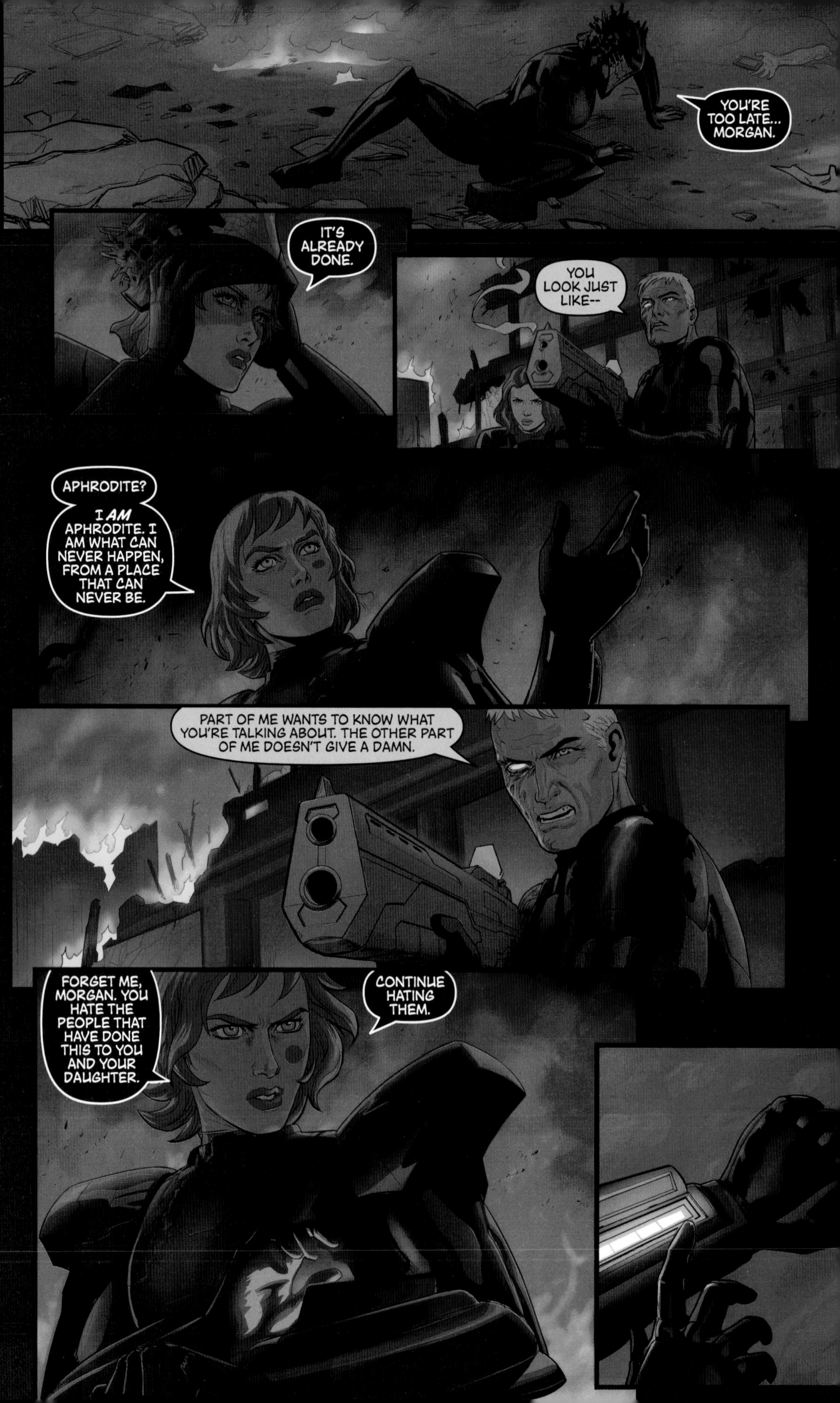
YOU'RE TOO LATE... MORGAN.
IT'S ALREADY DONE.
YOU LOOK JUST LIKE--
APHRODITE?
I *AM* APHRODITE. I AM WHAT CAN NEVER HAPPEN, FROM A PLACE THAT CAN NEVER BE.
PART OF ME WANTS TO KNOW WHAT YOU'RE TALKING ABOUT. THE OTHER PART OF ME DOESN'T GIVE A DAMN.
FORGET ME, MORGAN. YOU HATE THE PEOPLE THAT HAVE DONE THIS TO YOU AND YOUR DAUGHTER.
CONTINUE HATING THEM.

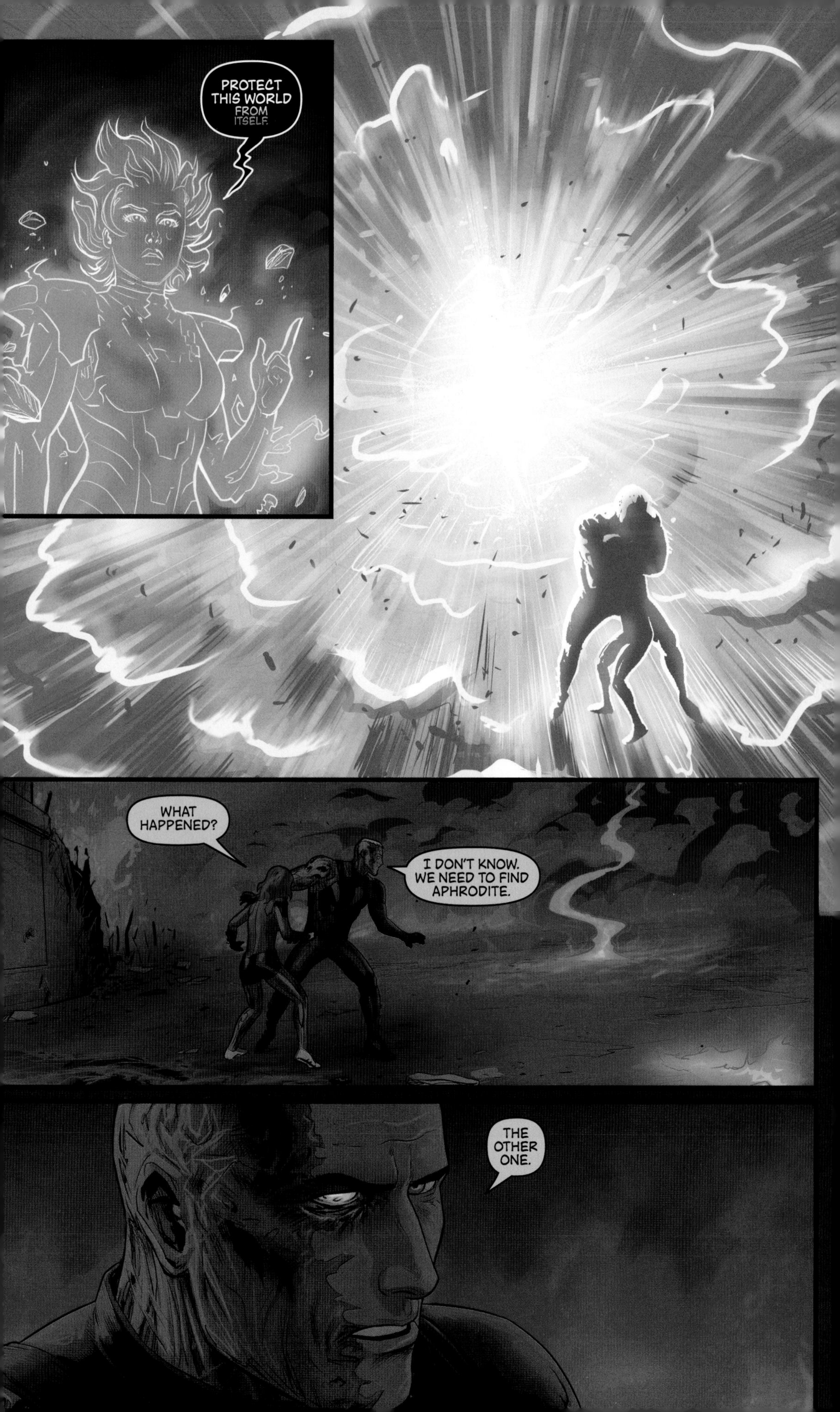
PROTECT THIS WORLD FROM ITSELF.
WHAT HAPPENED?
I DON'T KNOW. WE NEED TO FIND APHRODITE.
THE OTHER ONE.

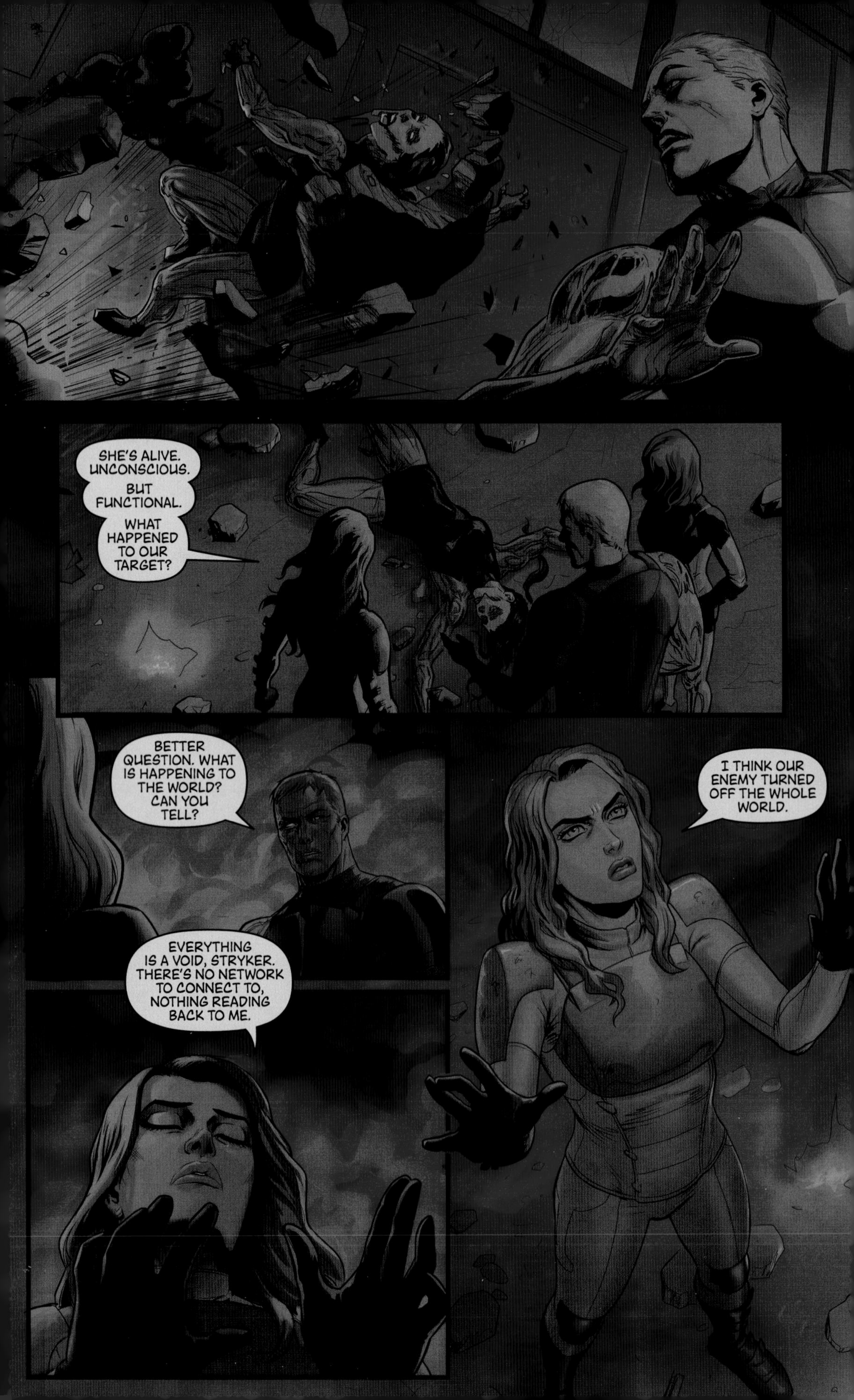
SHE'S ALIVE. UNCONSCIOUS.
BUT FUNCTIONAL.
WHAT HAPPENED TO OUR TARGET?
BETTER QUESTION. WHAT IS HAPPENING TO THE WORLD? CAN YOU TELL?
EVERYTHING IS A VOID, STRYKER. THERE'S NO NETWORK TO CONNECT TO, NOTHING READING BACK TO ME.
I THINK OUR ENEMY TURNED OFF THE WHOLE WORLD.

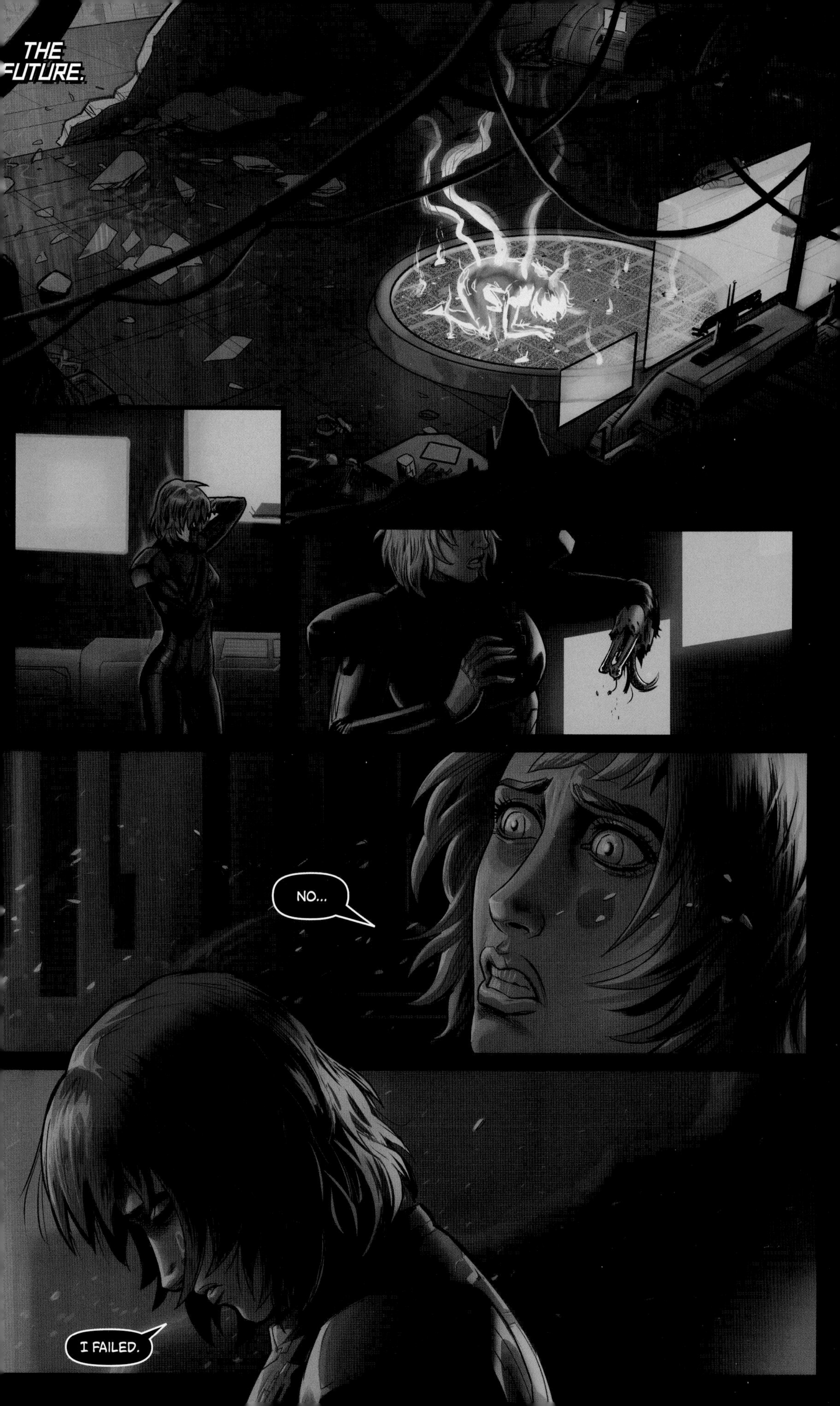
THE FUTURE.
NO...
I FAILED.

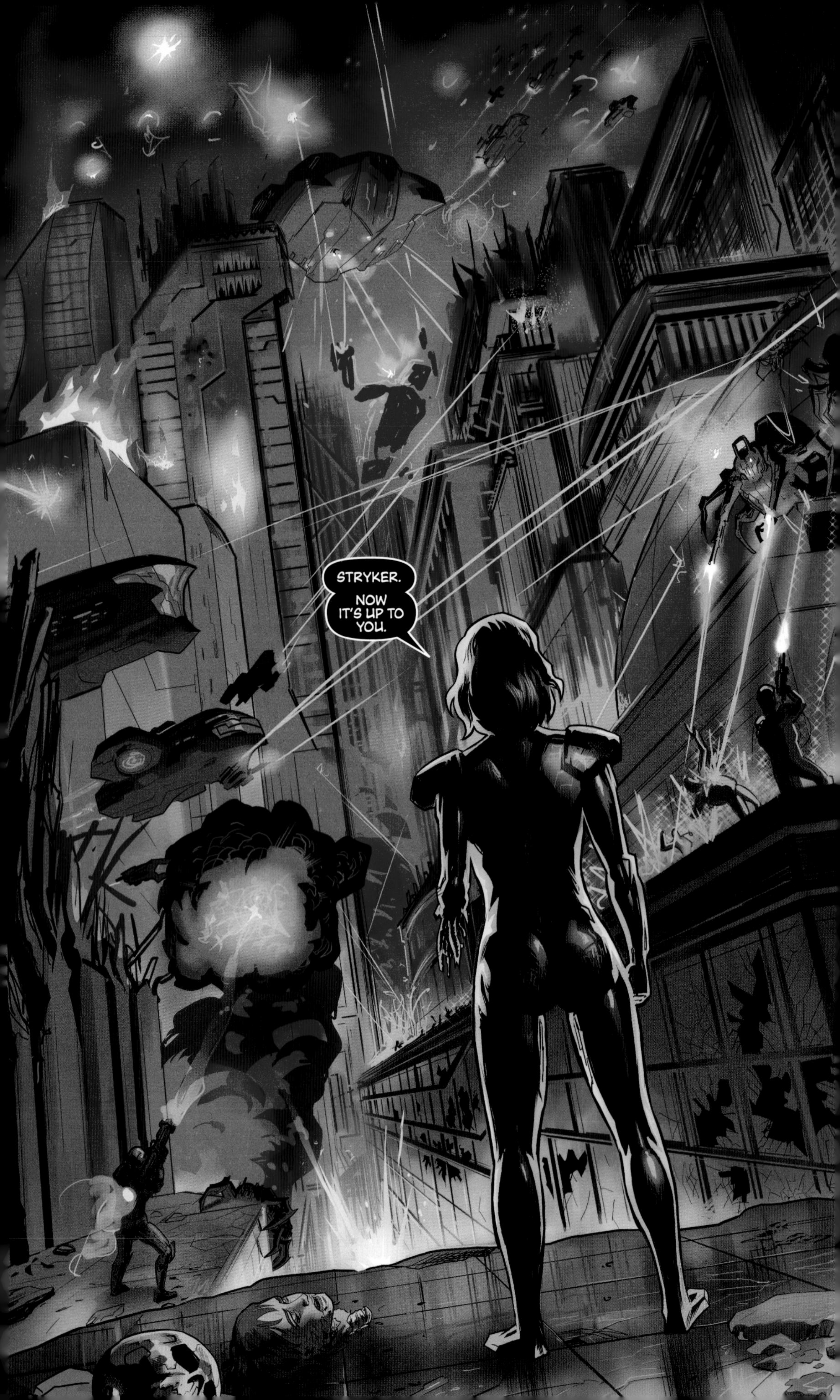
STRYKER.
NOW IT'S UP TO YOU.

COVER GALLERY

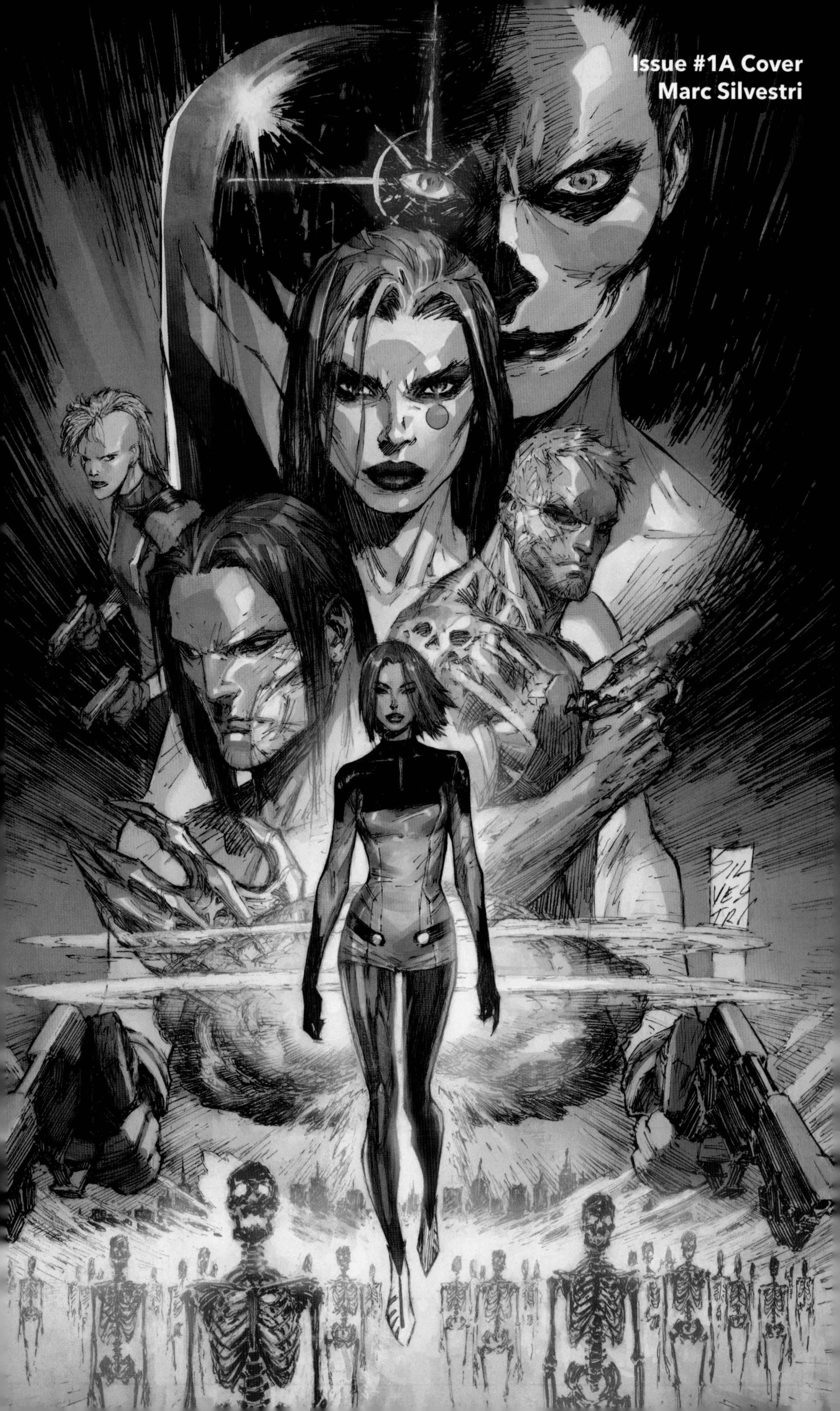

Issue #1A Cover
Marc Silvestri

Issue #1B Cover
Atilio Rojo

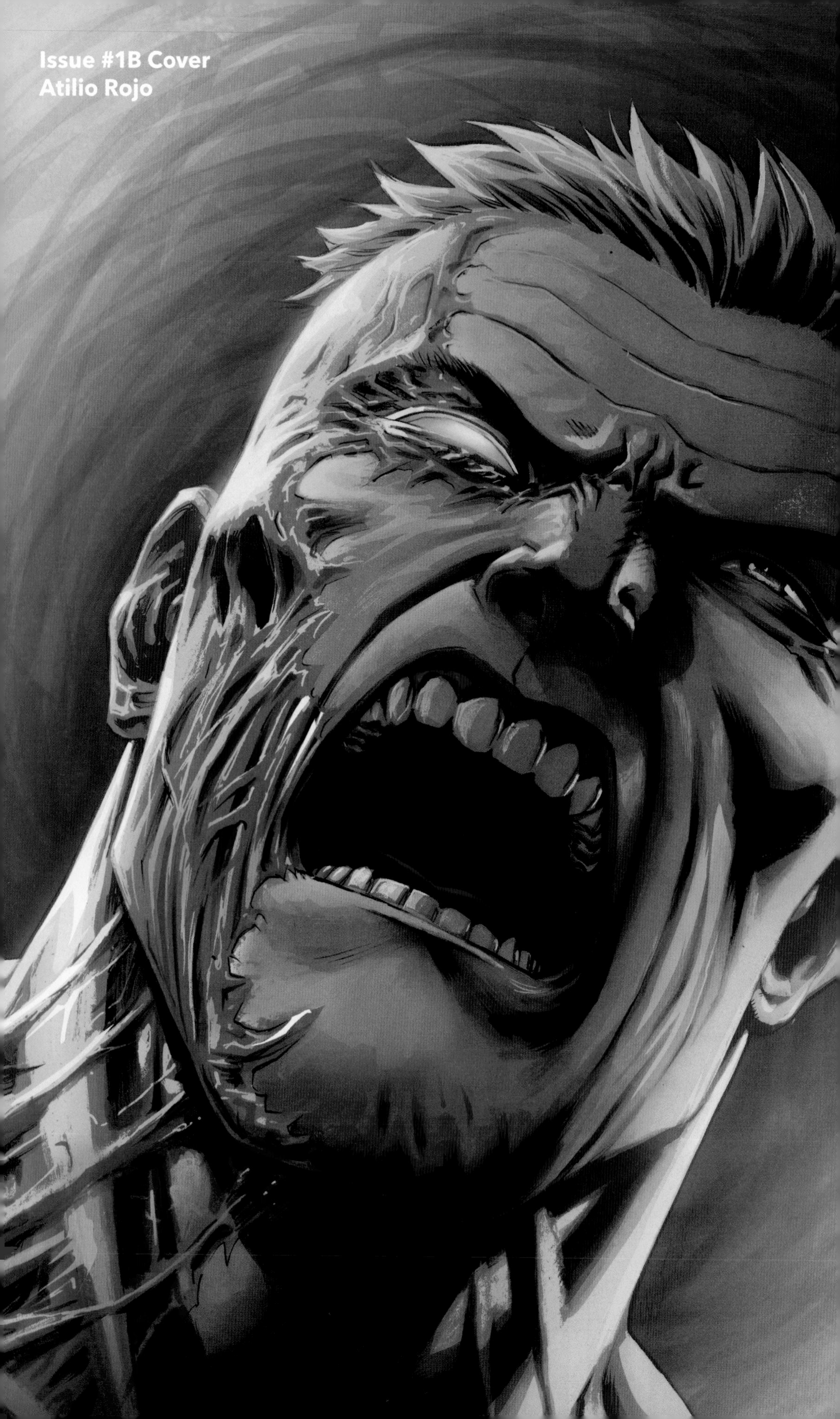

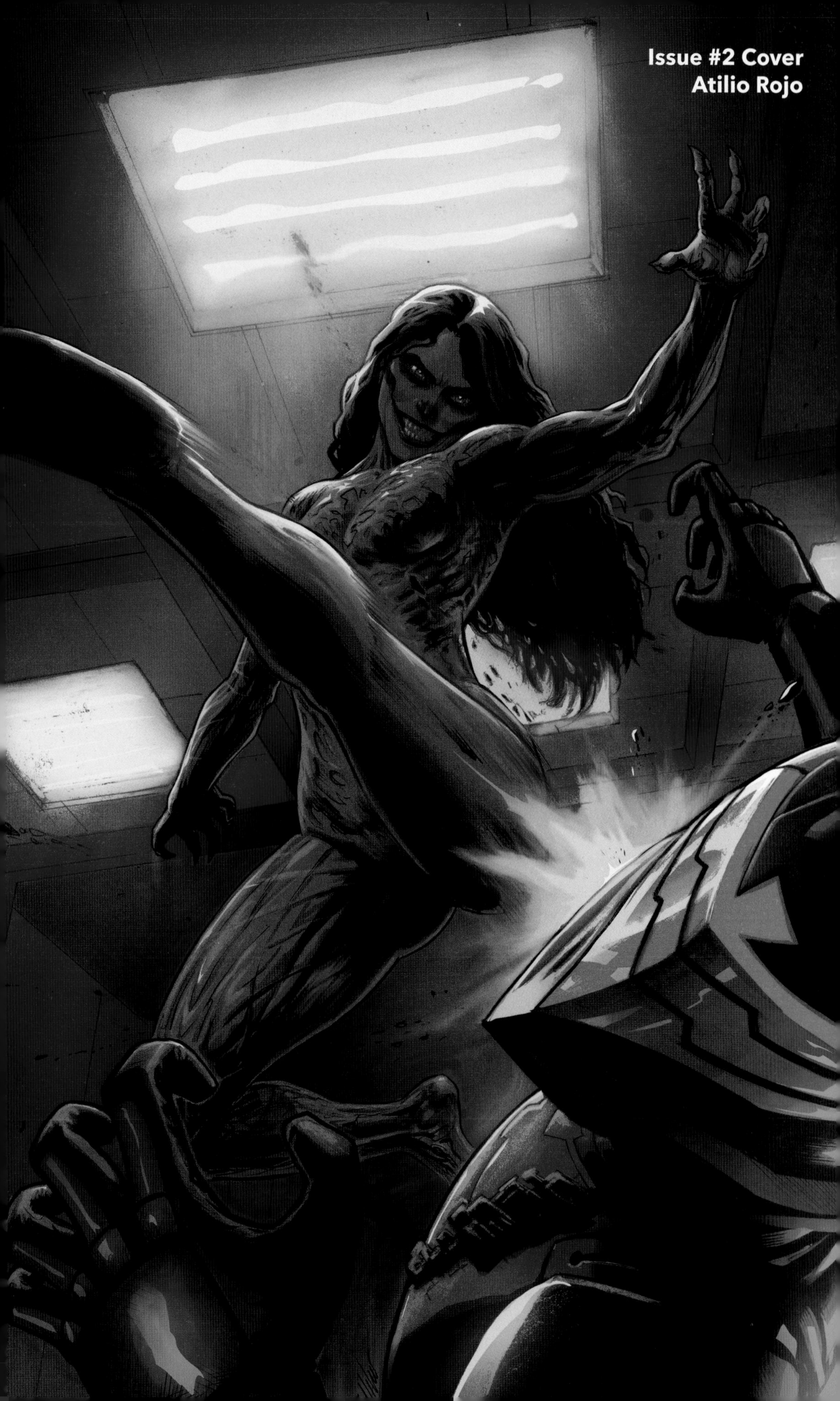

Issue #2 Cover
Atilio Rojo

Issue #3 Cover
Atilio Rojo

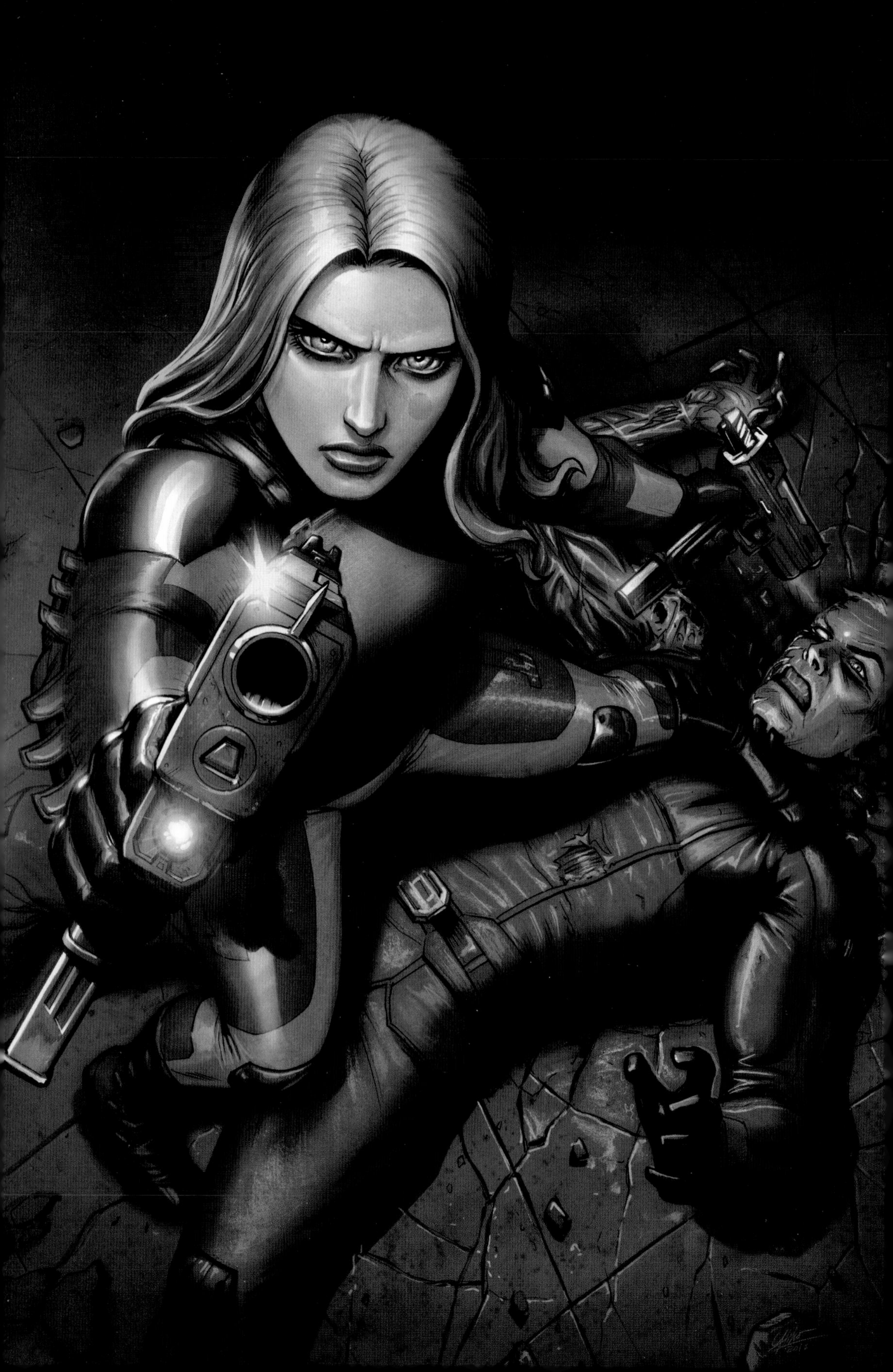

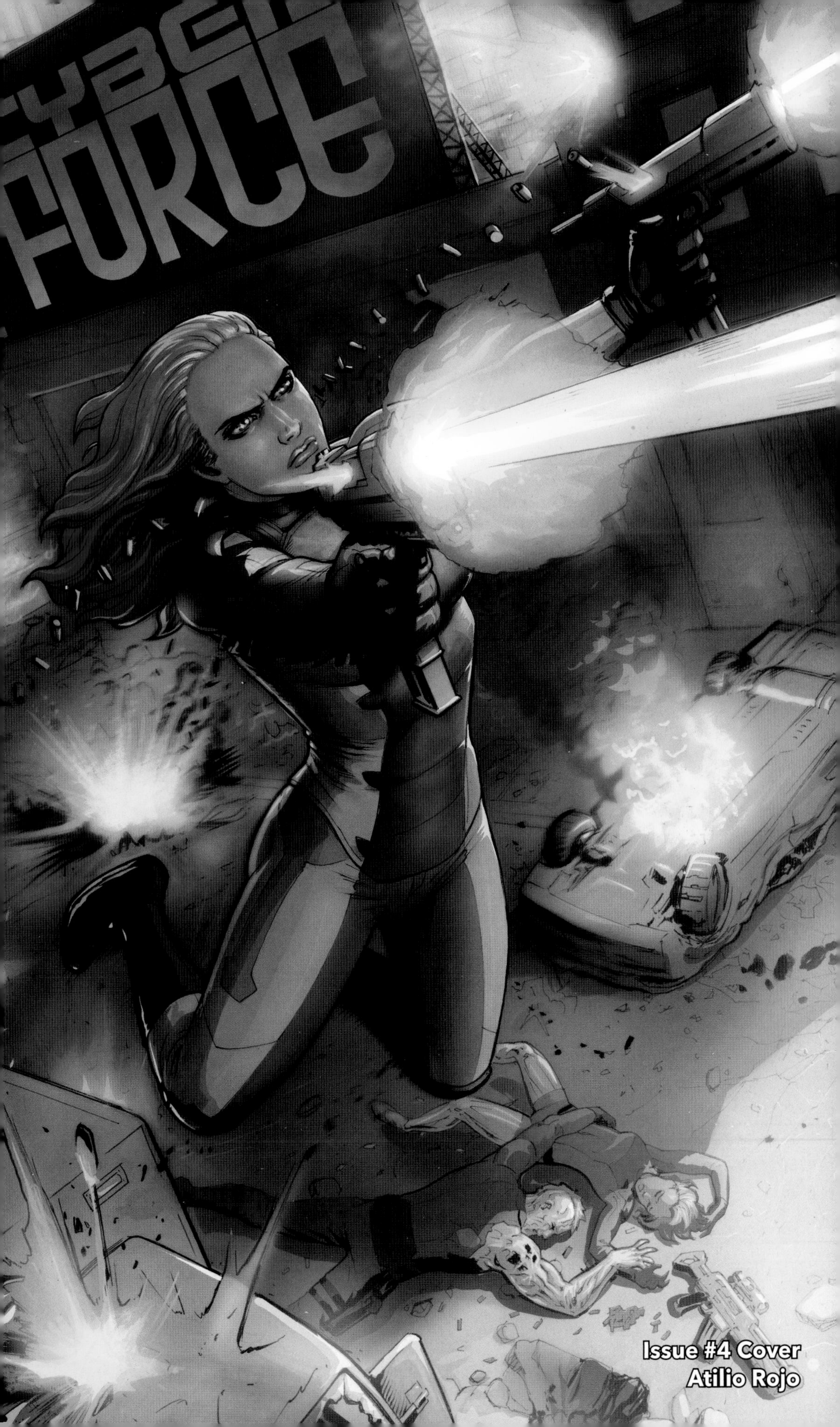
FORCE

Issue #4 Cover
Atilio Rojo

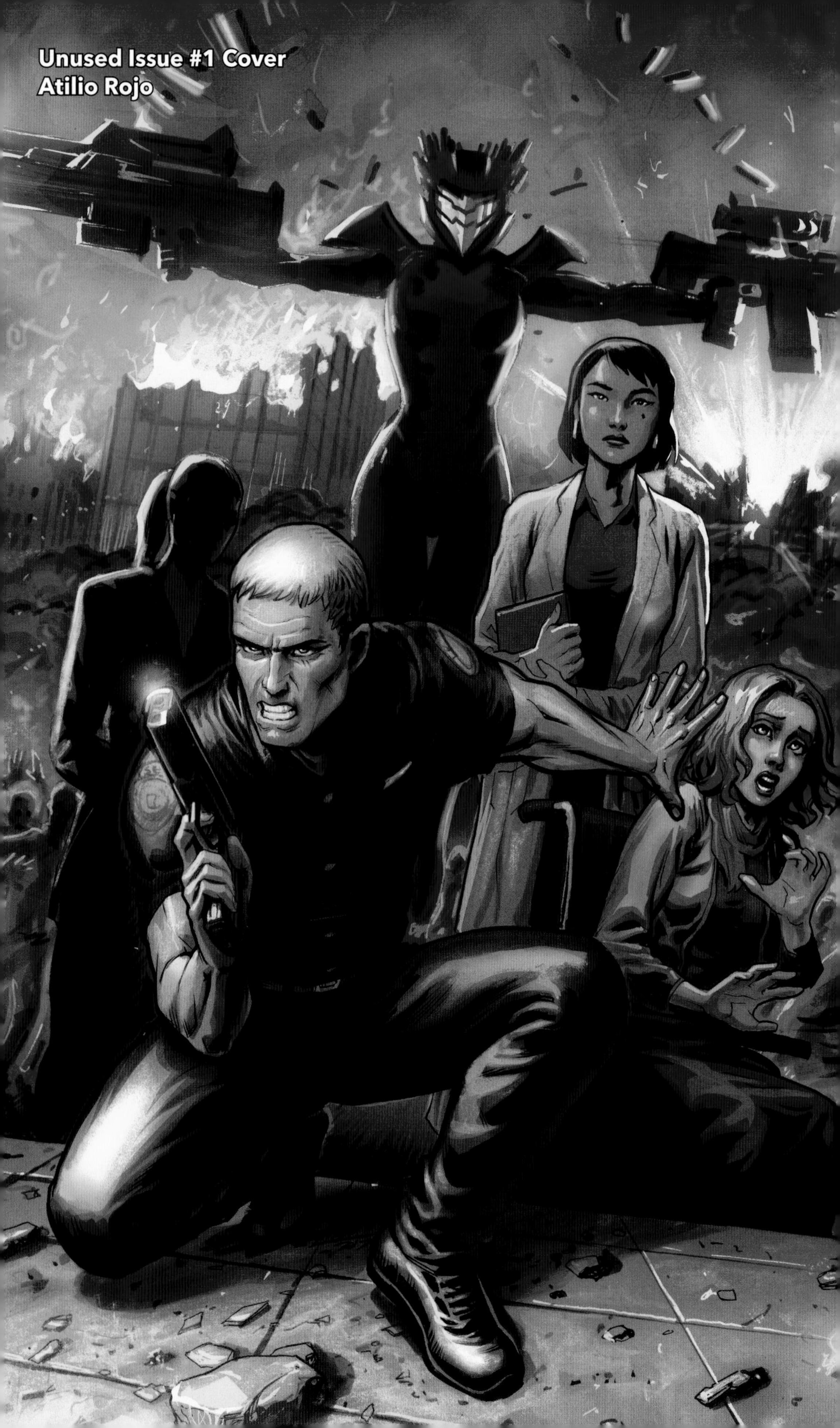

Unused Issue #1 Cover
Atilio Rojo

MATT HAWKINS
TWITTER: @topcowmatt
FACEBOOK: http://www.facebook.com/selfloathingnarcissist

A veteran of the initial Image Comics launch, Matt started his career in comic book publishing in 1993 and has been working with Image as a creator, writer and executive for over 20 years. President/COO of Top Cow since 1998, Matt has created and written over 30 new franchises for Top Cow and Image including *Think Tank*, *The Tithe*, *Necromancer*, *VICE*, *Lady Pendragon*, *Aphrodite IX*, and *Tales of Honor*, as well as handling the company's business affairs.

BRYAN HILL
TWITTER: @bryanedwardhill
INSTAGRAM: bryanehill

Writes comics, writes movies, and makes films. He lives and works in Los Angeles.

ATILIO ROJO
FACEBOOK: http://www.facebook.com/atilio.rojo.52

Atilio Rojo has been writing and drawing erotic comics since 2002. Rojo is best known for his work on *Transformers*, *G.I. Joe*, *Snake Eyes*, *Dungeons and Dragons*, *LOD*, *IXth Generation*, *Eden's Fall*, and *Samaritan: Veritas* (*The Tithe*).

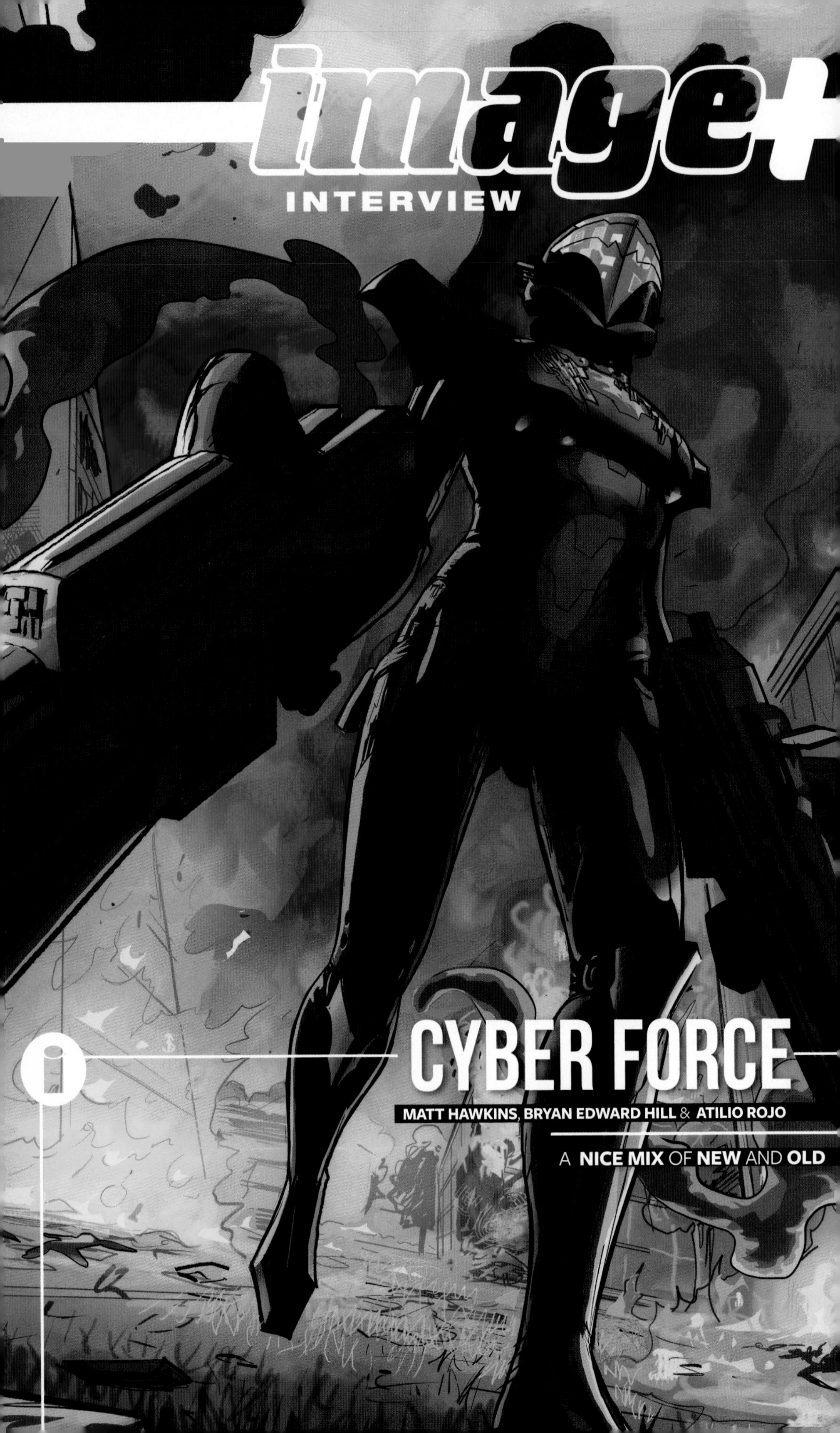

image+ INTERVIEW

CYBER FORCE

MATT HAWKINS, BRYAN EDWARD HILL & ATILIO ROJO

A NICE MIX OF NEW AND OLD

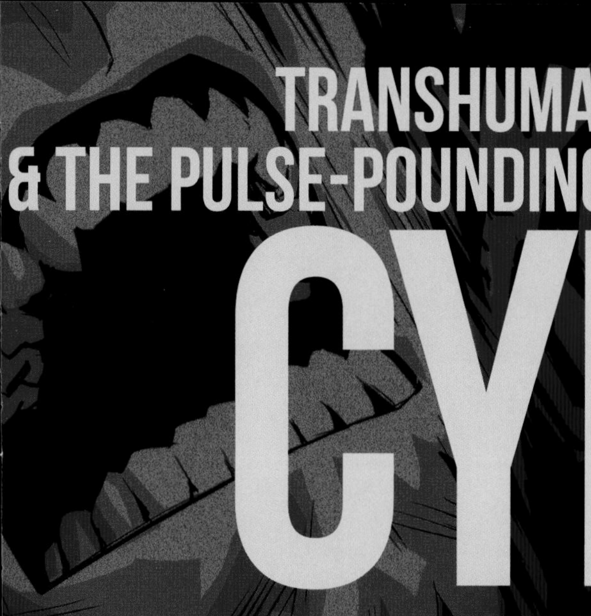

TRANSHUMANISM, TECHNOLOGY, & THE PULSE-POUNDING NEW DIRECTION OF CYBER FORCE

INTERVIEW BY **BRITTANY MATTER**

Have you been holding out for a cybernetic hero, or maybe... you've been missing your favorite characters from Marc Silvestri? Either way, **CYBER FORCE** is back and will save the day in this brand-new story from a well-seasoned team. Matt Hawkins, Bryan Edward Hill, & Atilio Rojo share some of the behind-the-scenes work they've been brewing for Top Cow's original hit, and their take pulls no punches.

ITTANY MATTER: *Matt, is this a continuation, an origin ory, or a reimagining of* **CYBER FORCE** *altogether?*

ATT HAWKINS: It is a combination of a continuation and origin story. Not to give too much away, but in the second ume of **IXth GENERATION**, Aphrodite IX killed someone in past that altered the time stream. This allows us to do a fresh ory that's both in continuity and a new gin. Ultimately, if you're reading this for first time, it's fine, and you don't need have read anything prior to this to fully everything.

"CLASSIC TOP COW COMICS HAVE ALWAYS BEEN VERY KINETIC."

emember the first meeting Marc and ad to discuss **CYBER FORCE** returning for the 20th anniversary Top Cow. We updated the team and its look. Rojo has done ne further design work off of Silvestri's designs that gives this even fresher feel.

ITTANY: *What were the most memorable moments from t or other* **CYBER FORCE** *meetings with Marc? Do you have ame for those meetings?*

ATT: We (pretty boringly) call them story meetings. Seems as creative types, we should be able to come up with something ter than that! Marc is very passionate about **CYBER FORCE**. an important property to him, and it's important that it's ated properly. I think for **CYBER FORCE: REBIRTH**, I was able convince him to get rid of some of the characters I thought re kind of lame [laughs]. The team is more focused on the ily dynamic now.

ITTANY: *What are you most excited about in this encore?*

ATT: This is the first **CYBER FORCE** storyline to be fully nned 25 issues in advance. We've got a long story arc planned, and one of the reasons we went with Atilio Rojo is he's so fast! With **POSTAL** coming to an end, it seemed a good time to launch a new planned long-arcing series. For the story itself, I love the idea that technology makes us less human. Playing with that dynamic is always fun, and it's front and center in this storyline.

BRITTANY: *Atilio, this first issue is nicely balanced between exciting action scenes and slower-paced emotional beats. What do you think makes a good action scene? How do you know when you've nailed an emotional moment?*

ATILIO ROJO: An action scene needs some powerful, dynamic images and a good narrative that's well choreographed to give emotion/meaning to the action, plus some intense colors in the strongest moments, the emotional moments. I see them the same as the action scenes but without choreography [laughs]. The most important thing here is to try to make the audience feel the same as the character, and I do, or try to do that, especially by way of facial expressions and body language. I have had a lot of practice with emotional stories, and I enjoy depicting those scenes.

BRITTANY: *The colors are remarkable as well. What feeling do you want the readers to get from your colors?*

ATILIO: With color, I try to get the readers into the story, to see the image as real. Although my style is not completely realistic, I try to create color palettes according to the

ABOVE:
CYBER FORCE #1 *panel artwork*

emotions of each moment, and appropriate lighting, whether it is an action scene or the more emotional moments.

BRITTANY: *How's your knowledge of cybernetics?*

BRYAN EDWARD HILL: I've been studying the societal ramifications of transhumanism for a while. I'm more interested in the effect of the technology on society than I am the details of the technology. Cyborgs are already here. It's been a world of pacemakers for a while.

From a certain point of view, you could consider social media a kind of cybernetic extension of the mind, like a collective hive mind we all join by compulsion. We have a near-organic relationship to our phones. They provide endorphins. They're fully integrated into our behavior.

Note: I'm not saying that any of this is a good thing.

BRITTANY: *Are you following the rules of the previous series, or was there some freedom in reimagining the future of human-cyborg technology?*

BRYAN: I'm certainly keeping the "high-octane spirit" of the original series, sure. I didn't want to reshape it into something static. Classic Top Cow comics have always been very kinetic, and that's a form I'm following.

Whenever you're writing about theoretical technology, you have to to make adjustments for the era you're in. When **CYBER FORCE** was created, there weren't smartphones. We didn't have Elon Musk. The world has advanced since the inception of that concept, so I have to consider all of that while writing.

> **"*CYBER FORCE* WAS ABOUT THE DEFINITION AND PRESERVATION OF HUMANITY AS WE EVOLVE THROUGH TECHNOLOGY."**

Ultimately, **CYBER FORCE** was about the definition an preservation of humanity as we evolve through technolog That core issue is as relevant as ever, so even while I'm adjustin things, I'm building on the foundation of what Marc created.

BRITTANY: CYBER FORCE *is a jewel in Top Cow's crown, f sure. How do you feel about working on this iconic title? Is the a lot of pressure?*

ATILIO ROJO: A lot of pressure.. lot! I think a lot of fans are waiting f Marc, and they will have to settle f my drawings! I expect a certain lev of hard criticism towards me, but i normal. I'm also a fan of Marc and th series in particular, so this is both a gre pleasure and a dream come true. At t same time, I feel pressured by my ov expectations and not only those of the public.

BRITTANY: *What are you most looking forward to showi the readers with this new story? Are there any new techniqu you're excited to show off?*

ATILIO: A lot of excitement and action, as well as a redesi of the characters! From what I've read from the script, I'm al excited about introducing another way to introduce the seri Time has passed, and some things that were wonderful in t '90s, today would not work as well, so we'll show fans a nice of new and old things.

BRITTANY MATTER *is a firecracker empath with a deep love for storytelling, ramen, and pour-over coffee, ideally all at the same time. You are most likely to find her immersed in a graphic novel, writing over cocktails, or looking after the people she loves.*

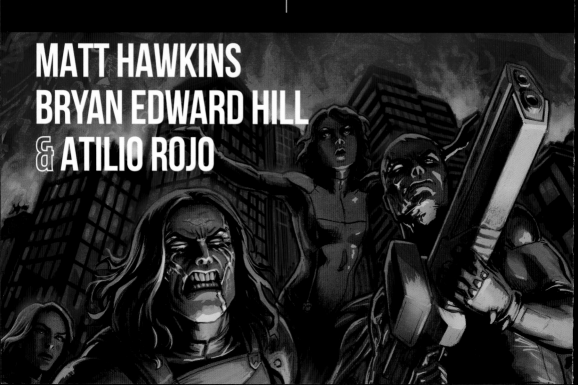

MATT HAWKINS
BRYAN EDWARD HILL
& ATILIO ROJO

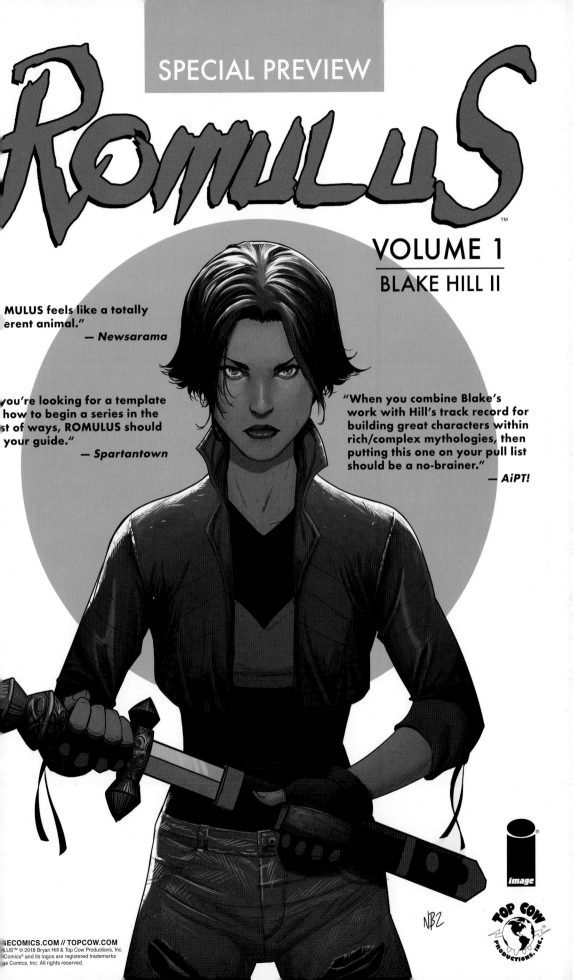

SPECIAL PREVIEW

ROMULUS™

VOLUME 1

BLAKE HILL II

"...MULUS feels like a totally ...erent animal."
— *Newsarama*

"...ou're looking for a template ...how to begin a series in the ...st of ways, ROMULUS should ...your guide."
— *Spartantown*

"When you combine Blake's work with Hill's track record for building great characters within rich/complex mythologies, then putting this one on your pull list should be a no-brainer."
— *AiPT!*

I'M BORN ON A MOUNTAIN DUSTED WITH SNOW.

I'M A *GIRL.* SO I GET TO *LIVE.*

TEN YEARS OLD.

I'M *MARKED* FOR THE *PATH.*

THE *SEVEN SPHERES* OF *PERFECTION.*

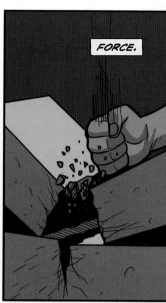

FORCE.

WAR.

FURY.

SPEED.

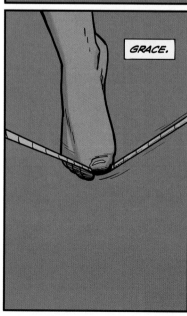

GRACE.

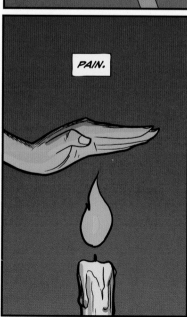

PAIN.

DEATH.

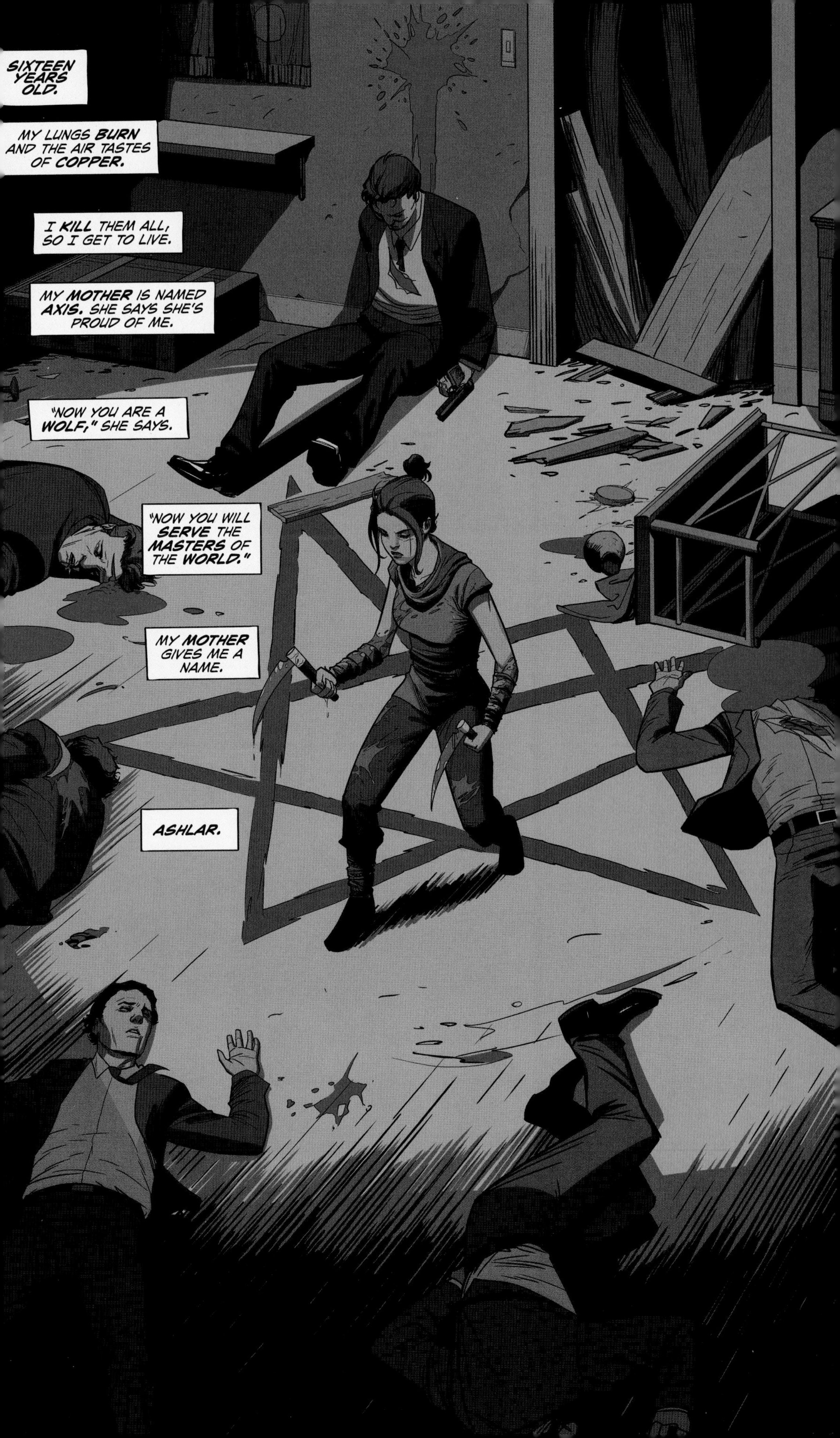
SIXTEEN YEARS OLD.
MY LUNGS BURN AND THE AIR TASTES OF COPPER.
I KILL THEM ALL, SO I GET TO LIVE.
MY MOTHER IS NAMED AXIS. SHE SAYS SHE'S PROUD OF ME.
"NOW YOU ARE A WOLF," SHE SAYS.
"NOW YOU WILL SERVE THE MASTERS OF THE WORLD."
MY MOTHER GIVES ME A NAME.
ASHLAR.

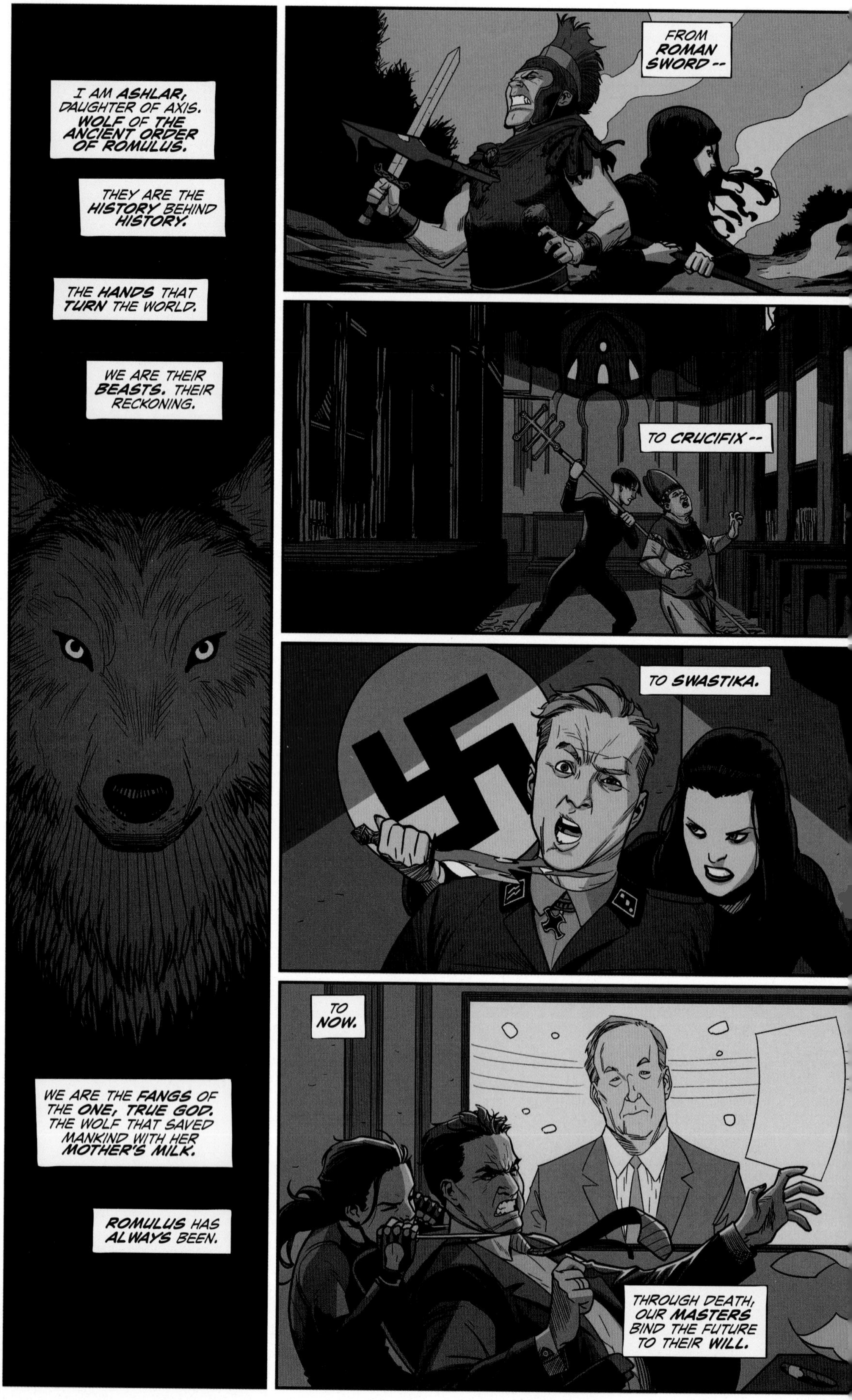
I AM ASHLAR, DAUGHTER OF AXIS. WOLF OF THE ANCIENT ORDER OF ROMULUS.
THEY ARE THE HISTORY BEHIND HISTORY.
THE HANDS THAT TURN THE WORLD.
WE ARE THEIR BEASTS. THEIR RECKONING.
WE ARE THE FANGS OF THE ONE, TRUE GOD. THE WOLF THAT SAVED MANKIND WITH HER MOTHER'S MILK.
ROMULUS HAS ALWAYS BEEN.
FROM ROMAN SWORD --
TO CRUCIFIX --
TO SWASTIKA.
TO NOW.
THROUGH DEATH, OUR MASTERS BIND THE FUTURE TO THEIR WILL.

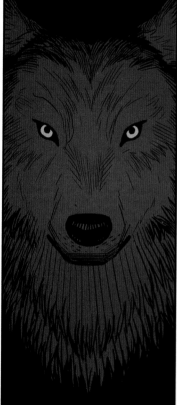

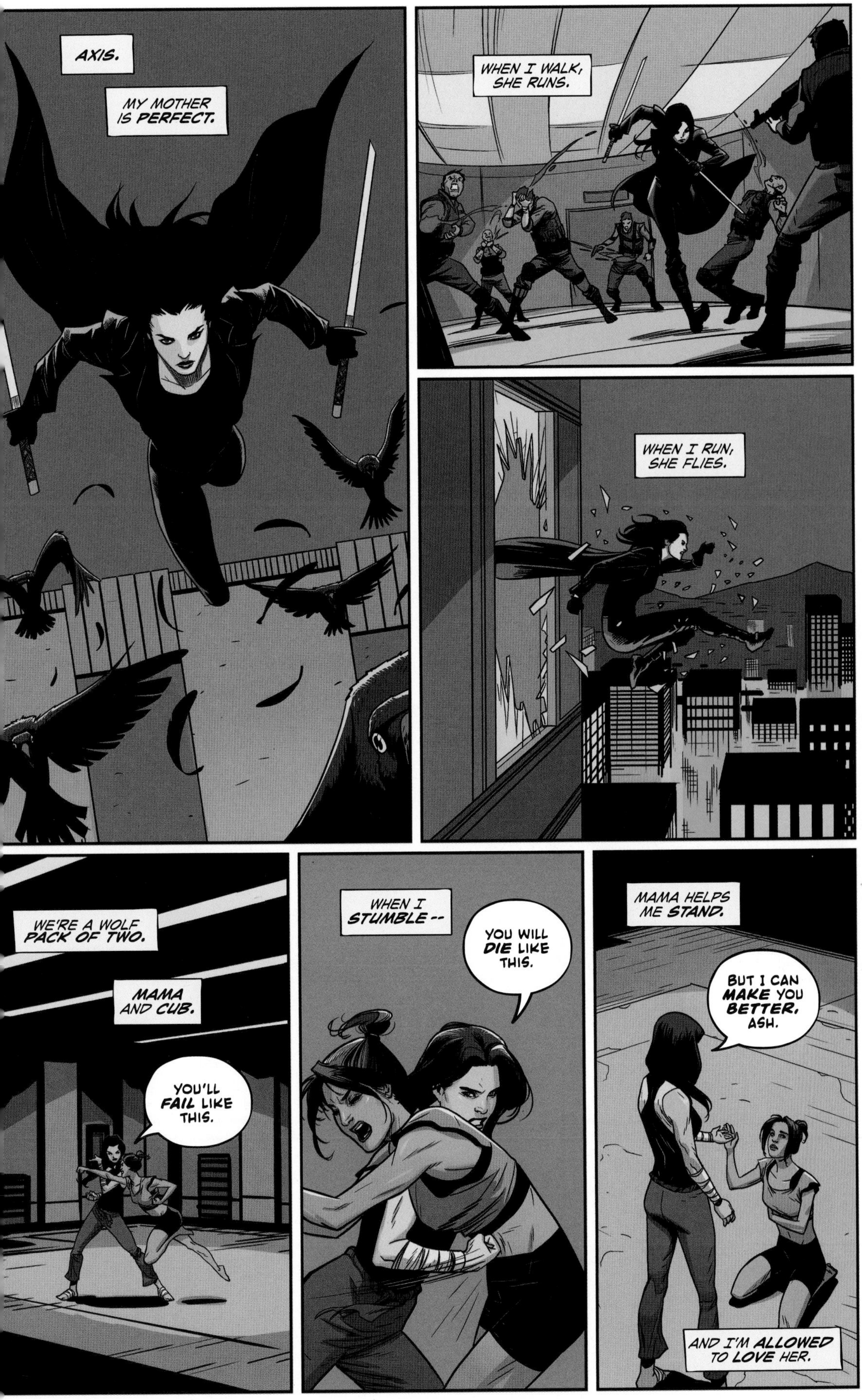
AXIS.
MY MOTHER IS PERFECT.
WHEN I WALK, SHE RUNS.
WHEN I RUN, SHE FLIES.
WE'RE A WOLF PACK OF TWO.
MAMA AND CUB.
YOU'LL FAIL LIKE THIS.
WHEN I STUMBLE --
YOU WILL DIE LIKE THIS.
MAMA HELPS ME STAND.
BUT I CAN MAKE YOU BETTER, ASH.
AND I'M ALLOWED TO LOVE HER.

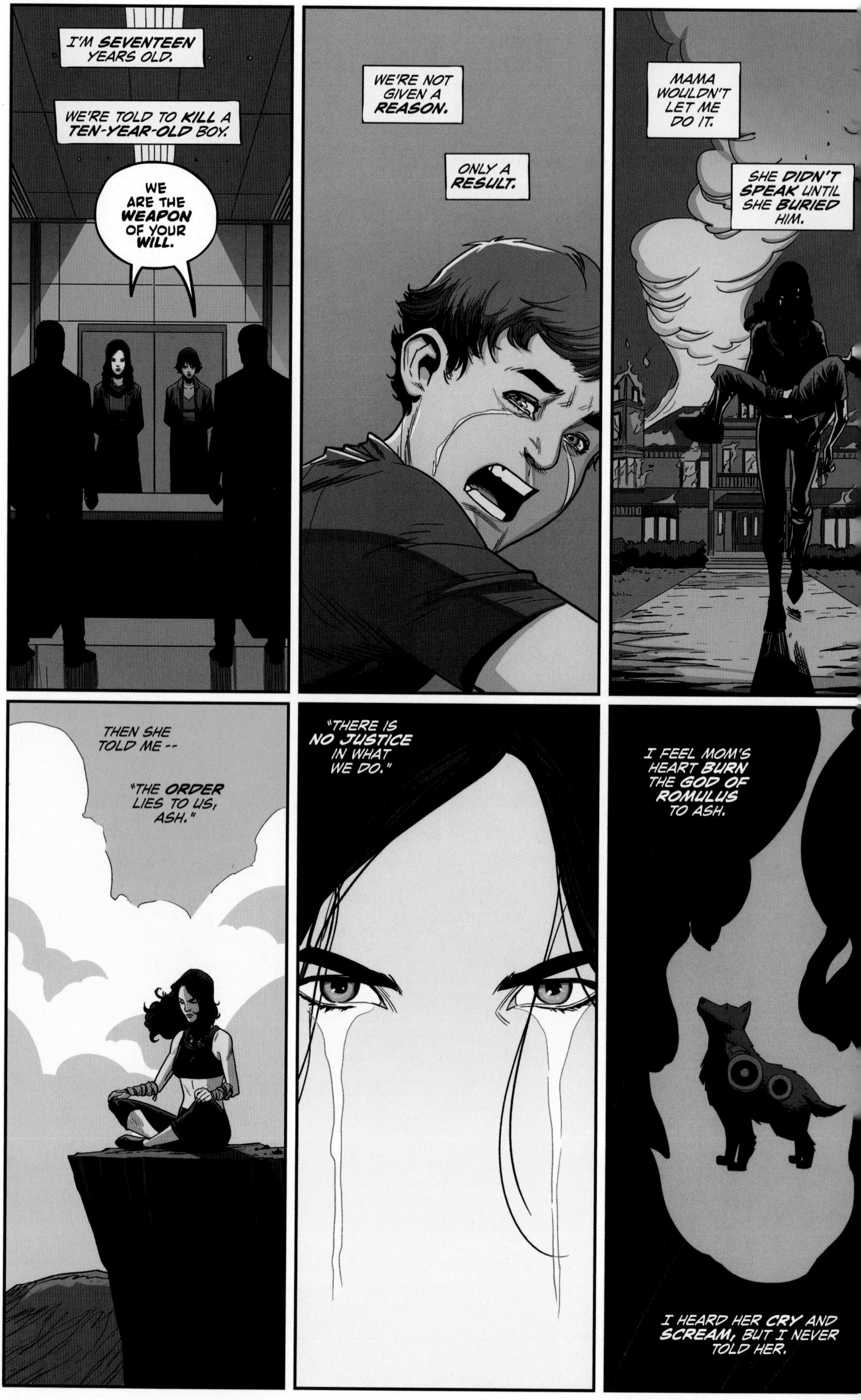
I'M SEVENTEEN YEARS OLD.
WE'RE TOLD TO KILL A TEN-YEAR-OLD BOY.
WE ARE THE WEAPON OF YOUR WILL.
WE'RE NOT GIVEN A REASON.
ONLY A RESULT.
MAMA WOULDN'T LET ME DO IT.
SHE DIDN'T SPEAK UNTIL SHE BURIED HIM.
THEN SHE TOLD ME --
"THE ORDER LIES TO US, ASH."
"THERE IS NO JUSTICE IN WHAT WE DO."
I FEEL MOM'S HEART BURN THE GOD OF ROMULUS TO ASH.
I HEARD HER CRY AND SCREAM, BUT I NEVER TOLD HER.

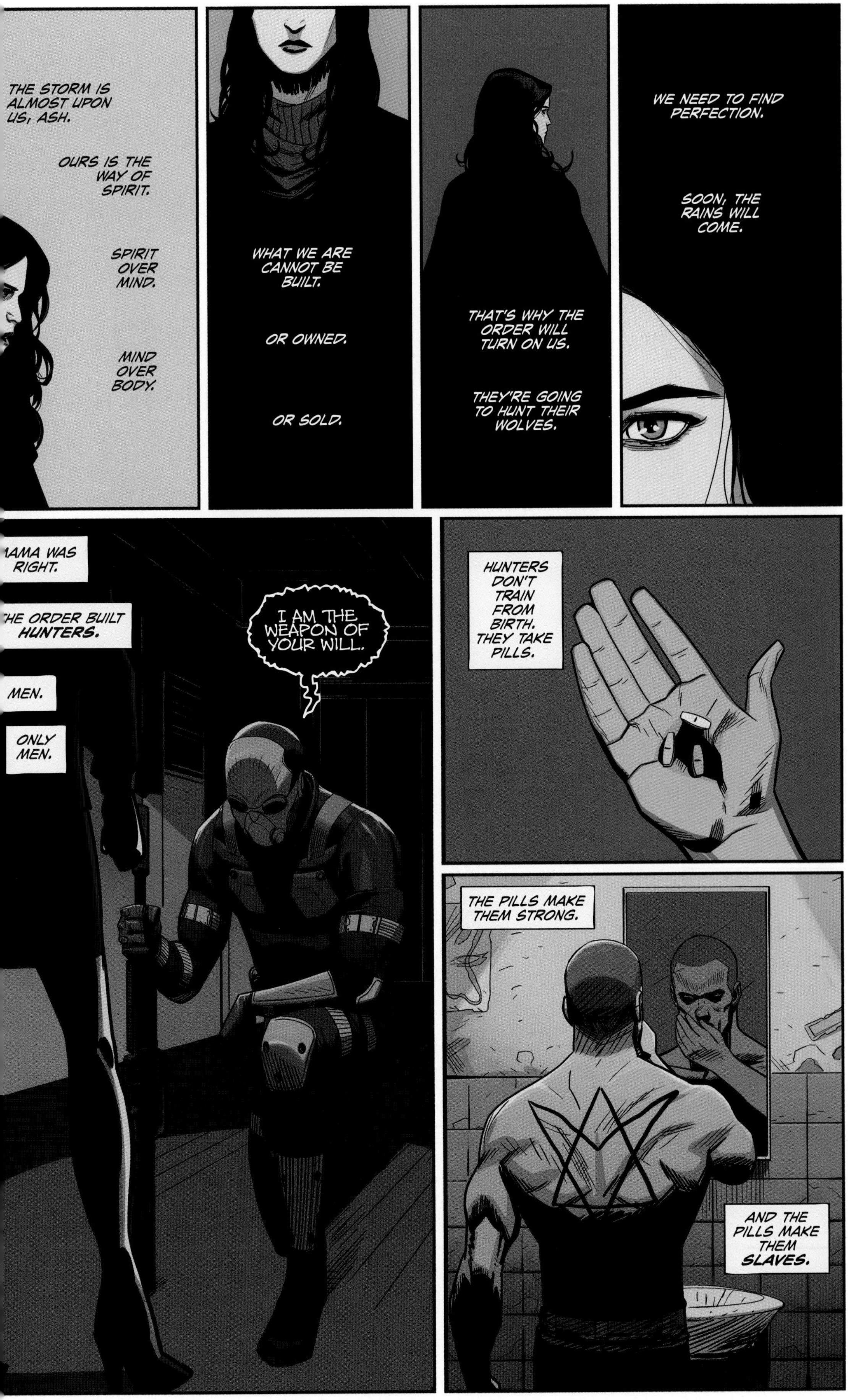

THE STORM IS ALMOST UPON US, ASH.
OURS IS THE WAY OF SPIRIT.
SPIRIT OVER MIND.
MIND OVER BODY.
WHAT WE ARE CANNOT BE BUILT.
OR OWNED.
OR SOLD.
THAT'S WHY THE ORDER WILL TURN ON US.
THEY'RE GOING TO HUNT THEIR WOLVES.
WE NEED TO FIND PERFECTION.
SOON, THE RAINS WILL COME.
AMA WAS RIGHT.
HE ORDER BUILT HUNTERS.
MEN.
ONLY MEN.
I AM THE WEAPON OF YOUR WILL.
HUNTERS DON'T TRAIN FROM BIRTH. THEY TAKE PILLS.
THE PILLS MAKE THEM STRONG.
AND THE PILLS MAKE THEM SLAVES.

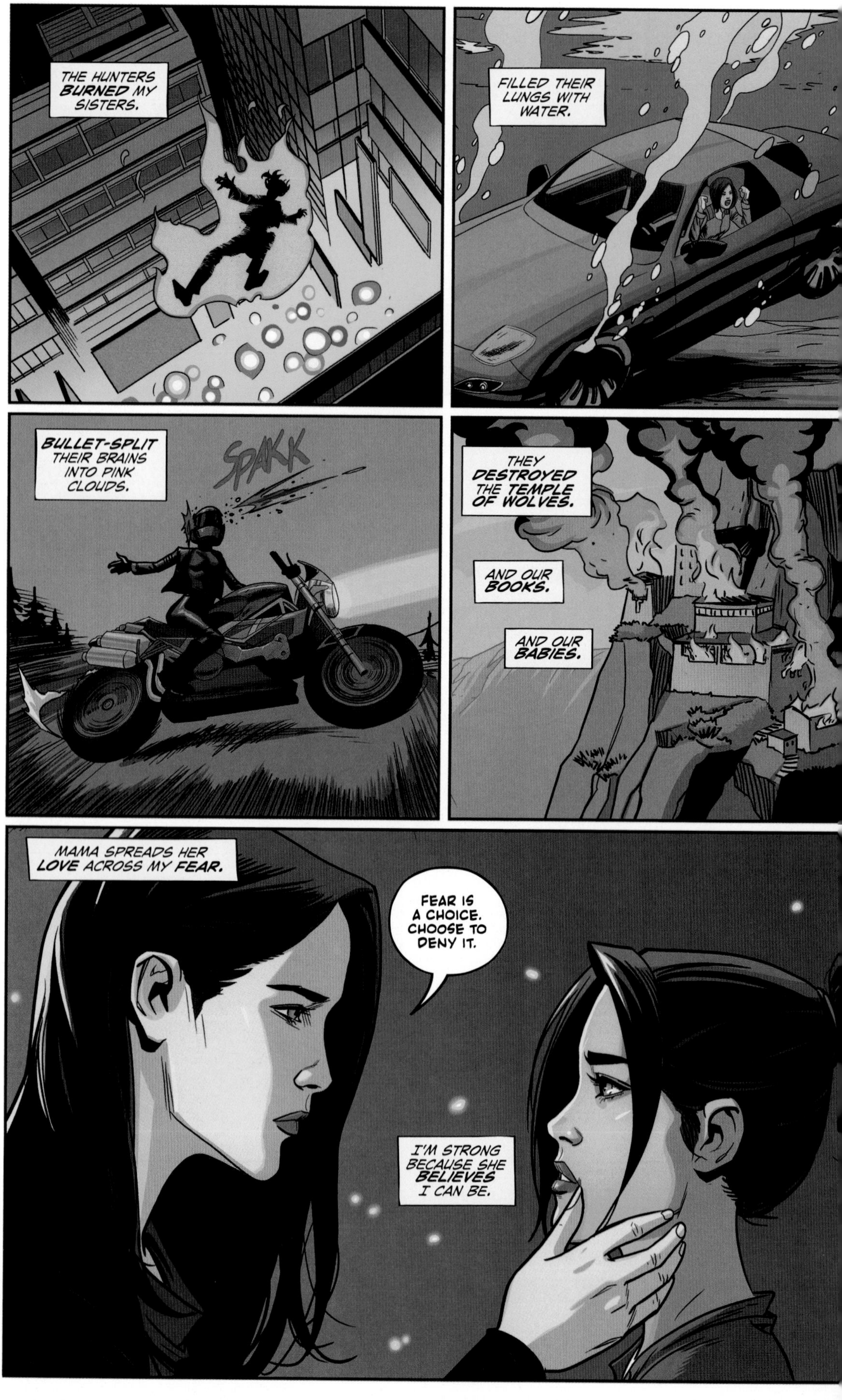
THE HUNTERS BURNED MY SISTERS.
FILLED THEIR LUNGS WITH WATER.
BULLET-SPLIT THEIR BRAINS INTO PINK CLOUDS.
SPAKK
THEY DESTROYED THE TEMPLE OF WOLVES.
AND OUR BOOKS.
AND OUR BABIES.
MAMA SPREADS HER LOVE ACROSS MY FEAR.
FEAR IS A CHOICE. CHOOSE TO DENY IT.
I'M STRONG BECAUSE SHE BELIEVES I CAN BE.

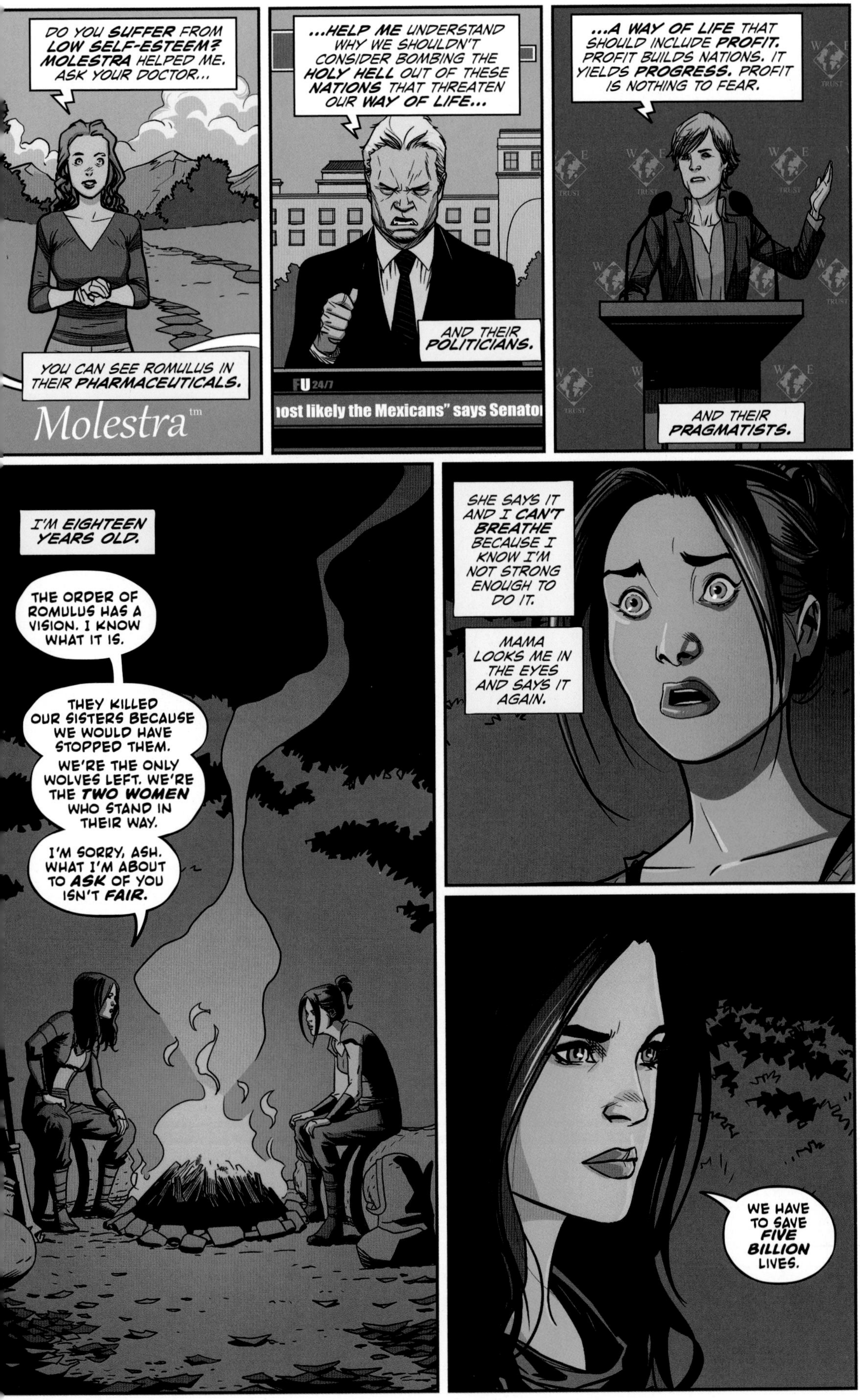

DO YOU SUFFER FROM LOW SELF-ESTEEM? MOLESTRA HELPED ME. ASK YOUR DOCTOR...
YOU CAN SEE ROMULUS IN THEIR PHARMACEUTICALS.
Molestra™
...HELP ME UNDERSTAND WHY WE SHOULDN'T CONSIDER BOMBING THE HOLY HELL OUT OF THESE NATIONS THAT THREATEN OUR WAY OF LIFE...
AND THEIR POLITICIANS.
FU 24/7
most likely the Mexicans" says Senator
...A WAY OF LIFE THAT SHOULD INCLUDE PROFIT. PROFIT BUILDS NATIONS. IT YIELDS PROGRESS. PROFIT IS NOTHING TO FEAR.
AND THEIR PRAGMATISTS.
I'M EIGHTEEN YEARS OLD.
THE ORDER OF ROMULUS HAS A VISION. I KNOW WHAT IT IS.
THEY KILLED OUR SISTERS BECAUSE WE WOULD HAVE STOPPED THEM.
WE'RE THE ONLY WOLVES LEFT. WE'RE THE TWO WOMEN WHO STAND IN THEIR WAY.
I'M SORRY, ASH. WHAT I'M ABOUT TO ASK OF YOU ISN'T FAIR.
SHE SAYS IT AND I CAN'T BREATHE BECAUSE I KNOW I'M NOT STRONG ENOUGH TO DO IT.
MAMA LOOKS ME IN THE EYES AND SAYS IT AGAIN.
WE HAVE TO SAVE FIVE BILLION LIVES.

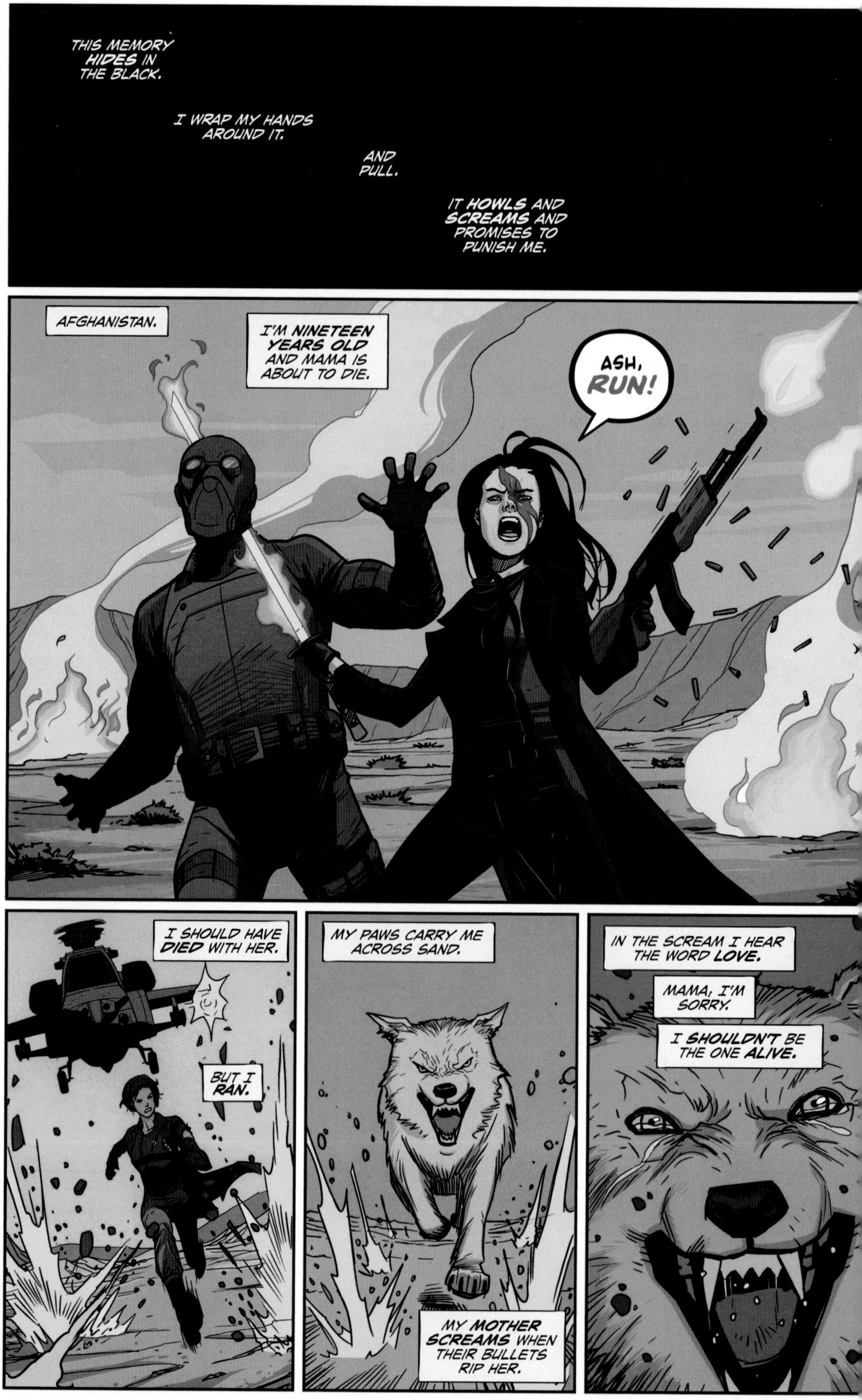
THIS MEMORY HIDES IN THE BLACK.
I WRAP MY HANDS AROUND IT.
AND PULL.
IT HOWLS AND SCREAMS AND PROMISES TO PUNISH ME.
AFGHANISTAN.
I'M NINETEEN YEARS OLD AND MAMA IS ABOUT TO DIE.
ASH, RUN!
I SHOULD HAVE DIED WITH HER.
BUT I RAN.
MY PAWS CARRY ME ACROSS SAND.
MY MOTHER SCREAMS WHEN THEIR BULLETS RIP HER.
IN THE SCREAM I HEAR THE WORD LOVE.
MAMA, I'M SORRY.
I SHOULDN'T BE THE ONE ALIVE.

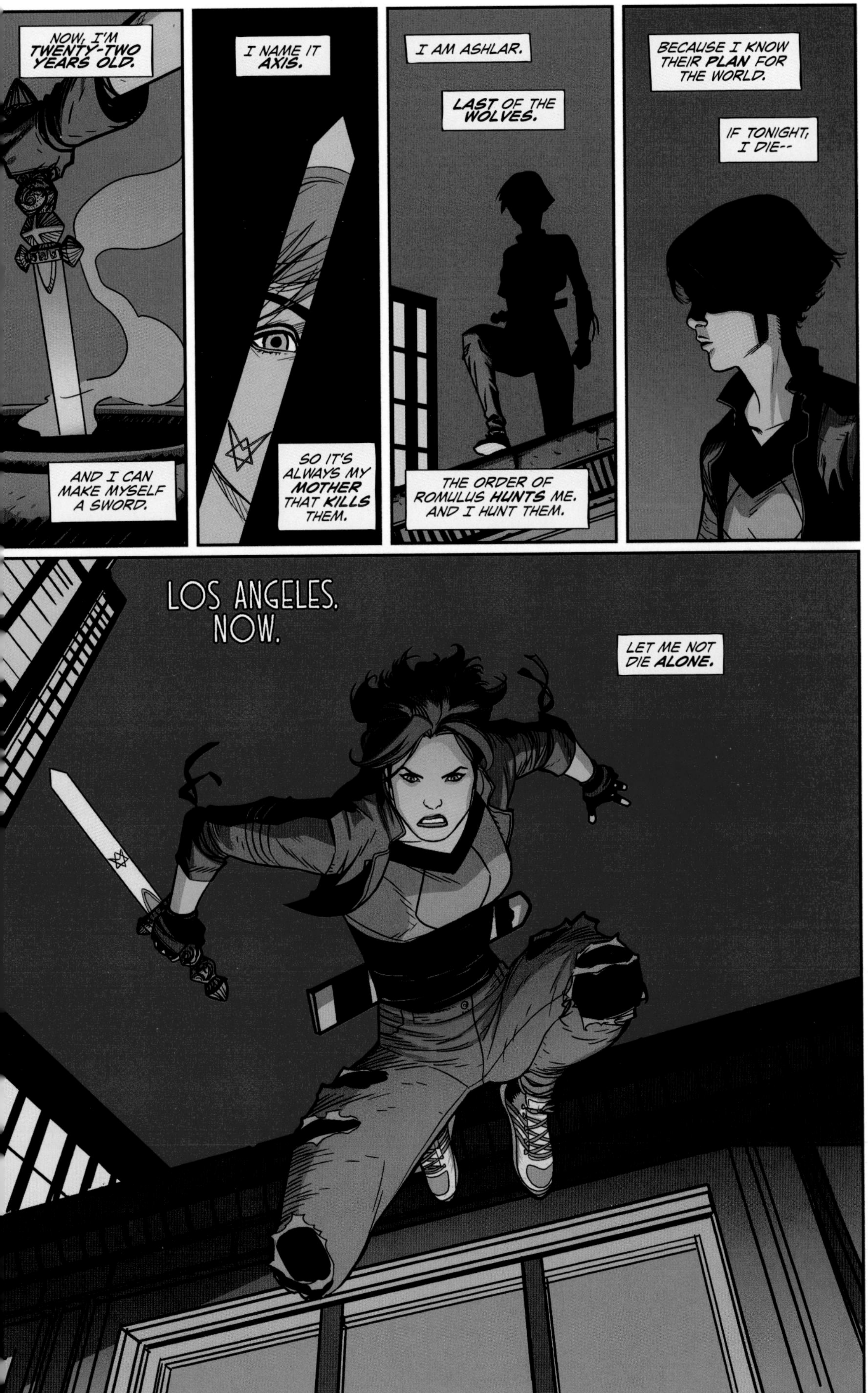
NOW, I'M TWENTY-TWO YEARS OLD.
AND I CAN MAKE MYSELF A SWORD.
I NAME IT AXIS.
SO IT'S ALWAYS MY MOTHER THAT KILLS THEM.
I AM ASHLAR.
LAST OF THE WOLVES.
THE ORDER OF ROMULUS HUNTS ME. AND I HUNT THEM.
BECAUSE I KNOW THEIR PLAN FOR THE WORLD.
IF TONIGHT, I DIE--
LOS ANGELES. NOW.
LET ME NOT DIE ALONE.

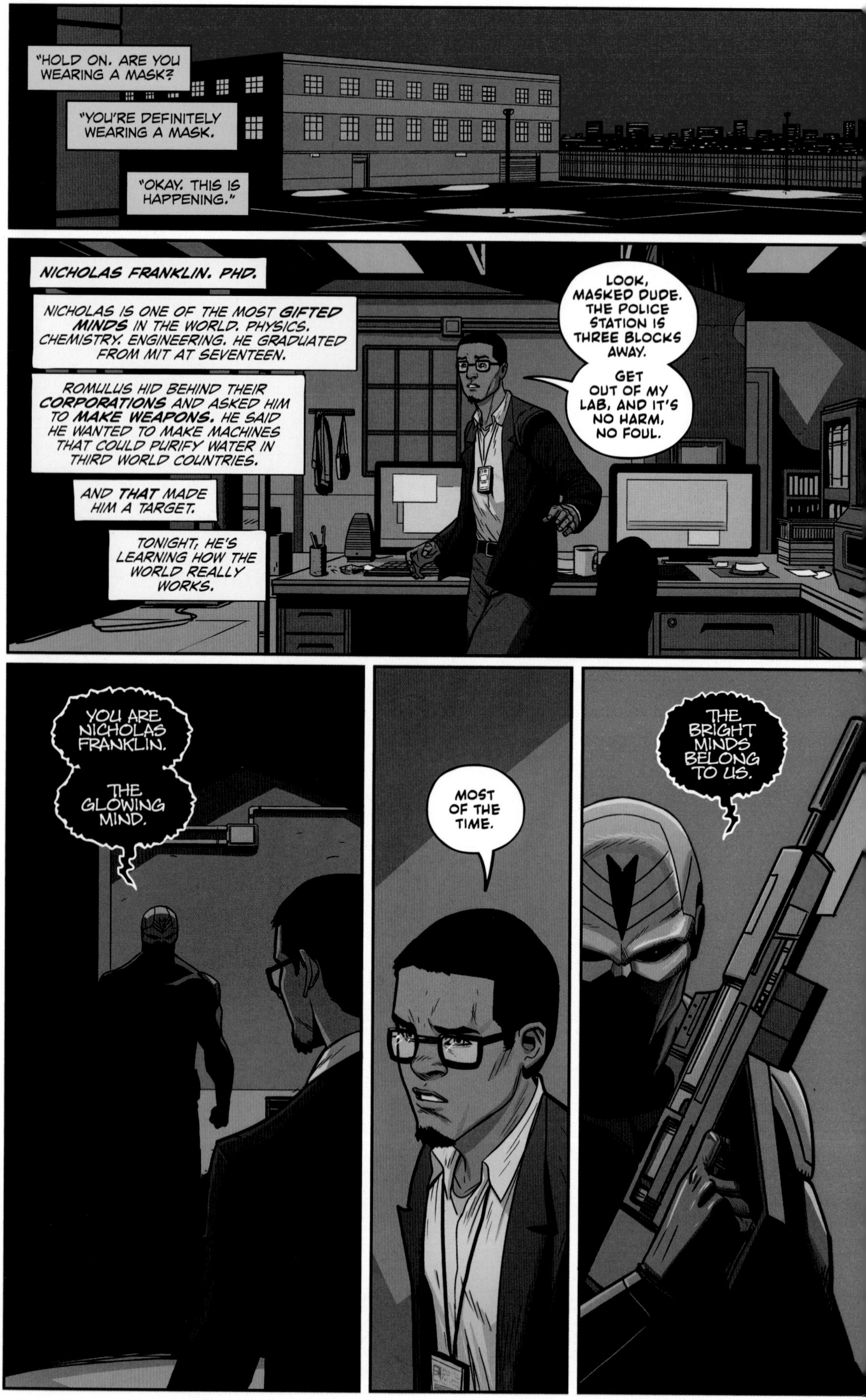
"HOLD ON. ARE YOU WEARING A MASK?
"YOU'RE DEFINITELY WEARING A MASK.
"OKAY. THIS IS HAPPENING."
NICHOLAS FRANKLIN. PHD.
NICHOLAS IS ONE OF THE MOST GIFTED MINDS IN THE WORLD. PHYSICS. CHEMISTRY. ENGINEERING. HE GRADUATED FROM MIT AT SEVENTEEN.
ROMULUS HID BEHIND THEIR CORPORATIONS AND ASKED HIM TO MAKE WEAPONS. HE SAID HE WANTED TO MAKE MACHINES THAT COULD PURIFY WATER IN THIRD WORLD COUNTRIES.
AND THAT MADE HIM A TARGET.
TONIGHT, HE'S LEARNING HOW THE WORLD REALLY WORKS.
LOOK, MASKED DUDE. THE POLICE STATION IS THREE BLOCKS AWAY.
GET OUT OF MY LAB, AND IT'S NO HARM, NO FOUL.
YOU ARE NICHOLAS FRANKLIN.
THE GLOWING MIND.
MOST OF THE TIME.
THE BRIGHT MINDS BELONG TO US.

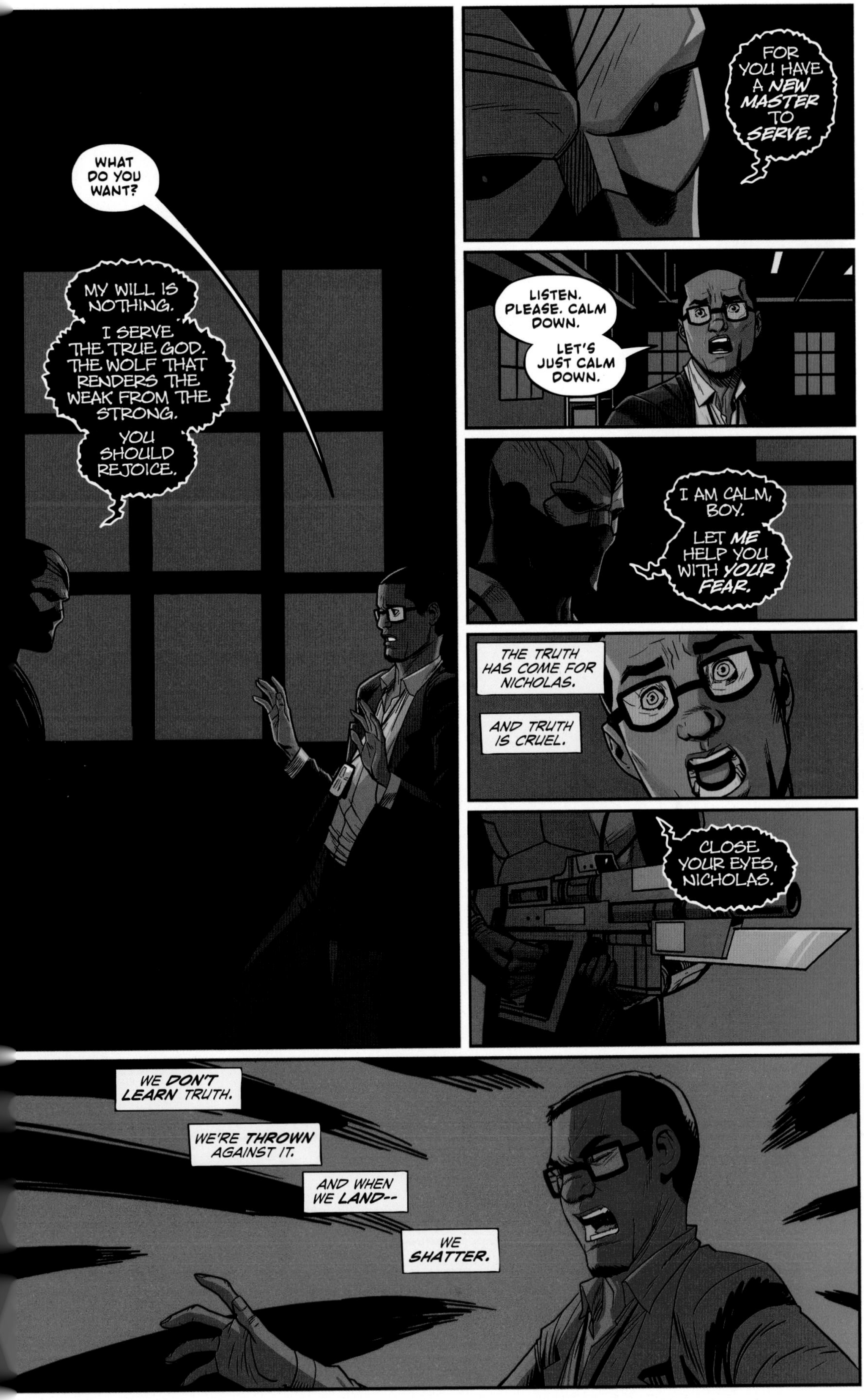
WHAT DO YOU WANT?
MY WILL IS NOTHING. I SERVE THE TRUE GOD. THE WOLF THAT RENDERS THE WEAK FROM THE STRONG. YOU SHOULD REJOICE.
FOR YOU HAVE A NEW MASTER TO SERVE.
LISTEN. PLEASE. CALM DOWN. LET'S JUST CALM DOWN.
I AM CALM, BOY. LET ME HELP YOU WITH YOUR FEAR.
THE TRUTH HAS COME FOR NICHOLAS.
AND TRUTH IS CRUEL.
CLOSE YOUR EYES, NICHOLAS.
WE DON'T LEARN TRUTH.
WE'RE THROWN AGAINST IT.
AND WHEN WE LAND--
WE SHATTER.

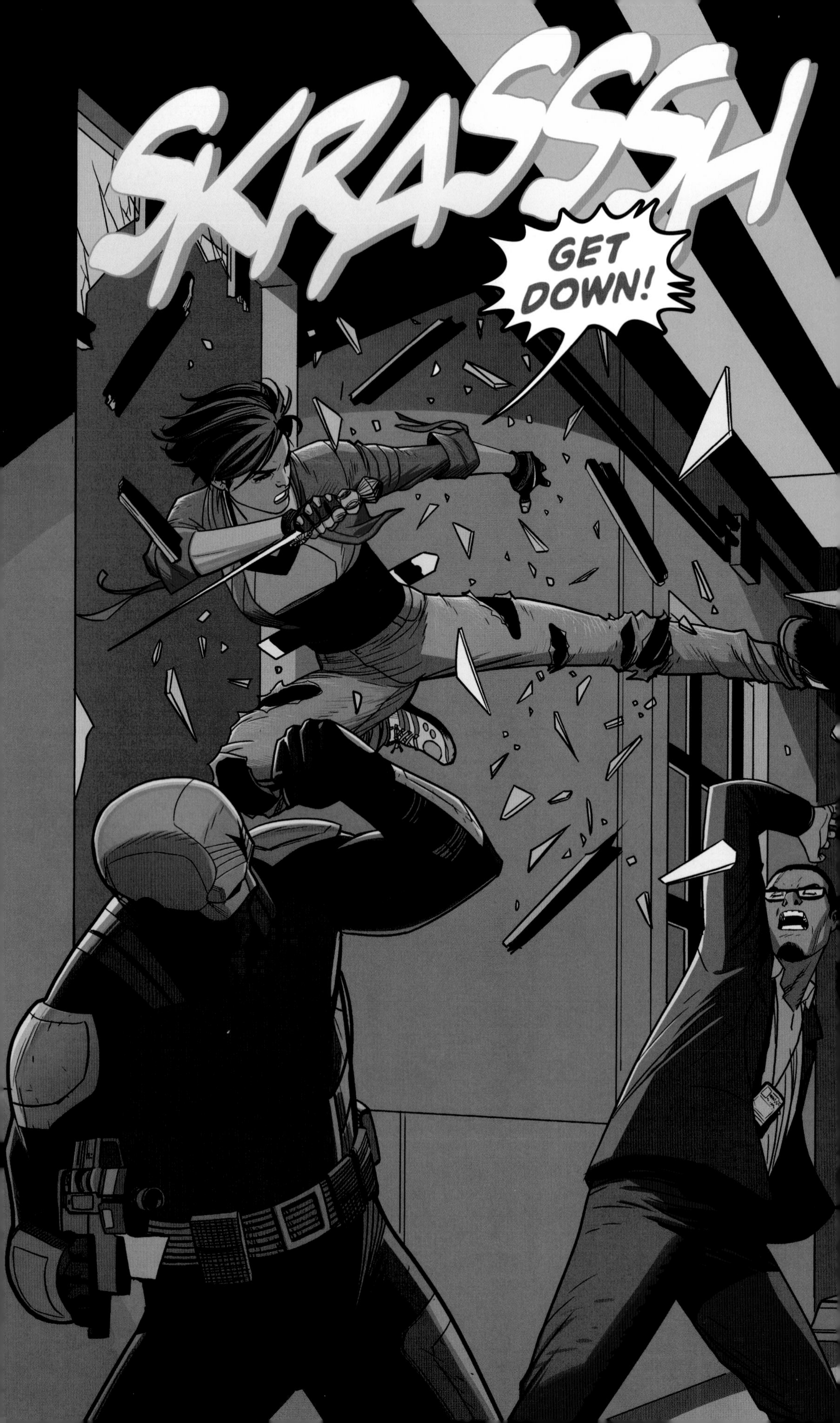
SKRASSSH
GET DOWN!

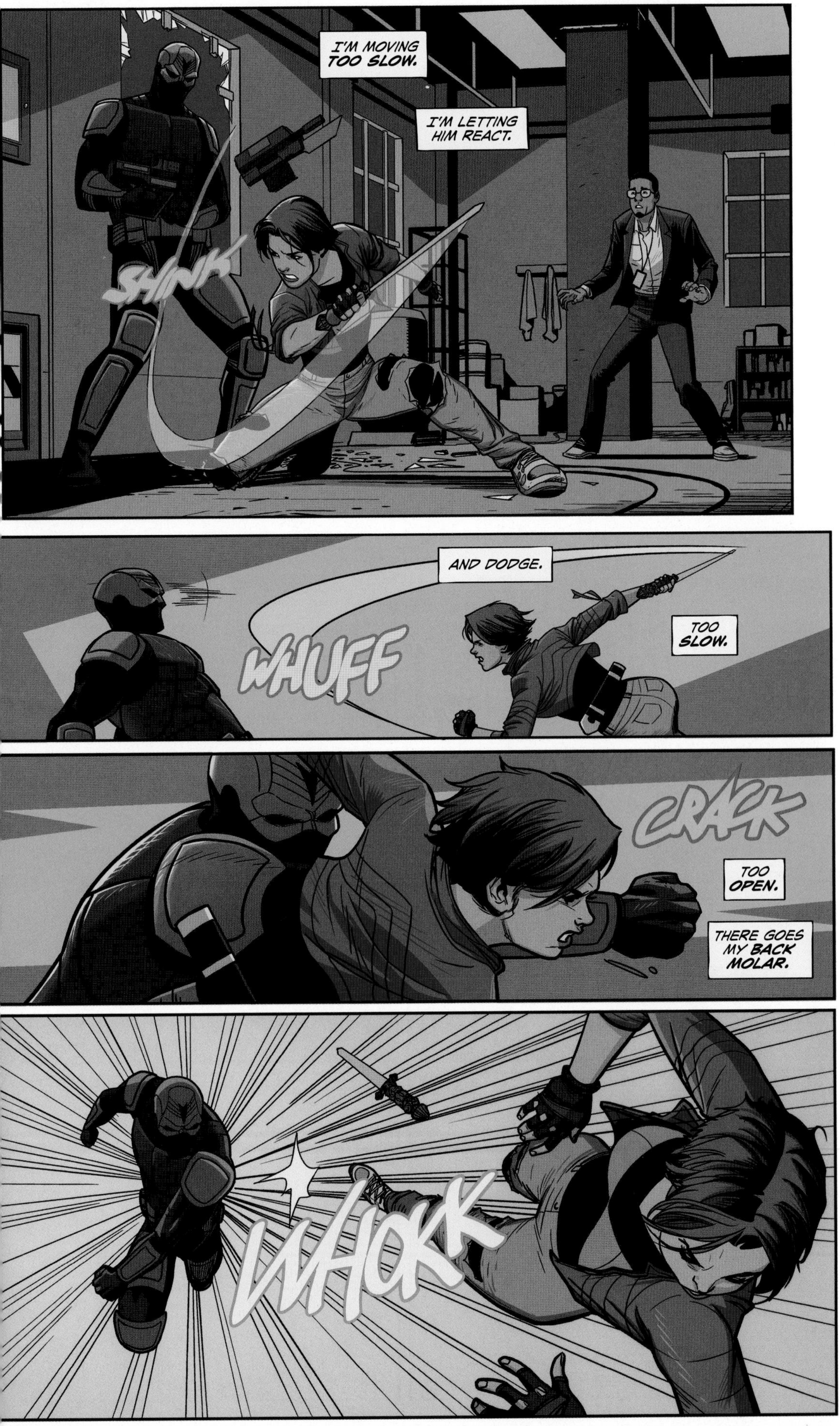
I'M MOVING TOO SLOW.
I'M LETTING HIM REACT.
SHINK
AND DODGE.
WHUFF
TOO SLOW.
CRACK
TOO OPEN.
THERE GOES MY BACK MOLAR.
WHOKK

KRASSSSH

THE TOOTH RIPS FROM MY GUMS IN WHITE-YELLOW PAIN.

BUT I DON'T NEED A TOOTH TO KILL THIS F%#&ER.

SKRITCH

I NEED ANGER.

DUMF

NICHOLAS IS WATCHING ME.

MY ANGER CAN SMOTHER HIS FEAR.

WHOMP

DON'T L[...] HIM WIN[...] ASH.

YOU C[...] DO TH[...]

BREATHE.

LET THE AIR COME UP WET.

SHINNG

TASTE YOUR OWN BLOOD.

REMEMBER WHAT HAPPENS IF YOU FAIL.

YOU CAN DO THIS.

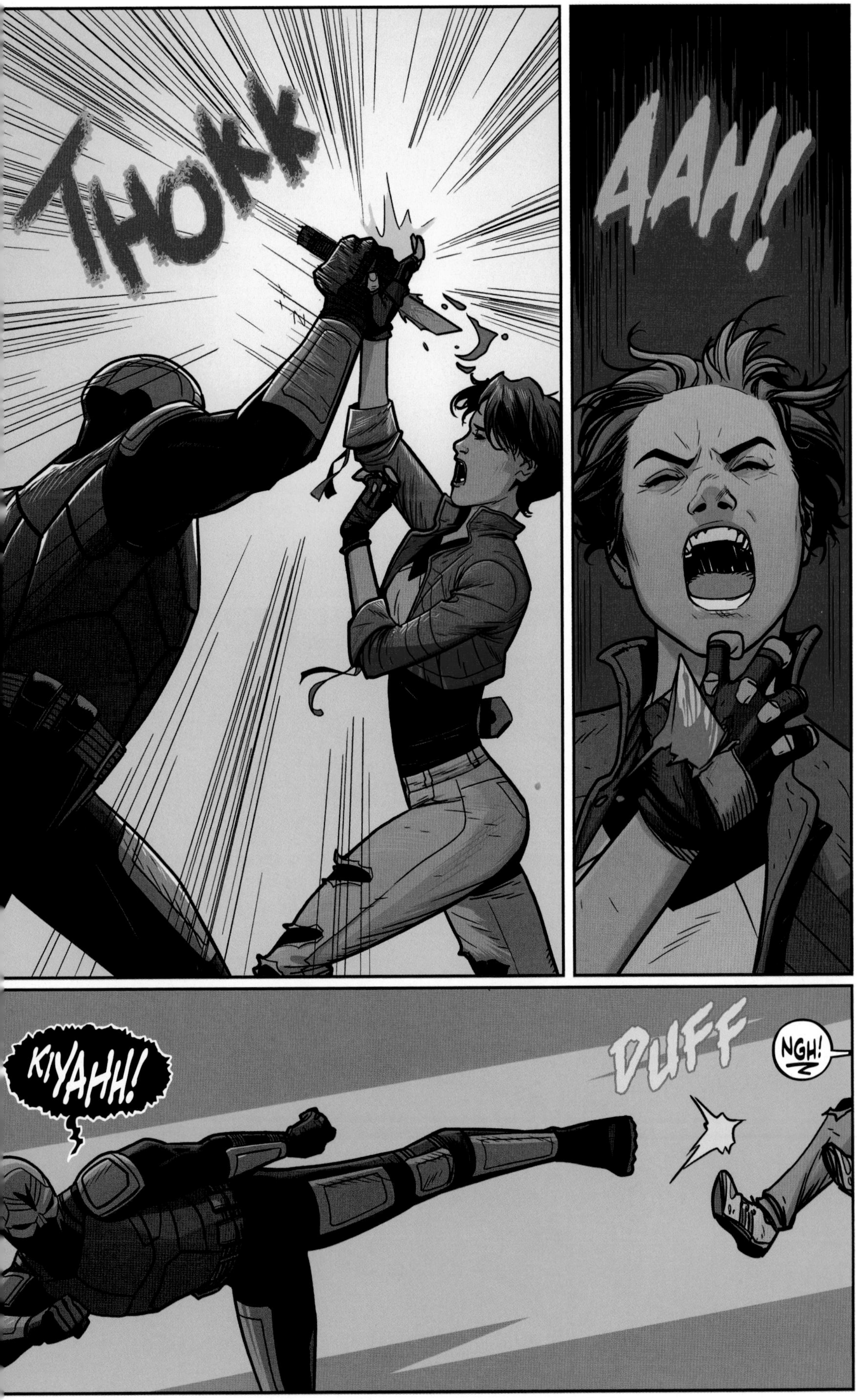
THOKK
AAH!
KIYAHH!
DUFF
NGH!

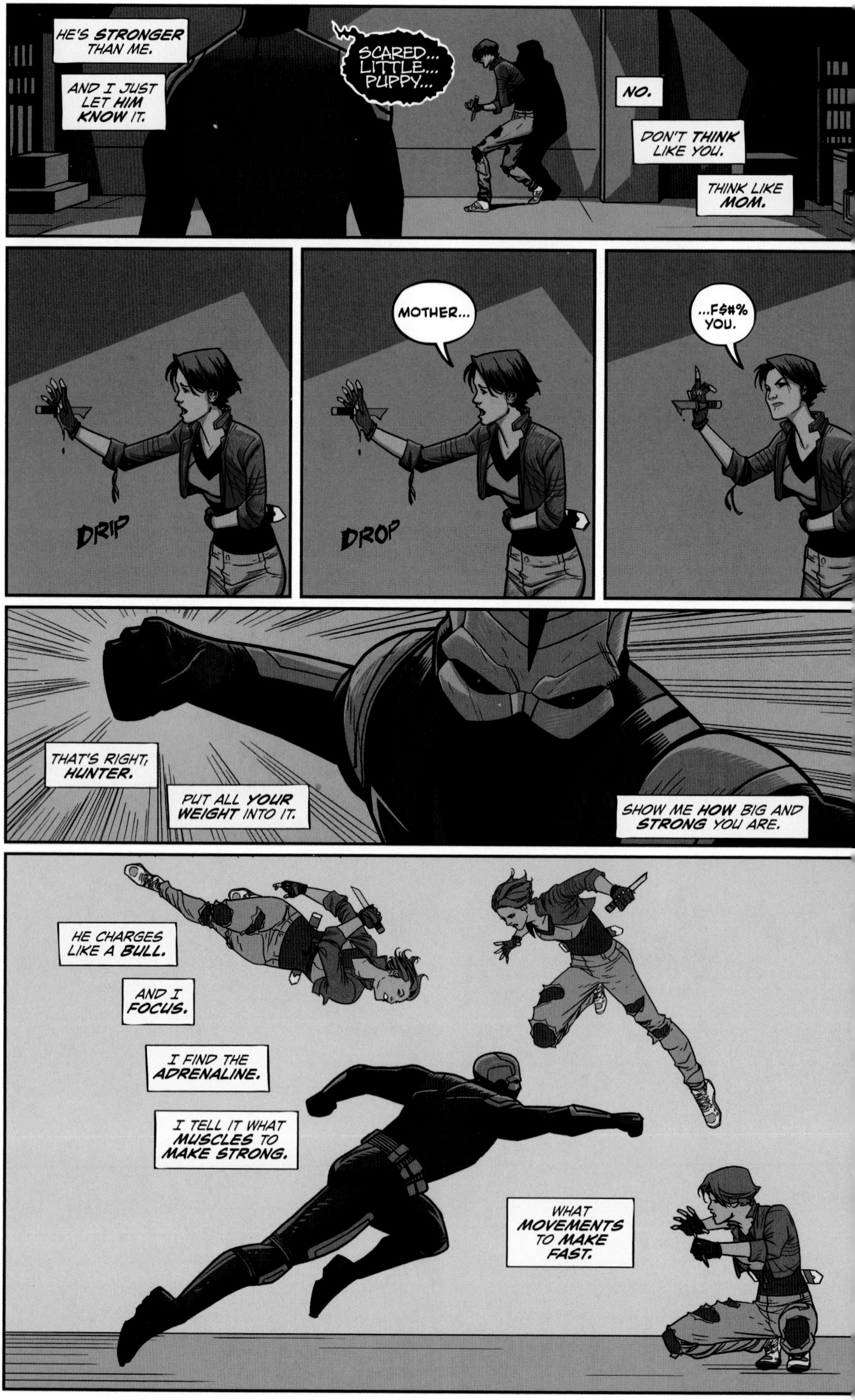
HE'S STRONGER THAN ME.
AND I JUST LET HIM KNOW IT.
SCARED... LITTLE... PUPPY...
NO.
DON'T THINK LIKE YOU.
THINK LIKE MOM.
DRIP
MOTHER...
DROP
...F$#% YOU.
THAT'S RIGHT, HUNTER.
PUT ALL YOUR WEIGHT INTO IT.
SHOW ME HOW BIG AND STRONG YOU ARE.
HE CHARGES LIKE A BULL.
AND I FOCUS.
I FIND THE ADRENALINE.
I TELL IT WHAT MUSCLES TO MAKE STRONG.
WHAT MOVEMENTS TO MAKE FAST.

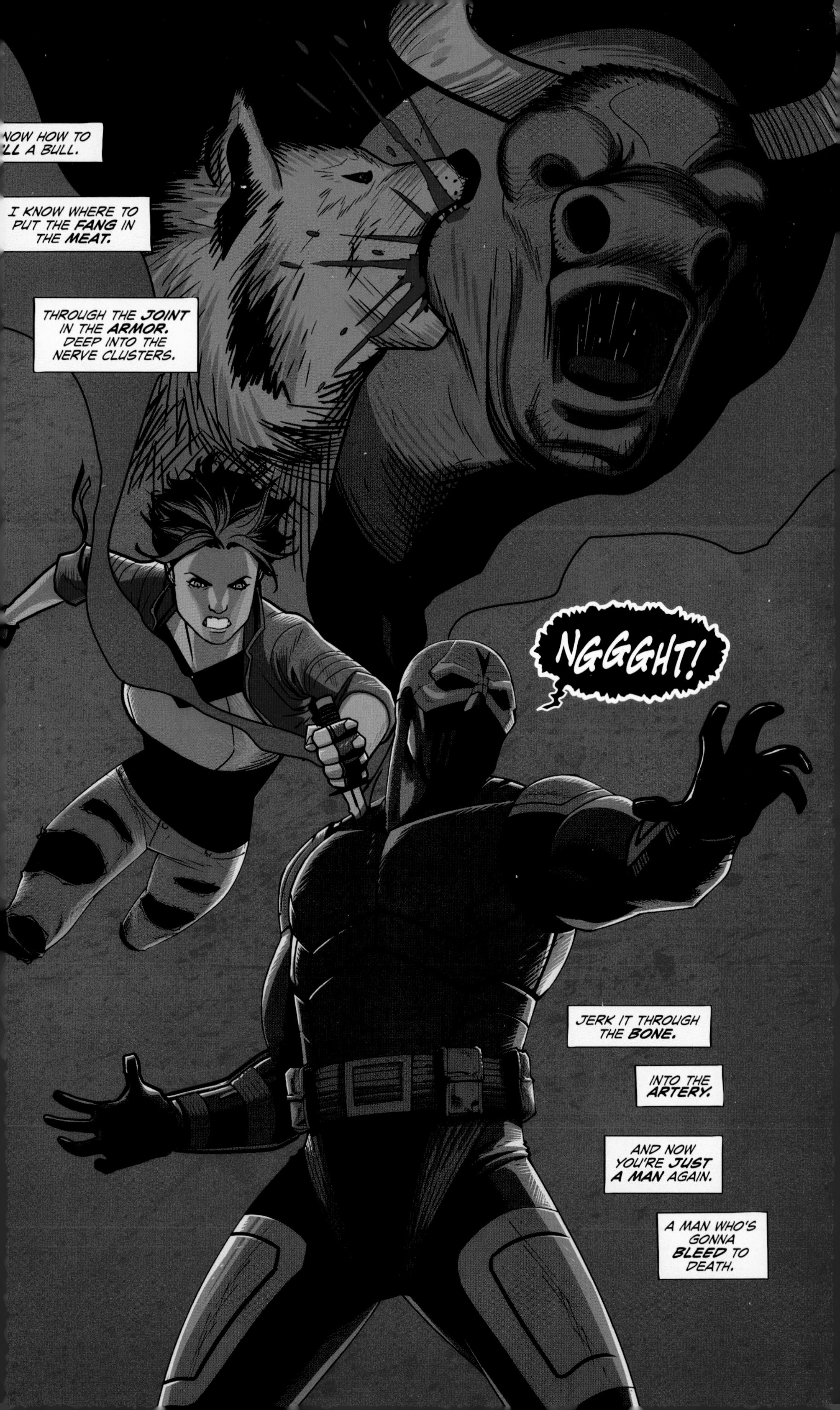
NOW HOW TO
LL A BULL.
I KNOW WHERE TO PUT THE FANG IN THE MEAT.
THROUGH THE JOINT IN THE ARMOR. DEEP INTO THE NERVE CLUSTERS.
NGGGHT!
JERK IT THROUGH THE BONE.
INTO THE ARTERY.
AND NOW YOU'RE JUST A MAN AGAIN.
A MAN WHO'S GONNA BLEED TO DEATH.

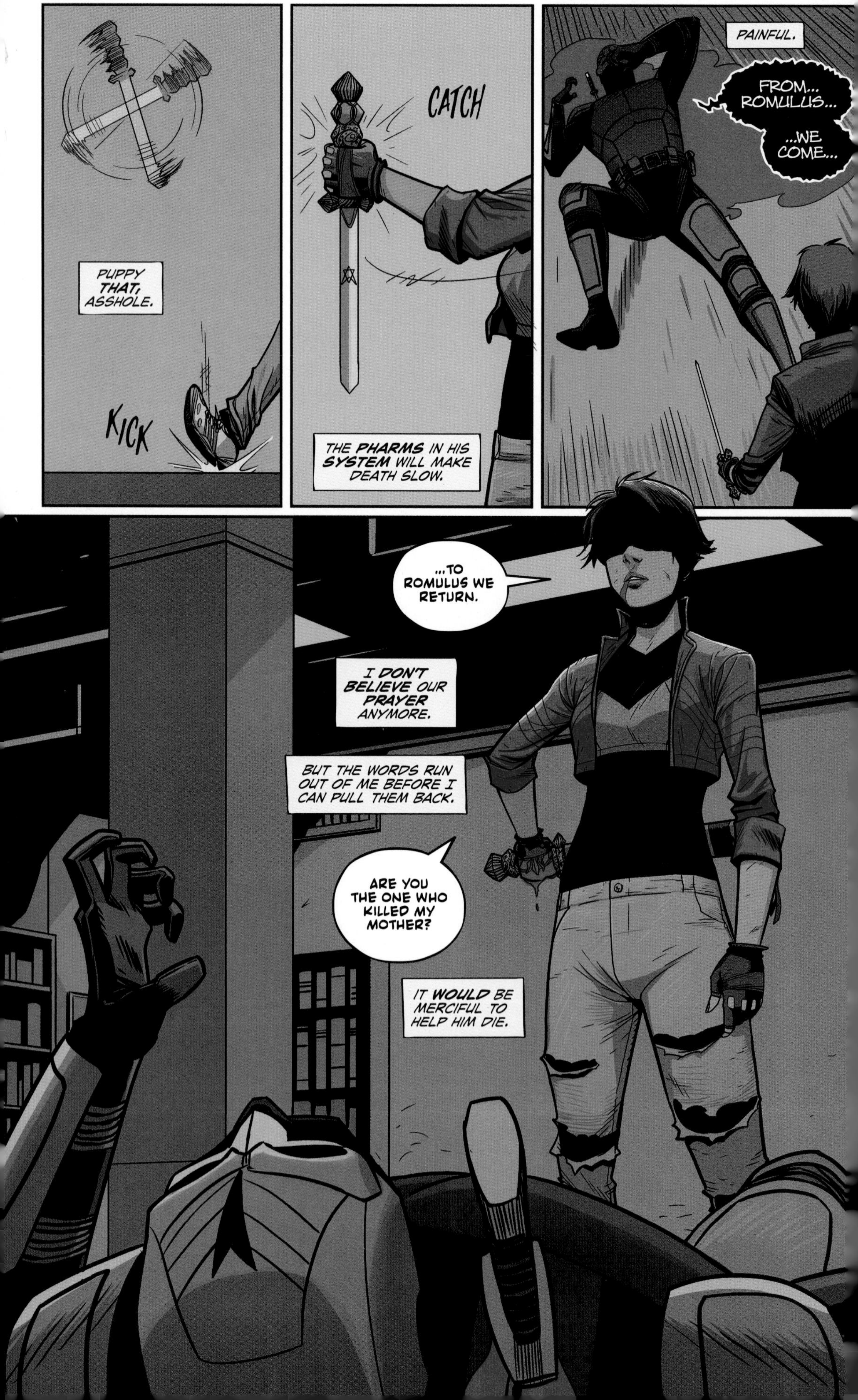

PUPPY THAT, ASSHOLE.
KICK
CATCH
THE PHARMS IN HIS SYSTEM WILL MAKE DEATH SLOW.
PAINFUL.
FROM... ROMULUS...
...WE COME...
...TO ROMULUS WE RETURN.
I DON'T BELIEVE OUR PRAYER ANYMORE.
BUT THE WORDS RUN OUT OF ME BEFORE I CAN PULL THEM BACK.
ARE YOU THE ONE WHO KILLED MY MOTHER?
IT WOULD BE MERCIFUL TO HELP HIM DIE.

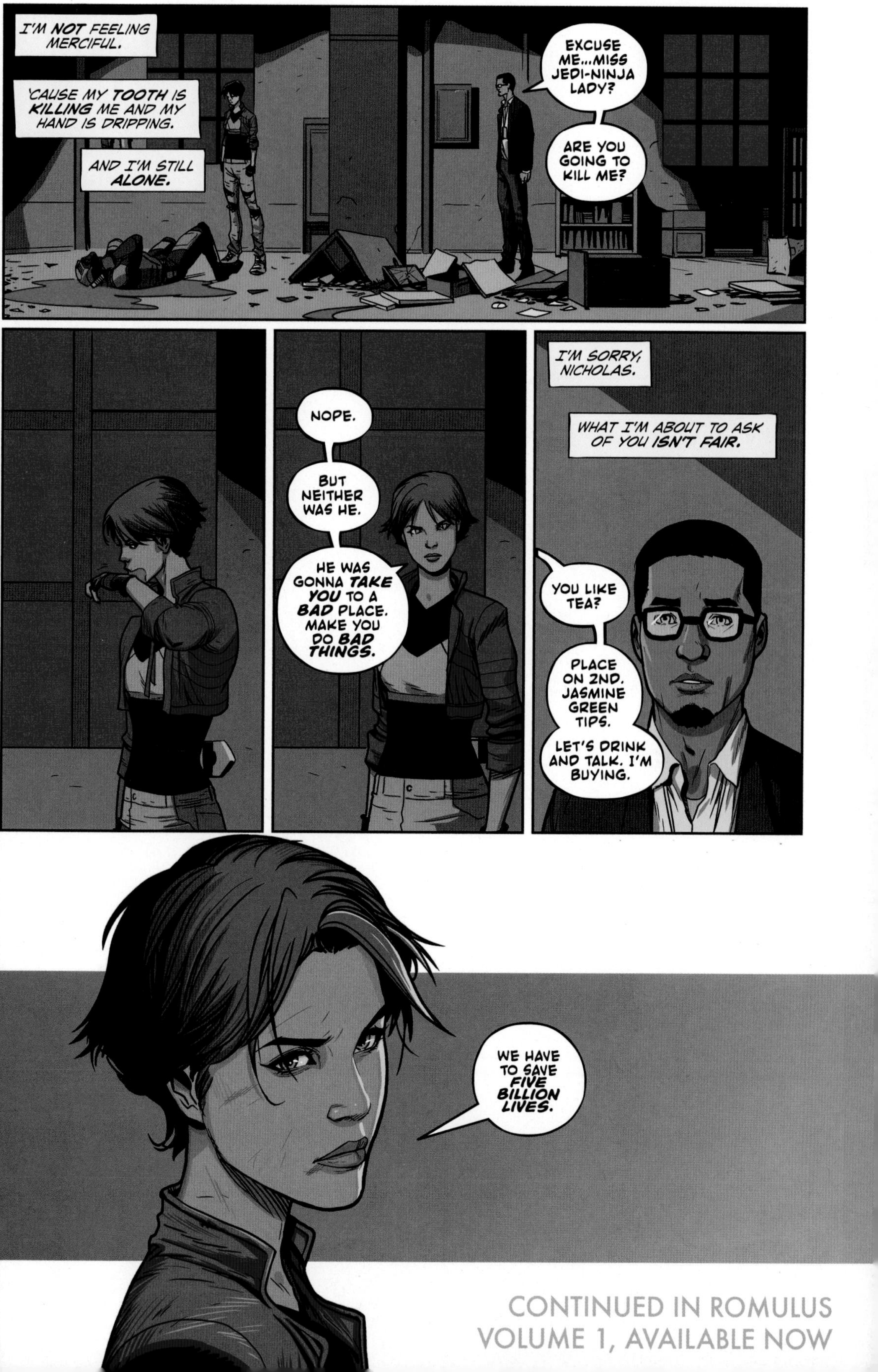
I'M NOT FEELING MERCIFUL.
'CAUSE MY TOOTH IS KILLING ME AND MY HAND IS DRIPPING.
AND I'M STILL ALONE.
EXCUSE ME...MISS JEDI-NINJA LADY?
ARE YOU GOING TO KILL ME?
NOPE.
BUT NEITHER WAS HE.
HE WAS GONNA TAKE YOU TO A BAD PLACE. MAKE YOU DO BAD THINGS.
I'M SORRY, NICHOLAS.
WHAT I'M ABOUT TO ASK OF YOU ISN'T FAIR.
YOU LIKE TEA?
PLACE ON 2ND. JASMINE GREEN TIPS.
LET'S DRINK AND TALK. I'M BUYING.
WE HAVE TO SAVE FIVE BILLION LIVES.

CONTINUED IN ROMULUS VOLUME 1, AVAILABLE NOW

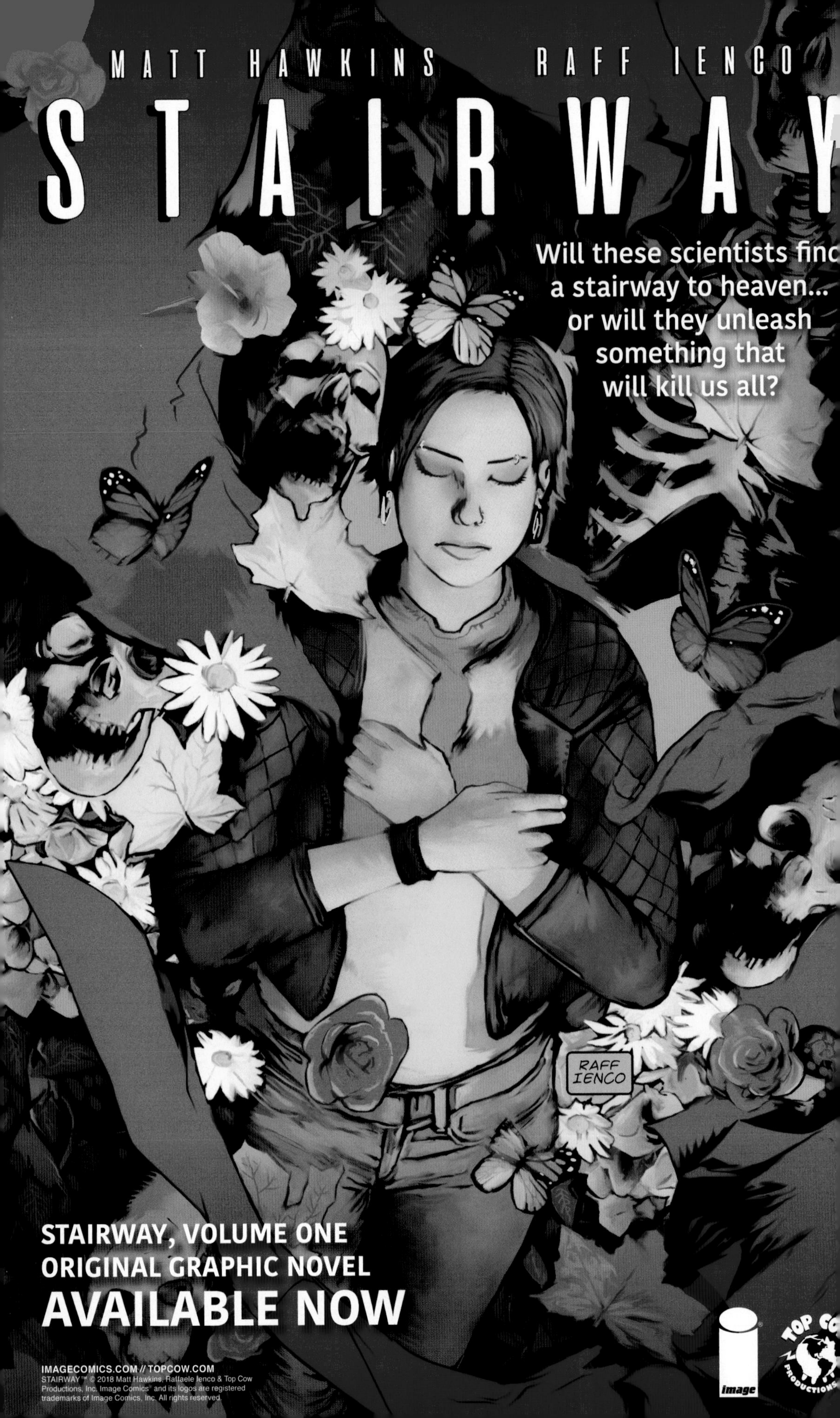

MATT HAWKINS RAFF IENCO
STAIRWAY
Will these scientists find a stairway to heaven... or will they unleash something that will kill us all?
RAFF IENCO
STAIRWAY, VOLUME ONE
ORIGINAL GRAPHIC NOVEL
AVAILABLE NOW
IMAGECOMICS.COM // TOPCOW.COM
STAIRWAY™ © 2018 Matt Hawkins, Raffaele Ienco & Top Cow Productions, Inc. Image Comics® and its logos are registered trademarks of Image Comics, Inc. All rights reserved.
image
TOP COW PRODUCTIONS

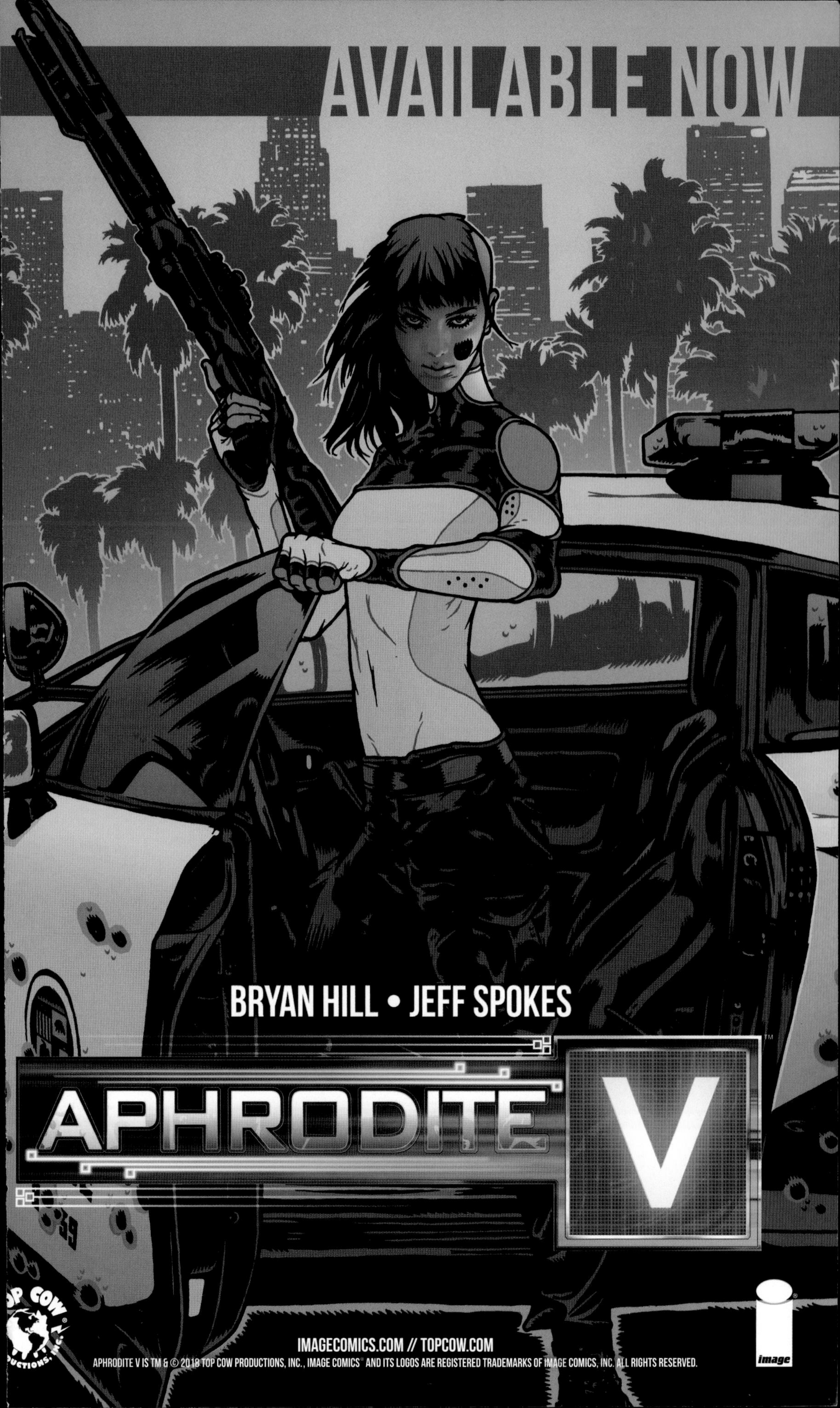
AVAILABLE NOW
BRYAN HILL • JEFF SPOKES
APHRODITE V
IMAGECOMICS.COM // TOPCOW.COM
APHRODITE V IS TM & © 2018 TOP COW PRODUCTIONS, INC., IMAGE COMICS® AND ITS LOGOS ARE REGISTERED TRADEMARKS OF IMAGE COMICS, INC. ALL RIGHTS RESERVED.

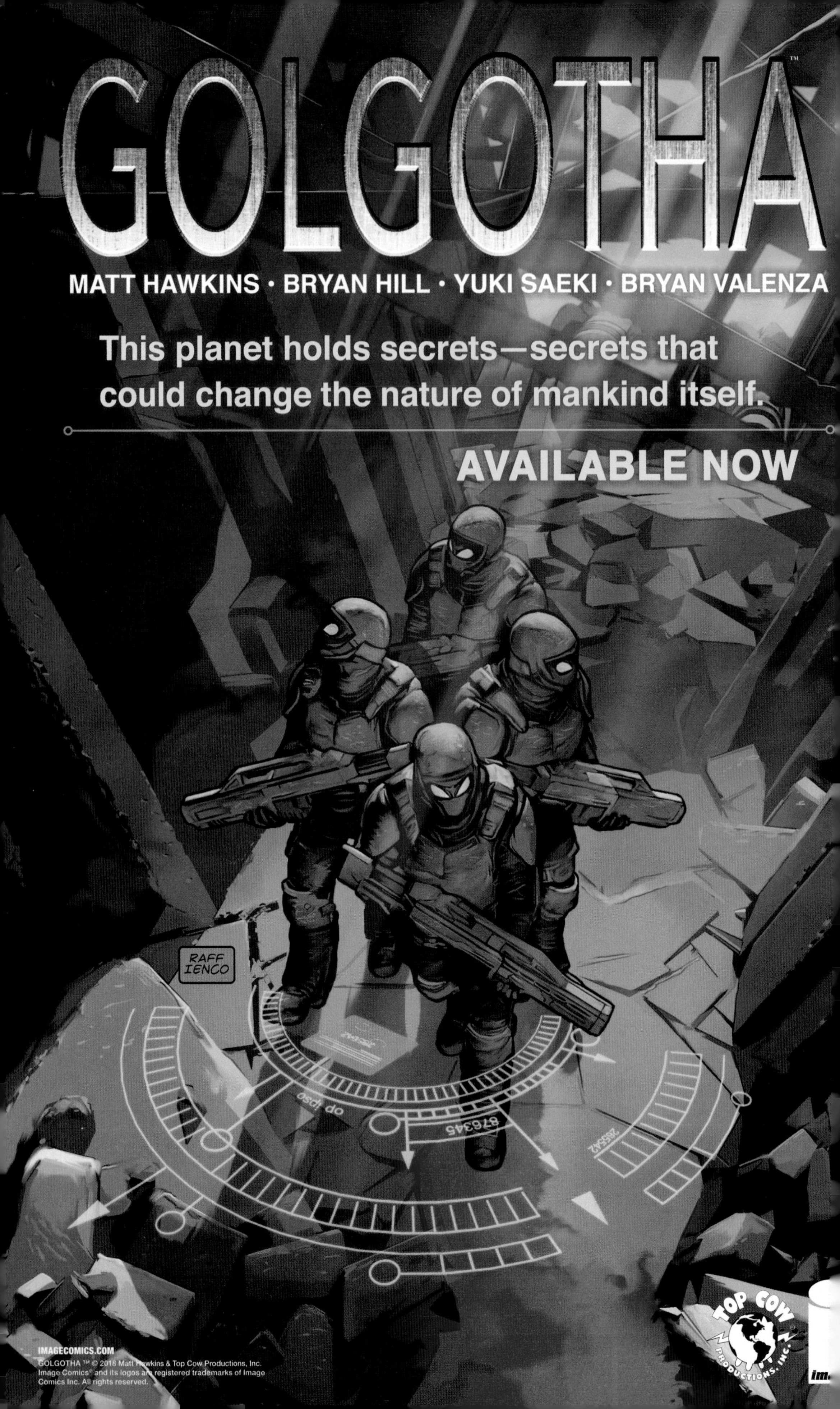
GOLGOTHA™
MATT HAWKINS · BRYAN HILL · YUKI SAEKI · BRYAN VALENZA
This planet holds secrets—secrets that could change the nature of mankind itself.
AVAILABLE NOW
RAFF IENCO
IMAGECOMICS.COM
GOLGOTHA ™ © 2018 Matt Hawkins & Top Cow Productions, Inc. Image Comics® and its logos are registered trademarks of Image Comics Inc. All rights reserved.

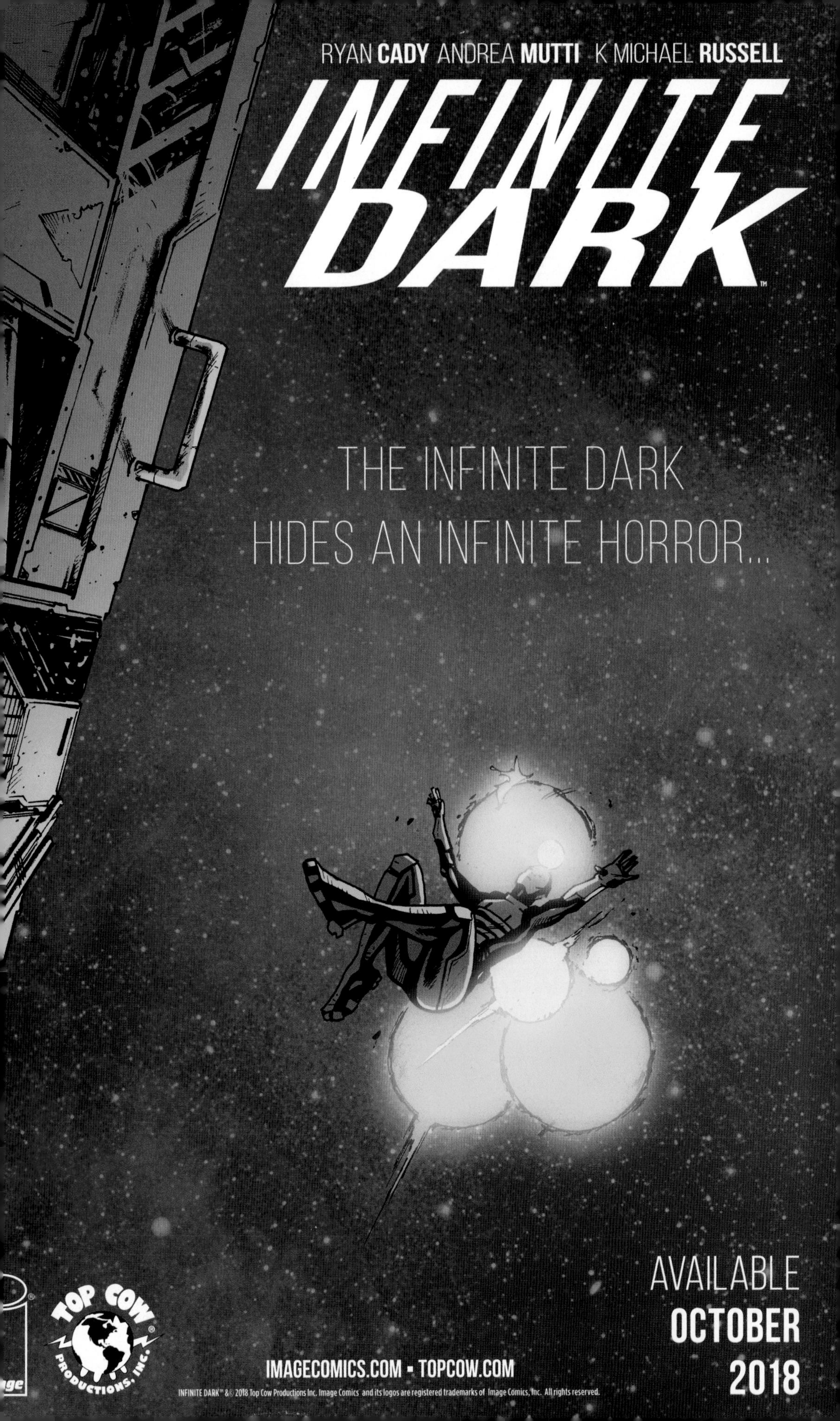

RYAN CADY ANDREA MUTTI K MICHAEL RUSSELL
INFINITE DARK™
THE INFINITE DARK
HIDES AN INFINITE HORROR...
AVAILABLE
OCTOBER
2018
IMAGECOMICS.COM • TOPCOW.COM
INFINITE DARK™ & © 2018 Top Cow Productions Inc. Image Comics and its logos are registered trademarks of Image Comics, Inc. All rights reserved.

The Top Cow essentials checklist:

IXth Generation, Volume 1
(ISBN: 978-1-63215-323-4)

Aphrodite IX: Rebirth Volume 1
(ISBN: 978-1-60706-828-0)

Artifacts Origins: First Born
(ISBN: 978-1-60706-506-7)

Blood Stain, Volume 1
(ISBN: 978-1-63215-544-3)

Cyber Force: Rebirth, Volume 1
(ISBN: 978-1-60706-671-2)

The Darkness: Origins, Volume 1
(ISBN: 978-1-60706-097-0)

Death Vigil, Volume 1
(ISBN: 978-1-63215-278-7)

Eclipse, Volume 1
(ISBN: 978-1-5343-0038-5)

Eden's Fall, Volume 1
(ISBN: 978-1-5343-0065-1)

Genius, Volume 1
(ISBN: 978-1-63215-223-7)

God Complex, Volume 1
(ISBN: 978-1-5343-0657-8)

Magdalena: Reformation
(ISBN: 978-1-5343-0238-9)

Port of Earth, Volume 1
(ISBN: 978-1-5343-0646-2)

Postal, Volume 1
(ISBN: 978-1-63215-342-5)

Rising Stars Compendium
(ISBN: 978-1-63215-246-6)

Romulus, Volume 1
(ISBN: 978-1-5343-0101-6)

Sunstone, Volume 1
(ISBN: 978-1-63215-212-1)

Symmetry, Volume 1
(ISBN: 978-1-63215-699-0)

The Tithe, Volume 1
(ISBN: 978-1-63215-324-1)

Think Tank, Volume 1
(ISBN: 978-1-60706-660-6)

Witchblade 2017, Volume 1
(ISBN: 978-1-5343-0685-1)

Witchblade: Borne Again, Volume 1
(ISBN: 978-1-63215-025-7)

For more ISBN and ordering information on our latest collections go to:
www.topcow.com
Ask your retailer about our catalogue of collected editions,
digests, and hard covers or check the listings at:
Barnes and Noble, Amazon.com,
and other fine retailers.

To find your nearest comic shop go to:
www.comicshoplocator.com